Two for Sorrow

Nicola Upson was born in Suffolk and read English at Downing College, Cambridge. She has worked in theatre and as a freelance journalist, and is the author of two works of non-fiction and the recipient of an Escalator Award from the Arts Council England. Her debut novel, *An Expert in Murder*, was the first in a series of crime novels whose main character is Josephine Tey – one of the leading authors of Britain's Golden Age of crime writing. She lives with her partner in Cambridge and Cornwall.

nicolaupson.com

Praise for *Two for Sorrow*:

'The death of the young seamstress . . . is a bravura essay in triumphant hideousness, its sinister sparkle enhanced by Upson's care over detail.' *TLS*

'Upson's style is compelling, meticulously researched and immaculately written. She creates a world you enter through her pages and are reluctant to leave at the end.' *Hunts Post*

'Scrupulously detailed descriptions . . . There is a heartfelt account of the condemned prisoner, a vivid picture of London life in the thirties and a carefully plotted mystery centred on a ladies' club in London.' *Literary Review*

'Upson expertly weaves fact with fiction in this haunting and brilliantly executed book.' *Stylist*

TWO FOR SORROW

Nicola Upson

faber and faber

First published in 2010
by Faber and Faber Ltd
Bloomsbury House
74–77 Great Russell Street
London WC1B 3DA
This paperback edition first published in 2011

Typeset by RefineCatch Limited, Bungay, Suffolk
Printed in England by CPI Bookmarque, Croydon

Quote from Noël Coward's *Tonight at 8.30* on page 445 by
permission of Alan Brodie Representation Ltd, agent for
NC Aventales AG, successor in title to the Estate of Noël Coward.
Taken from 'Still Life' (*Tonight at 8.30*), *Collected Plays: Three*,
Methuen Drama, an imprint of A&C Black Publishers Ltd.

The right of Nicola Upson to be identified as author of this work
has been asserted in accordance with Section 77 of the Copyright,
Designs and Patents Act 1988

A CIP record for this book
is available from the British Library

ISBN 978-0-571-24635-9

2 4 6 8 10 9 7 5 3 1

For Mandy. Two for joy.

Morning arrived, cold and frosty and defiant, as unwanted as
it was inevitable. Celia Bannerman looked up at two thin rows
of glass, seven tiny panes in each, and wondered again why
anyone had bothered to go through the motions of letting
daylight into such a godforsaken place. Even if the dirt from
the world outside had not made it all but impenetrable, the
window would have been much too high to see from. Soot
from the Camden Road was left to accumulate peacefully on
the glass, shielding those inside from a life which continued
without them. The cell was airless and oppressive. In the
absence of adequate natural light, a lamp burned throughout
the day and on into the night, denying the prisoner even the
comforting anonymity of blackness. Like many other things
about prison life, the brightness of the room was a compromise – never truly light and never truly dark, as if a denial of
such extremes could somehow keep their equivalent emotions
at bay.

From her chair in the corner, Celia watched the shadows
dance over the cell's familiar contents: a wooden wash-stand,
with its pathetic ration of yellow soap, and a single filthy rag,
meant to clean both mug and chamber pot but fit to touch
neither; a corner shelf with a Bible for those still able to find
comfort in its pages; and an enamel plate and knife, made
from folded tin and sharp as a piece of cardboard. A low, black

iron bedstead took up most of the room's thirteen feet by seven. The woman in the bed had turned her face resolutely to the wall, but Celia knew she was not asleep. As she thought of what lay ahead, she felt the customary tightening in her stomach and, for a moment, she was a child again, remembering the mornings when she herself had pulled the blankets over her head and prayed for time to stand still so that she did not have to face what the day held. At the time, those young fears had seemed terrible enough, but surely nothing could compare with what was going through Amelia Sach's mind in the hours before her death.

Quietly, Celia stood up and walked over to the far side of the cell, where a dark-blue serge cloak hung on a hook, placed halfway down the wall to discourage those who might be tempted to take fate into their own hands. The bottom of the garment lay crumpled and dusty on the floor, and Celia re-arranged the folds and smoothed the rough material as best she could, recognising the futility of the gesture but anxious not to let any opportunity of kindness go overlooked, no matter how small it seemed. In the three weeks between Sach's sentence and her execution, she was watched over constantly by two women at a time – strangers at first and then, as the days passed, allies, even friends. There was a peculiar intensity about the bond between wardress and prisoner: as she sat through her shifts, eight hours at a time, Celia shared every second of Sach's miserable existence, watching her as she washed and dressed, ate and cried, getting to know her habits and her preferences as she would have come to know a husband's in the early days of marriage. She had lived with Sach, and now she would see her to her death. Two warders had been brought in from another prison in case the distress

2

of the execution proved too much for their female counter-parts, but there was an unspoken determination amongst Celia and her colleagues to see this through to the bitter end: not because of suffrage or professional pride, not even – if she were honest – because they wanted to comfort the prisoner in her final moments, but simply because it was too late. The emotional damage had already been done. By the time the final week came, all but the most hardened of hearts found themselves counting the days as desperately as the condemned woman herself.

Long periods of sitting had created a numbness in her legs and back which she would willingly have shared with her other senses. She stretched her cramped limbs and wriggled her foot to get rid of the pins and needles, and her colleague – asleep in the other chair – sensed the movement and opened her eyes. The two women looked at each other, and Celia nodded. It was time. She walked over to the bed, holding her keys to stop them jangling – ridiculous, she thought, to suppose she could eliminate the reminders of incarceration, but it was another flicker of humanity to clutch at – and noticed Sach's body stiffen in anticipation of the hand on her shoulder. As Celia drew back blankets which were far too thin for the time of year, the smell of stale linen, sweat and fear rose up to greet her. Sach moved closer to the wall and tried to pull the covers back over her, but the hand was firm and she eventually allowed herself to be cajoled to her feet. In vain, Celia tried to reconcile the tall, gaunt woman in front of her with the arrogant, unfeeling creature who had filled the pages of the press since her arrest back in November. Sach looked much older than her twenty-nine years. Her face was grey with exhaustion, and her body looked barely strong enough to get her to the scaffold. How different she was from the woman who had entered prison with an incredulity bordering on indignation, who had believed that this could never happen to her. Right now, crowds would be gathering outside the prison gates, waiting for the customary announcement, but had any of them come face to face with Amelia Sach, Celia doubted that they would recognise the monster who lived in their minds.

She encouraged the prisoner to dress, trying not to adopt the expression of pity which she had noticed in every other visitor to the cell. Most of Sach's clothes were already on, worn in bed to fight the cold, but Celia helped her pull the standard blue shift – faded, and sufficiently shapeless to smother any sense of individuality amongst the Holloway women – over her head. Kneeling down to guide Sach's feet into shabby, ill-fitting shoes, she noticed holes in her stockings where the nails which held the shoes together had snagged the black wool and punctured the skin beneath. The feet felt so small and vulnerable in her hands that, for a few seconds, Celia found it difficult to breathe; the jury had been right, she thought – it must be so much worse for a woman to be hanged than a man. Or was that unfair? Did male warders feel this same raw despair when the time came for their prisoner to die? Too shaken to stand, she felt Sach's fingers rest briefly on her head; whether the gesture was a benediction or a silent plea for strength, she did not know, but it was enough. Pulling herself together, she began to scrape Sach's once-pretty auburn hair – now lank with neglect – back into a ponytail and fixed it in a bun, away from her neck, where it would not catch in the noose. It was a simple act, but it seemed to affect Sach more deeply than anything else and Celia took the cloak quickly from the hook,

4

trying to blot out a sound which was more like the whimper of an animal in pain than anything she had ever heard coming from a human being. As she wrapped it round Sach's shoulders, she wondered if terror – like dirt – could find a way of weaving itself into the fabric, accumulating with each poor soul who wore it. She turned the prisoner round to face her, desperate somehow to stem this outpouring of grief, but the woman's cries only grew louder and more coherent. 'Don't let them do it to me. I haven't done anything,' she repeated over and over again, drawing Celia into her hopelessness until the other wardress was forced to intervene.

'Come now, Mrs Sach,' she said, gently but firmly removing the hands that clung pitifully to Celia's dress. 'You haven't touched your breakfast. Try and eat something.'

'Can't we give her something stronger than bread and tea?' Celia asked angrily. 'What use is that to her now?'

The older woman shook her head and glanced quickly at her watch. 'There's no time,' she whispered. 'It's nearly nine.'

As though to prove her point, there was a noise in the corridor outside. Like most prisoners, used to spending so much time waiting and listening to events which could not be seen, Sach was quick to hear the approaching footsteps and eager to guess at their meaning. As they stopped outside the cell, then moved on again, the flicker of hope on her face was unbearable to Celia, who knew that only half the execution party had walked past; the other half would be just outside, waiting for the governor's nod. Staring at the door, she saw the slightest of movements as the hangman moved the peephole cover to one side to assess the mental state of the prisoner and then, after what felt like an interminable wait, the chime of the bells from the church next door signalled nine o'clock. Celia counted two strokes before she heard the rattle of the keys in the lock, three before the heavy iron door opened, and then the small group of men was in the cell, setting in motion a relentless sequence of events from which there was no escape, which could never be undone.

The hangman moved swiftly across the cell and began to pinion Sach's hands behind her back. As soon as she felt the leather straps against her skin, she seemed to lose what little strength she had left. Celia stepped forward to prevent her falling to the floor, whispering words of comfort, but they seemed to have the opposite effect and Sach had to be half-led, half-carried out into the corridor. A few feet to their right, at the door to the adjacent cell, a similar scene was being played out, but the contrast between the prisoners could not have been more marked. Annie Walters was a short, grey-haired woman in her early fifties, as sturdy and homely-looking as Sach was delicate, but it was their demeanour that set them apart, not their build or their age. The sight of the other woman only increased Sach's distress until it bordered on hysteria, but Walters remained cheerful and talkative, swapping casual remarks with the second hangman as if oblivious to the fact that these were her final moments. Looking at the two women now, brought face to face for the first time since their sentencing, it was hard to believe that they were conspirators in the brutal murders of babies – as many as twenty, some said, and most only a few days old.

Everything happened quickly from then on. The first hangman steadied Sach and prepared her for the short walk to the gallows. With a wardress on either side, the prisoners followed the chaplain towards the double doors at the end of the wing and into the newly built execution shed. It was only

6

a dozen steps or so, but far enough for Celia to notice that the prison seemed unnaturally quiet, almost as if a collective breath were being held. For three weeks now, the Holloway women had been restless and uneasy; the inevitable mixture of distress and sensationalism which greeted the sentence had been replaced by an angry helplessness, and everyone was touched by it, staff and prisoners alike. Celia knew she was not alone in longing to move the clock forward or back, to exist anywhere but in this present moment.

And then they were inside. Two nooses hung straight ahead of them, one slightly higher than the other, and the prisoners were led swiftly on to the trap. The executioners dropped to their knees to fasten the leg straps, their movements perfectly synchronised. Celia looked at Sach through the oval of rope, willing her ordeal to be over and refusing to look away in the face of death; it was the only help she had left to offer, and she held the woman's terrified gaze as a white cap – kept like a foppish handkerchief in the hangman's top pocket – was placed over her head and the noose adjusted. All the time she could hear the low, steady voice of the chaplain chanting out the service for the dead, but the words were indistinct. As the executioner moved across to the lever, the only thing she could focus on was the small circle of cloth moving in and out over Sach's mouth.

Afterwards, Celia could not say for certain if she had heard Walters calling out a goodbye to Sach shortly before the trapdoor opened, or if it had just been her imagination. But what she did remember of the seconds that followed – and she was sure of this because it came back to her sometimes, even now, in the early hours of a winter's morning – was the silence.

7

Chapter One

Josephine Tey picked up an extravagantly wrapped hatbox and used the perfect Selfridge bow to hook it on to the rest of her parcels.

'Are you sure you wouldn't like me to have that delivered for you, Madam?' the assistant asked anxiously, as if the hat's independent departure from the shop were somehow a slur on her standards. 'It's really no trouble.'

'Oh no, I'll be fine,' Josephine said, smiling guiltily at the group of young girls behind the counter. 'Carrying this will stop me going anywhere else today, and that's probably just as well – if I send many more packages round to my club, they'll be charging me for an extra room.'

Balancing her recklessness as best she could, Josephine took the escalator down to the ground floor. Its steady, sedate progress gave her plenty of time to admire the vast, open-plan design of the store, a look which was still so different from what most of London's shops had to offer. The whole building seemed to sparkle with an innate understanding of the connection between a woman's eye and her purse; even the prominent bargain tables were neatly stacked with beautiful boxes that gave no hint of their reduced price. December was still a week away, but staff were already beginning to decorate the aisles for the festive season and the familiar department-store smell – plush carpets and fresh flowers – had been replaced by a warm scent of cinnamon which only the drench of perfume from the soap and cosmetic departments could keep at bay. As a ploy to make Christmas seem closer than it really was, it seemed to have worked: even this late in the afternoon, the shop was packed with people and Josephine had to fight her way past the make-up counters to the main entrance and out into the bustle of Oxford Street.

She turned left towards Oxford Circus, following the long stretch of glass frontage to the corner of Duke Street. The shop windows were full of wax models, each a variation on the theme of Lot's wife, forever stilled in the midst of a gesture. Some beckoned to the curious to step inside, others carried on with their imaginary lives, oblivious to the flesh-and-blood women who studied every detail, but all were arranged against a background of light and colour which had been as carefully designed as any stage set. Josephine paused by a particularly striking bedroom scene. A ravishing wax figure, dressed in a crêpe de Chine nightgown, stepped out of a nest of silken sheets and pillows. Her pink foot rested lightly on the floor, and she stretched a perfectly manicured hand over to her bedside table, which held a morning paper, a novel – *The Provincial Lady in America*, Josephine noticed – and a tea tray with the finest bone china. Her dressing table – a magnet for feminine extravagance – gleamed with crystal, gold-stoppered bottles. It was a powerful image, but its message – that a life of comfort and intimacy was available to anyone who knew where to shop – was as painful for some as it was seductive to others. There was a whole generation of women for whom this would never be a reality, whose chances of happiness and security, even companionship, had been snatched away by the war, and no amount of satin could soften the blow of what they had lost. Glancing at the spinsters on either side of her – she used the word half-heartedly, aware of her own hypocrisy in treating them as a race apart – Josephine knew that the troubled look on their faces was about more than the lingerie's ability to withstand the November cold.

The pavement was only just wide enough to accommodate a double flow of pedestrians, and Josephine walked on slowly, recognising herself in the women from provincial towns who seemed utterly engrossed in their business, determined not to miss a thing. It was after five o'clock and, in the last hour, the pinks and oranges of a winter sunset had quickly given way to a sky the colour of blue-black ink. An unbroken line of street-lights stretched ahead of her like pearls on a string, drifting into the distance and relieving the mile-long stretch of shops – ladies' mile, as it was known – from the ordinariness of the day. Some of the smaller branches had already closed, empty-ing more workers out onto the streets, and a few shop-girls stopped to gaze wistfully into the windows of the larger stores, a long day on their feet having strengthened their desire to stand for once on the other side of the counter; most, though, headed quickly for the underground or for bus queues which grew longer by the second, muttering impatiently to them-selves and keen to make every second of freedom count before the daily routine began again.

As impressive as its sequence of huge stores was, Oxford Street was one of Josephine's least favourite parts of London, something to be endured for the sake of a weakness for clothes but never for longer than necessary. Gladly, she left its crowds and its clatter behind and cut through into the more select surroundings of Wigmore Street. There was something about the anonymity of walking through London in the early evening

11

that never failed to delight her, a sense of freedom in the knowledge that – for as long as she chose – no one in the world knew where she was or how to contact her. She had travelled down from Inverness ten days ago, but had so far managed to keep her presence a secret from all but a few casual acquaintances at her club. It couldn't last forever; there were several engagements booked for the following week and she would have to pick up the telephone soon and open a floodgate of invitations, but she was in no hurry to socialise before she had to. A world in which there were no timetables to be followed or deadlines to be met, and where messages left were never for her, suited Josephine perfectly. She was determined to enjoy it for as long as possible.

Even so, the sort of undemanding companionship offered by an afternoon of dedicated shopping was a relief after the solitary morning she had spent in her room – just her and a typewriter and a series of shadowy figures from a past which felt utterly alien to her. She was still not sure about the novel she was working on, and wondered if her desire to write something other than a detective story had been wise after all. When her editor suggested a book with a historical slant, a fictionalised account of a true crime seemed a good idea, particularly one with which she had a personal connection, but the claustrophobic horror of Holloway Gaol was starting to depress her and she had only just begun. Summer – both the real summer she had spent in Cornwall and the imaginary version which she had recently delivered to her publisher – seemed a long way away, and she found herself craving the warmth of the sun on her back and the comforting presence of Detective Inspector Alan Grant, hero of her first two mysteries. These early stages of a book, when all the characters were unfamiliar, were always the hardest to write. Getting to know them felt like walking into a room full of strangers, something from which her shyness made her recoil in horror; she would be pleased to get further on with the story, even if the world she was creating was unlikely to get any cheerier.

Across the street, the Times Book Club was still open and she was amused to see that books never failed to bring out the dormant shopper in a man. A lamp under the blind threw a welcoming yellow glow on to the shelves, where faded covers of popular novels and obscure political pamphlets were brought together as randomly as the people who browsed them. She considered going in, but decided that she was too laden with shopping to manage the sort of rummaging that books required, and pressed on instead to Cavendish Square. Here, the streetlamps were more forgiving, their pools of light interspersed with longer stretches of darkness, and there was a restful elegance about the area. The Square had been more fortunate than many of its London counterparts, where residential buildings were asked to rub along with modern offices, and it still consisted principally of beautifully proportioned old houses. It was home time and, as she made her way round to number 20, Josephine watched the lights coming on in the upper stories, imagining doors opening and voices calling up the stairs while life moved from the office to the sitting room.

The Cowdray Club occupied a particularly handsome eighteenth-century town house on the corner of Cavendish Square and Henrietta Street, at the heart of what was once the most fashionable area of Georgian England. The house had been bought from Lord Asquith – the latest in a line of distinguished owners – and, in 1922, established as a social club for nurses and professional women by Annie, Viscountess

Cowdray. Lady Cowdray – whom Josephine had never met but who had been, by all accounts, a formidable fundraiser and loyal supporter – had also paid for a new College of Nursing headquarters to be built in Asquith's old garden; thanks to some ingenious architectural thinking, the two buildings now functioned happily together, one providing for a nurse's working needs and the other for her rest and relaxation. Just over half of the Cowdray Club's membership came from the nursing profession. The rest were from all walks of life – lawyers, journalists, actresses and shop-girls, attracted by stimulating conversation, comfortable surroundings and the cheapest lunches in town – and Josephine was pleased to call it home whenever she wanted her time in London to be private and free from obligations to friends. Since Lady Cowdray's death a little over three years ago, the members had not lived together quite as harmoniously as the buildings: nursing was a political profession, and those left to run the club in its founder's absence had different views on its priorities and future. It was the same when any natural leader died or moved on, she supposed, but things were bound to settle eventually; in the meantime, she kept her head down and tried to avoid the bickering.

Outside the main entrance, she balanced her parcels precariously on one arm but the door flew open before she could reach it, and a young woman – one of the club's servants – rushed out, nearly knocking her to the ground.

'Am I missing the fire?' Josephine asked, a little more sarcastically than she meant to.

'Crikey, Miss – I'm so sorry,' the girl said, bending down to pick up the boxes that had skidded across the pavement and into the street. 'I wasn't looking where I was going.'

'Obviously,' Josephine said, but softened as she noticed how upset the girl seemed. 'I don't suppose there's any harm done. None of this is breakable.' She held out her hand to take the last of the parcels. 'What's the rush, though? Is everything all right?'

'Oh yes, Miss. It's just that I'm on my break and I don't get long. I'm already late to meet someone.'

'Even so, surely you've got time to go back for your coat?' She looked at the thin cotton dress and pinafore which all the club's housemaids wore. 'It's November – you'll catch your death going out like that.'

'I'm all right, Miss, and I'd rather get off. To tell the truth, I'm not supposed to use this entrance but it's so much quicker than going out the side door and all the way round. That's why I was in such a hurry – Miss Timpson on reception was showing someone through to the bar, so I nipped out the front while she wasn't looking.' She glanced across to the Square, then turned back to Josephine. 'I'd be ever so grateful if you didn't say anything, Miss, and I'm fine – honestly. I won't be out here long.'

'All right, then . . . ?'

'Lucy, Miss.'

'All right, Lucy – I won't hold you up any longer. But be more careful next time.'

'Yes, Miss – thank you.'

Josephine watched as Lucy hurried off towards the middle of Cavendish Square, then turned and went inside, glad to be out of the cold. The club's entrance hall was spacious and uncluttered, the focal point being a long reception desk made of diligently polished mahogany. A modest bronze tablet hung to the right of the desk, set in an oak frame which contained

15

the Cowdray coat of arms and recorded the gratitude of the first two thousand members to their founder; other than that, the walls were free of decoration, and the eye of any visitor was drawn instead to a number of beautifully furnished rooms which opened straight off the foyer. Miss Timpson was back at her post, and Josephine was treated to the full Cowdray Club welcome.

'Ah, Miss Tey,' she beamed from behind her desk. 'You've had a successful afternoon, I see. Can I get you your key?'

'That would be lovely,' Josephine said, matching the sincerity of the receptionist's smile and trying to think who the woman reminded her of. 'And there are some more parcels on their way, I'm afraid.'

'They're already here – Robert has just taken the last of them up to your room.' She cast a judgemental eye over the parcels, lingering on the scuff-marks where the boxes had hit the ground. 'Would you like him to give you a hand with those? I'm afraid the lift's out of order again.'

'No, no – I'll manage,' Josephine said, knowing that she had – in Miss Timpson's eyes at least – wasted quite enough of Robert's time already that day. 'They're not heavy.'

'If you're sure.' She reached up to take the key off its hook, and Josephine realised instantly that the resemblance she had been racking her brains to place was with the mannequin in the shop window: Miss Timpson shared that untouched-by-the-cares-of-the-world quality, an air of casual perfection which most women found insufferable, if only because they aspired to it themselves and always fell so short of the mark. 'Just say if there's anything else you require.'

'You'll be the first to know.' She took her key and headed for

16

the stairs, but hadn't got far before a familiar voice called her back.

'Josephine! Just the person I was looking for.'

She turned to greet Celia Bannerman and was struck – as always – by how little she had changed in twenty years. Her long dark hair, which Josephine had never seen worn any other way than scraped back from her face into a bun, was streaked with grey at the temples, and her glasses were needed too frequently now to be worn on a chain around her neck, but no one would have guessed that she was nearly sixty. They had first met during the war at Anstey, a Physical Training College in Birmingham where Josephine was a student and Miss Bannerman one of the senior teachers; by the time their paths crossed again at the Cowdray Club, Miss Bannerman – or Celia, as she had tried to get used to calling her – had become one of the most respected figures in nursing administration and was heavily involved in the management of the club. She had certainly come a long way since her earlier job as a warder at Holloway, but it was those years that interested Josephine now.

'I was just going to leave a message for you at reception,' Celia said, 'but you've saved me the trouble. Your note said that you've got something for me to read?'

'Yes, the first draft of what we discussed the other day. I wondered if you'd have a look at it, just to make sure it's reasonably accurate – and I have a few more questions, if you've time.'

'Yes, of course.' She looked at her watch. 'I'm free now for a while, if that suits you? Shall we say in fifteen minutes' time, just to give you a chance to catch your breath? I'll see you in the drawing room.'

She walked back into the lounge without waiting for an answer, and Josephine recognised the same confidence in her own authority that had earned Miss Bannerman the respect of all her students – respect tinged with just the right amount of fear. She had seen that authority falter only once, and then just briefly and under exceptional circumstances, and it never failed to bring out the schoolgirl in her. She headed for the stairs again like a straggler late for lessons, but was stopped once more in her tracks, this time by Miss Timpson. 'Oh Miss Tey, I nearly forgot – don't go upstairs without this,' she called, and at the higher volume her East End vowels were satisfyingly evident. 'It arrived for you earlier this afternoon.' She bent down to pick something up from the floor behind the desk and presented Josephine with an expensive-looking ornamental gardenia. Josephine held out her hand for the card.

'Sorry – that's it. There's no note.'

'Are you *sure* it's for me?'

'Oh yes. The boy from the shop was very particular. I had to sign for it.'

'But no one knows I'm here.'

'Then perhaps you have an admirer on the inside, darling.' There was no need to turn round to see where the suggestion came from: the voice – warm, attractive and full of innuendo – was an established feature of the Cowdray Club, as familiar to its members as the decor and just as expensive. The Honourable Geraldine Ashby fell into an unusual category of membership: neither nurse nor professional, she was one of a handful of women who were elected to the club at the discretion of the council and whose purpose was purely social. Geraldine's mother was more than happy to secure the position each year

18

with a generous cheque to the College of Nursing – after all, the association was the most respectable thing about her daughter – and Geraldine took her social responsibilities as seriously as the other members took their work. No one could deny that she livened things up considerably, and not just because she mixed the finest cocktails outside the Savoy: everything about her was daring, and that made a refreshing change from the cloud of earnestness that hung over so much of the club. It was impossible not to be drawn to her charm and good humour, and her beauty – a chic, adventurous beauty – sparkled as effortlessly in a tailored suit as it did in the latest Chanel. Forgetting for a moment the young girl on her arm – a pretty if rather dull-looking blonde – Geraldine smiled wickedly at Josephine. 'Just think – it could be any one of us. Who would you *like* it to be from?'

Experience had taught Josephine that a suitable response – flirtatious, with just the right amount of disdain – would only come to her later that evening, so she didn't bother to reply but picked up the flower with what she hoped was an enigmatic smile and strode determinedly up the stairs. She realised from the smirk on Miss Timpson's face that her admirer had been a matter of speculation from the moment the flower crossed the threshold, and tried to work out who could have sent it. Archie? It seemed unlikely – gardenias weren't his style; if he knew she was already in London, he would have chosen something far less showy and he would have brought them himself. It certainly couldn't be the Motley sisters – she doubted that Ronnie had ever done an anonymous thing in her life, and a flower from Lettice was always accompanied by a dinner invitation. Lydia, perhaps – it was a luxury beyond the budget of a struggling actress, but her friend was notoriously bad with

19

money and such an extravagance would be typical of her. Or perhaps Geraldine was right after all, and another member of the club had sent it. Just what she needed – awkwardness creeping into the only safe haven left to her. She shut her door with a sigh of relief, stuck the flower unceremoniously in the sink, and tried to forget about it.

The room was small but comfortable, and charmingly furnished with everything she needed and nothing more: a single bed, a solid writing table, a large wardrobe and plenty of cupboard space, and – her favourite feature – a tall window which took up most of one wall and looked out over Cavendish Square. She tidied the parcels away, freshened her make-up and found her glasses, then went over to the desk and picked up the sheaf of papers which she had been working on that morning. Scanning them quickly, she made a note of the questions which she hoped Celia might be able to answer and went downstairs, keen to find out as much as she could about the Finchley Baby Farmers.

There was no sign of Celia in the drawing room, so Josephine chose one of the blue horsehair chairs by the windows overlooking Henrietta Street and settled down to wait. It was the largest room in the house, extending the full width of the building on the first floor, and one of the most beautiful, with nicely proportioned panelled walls – painted in ivory-white enamel to maximise the reflection of light during the day – and a parquet floor. Fine rococo mirrors hung over original fireplaces – one at either end, suggesting that the space had once been two rooms – and there were other splashes of opulence in a gilt Louis XV couch with sapphire-coloured cushions and three enormous chandeliers, but most of the furnishings were quietly tasteful: simple mahogany bookcases housing an eclectic selection of fiction and non-fiction; plain velvet curtains; and comfortable Sheraton armchairs, alternately upholstered in blue and fawn and free of the tassels and loose covers that would have made the room look untidy. A number of women sat around in small groups or on their own, playing cards and reading newspapers, and the soft murmur of conversation filled the room, punctuated every now and then by laughter or the chink of cup against saucer. It spoke of privilege but most of the women had worked hard to get here, and Josephine could still remember how proud she had felt when she was first elected. For her, as for many women of her generation, the membership of a private club represented a new and cherished independence; ten years later, although her life had taken a different path from the one she had expected, her achievements as a novelist and a playwright more than justified her place here, but success had not dulled that early excitement. It was partly to do with the possibilities which the future now held for women – for the lucky ones, at least – but there was something more to it: in the Cowdray Club she had rediscovered the sense of female solidarity which she had known in her teenage years and early twenties, and she was honest enough to recognise in herself a need to belong which she resented but could not seem to outgrow.

'Josephine – sorry to keep you waiting but something came up unexpectedly.' Celia hurried over to the window, looking apologetic, and Josephine stood to greet her.

'It's fine,' she said. 'Please don't worry. We can do this another time if you're too busy.'

'No, no – it's nice to see you. And quite frankly I'm desperate to snatch half an hour away from committees and fundraising and politics, so you're actually doing me a favour.' She gestured to Josephine to sit down, and took the chair opposite. 'You know about the charity gala next week? Of course you do – you're friends with Ronnie and Lettice Motley, aren't you? They're making such a lovely job of the clothes. But Amy Coward seems to think I've got nothing else to do except plan for it and, as she's the only reason we're getting Noël for the evening, I have to be so careful not to disillusion her.'

Josephine laughed. 'You must have inherited a lot of that sort of work after Lady Cowdray's death. I can't imagine that this is an easy place to run – not smoothly, anyway.'

Celia gave her a wry smile. 'Is it that obvious?'

'Not at all. But with so many successful women in one place, it stands to reason that egos will clash sooner or later.'

'If it were just about personality, that would be fine, but it's a little more serious than that – it goes back to the very principles that the club and the college were founded on. Have you seen today's *Times*?' Josephine shook her head. 'The letters page is full of complaints from nurses about money being raised in their name and used to fund facilities for people who have never been near the sick in their lives. None of them mentions the club by name, but we all know what they mean.'

'Surely it works both ways – don't the subscription fees help to support the College of Nursing?'

'Of course they do, but the purists choose to forget that. If we're not careful, we'll find ourselves split right down the middle – and I don't know how the club *or* the college will survive if that happens.'

Having joined with a foot in the nursing camp but since abandoned that for another career, Josephine found it all too easy to see both sides of the argument. 'Where do you stand?'

she asked, nodding to Geraldine as she sat down at the next table and trying to ignore her grin.

Celia sighed. 'Oh, I'm all for mixing things up a bit. Lady Cowdray always said that women get far too narrow-minded if they don't spend at least some of their leisure hours with people from other professions, and I'm inclined to agree with her. Anyway, I feel obliged to fight for her original vision, but I fear that it's not going to be easy. And to cap it all – this is just between you and me, you understand – we've got an outbreak of petty theft on our hands. A couple of members have reported things going missing. Nothing very valuable – a scarf here, a bit of loose change there – but distressing, nonetheless, and I've had to involve the police. Discreetly, of course. Ah – here's Tilly with our drinks.' Josephine looked round and saw a young waitress carrying two large gins over on a tray. 'I took the liberty of having these brought up for us. If you want me to relive the story of the Finchley Baby Farmers, I'll need some Dutch courage, and I refuse to drink on my own.' She glanced at the papers on the card table. 'Is that what you'd like me to look at?'

Josephine nodded and pushed the typescript over to Celia, marvelling at how easy it was to slip back into the old teacher–pupil relationship. She looked on as the older woman read slowly through the pages, and thought back to the first time she had ever heard the names Amelia Sach and Annie Walters. It was during the summer of her final year at Anstey, shortly before the end-of-term examinations, when evenings were long and tempers short. The pressure of achievement – and, for the older girls, the urgency of securing a position in the world outside – weighed heavily on the whole college, and the common room was unusually silent as half a dozen of the seniors made the most of every last second of prep time.

Usually, Celia Bannerman's tall, authoritative figure could command a room from the moment she entered it, but that night she must have been there for some time before anyone noticed her: when Josephine glanced up, she was already standing over by the window, gazing at the girls in her care with an immense sadness in her eyes. One by one, they looked up and saw her and, when she had their full attention, she spoke, calmly but gravely. Elizabeth Price, a first-year student, had been found dead in the gymnasium; the body was hanging from one of the ropes and there was no question that the girl had committed suicide – a note had been discovered in her room. Miss Bannerman went on to explain that Elizabeth's real surname was Sach, and that she was the daughter of a woman who had been hanged for the terrible crime of baby farming. She was adopted as a young child and, until recently, had no idea of her true identity. Somehow, though, she had found out the truth, and her note made it clear that it was more than she could bear. The teacher normally moved with the grace of a dancer but, as she left the room that night, her steps were slow and heavy. Only later did Josephine learn that she blamed herself for Elizabeth Price's death.

Celia took her time in reading Josephine's manuscript and, when she had finished, she went back to check a couple of passages. Eventually, she put the papers down on the table and reached for her drink. 'You don't have to be kind,' Josephine said, annoyed with herself for feeling the need to break the silence. 'I can take criticism these days.'

Celia smiled. 'Kindness doesn't come into it. It's very powerfully done. A little too powerfully for my taste, perhaps – reading that brings it all back. No one can really know what it's like to live through an execution unless he or she has been

there – but this is close. Can I make a couple of comments?'
Josephine nodded. 'It's up to you, of course, and it depends how far you're prepared to let truth stand in the way of a good story, but those last few hours would never be that peaceful. I can see that you want to highlight the relationship between the prisoner and the warder but, if you'll excuse a rather tasteless pun, it was actually like Finchley Central in that cell. The world and his wife passes through on the morning of an execution: first the governor, and then the chaplain. I can't speak for Walters, of course, but the chaplain was with Sach for some time. Oh, and the governor always asks the prisoner if she wishes to make any final statement.'

'And did she?'

'No.'

'No last-minute confession, then?'

'No. Neither Sach nor Walters ever made any sort of confession. Somebody once told me that Walters said she didn't mind dying as long as Sach did, too, but I don't know if that's true. There was a great deal of bitterness between them at the end. Walters felt betrayed by Sach, who did everything she could to save her own skin; and Sach by the justice system, because she genuinely believed she was innocent. It was Walters who did the actual killing, you see, and Sach was careful never to get blood on her own hands. She was always very keen that we understood that, me and the other women who looked after her.'

'Isn't that worse? Getting someone else to do your dirty work?'

'She certainly didn't see it like that. In fact, I was surprised that her defence didn't argue more strongly along those lines during the trial.'

'So how exactly did Sach and Walters work things between them? The newspapers only tell half a story, and I'd rather hear it from someone who knew them.'

'Well, Sach ran a nursing home and took in young women for the period of their confinement. Most of them were unmarried mothers, desperate to hide their shame and willing to go along with anything that would get them off the hook. Apparently, Sach told them she knew lots of women who were keen to adopt a child and offered to find their baby a good home.'

'For a small fee, I suppose.'

'Not so small. Most of them paid around thirty pounds, which was a lot of money then, especially for women of their class.'

'So they handed over the money and never saw their baby again?'

'Exactly. They all believed the children were going for adoption – or so they said, although I think some of them were too desperate to care what really happened – but in fact Walters took them and disposed of them. She was found carrying a dead child one day, and wasted no time in leading the police straight to Sach. Sach denied all knowledge of the killings, but no one believed her.'

'Do *you* think she was guilty?'

'You can't think about innocence and guilt when you're in that position – it's not your job, and the only way you can do what you're asked to do is by placing your faith in the system. Looking back, I think it was the right verdict, although both women felt very hard done by. They didn't set eyes on each other from the moment of sentencing until the morning of the execution, but they were in adjoining cells and you could often hear them banging on the walls and accusing each other of being the guilty party.'

'Was it your first execution?'

'First and last, thank God. It was three years since a woman had been hanged in this country. Much was made at the time of its being the first female execution under the new king, as if a change of reign were somehow going to make a difference. And it was the very first hanging at the new Holloway. I suppose you could say they were trying it out.' The bitterness in her voice was unmistakeable, and Josephine wasn't surprised: hanging was a terrible death, and the fact that it was organised was scarcely likely to remove any of its horror. 'None of us had ever assisted at anything like that before, and the fact that it was a double execution made it unbearably grim. To tell the truth, we were all hoping for a reprieve so that we didn't have to go ahead with it. Even the hangman was dreading it, apparently.'

'That was Billington?'

'Yes, with two assistants – his younger brother and one of the Pierrepoints.'

'It must affect you very deeply, being that close to a prisoner,' Josephine said quietly, aware that she was stating the obvious but keen to get a better understanding of how Celia had really felt. 'It's a very strange relationship.'

'I suppose it takes people in different ways. Some of the older warders were hardened to it by the time I met them. I'm sure they'd spent years trying to shake off the emotional impulses that are so instinctive to most of us. Some were so terrified by it that they had to leave the prison service altogether. But you're right – no one was immune to it. It was destructive to us all in some way.'

'And I dare say one or two enjoyed the notoriety. I can see that the more sadistically minded could dine out on it for years.'

'I think you're confusing us with crime writers.'

Celia smiled, but the sharpness of the rebuke was not lost on Josephine. 'You don't approve?'

'Of your writing about this for pleasure? It depends how you do it, I suppose, but I do question why someone would choose to put herself through those emotions if she doesn't have to – and why somebody would read about it to be entertained. Can I ask why you're doing it?'

Josephine thought carefully before she answered. 'I've never forgotten that night at Anstey,' she said eventually. 'When you broke the news to us, it was such a shock. We didn't see anything, of course, and you saved us from the details of how Elizabeth must have suffered, but that made her death all the more powerful in our imaginations. You know how fanciful girls of that age can be and we were at a vulnerable time in our lives, worrying about our futures – I suppose we all felt the poignancy of how easily that future could be snuffed out. I remember being intrigued by what her mother must have been like and what drove her to do what she did. It wasn't that long ago, and yet it seemed like a crime from a different age, something that Dickens would write about but not something we could reach out and touch in our own memories.'

Celia nodded. 'Yes, I suppose it must have felt very alien to a group of modern young women.'

'And of course we never found out who discovered Elizabeth's secret and taunted her with the past, so there was a mystery there, something that we could speculate about for hours even though it was never likely to be solved. I spent days afterwards trying to put myself in that poor girl's position, wondering about my own past and what I would find too terrible to live with.'

'And?'

'I don't think shame would make me do it, if I'm honest, but I can understand how terrible it must be if you suspect you might be disposed to that sort of violence somewhere in your genes. Perhaps she thought there was a deep-seated cruelty in her which made her afraid of her own future – the sins of the mothers, and all that. It could be why she chose to end her life in that way – she thought her mother's fate might one day be hers, so she took the punishment into her own hands.' She smiled defensively. 'Or perhaps that's still the imagination of an eighteen-year-old talking.'

'No, I think there's something in that,' Celia said seriously. 'You know, Sach worried about her daughter all the time she was in prison. It's ironic when you think about how callously she dealt with other people's children, and I suppose it shows how far she was able to distance herself from what she was doing, but she was forever fretting about whether her husband would remember to save for the child's new boots or what she'd be told about her mother when she was older. And she was right to worry – the child's father washed his hands of everything the minute the trial was over. During those last few days, she begged me to make sure that Elizabeth was looked after and it seemed such a small thing to promise at the time. I never dreamt that I'd let them both down so badly.'

'You can't keep blaming yourself,' Josephine said gently. 'We were all at fault to some extent. Elizabeth was a hard girl to like – she could be sly and manipulative – but if we'd tried harder to make her feel at home, then perhaps she'd have felt able to cope with what she found out about her mother. She needed a friend, and that wasn't your fault.'

'Perhaps,' Celia said, unconvinced.

'Had you kept in touch with her regularly while she was growing up?'

'Not her directly, but I contacted her adoptive parents from time to time and kept an eye on her education – she was a bright girl, for all her faults. And I arranged for her to come to Anstey, of course. Perhaps I shouldn't have done that – apart from anything else, it wasn't fair on all of you who worked so hard to earn a place in the proper way. But I honestly believed it would be the making of her.'

'And perhaps it would have been if she'd had time to make the most of the opportunity. But someone else denied her that, not you.'

'Even so, I should at least have got to the bottom of who drove her to it.'

'What good would that really have done? It wouldn't have changed anything for Elizabeth, and I'm sure whoever it was never meant things to go that far – she's had to live with that, and it's probably worse than any punishment you could have dished out. Look, I shouldn't even be asking you about this,' Josephine added, genuinely sorry. 'It's insensitive of me to rake over the past and expect you to fill in the gaps for the sake of curiosity and entertainment.'

'It's painful, certainly, and I do still feel guilty. Not just about Elizabeth, but about her mother. That execution changed my life for the better, and it seems so wrong to profit by someone's death.'

'Profit in what way?'

'It's hard to explain, but the thing that really stands out for me about that terrible morning was the moment when we got to the execution chamber. You're absolutely right in your description of Sach's mental state – she was so frightened that she could barely stand, but the prison doctor was waiting at the door and that seemed to give her strength. She recovered for a moment – only very briefly, but long enough to thank him for the kindness he'd shown her. I'll never forget it. Sach and Walters both called themselves nurses – certainly Sach was a qualified midwife – and yet they took the lives of those innocent babies in the most cold-blooded way imaginable, and made capital out of desperate women who came to them for help because society drove them to it. That doctor was a fine medical man, and those two women had made a mockery of his profession. He could have been forgiven for refusing them any humanity at all, but he didn't. He put his hand on her shoulder and told her to be strong, and that struck me as such a remarkably compassionate thing to do.' She laughed nervously, and Josephine got the impression that she was embarrassed at having dropped her guard quite so readily. 'I suppose I've been trying to live up to it ever since.'

'Did that make you decide to take up nursing?'

'To go back to it, yes. I'd already done some training before I went into the prison service, and I spent some time on the hospital ward before I left. Believe me – if you ever need a salutary reminder to stay on the right side of the law, that's the place to be. Those women have no shred of privacy: they're always under the eagle eye of a nurse, and the more infamous ones are subjected to intolerable scrutiny from other prisoners. You can imagine the sort of atmosphere that's created when women like that are forced together.'

'Do I have to imagine it?' Josephine asked drily, looking around at the other tables.

Celia laughed. 'Trust me – the food's better here. Seriously though – we're supposed to be innocent until proven guilty, but sometimes I wonder. How can anyone prepare for an ordeal in court under those circumstances?'

'Is there anyone else from the prison who might be willing to talk to me? What about the doctor?'

'He died in the war, I believe,' Celia said, 'and I can't think of anyone else off the top of my head. I kept in touch with Ethel Stuke – the other warder – for a while, but she was killed in a Zeppelin raid in 1915. Billington might be about still, I suppose, but God knows where – he was only hangman for a few more years. I've no idea what happened to the chaplain, but he was an elderly man even then. The best I can offer you is Mary Size – do you know her?'

'No.'

'She's the present deputy governor, and she's done some remarkable things for Holloway and for prisons in general. She's also a member here, so I'd be happy to introduce you. Sach and Walters were long before her time, but she could talk to you generally about prison life if that would help.'

'I'm sure it would – thank you. What about their families, though? You mentioned Sach's husband?'

'Yes, but I don't know how you'd find him – assuming he's still alive of course.' She thought for a moment. 'Walters had two nieces – they came to visit her several times, but I can't remember what their names were and I'm not sure how much they could tell you, even if you traced them. She didn't strike me as a family woman.'

'And the trial? There must have been witnesses?'

32

'Again, that's something you'd have to look up. It's all so long ago now, Josephine, and I start to feel like a very old woman when I think about everything that's happened in between. It's hard to look back at the beginning of your career when you find yourself too near the end – you'll understand that one day.'

Feeling a little patronised, Josephine made a note of Walters's nieces and finished her drink. 'I've got a lot more newspaper reports to look at,' she said, gathering up her papers. 'And if the worst comes to the worst, I'll call in a few favours from the police.' Celia raised an eyebrow questioningly. 'One of my closest friends is an inspector at the Yard, and God knows I've helped him often enough. No point in having police connections if you don't use them.'

'Make it up, Josephine – isn't that what you do best? Truth isn't always stranger than fiction, you know. I'm not trying to tell you what to do – I stopped that twenty years ago – but for my own peace of mind I must say this: what happened back then wasn't mysterious or fascinating, it was squalid and depressing. Sach and Walters weren't anything special – their crime was ten-a-penny and they weren't even particularly good at it. If you want to write about baby farming, look at Amelia Dyer – she managed four hundred before they hanged her. Don't make these women into something they weren't. There was nothing noble or heroic about the way they lived *or* died.'

'It's not the killing that interests me,' Josephine said, irritated at being lectured to and all the more annoyed because she knew in her heart that Celia was right. 'It's the relationship between two women who commit a crime, and the story of how trust breaks down when it all goes wrong. That's what

33

struck me when we talked about it last week – the acrimony between them when they went to their deaths.' She sensed now that she really had overstepped the mark: to Celia, her interest in something that had clearly been traumatic must make her akin to those who crowded to the scaffold before legitimised killing became a private affair. 'I'll bear in mind what you've said, though.'

'And I'm sorry for being so discouraging. It doesn't mean that I won't help you in any way I can. Is there anything else at the moment?'

'Just one thing. What happens immediately after the execution? I wanted to go on, but I realised I have absolutely no idea.'

'Well, the bodies are left to hang for an hour, then they're taken down and washed, ready for the coroner and a jury to see them.'

'A jury?'

Celia nodded. 'They're laid out in coffins under the trap-door – nothing elaborate, of course, just rough wooden boxes. The doctor goes through the usual stuff about the execution being skilfully carried out and confirms that death was instantaneous – you know, the sort of thing that makes a democracy feel better about what it's just done. In this case, it happened to be true, but I gather that others weren't so lucky.' She paused, and Josephine guessed that she could still visualise that scene as if it were yesterday. 'There was something unusual, though – someone had put a bunch of violets on each of the women's bodies.'

'Someone? Am I allowed to guess who?'

'It's your book,' she said, smiling. 'And thank you for giving me such courage at the end, but I'm afraid that part isn't very accurate. When it came down to those last few seconds, I couldn't look Sach in the eye, and that's not something I'm proud of.'

'What was going through your mind?'

'There but for the grace of God, Josephine,' she said without hesitation. 'It's all anyone could possibly think at a time like that.'

(untitled)
by Josephine Tey
First Draft
Claymore House, East Finchley, Wednesday 12 November 1902

Amelia Sach held the baby close to her chest and stared impatiently at the longcase clock, whose steady, purposeful ticking dominated the front parlour of the house in Hertford Road. These days, it seemed that her life was governed by waiting – waiting for babies to arrive, waiting for them to depart, waiting for the next timid knock at the door which would start the whole process again. It was twenty minutes past the time she had specified in her telegram, and there was still no sign of Walters. Sometimes she thought the woman was late on purpose, making herself seem indispensable by giving Amelia time to contemplate what she would do if left on her own with another woman's unwanted child. The baby wriggled in her arms and gave a soft gurgle of contentment. She was a beautiful little girl, only a few hours old but already comfortable with the strange new world which she had entered in a business-like fashion, free from fuss or struggle. It had been an easy birth, with no reason to call in the local doctor, and Amelia looked gratefully down at the child, making sure that she was warmly wrapped in the bonnet and shawl that her mother had painstakingly knitted. In fact, there had been only one anxious moment: when she took the baby in to her mother for the final goodbyes, the woman had looked at her with such longing and desperation that Amelia half-expected her to change her mind; now, in her heart, she almost wished she had.

The warmth of the baby in her arms reminded her – as it always did – of how she had felt when she first held her own daughter. It was more than four years ago, but she could remember it as if it were yesterday and she experienced the same stab of joy and pride now every time she looked at her little girl, her Lizzie, who – with her auburn hair and delicate features – was a miniature version of her mother. Her own pregnancy had seemed like a miracle after years of hoping for a baby, and her life now was dominated by thoughts of her daughter's future. She was determined that Lizzie would never be faced with the difficult choices that she had made and comforted herself with the knowledge that, having made those choices, she was at least making a success of things: her business was growing by the day. A change of monarch had made no difference whatsoever to women so much further down the social scale, and there were still plenty who needed someone to take their humiliation off their hands; if she didn't do it for them, she told herself, then someone else would. The Hertford Road premises were the largest she had taken yet, and Claymore House was a superior-looking building which made a fine maternity home and had been easy to adapt for nursing purposes. There were four rooms available, although, to stay within the law, she should really only accommodate one child at a time – but Finchley lay just outside the area in which London City Council inspectors exercised control and, in any case, the authorities were less keen to uphold regulations than the legislators were to make them. Not that she had anything to hide: when she placed her advertisements in the weekly journals, offering moderate terms, skilled nursing and every care taken, she was only telling the truth. More than twenty women had passed through her doors in the last eighteen months, and she would be surprised to hear a complaint from any of them; they travelled from all over the country for the benefit of her discretion, and they wouldn't find better.

Outside, she heard the iron gate close but the footsteps coming up the path – although familiar – were not the ones she was waiting for. The front door slammed and her husband called her name. 'In here, Jacob,' she answered brightly, rocking the child gently as she began to cry, but her smile of welcome faded as she saw his expression change. He looked long and hard at the baby and then at her, and began to put his coat back on. 'Jacob? Where are you going? Don't be silly, love – you've only just come in. Stay with me now, Jacob – *please!*'

'How many times do I have to tell you?' he asked, the suppressed anger in his tone making his words seem far more threatening than if he had shouted them at the top of his voice. 'I don't want that woman in my house when I'm here, and I won't have anything to do with what you and her get up to. I'll say this for the last time, Amelia – whatever it is, get it over and done with by the time I get home. Do you understand me?' For a moment, she thought he was going to strike her and she lifted her hand to shield the baby, but he turned and left without another word.

'So you don't want anything to do with it?' she shouted after him. 'You're happy enough to spend my money, though, aren't you? And to call this house yours when it suits you, and lay down your laws. The only thing you can't seem to do is spend any time with your wife and daughter.' But she was talking to an empty hallway. The front door slammed behind him, and the baby's cries grew louder. 'There, there,' she said softly, but her attention was no longer on the child: she was thinking

39

about Jacob, and how he'd be spending the rest of the night in the Joiner's Arms, washing away his self-pity. Was that really what she was doing this for? So Jacob could afford to drink himself to death and risk everything she'd worked for with one slurred indiscretion? If only the wretched child would stop crying, she thought impatiently, hugging the tiny body closer to her. And where the devil was Walters? This was all her fault.

She went back into the sitting room and drew aside the curtain in the large bay window, talking absent-mindedly to the child all the time. Peering out into the darkness, she saw Walters at the bottom of the street, sauntering along as though she didn't have a care in the world. And perhaps she didn't. Perhaps her reliance on drink or on drugs – Amelia didn't know which and didn't care to find out – had created a detachment from life which made her ideal for a particular sort of work. Theirs was a strange, twisted relationship, she thought, as she watched the older woman's slow progress along the pavement. They were bonded by their work and had to rely on some sort of trust, but with that came a resentment that neither could flourish without the other. In her darker moments, distanced from her husband and fearful for her child, Amelia felt trapped by circumstances from which she could see no escape. While she knew that the trap was of her own making, she hated Walters, both as an unwelcome reminder of her situation and as a scapegoat for it. It did not require a great deal of understanding to know that the feeling was mutual.

She opened the door before Walters had a chance to ring the bell, and stood aside to let her into the hallway. 'Where the hell have you been?' she whispered angrily. 'I said five o'clock.'

Walters was dressed respectably enough in the brown cape which she always wore, tied tightly with a black ribbon at the throat, but her smile seemed grotesquely out of place in a face which had been destroyed by hard living and which looked much older than its fifty-odd years. It reminded Amelia of the terrible old women who haunted the fairy tales that she read to Lizzie, and the impression was hardly dispelled by Walters's response. 'A few minutes isn't going to make any difference to the little one, is it?' she said, and held out her arms. Amelia noticed the dirt under her ragged fingernails, and hid her disgust as she handed the baby over: she needed help, no matter what form it took; Walters knew it, and never missed an opportunity to exploit the fact. On a previous visit, when Amelia had been called away for a moment by one of her patients, she had come back into the parlour to find Walters holding Lizzie in her arms, and the triumphant expression on her face was enough to remind Amelia how easily they could destroy each other; there was no doubting who had the most to lose. Now, Walters kissed the newborn's forehead and the child stopped crying immediately. 'She's a pretty little thing,' she said softly, laughing as the child stretched out a tiny hand to touch her face. 'I'll be sorry to see her go.'

'I've told you before,' Amelia said angrily, realising how like her husband she sounded, 'I don't want to know what happens after you leave here.'

She went hurriedly over to a small bureau in the corner, unlocked the top left-hand drawer and removed a cash-box, feeling Walters's eyes on her all the time. As she counted out thirty shillings on to the table, the other woman laid the child carefully down on the settee and scraped the money into her purse without waiting to be asked. 'It's not much to pay for a clear conscience,' she said quietly. 'Not when you expect me to do all your dirty work.'

'It's what we agreed.'

Walters picked the baby up and wrapped her in the thick blanket which Amelia had put ready. 'That was a long time ago, though, and you've kept me very busy just lately. Seems to me you should face up to the truth or pay a bit more for your ignorance.'

'I'm not listening,' Amelia said, still clutching the rest of the money. 'Just take the child and go.'

'What will it be this time, I wonder?' Walters mused, running her hand lightly across the baby's cheek. 'River or rubbish dump? Which do you fancy, my little one?'

Amelia turned away and put her hands over her ears. 'Stop it!' she screamed. 'Get out – *now*!'

There was a tentative knock at the door and a young woman looked in on them. She was the latest intake, and it was obvious from her swollen belly that the birth was only a matter of days away. 'Is everything all right?' she asked, looking curiously at Walters and the baby.

'Yes, Ada, we're fine,' Amelia said, pulling herself together. 'Go back upstairs – you should be resting.'

'You're kindness itself, aren't you?' Walters said sarcastically as soon as they were alone again. 'Always so concerned for their welfare. But what about my welfare, eh? Who looks out for me? I'm taking all the risks here, while you sleep easy in your bed. How do I know you won't turn me in?'

'Because we're in this together,' Amelia said, horrified at how true it was. 'Now just leave.' Walters opened her mouth to speak but changed her mind, and turned to go with nothing more than a defiant glance. Amelia heard the front door close and, in response, footsteps from the room above, and realised that the baby's mother – still weak after the birth – must have struggled out of bed and walked over to the window for a final glimpse of her child. What in God's name must she be thinking? Amelia wondered. Was she trying to imagine the fine, wealthy lady who would bring her daughter up, or did she know in her heart that Walters's was the last touch which the baby would know? The thought made her desperate to see Lizzie and she hurried up to the nursery. When she opened the door, the child was standing over by the window and she turned an excited face to her mother.

'It's so cold now, Mummy. Do you think it's going to snow?'

'Oh, it's bound to soon,' Amelia said, bending down to cuddle her. They looked out of the window together, trying to see beyond their own reflection to the darkness of the yard and the houses opposite and, as she caught sight of herself next to her daughter's innocence, it seemed to Amelia that her own face had grown so much older in the last few months. If only it were just the physical shell that decayed with age, she thought, and not the heart: the world – her world – would be a very different place.

'What's that, Mummy?' Lizzie asked, pointing to the handful of five-pound notes that her mother had forgotten to put back in the bureau before coming upstairs.

'That's Christmas,' she said, smiling.

Lizzie frowned. 'But Christmas is too far away.'

'Oh, it's only a few weeks, and they'll fly by quickly enough as long as you're good.' She hugged her daughter tightly. 'And I promise you – it will be the best Christmas that any little girl could have.'

Chapter Two

Josephine tore the sheet of paper out of the typewriter and added it to the others on her desk, pleased to see that the pile was steadily growing but relieved to be able to step back into the present for a while. She couldn't quite put her finger on why, but the conversation with Celia had unsettled her and she found retracing the origins of Lizzie Sach's suicide unaccountably depressing. Standing up to stretch her legs, she looked around the room and realised that its measured comfort and privacy were suddenly not at all what she wanted; right now, she felt like some company. It was a little after nine o'clock and still early enough to while away a couple of hours in the bar, but she was reluctant to run the risk of getting embroiled in the club's politics and, in any case, small talk with comparative strangers wasn't really what she was looking for. Perhaps it was time she owned up to being in town and went to see Archie? He wouldn't mind being interrupted at this time of night and she knew she could rely on him to dilute Celia's disapproval with a genuine interest in what she was doing. Even if he was out, a walk through the West End at night would cheer her after an evening spent with Sach and Walters.

She changed quickly and found Archie's flat-warming present among the pile of packages that Robert had brought up earlier, then went downstairs to the bar to collect a bottle of wine. It was quiet for the time of night and the only person Josephine recognised among the handful of women was Geraldine Ashby. She sat alone at a table, and Josephine was surprised to see that – unguarded and, as she thought, unscrutinised – Geraldine's face wore a very different expression from its usual blasé cheerfulness. Tonight, as she stared across the room at a group of young nurses who had obviously just come off duty, her sadness made her seem remote and untouchable. The mask fell effortlessly back into place as soon as she realised she had company, but the contrast made her fleeting melancholy even more striking.

'Josephine – thank God,' she said, coming over to the bar. 'This place is like a morgue tonight. You'll have a drink with me, I hope?'

'I can't, Gerry – I'm sorry. I've only popped in to get a bottle.' She chose from the list and waited while the wine was brought up from the cellar. 'Where were you, anyway? You seemed miles away.'

'Oh, you know – a collection of pretty young women in uniform. It's easy to get distracted.' The comment was perfectly in character but, from what Josephine had seen a moment ago, casual flirting could not have been further from Geraldine's mind. 'And talking of idle distractions,' she added, 'if you're ordering fine wines to take off the premises, you must have tracked down your mystery admirer. Am I right?'

'I'm not sure, but there's only one way to find out,' Josephine said, smiling. 'I'll let you know tomorrow.'

It was a beautifully clear night, but cold, and Josephine pulled her fur closer round her as she walked briskly down Oxford Street and into Charing Cross Road. Archie's new flat was in Maiden Lane, and she had been amused to hear that his cousins, Ronnie and Lettice, had heard about his lucky find and had immediately snapped up the remaining three apartments in the same building for themselves and their housekeeper, Mrs Snipe. It would hardly be the peaceful bachelor pad Archie had had in mind, but it was unlikely ever to be dull. At the junction of Cranbourn Street and Long Acre, she paused briefly to look down St Martin's Lane towards the New Theatre, where three of her plays had been staged in the last eighteen months, and realised how relieved she felt to be in London with no responsibilities and no obligations to attend a first night or promote her work in any way. Shakespeare was welcome to the limelight for a bit, she thought, noticing the posters for *Romeo and Juliet* which covered the front of the theatre; she was happy now to sit quietly in the audience and enjoy the fruits of other people's labours. Across the street from the New, the lights were still on in the Motley workrooms. Josephine knew from past experience that Lettice and Ronnie were likely to be there long into the night, somehow fitting the Cowdray Club gala in around whatever theatre productions they were currently working on. She resisted the temptation to stop by and say hello – there was no such thing as a quick chat with the Motley sisters – and quickened her step, making short work of Garrick Street.

Maiden Lane was a narrow road which ran parallel with the Strand and was used, it seemed, as a shortcut between Bedford Street and Covent Garden. Josephine walked along the cobbles, past a series of restaurants which were quiet at the moment but bracing themselves for the post-theatre crowd, and found the number she was looking for next to the stage door of the Vaudeville Theatre. It was a tall, narrow building, and she was pleased to see a light on in the top flat; the rest of the house

47

was in darkness. None of the doorbells outside was labelled, so she rang them all and waited. A couple of minutes later, she heard footsteps thundering down the stairs and Archie pulled the door open, looking furious.

'Josephine!' His impatience turned to delight as soon as he saw her. 'I didn't think you were in town until the weekend. What a lovely surprise!'

'I won't stay long if this is a bad time,' she said, kissing him. 'You didn't look like a man who needed visitors when you answered the door.'

'Don't be silly – I thought you were Ronnie. She's locked herself out five times in the last two days, and I swear she's started to do it deliberately just to keep me fit.' He smiled, and stood aside to let her in. 'It's wonderful to see you. Why the change of plan?'

'Oh, there's some research I need to do for a new book idea,' she explained casually, hoping he wouldn't ask exactly how long she'd been in London. 'I thought I might as well build it in around the gala night next week. And now I'm here, I'm dying to see your new pad.'

'As long as you're not expecting too much – nothing looks very impressive at the moment. I haven't even unpacked yet and none of the furniture's arrived – but the most comfortable box is all yours.' He took the bottle she offered him and looked approvingly at the label. 'You might have to be patient while I look for some proper glasses, though. We're not drinking this out of a mug.'

She followed him up three flights of stairs to the top of the house. 'Are Ronnie and Lettice working late? I saw the lights on in the studio as I came past.'

'Oh, someone's bound to be there,' Archie said. 'They're

48

snowed under at the moment, and there's been much muttering about extra staff and overtime rates, as you can imagine. But they're actually having some time off tonight – it's the Snipe's birthday, and they've taken her to see *Romeo and Juliet*.'

'Lucky her. I can't wait to see it.'

'Mm. I'm not sure how much of a treat the Snipe regards it as. When she left this evening, she was still muttering that if she wanted to see two families at each other's throats, she could have stayed at home and saved them the expense of an extra ticket. At least they're taking her for supper afterwards.'

Josephine laughed. 'I think even the Snipe will be won over. Peggy's supposed to be magnificent as Juliet, although I shall have to tell Lydia that she's awful if I'm put on the spot. She still hasn't forgiven Johnny for not casting her – and with nothing else in her life at the moment, a snub like that is bound to hurt.'

'It's not like Lydia to be without a girl on her arm for so long, is it?'

Archie's comment was light-hearted, but it was true enough: the actress's reputation for attracting and tiring of a succession of lovers was legendary; only once had Josephine ever seen her truly settled, but the relationship had ended in difficult circumstances the year before, with Josephine caught in the middle of it. 'I think she's hoping to make a new start with Marta eventually,' she explained as he showed her into his flat. 'She's never been as happy with anyone else.'

'Has she heard from Marta, then?'

'Not as far as I know.' She left Archie rummaging around in a tiny kitchen to find a glass to match the quality of the wine, and walked through to the living room. It was even more chaotic than he had suggested, but the piles of boxes – some half-unpacked, apparently at random – could not hide what a beautiful space it was. Archie had obviously been working before she interrupted him. A makeshift desk and chair had been fashioned from a couple of large book trunks, and a ciga-rette burned slowly down in an ashtray next to an untouched mug of coffee and a pile of folders and paperwork. Idly, Josephine glanced down at a series of black-and-white photo-graphs; by the time she realised what she was staring at, it was too late to walk away. A dark-haired woman of around forty was lying back on a bed with what looked like a silk stocking tied around her neck. Her left leg was bare. A tassel attached to the jumper she was wearing seemed to be caught in the liga-ture, and there were bruises on her neck and around her throat. On the pillow, a few inches from the woman's head, there was a thin dental plate, presumably dislodged from her mouth as she struggled.

'Oh shit,' Archie said from the door, 'I'd forgotten they were out.' He put the glasses down and hurriedly gathered up the files. 'Sorry – you shouldn't have seen those.'

'My fault for looking,' Josephine said, still a little shocked. 'Poor devil – what happened?'

'I'm not sure yet. The maid found her strangled in her flat in Piccadilly. She was in debt to the tune of forty guineas for some furs, and there was talk of suicide but Spilsbury's convinced it was murder. One of the neighbours heard her arguing with a man about money the night before.'

'And you don't know who he was?'

'No, but there's no shortage of candidates – she'd been up in court on seventy-four counts of prostitution before she died.'

'Then I can see why you haven't unpacked.' She chose a box

next to the fireplace and sat down. A fire was already laid in the grate – the only impression that Mrs Snipe had been allowed to make on the room as yet – and Archie threw her some matches to light it.

'That's just the beginning,' he said, carefully uncorking the bottle. 'There are three other cases on the go, not to mention a load of extra paperwork. It's always the same after a general election – they want to reassure people that they're safe in their beds so we have a complete overhaul of all the procedures, only to carry on in exactly the same way.' He sighed and gestured towards the boxes. 'So it might be some time before this lot gets sorted. I think I'll just wait a month and assume that anything which hasn't surfaced by then is surplus to requirements. That way, I can give all the unopened boxes to the deserving poor. We'll let this breathe in the glass, shall we?'

Josephine nodded, and held both drinks while he pulled another box up to the hearth. 'Do you want some help?' she asked, glancing round at the chaos.

'God no – let's just enjoy a drink. I'm spending so little time here at the moment that it hardly matters.'

'Well, start by opening this,' she said, handing over the flat, square parcel. 'At least the walls are peaceful – you might even be able to see it.'

Intrigued, Archie unwrapped the brown paper and stared in delight at the painting, a delicate watercolour of a lake surrounded by woodland and the perfect likeness of his home in Cornwall, where he and Josephine had spent some time together during the summer. Regardless of its personal meaning, the painting was superb and the artist – like all the best watercolourists – had made the medium look deceptively simple. The minute detail of the trees contrasted with spon taneous washes of colour for the sky and the surface of the water and, looking at it now, Josephine felt as though she would sense the magic of the place even if she had never been there.

'Loe Pool!' Archie exclaimed. 'Where on earth did you find this?'

'I got it while I was there,' she said, pleased that he liked it so much. 'There was a painter on holiday – he was staying in the village, but he was by the lake whenever I went for a walk; I must have seen him do at least fifteen pictures. I pestered him to let me buy one, and eventually he agreed – just to get rid of me, probably. It came back from the framer this afternoon.' She watched his face as he looked down at the painting, and knew that he was thinking about the tragic events that had taken place there just a few months earlier. 'I thought it might help to remind you of how beautiful the place is,' she added gently, 'and perhaps wipe out a few images that aren't so pleasant.'

Archie looked across at her. 'Thank you,' he said quietly. 'It's perfect.' He stood up and held the painting against the wall, where a previous occupant had obligingly left a picture hook. 'Over the fireplace, I think, don't you?' She nodded, and he hung it in place, then picked up his glass. 'To a quieter winter.'

'I'll drink to that.'

'Now – tell me about this new book.'

Josephine accepted a cigarette, and Archie listened while she outlined the crimes of Sach and Walters and explained her own connection with Sach's daughter. 'Have you heard of the case?' she asked when she'd finished.

He shook his head. 'No, although the crime's familiar and I know about Dyer. She tends to eclipse everyone else, simply because she was so prolific. It's funny you should mention it now, though – it's very topical. Baby farmers are high on the government's new agenda.'

'What? You mean it still goes on?'

'Absolutely. The Home Secretary's just announced a new committee to look into the whole adoption issue. Wait a minute.' He got up to rummage through a pile of newspapers, and handed her a copy of Tuesday's *Daily Mail*. 'Here you are – "Government Drive against Baby Farmers". The process is different these days, of course – it's more a case of selling babies to countries where it's illegal to adopt native children – but the principle is exactly the same. Making money out of unwanted children.' He refilled their glasses while she read the newspaper article, then asked: 'What will the book be? A fictionalised account of the Sach and Walters case, or a modern version of it?'

'I haven't really decided. It's so different from anything I've written recently that it hasn't found its shape yet. I suppose *Kif* is the closest I've come to looking at the story of a crime without turning it into a detective novel, so it's a bit like going back to the first book I ever wrote, but with a true case. Anyway, I'm going to have a look through all the newspaper accounts of the trial tomorrow and find out as much as I can about the two women to see what that throws up, but I think what really interests me is the impact the crimes had on everyone else around them. When Sach met Walters – however that happened – they set up a chain of events which didn't just stop with their execution, and so many people were drawn into it; their families, the mothers of the children, the people who were responsible for them in prison. It's a whole cast of characters, unconnected except by these two women and changed by them for ever. Look at what happened to Elizabeth Sach, for God's sake, and that was nearly fifteen years later. I don't think I'd be taking this on if I hadn't known her and seen first hand how crimes can linger.'

'That's interesting. It sounds like your book starts where most of them finish.'

'Yes, I suppose it does.' She smiled. 'I think I've only just realised that myself. You don't often get the aftermath in detective fiction – the sense of life going on, I mean. Or not going on, in Lizzie's case. It's funny, and I hadn't thought about it before, but Lizzie would never have been able to come to terms with what her mother did because she wasn't given the chance to talk to her about it. The death sentence doesn't allow for that sort of solace.' She set down her glass for a second to put some more coal on the fire. 'I'm glad you think it sounds interesting, though – I was beginning to have my doubts after talking to Celia earlier. She wasn't exactly encouraging.'

'Her name sounds familiar. She was one of the warders, you say?'

'That's right. And she does a lot of charity work, so her name's often in the papers – usually mentioned in the same breath as the Queen.'

He laughed at her expression of distaste. 'The society pages aren't exactly the ones I'm drawn to first when I pick up *The Times*.'

'No, nor me. But she did tell me she's called your lot in to the Cowdray Club – perhaps that it's, although I wouldn't have thought it was serious enough to bother the inspector with.'

'Ah, the anonymous letters – that's it. I knew I'd heard her name recently.'

'Letters?'

54

'Yes. Sorry – I shouldn't have said anything, but it sounded like you already knew.'

'I don't know anything about anonymous letters. Celia told me it was theft.'

'Yes, there's been some of that, too, apparently, but you're right – that wouldn't concern us. Unpleasant letters to the great and the good, however, are a different matter altogether. The chief constable's wife is a member.'

'Unpleasant in what way?'

'I suppose spiteful would be the best word to describe them. There's nothing threatening or violent about them, but they play on people's vulnerabilities with remarkable skill. Four members of the staff or committee have had them so far, including Miss Bannerman herself.'

'And do they come from another member or from outside the club?'

'We don't know yet, and I can't go into details, but they imply a knowledge of the recipients rather than just random targeting.'

'How upsetting. Celia said there'd been trouble between the nurses and the other members – I wonder if it's anything to do with that?'

'Possibly. I don't think you need to worry, though – it's not the members themselves who are receiving them; only people closely involved in the running of the club. You haven't had anything, have you?'

Josephine decided to come clean. 'Nothing like that, no – only a mysterious gardenia that no one seemed to want to put a name to.'

'What?' he asked in mock offence. 'You mean someone's welcomed you to town before I did? I'll have to up my act.'

'Well, at least wait until the other one's died – the room's too small to look like a florist's shop.' She drained her glass. 'I'd better go – it's late, and I've got a long morning at the British Museum ahead of me.'

'I'll walk you back – unless you'd rather take a cab?'

'No – let's walk.' They went out into the street and headed towards Leicester Square, and Josephine took his arm, enjoying the easy way that she and Archie seemed to fall into each other's company these days, no matter how long it was since they were last together. It hadn't always been that way: when Josephine's lover – Archie's closest friend – had been killed at the Somme, Archie had blamed himself, and the subsequent distance between them, the impossibility of ever understanding how the other truly felt, was one of the many ways in which the war had blighted the lives of those who survived it. She knew that their relationship would never be straightforward – neither of them had the temperament to make it so – but they had both learned to accept its limitations, and to rely on an honesty and understanding which they found only in each other. 'I wonder why Celia didn't mention anything about those letters to me?' Josephine asked as they picked their way through the late-night revellers in Piccadilly.

'Nothing more sinister than an eye on the club's reputation, I should think. You're a client as well as an acquaintance, don't forget, and she won't want to unsettle the members. She's got books to balance, and discretion and privacy are what her customers pay for. News of this getting out is the last thing she needs, especially with the gala coming up on Monday. That's bound to attract publicity.'

'You're still coming with me, I hope?'

'Of course, although I'm heartily sick of it already. Whenever I do see Lettice and Ronnie, it's all they seem to talk about.'

'It's quite a coup for the club, though, getting Noël and Gertie – especially when *Tonight at 8.30* hasn't even been seen in London yet.'

'Isn't some relative of his involved in the Cowdray Club?'

'His aunt, yes. He agreed to do it for her as long as some of the money goes to the Actors' Orphanage. He's president, and he takes his role very seriously, apparently. I suppose that'll be another bone of contention – even less money for the nurses.'

'It could turn into quite an interesting evening – anonymous letters, charities at each other's throats. I suppose it's more interesting than just waiting to see what plum role Noël's written for himself this time.'

She hit his shoulder playfully. 'Don't act the cynic with me. You loved *Private Lives* when we went to see it. In fact, I seem to remember you were quite tongue-tied with awe when Gertie spoke to you at the party afterwards, and we could all hear the ice cubes rattling when she asked you to hold her drink.'

'All right, all right,' he said, holding his hands up in defeat as they turned into Cavendish Square. 'I do have a soft spot for Miss Lawrence but I'll try to curb it on the night.' They stopped outside the club. 'Listen, I don't know how much time I'll have over the weekend, but it would be nice to see you. Do you have any plans?'

'Only to get some more work done, and to call in on the girls to try the dress they've made me for the gala. They haven't told me anything about it, but they've made enough clothes for me by now to know what I like.'

'I've seen it, and I don't think you'll be disappointed. Shall I telephone when I know what I'm doing?'

'Yes, do. There's a new Hitchcock on at the Odeon – we could go to see that.'

'Excellent, but it might be short notice.'

'That doesn't matter. I'll be here most of the time.'

'Am I allowed in if it's not on official business?'

'Only if I vouch for you, so no more talk of Gertrude Lawrence.' She kissed him goodnight and ran up the steps to the club, feeling much more cheerful than when she had left it. The lift was still out of order, so she took the stairs reluctantly, thinking how ashamed Celia Bannerman would be if she saw her pause for breath at the second flight: Anstey girls were not supposed to pant, even in the grip of approaching middle age. Ashamed of herself, she pushed on to the third floor and was surprised to see her bedroom door ajar. There was a light on inside, although she knew she had left the room in darkness, and the spiteful letters – which had seemed a world away in the warmth of Archie's flat – suddenly seemed much closer to home. Gently, she pushed the door open a little further. The lamp was on at her desk, and the girl she had met earlier – the one who had knocked her parcels to the floor – was standing by the chair, reading through the pile of papers which Josephine had left by her typewriter before she went out.

'What are you doing here at this time of night?' she asked, relieved and annoyed at the same time.

The girl jumped and threw the pages down as though they had scalded her. When she turned to face Josephine, it was obvious that she'd been crying. 'I'm so sorry, Miss. I brought you the vase that you asked for earlier, and I . . . I just . . .' Unable to control her tears, she pushed past Josephine and ran down the corridor towards the stairs.

Still a little shaken, Josephine glanced quickly round the

room to make sure that nothing was missing, then bent down to pick the pages up. She put them back in order, noticing that the ink on the most recent work was smudged in several places. Was this what had upset Lucy? she wondered, as angry at herself for leaving the work out in plain view as she was at the girl for reading what did not concern her. Or had something else happened in the club? Worried now, she walked quickly back to the main staircase, hoping to be able to call Lucy back and talk to her – but the girl was nowhere to be seen.

Chapter Three

'Fucking charity,' said Ronnie, shutting the door to the work-room behind her and leaning heavily against it as though something savage were at her heels. 'It may well begin at home, but I didn't expect to have to live with it morning, noon and night. I don't know why we do it to ourselves.'

Lettice looked up from the design she was working on and rinsed her paintbrush vigorously in a Staffordshire harvest jug which stood on her desk, chipped and missing its handle like most of the antiques she collected. 'Cheer up, darling,' she said brightly. 'It's nearly over.'

'Is it, though? I know we've almost finished the costumes, but somebody' – Ronnie looked pointedly at her sister – 'somebody agreed to make the do-gooders' evening gowns for them and donate all the profits to the charity. So now we've got to clothe the whole of the bloody Cowdray Club as well as their ridiculous gala night.' Lettice caught her eye accusingly. 'All right, I know there are only eight of them, but it *feels* like the whole club.'

'Seven, darling – you can't count Josephine. It'll be so nice to see her.'

'Of course it will, but I'll never understand how she can bear to rattle around with those harridans in Cavendish Square for weeks at a time.'

'It's convenient for her, and she couldn't have come to us

this time – it's chaos here and even worse at Maiden Lane. She says the club's very comfortable, though.'

'I'm sure it is, but all those women in one place . . .' Ronnie shuddered. 'It can't be healthy, and they're so *dull*. It's as much as I can do to stay awake for the duration of a fitting. Fittings that your generosity has thrust upon us, I might add.'

'I thought it would be a nice gesture to make the dresses as well,' Lettice said defensively, sucking the tip of her paintbrush to make a fine point. 'The nurses are a very good cause, after all, and those ladies on the committee work so hard to raise money for them.'

'Hard my arse! Swanning around with a glass of free champers in their hand?'

'Oh, I'm sure it's not all galas.'

'No – you're right. Twice a year they swap their designer gowns for some overalls and imagine they know what it's like to be a working girl. Jesus!' She held up her hands in exasperation. 'I can think of a nice gesture, too, but I can make mine sitting down.' She lit a cigarette and demonstrated. 'It *would* all have to happen when we've got work coming out of our ears, wouldn't it? There's all of Wendy's ballet to do before Christmas and we haven't even thought about *Bitter Harvest* yet – it's only a matter of time before the director asks to see the designs. In fact, we seem to have forgotten that we work in the theatre at all. Celia Bannerman and Amy Coward will be laughing their way to the bank in a haze of silk and chiffon, while our whole business goes to the dogs in tatters.'

'Oh for goodness' sake, darling – you do exaggerate.' There was a knock at the door, and an attractive dark-haired girl poked her head round without waiting for a response. It was a face which would have been more at home on a cinema screen than behind a sewing machine, and Lettice smiled at her, glad of some respite from Ronnie's tirade. 'Yes, Marjorie – what is it?'

'Mrs Reader says we've run out of black bugle beads, Miss, and someone from the club has just telephoned to see where the samples for the accessories are. Apparently you said one of us would drop them round to Cavendish Square. Do you want me to kill two birds with one stone?'

'Only if I can choose the birds,' Ronnie muttered sarcastically.

'Ignore her,' Lettice said, 'and yes please – that would be very helpful. There might be some other things we need from Debenhams, though – give me five minutes and I'll bring you a list.'

Marjorie shut the door behind her and Ronnie raised an eyebrow. 'So I exaggerate, do I? Accessories? They only have to snap their expensively manicured fingers for us to jump – and for what? The self-glorification of half a dozen bored women with more time and money than they know what to do with. Go on, admit it – you know I'm right.' She got up and looked over her sister's shoulders. 'God, that's good,' she said, admiring the delicate image which was just receiving its finishing touches. 'Please tell me we're not giving it away.'

'Of course we're not.' Lettice tore the sheet of thick white paper impatiently from its pad and waved it back and forth a few times to dry the paint. 'While you've been holding forth, I've been hard at it,' she said, and handed the page over smugly. 'I think you'll find that Wendy's ballet has been taking shape without you.' Enjoying the surprise on Ronnie's face, she continued: 'Anyway, not all charity is selfless – we took Marjorie on trust from prison and she's turned out to be the best seamstress we've got.'

'All right, all right – I agree with you completely about that, but rehabilitation is a very different thing from meddling and fundraising. I'm proud that we've been able to give Marjorie a fresh start – she's not even quite such a cheeky little madam as she was when she first arrived.'

Lettice laughed. 'I'm sure a girl needs a bit of spirit where she's been. Anyway, I always like to meet someone who can give you a run for your money.' She stood up and walked over to the glass that separated the main workroom from the small design studio which the sisters shared. 'And the other girls seem to like her. I was worried they'd give her a hard time at first, but she settled in right away. It's hard to believe she's only been with us for six months.'

Ronnie stubbed her cigarette out and joined her sister at the window. 'It's hard to believe that this is here at all,' she said, looking across at the roomful of women, engrossed in a series of small individual tasks that made up a remarkably successful whole – a business which now occupied two houses in St Martin's Lane and kept sixty people on the payroll, including thirty fulltime seamstresses. 'The last eighteen months have been extraordinary, haven't they? First *Hamlet*, and now *Romeo* – we've never had better notices than the ones we're getting at the moment. Johnny's certainly been lucky for us.'

'And Josephine – if it weren't for the success of *Richard of Bordeaux*, I'm not sure any of us would have had the freedom we've enjoyed since.'

They watched as their head cutter showed one of the newer girls how to work with a length of beautiful soft crêpe, re-assuring her when she got it wrong and patiently starting again at the beginning. 'Look at Hilda,' Ronnie said affectionately. 'Do you remember when she taught us to cut fabric and make

64

up costumes like that? She was the village dressmaker's niece and we couldn't tell one end of a needle from the other – who'd have thought that we'd all end up here?'

'And thank God she still enjoys it as much as we do. I suppose we could have our pick of cutters and supervisors now, but I honestly think the whole place would fall apart if Hilda left us.'

'Then let's just pray that she doesn't – and if good works will keep the sun shining down on us, then I suppose we can afford a few free frocks. You'd better get that girl over there sharpish with her samples.'

Lettice jotted some items down on a bit of paper and went out into the workroom to deliver her list. 'Ask them to put it all on our account,' she said, piling a glut of brightly coloured materials into Marjorie's arms to be parcelled up. 'And deliver the samples to Miss Bannerman at the club, with this letter. We've only got a few days to make any alterations, so if she can send a couple of the women round this afternoon, that would be helpful. But don't be long – there's still so much to do today. Take the bus, and get back here by lunchtime at the latest.'

'With the change from the bus fare,' Ronnie called, winking at the girl. 'We know what you're like.'

'If you did, Miss, you'd blush,' Marjorie said good-naturedly, winking back. 'I'll see you later if I don't get a better offer.'

Marjorie went down the corridor to the small back room where the girls kept their outdoor clothes and rifled through the layers of coats and scarves which accumulated each morning, looking for her own modest raincoat. The racks held a hotch-potch of clothing, which functioned as a catalogue of styles from the last twenty years or more – the Motley sisters were fair with their wages but a good coat, once afforded, was unlikely to be replaced quickly for the sake of fashion, even here. The varying shapes and sizes reminded her of her last day in prison, walking down the line of discharge cubicles to the one where her own clothes awaited her, past a series of outfits which would have been the envy of any jumble sale in London – petticoats, skirts and hand-knitted jumpers, some in preposterous colours, others faded and drab; some torn and stained, others smarter and more respectable. It was a brief glimpse of lives waiting to begin again, and it mattered because it was the moment when women found their old selves, free of the levelling effect of prison and the loss of individuality – femininity, even – which was standard Holloway procedure.

She found her coat and tied the belt tightly round her waist, remembering how, at the end of her last sentence, a fur coat had graced one of the cells, removed from its mothballs and looking as good as new after months of careful storage. A black crêpe de Chine dress was on a hanger next to it and, on the bench, washed and neatly folded, lay a pair of black silk panties, some stockings and a pale pink brassiere. Marjorie had stopped for a moment, transfixed by clothes which were so unfamiliar, and had tried to imagine how the underwear would feel against her skin. What sort of life would she be returning to if she owned clothes like that? she wondered, but the prison officer moved her roughly on to the end of the row before she could decide and she became Marjorie Baker again, equal to the best of them while she was inside but nothing special anywhere else. The sight of her own clothes mocked any illusions she might still have harboured. There was no need for a hanger here: the worn woollen cardigan, second-hand skirt and loose-fitting stockings – mended and torn again, just like her life –

sat in a shapeless pile on a chair. She had been brought in to Holloway in winter; now it was May, but no one at home could be bothered to bring her clothes better suited to a summer release and she had been too proud to accept the offer of something from the prisoners' aid store. Shaking off the memory, Marjorie picked up the parcel and envelopes, then, as she noticed a lipstick poking out of one of the girls' pockets, put it down again and helped herself. It would have been easy to take a few bob from these pockets, but the theft would surely be traced back to her and, in any case, she had never had the stomach for stealing from her own sort. She examined her reflection in a small powder compact which someone had obligingly left out, then put the lipstick back where it came from. Even now, six months after her release, she found it hard to get the thought of those other clothes out of her head. But that was her trouble – her mother had often said so, and Marjorie knew she was right. She was never satisfied, never had been. She always wanted something more.

Not that there had been much to be satisfied with until now, she thought, picking her way carefully down the iron staircase which led out into the cobbled courtyard at the back of the premises. Being brought up in Campbell Road – the sort of street you had to lie about living in if you were to stand a chance in hell of getting work – wasn't exactly the perfect start in life. Seven households shared number 35, and the Bakers had a room at the top, across the landing from a knife-grinder and his family. There was nothing unusual about their slum; the pattern was repeated all the way up the street, and she'd had to laugh back in May, just after she came out, when the old Poor But Loyal bedsheet banner was dragged out for the Jubilee, just like it always was for any day of national celebration. There it hung, amongst the tattered bunting and faded Union Jacks – but loyal to what? she had wondered. To a king who didn't even know they existed? Or to the good old days of community life, when Campbell Road muddled through, immune to interference from outsiders? Surely the only people who truly believed that were the ones who had never lived there. As far as Marjorie was concerned, the only thing the street had going for it was its proximity to Holloway; at least she never had to worry about finding the bus fare home when they let her out.

She crossed St Martin's Lane and cut through Cecil Court, passing between two theatres to get to Charing Cross Road. A bus was already in sight and she had to run to catch it, but the pavements were quiet at this time of the morning and she reached the stop in plenty of time. Although there was scarcely anybody on board, a man gave up his seat for her at the front of the lower deck. She accepted it with a polite smile, then looked steadfastly out of the window, making it impossible for him to benefit from his gallantry by forcing a conversation. If there was one important lesson that her father had taught her, it was that men were not to be relied upon for anything in life, and she had long since perfected a way of discouraging them from believing that her good looks were any reason to be hopeful. He was a waster, her dad – and had been for as long as she could remember. A builder's labourer by trade, he travelled all over north London but they were lucky if he came home with thirty shillings a week and, when he wasn't working, he was in and out of jail on a series of petty charges. He was a philanderer, too – she had known what that was long before she ever heard the word – and he had made the years that followed the war work for him, taking advantage of women who, with a shortage of men and no prospects of their own marriage, were prepared to lower their standards and settle for a share in somebody else's. She hated his weakness and his cheap opportunism, but despised her mother even more for allowing it to happen. In her mother's unquestioning acceptance of her lot, Marjorie had seen the image of her own future. It rang a warning bell in her head, louder and more lasting than any deterrent which an institution could throw at her, and it told her to make self-reliance her guiding principle – no matter how much trouble that brought or what the consequences were.

She rang the bell for the bus to drop her at Oxford Circus and strolled slowly down Holles Street, savouring the novel experience of walking through a decent part of town and having a reason to be there. This time, surely, things ought to be different? She had a new job – one that she was good at, which wasn't the same, day in, day out; she had friends, some from Holloway and others found within the easy camaraderie of the Motley girls; and, for the first time in her life, she could see a way out of Campbell Road. It ought to be enough. Yet still the dissatisfaction gnawed away at her, still she knew that – sooner or later – she'd be chasing something else, proving her mother right. 'We know what you're like,' Miss Motley had said and, while Marjorie knew that no malice had been intended by the comment, the predictable future which it hinted at – the impossibility of change – depressed her. She hesitated for a moment outside 20 Cavendish Square; then, when she was sure she was tidy and presentable, she walked boldly through the Cowdray Club's doors, marvelling at how readily they opened for her. It was true, people *did* know what her sort was like – but they didn't know what she *could* be; she didn't even know that herself. Perhaps this time she'd have the chance to find out.

She stood patiently in the entrance hall, waiting for the woman behind the desk to finish speaking on the telephone. Prison taught you to see people as types rather than human beings, and – as the receptionist stretched out her conversation for as long as possible, making her wait and throwing practised smiles at the members as they passed through, thinking she was one of them – Marjorie could tell instantly what sort of creature she was. This small area, where people came and went but never stayed for long, was the only empire she would ever know, and she was welcome to it; there was a big, wide world out there, and she was not about to be made to feel uncomfortable by a glorified message-taker. 'Can I help you?' the woman asked at last, looking grudgingly at Marjorie.

'I've come from Motley to deliver these for the gala evening,' she said, putting the parcel of materials down on the counter. 'They're for Miss Bannerman.'

'Leave them with me. I'll make sure she gets them,' the receptionist said with a dismissive nod.

'There's a note here from Miss Motley, too,' Marjorie continued, undaunted. 'She'd be obliged if you could let Miss Bannerman have everything straight away.'

There was a heavy sigh. 'Miss Bannerman is very busy this morning, but I'm sure she'll attend to . . .' – she waved her hand vaguely at the parcel – 'to whatever seems to be so urgent as soon as she has a moment.'

Marjorie was about to argue when she felt a hearty slap on the shoulder. 'Baker – how nice to see you!' The Irish accent was unmistakeable, warm but full of authority. Enjoying the surprise on the receptionist's face, Marjorie turned round to greet Mary Size, but her sense of one-upmanship was not the only reason why she was genuinely pleased to see the deputy governor of Holloway. Like most of the girls who had passed through prison on her watch, Marjorie had an ungrudging respect for Miss Size and the way she approached a difficult and often unrewarding job. Despite her vast list of responsibilities, Marjorie had never known her to refuse to see anyone, inmate or member of staff, and she listened to the most trivial request or serious complaint with patience and a fair mind – qualities which were more valuable to those on the receiving end of them than any other. Miss Size had an instinctive understanding of what mattered to women in prison and, although her reforms fell far short of her ideals, her passion for improvement was strong. Thanks to her, the women now had looking glasses in their cells and photographs on their walls, and Marjorie was not the only discharged girl to owe her first job to Miss Size's quiet but imaginative scheming.

'Baker and I go back a long way, Miss Timpson,' the governor explained, seeming to enjoy the receptionist's astonishment as much as Marjorie. 'Don't we, Baker?'

'Yes, Miss – three stretches now, isn't it?'

'You haven't lost your sense of humour, I see. What brings you to this part of town? Are you here to see Peters?'

'No, Miss, I'm on an errand from Motley – it's for the gala next week.'

'Ah, yes – I'm looking forward to that. Which reminds me – am I supposed to pick the dress up or something?'

'No, Miss – we'll deliver them to the club. But you do need to stop by and have a final fitting first, just to make sure every-thing's all right. In fact,' she added, looking pointedly at the Timpson woman, 'that's partly why I'm here. Miss Motley needs to see everyone as soon as possible in case we have to make any alterations.'

'Fine, fine – I'll come after lunch on my way back to the prison. Will that be all right?'

'Yes, Miss, of course – and anyone else who's free today.'

'Wait here – I'll see who's about.' Marjorie did as she was told, smiling infuriatingly at Miss Timpson, while Mary Size put her head round the door of the bar. 'Gerry,' she called, 'you're going to the gala, aren't you? Come out here a minute.' The woman who came out into the hallway wore a stunning Schiaparelli trouser suit, and Marjorie remembered her from an earlier visit to Motley; in fact, she was the sort it would have been impossible to forget. 'We're needed for another fitting. Could you do Miss Baker here a favour and pop round to St Martin's Lane this afternoon?'

Geraldine smiled. 'It would be a pleasure.' She walked over to Marjorie and brazenly stroked her cheek. 'Nice to see you again, Miss Baker. Will you be looking after me again this afternoon?'

'I don't know, Miss,' Marjorie said modestly. 'It depends what Mrs Reader has got lined up for me when I get back. I suppose I could say you'd asked for me personally.'

'Yes, why don't you do that? I'll be there around five but, if I'm late, I'm sure you'll wait for me.'

'I'll put you in the book. It's Lady Ashby, isn't it?'

'That's right,' she said, drifting back towards the bar. 'Sweet of you to remember.'

'You're still in touch with Peters, I hope?' Miss Size asked as Marjorie made a note of the appointment. 'You were a good friend to her during her spell with us, and I'd like to know you're keeping an eye on her now you're both out.'

'Oh yes, Miss – we go out and have a bit of a laugh when we can. We had a day out last weekend and I saw her yesterday. She was all right – a bit quiet, that's all.'

'Well, that's only to be expected, but she'll perk up again, I'm sure. Are you going to say hello to her now, as you're here? I'm sure Miss Timpson would be only too happy to fetch her for you.' Her manner was courteous enough, but there was a twinkle in her eye as she turned back to the desk. 'That would be all right, wouldn't it?'

'Lucy Peters isn't due her break for another ten minutes,' the receptionist said, standing her ground as best she could. 'I'll let her know that Miss – uh – Miss Baker would like to see her, though.'

'Excellent. And I'll see you later, Baker.'

She walked off into the club and Marjorie was left alone with Miss Timpson's thinly disguised pique. 'If you'd like to wait outside, I'll tell Lucy you're here,' she said. 'We don't allow staff to fraternise on the premises.'

Marjorie couldn't be bothered to argue over the battle when the war was so clearly hers, so she did as she was asked and strolled over to one of the benches in the middle of Cavendish Square. It was cold but not unpleasant, and the sun was out, so she sat down and lit a cigarette, keeping a nervous eye on the clock which graced the front of the Westminster Bank. It wasn't the day to get into trouble with the Motley sisters, not with the deputy governor due, and she was about to give up and carry on with her list of errands when Lucy appeared at the corner of Henrietta Street. Marjorie waved, and beckoned her over. 'Where the bleeding hell have you been?' she asked. 'I've been here fifteen minutes, and I'll be out on my ear if I'm not back by lunchtime.'

'Sorry, but that bitch on reception made me wipe all the ashtrays in the drawing room before she'd let me out.' Lucy accepted a cigarette gratefully. 'I'm glad you're here, though – there's something I need you to do for me.' She reached under her coat and took a small silver photograph frame out of the pocket of her apron. 'Will you look after this for me for a bit?'

Marjorie took it from her and looked down at the image of a woman and her young baby. 'Where did you get this?'

Lucy wouldn't meet her eye. 'I found it on one of the women's writing desks. I know I shouldn't have taken it, but I couldn't help myself – she's such a lovely little thing. I can't keep it in my room,' she explained, and Marjorie could see that she was close to tears. 'I overheard Bannerman talking about getting the police in, and they're bound to come to me first – they always do.'

'Well this is hardly worth getting caught for, is it?' Marjorie said, angry at her friend's stupidity. 'What the hell are you thinking of?' Then, as she saw the sadness on the young girl's face, she softened. 'Look, Lucy, you've got to be careful,' she continued, putting her arm round her. 'You've got to put all that behind you and get on with your life, and you won't change anything by nicking worthless bits of tat.'

'It's all right for you – you've got a good job and some girls to have a bit of fun with – and a bloke who'd look after you if you'd let him.'

Marjorie gave a scornful laugh. 'It's himself he'd be looking after, not me,' she said. 'You should know that after what you've been through. They're all the same, men, wherever they come from, and a girl's got no chance of a life if she waits for a bloke to help her. You make your own luck, Luce, but not like

74

this.' She held up the stolen frame, then put it in her pocket. 'I'll keep it safe for you, of course I will, but don't go nicking anything else – I've got something much better than that lined up.' She smiled and pinched Lucy's cheek, trying to cheer the girl up. 'Something that'll be enough for us both. If we're going back down, we might as well go properly, eh?' It was a joke, but the worried look on Lucy's face exasperated her. 'Don't you want anything better than this?' she asked impatiently. 'Scrubbing tables while that lot look down their noses at you?'

'It's not so bad,' Lucy said defiantly. 'I've got somewhere to live and a bit of money coming in.'

'Yeah, and for that you're supposed to spend every waking hour being grateful to them. Have you forgotten all those things we talked about? A flat of our own one day, flowers on the table and friends to visit. A gramophone. The odd trip to the pictures, even?' Lucy began to smile again. 'That's better,' Marjorie continued. 'There's no one in the world who can stop us having that if we're clever.'

'I suppose not, but won't you even tell me what you're up to?'

'Best that you don't know at the moment. But you trust me, don't you?'

Lucy nodded reluctantly. 'I'd better get back,' she said. 'I don't want any more trouble today.'

Marjorie gave her a hug, and they walked back towards the club. 'Looks like you got out just in time, Luce,' she said, glancing across the road to where a middle-aged man was getting out of a car. 'That's a copper if ever I saw one.' Lucy followed her gaze, and Marjorie saw the fear return to her eyes. 'Chin up, girl,' she said. 'You'll be all right. There's nothing else dodgy in your room, is there?' Lucy shook her head. 'Good – then you've got nothing to worry about. Is it your afternoon off tomorrow?'

'Yeah, I'm off at one.'

'Then I'll meet you here and we can go for a walk. I might have some good news for you by then.'

'News about what?'

'About our future.' She threw the end of her last cigarette on to the pavement and ground it under her shoe, then kissed Lucy quickly on the cheek. 'Start making a list of films you'd like to see,' she called back over her shoulder.

'Tell the sergeant I'll be with him in a few minutes.' Celia Bannerman put the receiver back on its cradle and sighed heavily. Miss Timpson's announcement of Scotland Yard in her foyer felt like a personal blow, and she did not need the disapproval in the receptionist's voice to tell her that a policeman's arrival undermined everything she had done for the Cowdray Club over the years, and threatened all that she still hoped to achieve. She had had no choice but to involve the police – the women who had received the letters had insisted on it – but, now they were here, a process had been set in motion which was no longer entirely under her control and she felt uneasy, perhaps even a little afraid. How many of those women would thank her, she wondered, when their privacy was disturbed, their pasts raked over? Surely she was not the only one who had done things in her life which she regretted? And even if the matter was resolved satisfactorily, the fact that she had allowed it to arise at all would still hang over her as a mark of failure, proof that she was undeserving of the trust which Lady Cowdray had placed in her.

She would have to tell the president, of course. Although the club functioned independently, it was linked to the College of Nursing by funding and by reputation, and any trouble in one body would soon seep through to the other. She was lucky that she had been able to contain it until now, but the last thing she needed was for Miriam Sharpe to bump into Scotland Yard with no warning. They came from two different sides of nursing: Sharpe was a hands-on traditionalist through and through, scathing about so many of the changes that had taken place in medicine over the years, and they had never had an easy relationship. While Lady Cowdray was alive, she had harnessed their different skills into a fragile but effective alliance; now, their differing viewpoints hovered constantly on the brink of outright animosity. But Celia was on the defensive here and she should, out of courtesy, give Sharpe the opportunity to sit in on the discussion she was about to have. Reluctantly, she picked up the telephone.

'Miriam Sharpe.'

'Miriam – are you free at the moment? I need to speak to you urgently – can I come and see you on my way downstairs?'

'Don't bother, Celia – I was just on my way up to you.'

The line went dead and, less than a minute later, there was a knock at the door. 'Come in,' Celia called, but the president of the College of Nursing was not in the mood to wait for an invitation. She strode across the room, ignoring the chair that was offered to her, and threw a copy of *The Times* across the desk. 'What is the meaning of this?' she asked, her face white with rage.

'It's an advertisement for the gala.'

'I know what it is – and it's bad enough that you deprive

nurses of their economic and professional independence by seeking charity at all, but to raise it in their name without mentioning that the proceeds are to be siphoned off into a private women's club is despicable beyond belief.'

'Oh for God's sake – nothing is being "siphoned off", as you put it. We're raising money to support two mutually dependent organisations,' she added, deciding that now was not the best time to admit that further funds were to go to the Actors' Orphanage in order to secure Noël Coward's support for the gala. 'You make it sound like fraud.'

'That's exactly what it is. Can you honestly tell me that people reading this won't suppose that their money is going directly to support the everyday needs of our nurses? It's worded deliberately to suggest that.'

'The whole purpose of the club is exactly what you've just mentioned. Aren't nurses allowed to enjoy a little relaxation and luxury? Don't you think they work more effectively and with a better heart if they're offered that? You're behind the times, Miriam – they're women, not machines. It's not like it was when we were young.'

'Oh? So what's changed? The dedicated are still trodden on or passed over, just like they always were. It was exactly the same after the war – how much of the money raised to support nurses in distress actually went to them? It was all put into bricks and mortar or administration. When will you realise that we're tired of being thrust forward as some sort of unblushing mendicant every time funds are needed? There's no room for politics in nursing, and there never will be.'

'You really expect me to believe that you're oblivious to the value of politics? All those letters to *The Times* haven't come out of thin air. You're behind them, any fool could see that –

you've virtually just quoted them word for word. But if you think I'll allow you to split this place down the middle, then you're mistaken.' She took a deep breath and tried to control herself before she really went too far: she hadn't wanted to antagonise Sharpe – it would only make things worse when she told her who was waiting downstairs. 'Anyway, I didn't call you in for that,' she said impatiently. 'I'm sorry to say that we've had a number of thefts in the club, and one or two members of the committee have received some unpleasant letters – anonymous ones. Obviously it doesn't affect the college, but I've had to call the police in and I thought you should know.'

'Doesn't affect the college? How can you say that? You're even more deluded than I thought you were, Celia. Of course it affects us – that sort of notoriety doesn't stay conveniently in a box just because you'd like it to.'

'You're blowing it out of all proportion. It's simply . . .'

'It's simply that you decided to bring ex-prisoners into this organisation. I told you what would happen if you did, but you wouldn't listen. Once more, nurses have to be guinea pigs in your precious rehabilitation schemes.'

'There's no reason to suppose that any of the Holloway girls are behind either the thefts or the letters, although of course we'll look into it.'

'Of course it will be one of them! A leopard doesn't change its spots.'

'You'd lock them all up and throw away the key, I suppose. Has it ever occurred to you that they might deserve a second chance?'

'And has it ever occurred to you that if you wanted to help convicts, you should have stayed in the prison service? You talk so eloquently of expanding a nurse's horizons – by showing her how to cheat and steal? I can only imagine what Lady Cowdray would have thought to that.'

Incensed, Celia stood up and slammed her hand down on the desk. 'I knew Lady Cowdray better than anyone here, so don't tell me what she would and wouldn't think.' The telephone rang, and she snatched the receiver up. 'Yes? No, Miss Timpson – of course I haven't forgotten he's here. Don't be ridiculous. I'll be down shortly.' She made an effort to regain her composure and looked at Miriam Sharpe. When she spoke again, her voice was unnaturally calm. 'I have to go now and talk to this policeman. Do you want to come and listen to what he has to say?'

'Why would I want to do that? This is your mess and, as you pointed out, it's got nothing to do with me.' Sharpe turned and walked to the door without another word, but paused before leaving. 'You've taken your eye off the ball lately, Celia. Don't expect any help from me when your empire starts to crumble.'

It didn't take Marjorie long to collect the things she needed from Debenhams, and she ran up the back steps to the workroom at precisely a quarter to one. 'Everything all right at the club?' Hilda Reader asked as Marjorie put the beads down on her worktable.

'Yes, Mrs Reader. Miss Bannerman was busy, but I spoke to Miss Size and she and Lady Ashby are coming over this afternoon for their fittings.'

'Good girl. You might as well take your lunch break now – you've got a visitor.'

'What?'

'Your father turned up – he said you were expecting him.' Marjorie knew that the expression on her face must have exposed the lie, but Hilda Reader was too discreet to comment. 'He said he'd wait for you across the road.'

In the pub, no doubt, Marjorie thought as she hurried back down, wondering if her fury and embarrassment were written all over her face. Sure enough, her father had taken a corner seat in the Salisbury Arms and was just draining his pint glass as she walked in. 'What the bloody hell are you doing here?' she asked, sitting down opposite him.

'Come on, love – that's not very friendly, is it?' he said. 'It's Friday – I thought you might have some wages for me.'

'Then you thought wrong. We don't get paid till the end of the day, but don't get your hopes up. I wouldn't give you anything even if I had it, so you'd better make that your last drink.'

'But it's your mother's birthday on Sunday, love. You want her to have something nice, don't you?'

'The best present you could give her would be to clear off and leave us to it.'

'You know you don't mean that. Why don't you nip back to work like a good girl and ask that nice lady if you can have your money now? It's not like you're going to bunk off this afternoon, is it, and I'm sure she'll understand if you tell her it's for your old dad.'

'Like hell, I will. I've got a chance here now, and I'm not about to let you ruin it for me.'

She stood up to go, but he reached across the table and took her wrist in his hand. 'Don't kid yourself,' he scoffed. 'You know as well as I do that your new friends aren't all they're made out to be. You'll never be anything other than a cheap little crook. It's in your blood – and I should know. You'll be back inside before you know it, and I'm bloody well going to get what I can out of you before that happens.'

Marjorie wrenched her hand away, accidentally catching the glass as she did so and knocking it to the floor. Blinded by anger and terrified that her father spoke the truth, she picked up one of the broken pieces and thrust it towards him. As he held his hands up to protect his face, Marjorie – for the first time in her life – felt stronger than he was. The balance of power in their relationship had suddenly shifted. How could she not have noticed that he had become an old man? The realisation seemed to shock her father as much as it did her: he made no attempt to speak to her as she placed the glass gently back on the table and left the pub.

Chapter Four

Josephine emerged from the newspaper room at the British Museum with her hands as covered in ink as her notebook, her mind full of the varying press accounts of the trial: the verbatim witness testimonies found in *The Times*; the lively opinions put forward by the *Echo*; and the *Telegraph*'s lengthy descriptive commentaries. Before leaving the building, she couldn't resist straying for a moment into the Museum's great domed Reading Room. She sat down at one of the leather-covered reading desks which extended like spokes from the circles of bookcases in the middle of the room and, while the reports were still fresh in her mind, summarised the most interesting aspects of the Sach and Walters case. She had no idea yet how the story would be told but, when she had finished, she was pleased to see that there was a compelling series of scenes to recreate. To a mind untrained in law, the trial and lack of evidence for the defence threw up a number of questions which she looked forward to talking through with Archie. Having read more about the case, though, it seemed that her original instinct had been a good one: it was the balance of power between the two women which would drive the novel, and the effect it had on those around them. The social circumstances of the time were interesting, too: she had been astonished at how many other accounts of child neglect, cruelty and abandonment she had found in the pages of the press without looking very hard for them. Celia had been right: Sach and Walters were certainly not unique in their crimes; she had identified at least four other baby farmers operating during the same period.

She walked out into a pleasant haze of winter sunshine and headed back to the Cowdray Club for lunch, her spirits lifted after the misery of the morning by the brisk freshness of the day. In fact, if the last week was anything to go by, November in London certainly didn't deserve its bad press. It was cold, certainly, but the trees in Cavendish Square were still in leaf and, although the drift of gold that ran through the branches was a muted, poignant affair, there was no doubt that this month of scarlets and yellows held its own beauty.

'Miss Tey! What a lovely surprise!'

Josephine glanced across the street and was astonished to see Archie's detective sergeant, Bill Fallowfield, standing at the entrance to the club. Celia was with him and, judging by the impatient look on her face, he had broken off an important conversation to greet her.

'The surprise is mutual, Bill,' she said, smiling warmly. She had a soft spot for the sergeant, and admired the loyalty and good humour that – by Archie's own admission – saw them both through the most difficult of times. 'What brings you to this side of town? A spot of early Christmas shopping?'

'I should be so lucky, Miss,' he said. 'No, I do all mine on Christmas Eve, I'm afraid.'

He stopped discreetly short of revealing his business at the club, and Josephine was careful to hide how much she knew. 'The stealing?' she asked, turning pointedly to Celia, who nodded. 'Is it really that serious?'

'I'm afraid so. Nothing very valuable has been taken, as I

said, but that's not the point. We can't be seen to be lax about security, not if we want to maintain the reputation of the club. If word gets out about this, the membership is bound to suffer.'

'We'll do all we can to put a stop to it before it gets out of hand, Miss Bannerman, and what you've told me today has been very helpful.' He turned to Josephine. 'Inspector Penrose didn't even tell me you were in London,' he said, feigning indignation. 'I'll have to have a word with him when I get back to the Yard.'

Josephine looked guilty. 'He didn't know himself until last night, Bill. I had the chance to come down a day or two earlier than planned,' she explained, hoping that she could rely on Celia not to be more specific, 'and I've had a lot of work to catch up with.'

'A book or a play?' he asked cautiously.

'A book,' she said, knowing that this would please him. Fallowfield was a great fan of her novels and an avid reader of detective fiction in general, but he didn't 'hold' with plays and privately considered that she was wasting her talents in writing them. 'Actually, Bill,' she added, looking at him thoughtfully, 'you might be able to help me.' Fallowfield was in his fifties, although he looked younger, and would know from experience what policing was like at the time she was investigating. 'Do you know anything about the Finchley Baby Farmers?'

He looked intrigued. 'Sach and Walters, you mean? Blimey, that takes me back. I haven't heard their names mentioned in years.'

'Takes you back?' Josephine prompted, scarcely daring to hope.

'Yes, Miss,' he said. 'It's funny you should ask about them – I was in the car that took the Billingtons into Holloway the day before they hanged them.'

'You drove the executioners into the prison?' she asked, resisting the impulse to hug him.

'Yes, with my sergeant at the time. There were always two of us on a job like that in case of any trouble. Thirty years ago or more, that must have been.' He shook his head, as if he couldn't imagine where the time had gone. 'I hadn't been in the force long, and it was one of the first jobs I was given – certainly the first job like that. I'll never forget it.'

His words echoed Celia's, and Josephine was struck by how many people – young, impressionable and just starting out in their careers – had been affected by the crimes of these two women. 'Would you tell me about it when you've got time?'

'Of course, Miss. I'd be glad to help, and I might be able to find you a few more people to talk to, as well – I've kept in touch with some of the lads from back then.'

Celia cleared her throat. 'As long as the sergeant has some time left to concentrate on crimes that *haven't* been solved yet,' she said archly. 'Petty theft isn't as glamorous as baby farming, I know, but it seems a little more pressing to those whose belongings are at risk.'

Having delivered such a satisfactory parting shot, she went back into the club with a purposefulness that suggested others might also do well to get on with their work. Josephine and Bill looked at each other, and Bill raised an eyebrow. 'Now why do I feel like I'm back at school?' he asked.

'Imagine how *I* feel,' Josephine confided. 'She really did teach me.'

'Oh?'

'Yes, and she was Sach's wardress in Holloway. In fact, it was

86

her that got me started on all this. She was there at the execution.'

'Crikey,' Bill said, looking after Celia with a new respect. 'That'll teach me to assume that people who run posh clubs don't know about the real world. It takes some guts, looking after someone in the condemned cell. Makes our part of the job look easy.' He smiled at Josephine. 'Have you been to Claymore House yet?'

'Sach's nursing home? No, not yet. It's still there, then?'

'Yes, although the area's changed a fair bit. Listen, I've got a bit of business near Finchley, as it happens, and there'd be no harm in doing it this afternoon. How about I show you and we can talk on the way?'

Josephine could only imagine what Archie would say when he found out that she'd been sightseeing with his sergeant at a time when they were so busy, but it was too good a chance to miss. 'On one condition,' she said. 'Lunch is on me.'

From the drawing-room window, Lucy watched as the policeman drove off with the woman who had walked in on her last night, and wondered how long it would be before they came for her. It was kind of Marjorie to look out for her, but nothing would ever come of it: Marjorie's schemes always petered out, and Lucy didn't much care what happened to her now anyway.

Every time she thought about her own child, a knife twisted, reopening old wounds. She could hardly remember anything about the day she had said goodbye – the weather, who else had been there, what she had said as she looked down at the little girl for the last time. The only thing she had to convince her that it really had happened was the pain, which refused to lessen with time. Everyone had said it was for the best, and her own voice had been lost amid a clamour of good intentions; she supposed they meant well, but they could never know how the knot of anger and resentment grew inside her, replacing what was lost, or how it moved and kicked and screamed every time she remembered.

'What were the Billingtons like?' Josephine asked as they drove through Kentish Town. 'They were brothers, weren't they?'

'Yes, William and John – John was the youngster of the family, and there was another brother who was in the trade as well, but I never met him.'

'It's a real family business, isn't it? Aren't there several Pierrepoints doing it at the moment?'

'Yes. Now you mention it, Henry Pierrepoint was the assistant for Sach and Walters. But it's natural to keep it in the family, I suppose. Hanging's a competitive business, although I've never understood that myself, and they all want to be number one: if you bring your sons in, you hold on to the top spot for as long as you want it. All the Billington boys were taught by their father. He was a bit before my time, but he was a rum character by all accounts – a barber originally, but they say he wanted the job so badly that he built a miniature scaffold in his own back yard to practise on.' Fallowfield shook his head at the vagaries of human nature. 'It was a bit more organised by the time that interests you. In fact, I think William was the first hangman to be properly trained.'

Josephine was horrified. 'You mean they let people near a rope without any formal training before that?'

He nodded. 'I suppose it was like any other profession. People observed the craft and learned on the job.'

'You wouldn't want to get an amateur when it was your turn, though, would you? And it must have been a terrifying thing to do for the first time – it's not as if you could take another run at it if you got it wrong.'

'No, and I dare say there were a few more accidents than anyone would like us to know about. But the Billington boys seemed to know what they were doing. Earnest chaps, they were – I can see them now: two pale-faced young men in dark suits with bowler hats, sitting quietly in the back of the car. They hardly said a word during the whole journey, but there was something calm and composed about them – you'd never have guessed what they were on their way to do.' He paused for a moment to negotiate a busy junction at the head of Archway Road, then swung boldly into the traffic between two oncoming cars, raising his hand to thank the second driver for a courtesy which had not been his choice. 'I remember looking at the two of them in my rear-view mirror and thinking how young they were to take a life – in peacetime, at any rate. They weren't much older than I was, and I found it unnerving enough just to drive them into the prison.'

'I've often wondered what sort of man it takes to do a job that most of us would balk at. Justice is a luxury when you don't have to carry it out yourself, and they can't be unmoved by it – it's quite noble, I suppose.' Bill gave a dismissive snort, and Josephine looked at him. 'Am I being naive?'

'I shouldn't speak out of turn, Miss, but they certainly weren't saints. It's a position of power, don't forget, and I've heard that a lot of them turned the notoriety to their own advantage, although they were never supposed to brag about what they did. And they weren't always on the right side of the law themselves, either. William spent a month in prison for refusing to keep his wife and two kids – they ended up in the workhouse – and Henry Pierrepoint turned up drunk to an execution once and had a punch-up with his assistant on the scaffold. The warder had to break it up. God knows what the poor sod on the gallows was thinking. Mr Churchill dropped Henry from the list after that.'

'What happened to them? Are they still about?'

'Henry's long gone now. William was dropped a couple of years after Sach and Walters for refusing to attend the inquest after a hanging in Ireland – he's still alive, though, I think. And John ...' He paused, and Josephine noticed a smile playing on his lips. 'I shouldn't laugh, really – it was a terrible accident and he can't have been more than twenty-five, but it would take a better man than me not to see the funny side.'

'Why? What on earth happened?'

'He fell through his own trapdoor while he was rigging a drop up in Leeds. Recovered sufficiently to do the hanging, but died a couple of months later.'

Josephine tried not to laugh. 'That's awful,' she said, but took a while to compose herself. '*Did* it get to them, do you think?' she continued more seriously.

'Like you say, they can't have been completely immune to it. James – that's Billington senior – took to drink eventually. He had to execute a friend, apparently, and they say that finished him off.'

'Surely that should never have been allowed? It must make a huge difference when it's personal.' They passed East Finchley tube station, and Josephine began to take a keener interest in her surroundings. 'It's funny – I wrote a whole play about how Mary, Queen of Scots must have felt in the days before her execution, but it never affected me like this. It's because it's in living memory, I suppose – it's much more real. Thirty-odd years isn't long, is it? Sach and Walters could still be walking these streets if things had been different.' She looked ahead of her at the wide road, flanked with busy shops, and thought again about what Celia had said to her. 'They weren't noble or special, and the ordinariness of it makes a difference somehow. It could be any of us.' They stopped in a long line of traffic at a crossroads, and she said: 'Tell me, Bill – what was that day like? I'd like to be able to recreate it in the book. It would have been the day before the execution?'

He nodded. 'They had to be at the prison by late afternoon, so we collected them from the station and took them on to Holloway. They weren't carrying anything with them – the luggage had been sent on ahead, and I remember thinking it was like going on a bloody holiday except for the weather. It was bitterly cold – am I right in thinking it was just after Christmas?'

'The beginning of February, yes. They were committed on Christmas Eve, of all days, and tried in January.'

'That's right. It was starting to get dark by the time we got down the Camden Road, but that hadn't put the crowds off.'

'Abolitionists or sensation-seekers?'

'Oh, mostly sensation-seekers. There wasn't the strength of feeling against it all that there is now. That didn't really start until the trouble over Edith Thompson. No, most of this lot were in good spirits, laughing and joking with our lads at the gate – more like a state occasion or a football match than a wake. They might have missed out on watching the hanging itself by thirty years or so, but they were determined to get what they could out of it.' The car moved forward a few feet but the lights turned red again before they got to the front of the queue and Fallowfield continued with his story. 'It was the executioners they all wanted to see – they were the stars of the show, so there was quite a commotion when they saw us approaching. Greeted like heroes, they were, and it was a while before we had a clear path through – lots of banging on the car and cheering as we went in.'

'The power of fame,' Josephine said cynically.

'To be fair, not all of them were there just for the spectacle. Baby farming caused quite a stir, you know, and there was a lot of strong feeling about it. Hundreds went to Newgate when Dyer was hanged. Sach and Walters didn't pull in as many as that, but there were a fair few waiting, and a lot of them were women.'

'I wonder if any of the mothers were there? It must have been terrible to read about the trial in the newspapers if you'd left Claymore House believing your child had found a good home.'

'I shouldn't be surprised but, if not, there were plenty of others around to be outraged on their behalf.'

'It's funny, isn't it? If you wanted to be cold about it, you could argue that they were only doing what women have done for hundreds of years – getting rid of children whom society couldn't afford to care for or even acknowledge. They probably told themselves they were providing a service. I suppose it's the professional aspect of it that frightened people, though. It's one thing to manage the population quietly within your own family, but quite another to undermine the social set-up by turning it into a business.'

'In my experience, for all the talk of justice and compassion, people react to crime by how threatened it makes them feel – and none of us want to believe that women can kill children. It unsettles everything we take for granted.' The lights were changing again, but this time Fallowfield scraped through on amber. 'Hertford Road's just up here on the right,' he said, and Josephine felt a rush of excitement and curiosity: as much as she loved fiction, there was nothing quite like delving into the lives of real people, and imagining them in their everyday surroundings helped her understand them better than anything. A couple of minutes later, they turned into a side-street and parked in front of a gate. 'That's it,' he said, pointing to one of the terraced houses on the other side of the street. 'Claymore House.'

Josephine had not known quite what to expect, but the grandeur of the name had led her to imagine something more individual and imposing than this unassuming, red-brick building, the mirror image of its neighbour and indistinguishable from most of the houses along the row. From the outside, Claymore House looked moderate in size, but the number of chimney pots suggested that appearances were deceptive; certainly, from what she had read in the newspapers, Sach's nursing home had housed several occupants at a time as well as her own family; it would have to be quite spacious inside and, she noticed, looking more closely, there was a basement and possibly an attic to provide additional accommodation if necessary. A tiny front garden separated the house from the street, and a couple of steps led up to an open porch and solid front door, where stained-glass panels offered one of the building's few unique features. As her gaze moved upwards towards a turreted bay window – presumably the master bedroom – she noticed that the plaque which should have held a name was blank; after the notoriety, it was perhaps not surprising that subsequent occupants would be reluctant to acknowledge the existence of Claymore House. 'I don't know why, but I expected it to be detached,' she said to Fallowfield as they got out of the car. 'It's very overlooked, isn't it? You'd be hard pushed to hide any comings and goings.'

'But in a respectable street like this, you wouldn't expect to see anything out of the ordinary. That's what was clever about it.'

Josephine nodded. 'And I suppose all there was to see was exactly what you'd expect from a nursing home. Listen – why don't you leave me here for a bit and do what you need to do? I'd like to walk up and down the street and try to get a feel for what it was like back then.'

Fallowfield looked doubtful. 'Are you sure you'll be all right on your own?'

'Of course I will. As you said – it's the height of respectability. Come back and fetch me when you're ready.'

'All right, but I'll be half an hour at the most.'

She watched him turn the car round and force his way back into the busy traffic on the High Street, then crossed over to get as close a look at Claymore House as she could manage without drawing attention to herself. The terrace was late Victorian and must have been almost brand new when the Sach family took it. Where had the money come from? she wondered. Was it Amelia's growing business that had made the move possible, or did the family have other means, either through her husband's earnings or some sort of private income? She looked long and hard at the house, which was an enviable residence even by today's standards. Having read widely about the times, she was mindful of the conditions that drove women to kill, but this wasn't poverty – this was climbing your way up the social scale in a calculated manner, and she was even more convinced that Sach's guilt was the greater of the two, bloodless as it was. Sach had trained as a nurse and midwife – why was an honest living not enough for her? Josephine thought about all the hard-working young nurses she nodded to each day at the Cowdray Club, and all the dedication she had witnessed in her own life; admittedly, great advances had been made in the status of nurses as professionals over the last thirty years but they were still very poorly rewarded in comparison with other working women – materially, at least. Yet how many of them would countenance putting their training to illicit ends purely for money, taking advantage of vulnerable people who had no choice but to depend on them? She could think of no profession which was easier to abuse, and no line that would be harder to cross.

Peering through a gap in the terrace, Josephine could just about see to the rear of the houses, and tried to imagine what Sach had thought as she watched her daughter playing in one of those yards. Could she really have believed that she was building a secure future for Lizzie? Or – and this was a terrible thing to think – was her own child merely a smokescreen for her crimes, the perfect alibi in a world where, as Fallowfield said, women bore children but did not kill them? She walked to the other end of the road so as not to appear too ghoulish, then took out her notebook and jotted down her first impressions of the house and neighbourhood, mentally revising the few details that had already been sketched out in the draft she had written the night before. As she was doing so, a man came out from the house opposite and looked at her curiously. 'Taking an interest in Hertford Road?' he asked, smiling at her. 'You must be after the child killers. A journalist, perhaps?'

'No, nothing quite that sensational,' she said, then added vaguely: 'I'm just doing a bit of research for a book.' He looked interested, but was too polite to question her further. 'I don't suppose you were here at the time?' she asked hopefully.

He shook his head. 'No, sorry. My wife and I moved in just after the war and I don't know anyone who's been here longer. But we've all heard about the woman who ran the nursing home and killed babies.' Josephine didn't put him right, but she was interested to see how stories were corrupted in the telling: Sach would be mortified to know that, after all her careful work to distance herself from the actual bloodshed, history had her down as the murderer. The man shuddered. 'It doesn't bear thinking about, does it?' he said, walking on.

By the time she had finished making notes, her chauffeur was back in place at the end of the street and she walked over to meet him. 'Have you seen all you need to?' he called through the window, and Josephine nodded. 'Then how about a quick trip over to Islington to see Walters's lodgings? If we go straight there, it'll still be daylight.'

'Have you honestly got time to take me all the way to Islington? I know how busy you are – Archie said things were frantic at the moment.'

'It's amazing how long you can wait to talk to a witness, you know, and the traffic in Finchley can be shocking at this time of the day.' He winked at her. 'Anyway, what Inspector Penrose doesn't know can't hurt him.'

She got in, and the aroma of bacon rose up from a parcel on the dashboard. 'It's way past lunchtime and I thought you might be hungry,' he said. 'There's a good cafe round the corner, but if we stop there we won't get to Danbury Street before dark.'

Touched, she unwrapped the greaseproof paper. 'I said lunch was on me, Bill. You're doing me enough favours as it is.'

'It's a pleasure, Miss. Your treat next time.'

They set out again, driving back the way they had come for a while, then striking off to the left. As the sergeant negotiated a network of smaller streets off the Caledonian Road, Josephine admired the unhesitating way in which he chose his route; not a Londoner by birth, Fallowfield nevertheless belonged to the city in the way that incomers often do, held there by a bond which was all the stronger for its element of choice. It was hard to imagine him as the new boy which he must have been during the time of Sach and Walters. 'Do you remember much about the case?' she asked, finishing her sandwich and, as directed, dropping the bag by her feet, where it joined the remnants of a week's worth of lunches eaten on the move.

'Not really, I'm afraid,' Fallowfield said. 'To be honest, you're so busy during those early years trying to keep on top of the cases you *are* involved with that there's precious little time to take an interest in those that don't really concern you. I'd heard about it, obviously, and there was a lot of talk about it at the Yard because Walters lodged with a couple of coppers, but the trial was all done and dusted by the time I had anything to do with it. Delivering the Billingtons was as close as I got to it.'

'I was astonished when I found out where Walters lived,' Josephine said. 'Why on earth would she take a room in a house with two policemen?'

'Well, she wasn't too bright, by all accounts.'

'She certainly wasn't well educated if any of her statements are to be trusted, but I'm not so sure about bright. I wonder if that was just a card she played – wanting to be thought more stupid than she really was.'

'Perhaps it was a sort of double bluff, then – the most brazen thing she could think of. Killing children under a copper's nose is almost too ridiculous to be true.'

'If so, then it backfired.' He looked questioningly at her. 'They got suspicious about the babies she brought home with her – although God knows why she took them there at all – and had her followed. She was caught red-handed with a dead child. I wonder if she'd ever have been rumbled if she'd chosen to live somewhere else?'

'What other evidence was there?'

'Well, there was one witness who said she'd seen Walters in a cocoa-house in Whitechapel a day or two before, holding a baby wrapped in a blanket. She was suspicious because the child didn't move or make any sound at all, but Walters came out with some nonsense about its being under anaesthetic. Then there was another woman – Evans, I think her name was.' Josephine rummaged in her bag for her notebook and turned back a few pages, holding the words at arm's length so that she could read them without glasses. 'No, sorry – Nora Edwards. It seems to me that she hanged them both, really. She'd answered Sach's advertisement in the newspaper and had gone to the nursing home to have her child. Sach tried to get her to give the baby up, apparently, but she refused because she wanted to keep it. She stayed on at the home, though, and started to work for Sach as a servant. At the trial, she testified that Walters took babies away from Sach's premises on a regular basis, and that she was told never to tell the mothers where they went, or with whom.' She put the notebook back in her bag and thought for a moment. 'You know, when I read the trial reports, that was the part I really couldn't understand. Edwards must have known what was going on – I'm even more convinced of that now I've seen the sort of premises that Sach used – so why did she stay? How could she do that, knowing that her own child had so nearly met the same fate? At best, she was enabling it to happen by turning a blind eye – at worst, I wonder if she had more to do with it than was ever suggested. Perhaps she turned evidence against Sach and Walters to save her own skin.'

'Possibly, but don't forget she was an unmarried mother. There won't have been many options open to her, and it sounds like Sach offered her security – a roof over her head and no questions asked about her circumstances. That must have been like a gift from heaven. Principles are one thing, Miss, but the moral high ground may as well be Timbuktu if you're lying in the gutter.' Josephine was quiet, thinking about what he had said. 'I'm not saying that this girl was in the right,' he added, 'and I'm certainly not condoning what Sach and Walters got up to – but let's not forget that women went to that nursing home for a reason, and I don't see anybody rushing to make the men who got 'em pregnant take their share of the blame.'

'It's funny you should say that,' she agreed. 'I found it outrageous that the men who gave evidence in court – the fathers, I mean – were all allowed to stay anonymous while the women had their names and descriptions plastered all over the newspapers.' She looked at Fallowfield, ashamed that a man in his fifties who worked in a notoriously chauvinistic profession had been less judgemental of her own sex than she was. 'You're right, of course – there's more than one way to destroy a life. It's a pity there aren't more men about like you, Bill.'

He smiled. 'I'm sure it's easier to be fair-minded when you're a bachelor and long past the courting age. Look – there's the Angel. We're only a couple of minutes away now.' The traffic was at its height here, where several of the great northern roads converged. They drove slowly past the underground station, then a substantial Lyons Corner House, which looked shiny and familiar in comparison with the shabbiness of the other public buildings, and Josephine was relieved when Fallowfield turned left into the peace of Colebrook Row. A pleasant line of public gardens stretched half the length of the street, separating it from the neighbouring terrace and providing a welcome contrast to the elegant but relentless Georgian housing on either side.

Danbury Street ran parallel with Colebrook Row and was reached via another string of uniform houses. The buildings here were slightly more modern – early Victorian, Josephine guessed – and not as spacious; most had just three floors, including a basement. The area was closer to the heart of the city, and many houses showed signs of multiple occupancy, suggesting that a lot of the accommodation was still rented rather than privately owned. 'Which one was it?' she asked, opening the car door. Fallowfield pointed over to his left. Josephine looked up at the building in which Annie Walters had killed at least twice, and was interested to see that it was one of the few houses which looked genuinely loved. It was nearly dark now, and the November evening was hinting at snow to come, but the warmth of the softly lit rooms could not have been further from the drab, suffocating boarding house that she had imagined from the newspaper descriptions of Walters's lodgings. Better kept than most, the house was obviously in the middle of preparations for a family celebration: a child's toy hung in one of the upstairs windows, and a pile of presents stood proudly in the window to the right of a smart front door. As she watched, an attractive woman led a girl of three or four to the sink in the basement kitchen, and lifted her up so that she could wash what looked like pastry off her hands. The woman glanced up at them and smiled, but Josephine – embarrassed to have been caught staring – moved hurriedly away, pulling Fallowfield with her.

'It's the same time of year that Walters was arrested, almost to the day, but it couldn't be more different, could it?' she said, as the two of them loitered suspiciously further up the street. 'It chills me to see a child there. I've always thought that buildings must hold some sort of trace of what's happened in them, but I doubt that family has any sense of the sadness which one of those rooms witnessed. And thank God – they'd be horrified, I'm sure. It's one thing to gawp at a house of notoriety, but quite another to live in it.' She looked around her, trying to build up an impression of the sights that had greeted Walters as she came and went from her lodgings each day, and something further up the street caught her eye. 'That's not a canal up there, is it?' she asked.

'Yes, Miss – it's the Grand Union,' Fallowfield said, intrigued by her surprise. 'Why? Is that important?'

'I don't know about important,' Josephine said, walking up the road to take a closer look, 'but there's an account in the newspapers of the journey that Walters took to dispose of the dead baby on the day she was arrested. She went all the way to South Kensington Station, partly on foot and partly by bus, and I'd assumed that was because there was nowhere safe for her to get rid of it closer to home. But surely it would have been much easier to weigh the body down and throw it in the canal?'

'Like Dyer, you mean.'

'Is that what she did?'

'Yes – she got away with it for years. Then the stupid woman wrapped a dead baby up in some brown paper that had her address all over it.'

They stopped at some railings and looked down into the water. 'Why would you risk tramping all over London with a dead baby clutched to your bosom when you have a canal less than a hundred yards from your doorstep?'

'Maybe it was *too* close to home,' Fallowfield suggested. 'Or maybe she liked the danger. Some people do, you know. Then they push their luck too far – and God bless 'em for their arrogance, otherwise we'd never catch them.'

Josephine had gone quiet, trying to imagine what it felt like to carry death so close and to picture the sort of woman who would choose that rather than take the easier option. She thought again of how Walters had stopped to drink cocoa with a lifeless bundle in her arms, how she had taken the children home with her rather than dispose of them as quickly as possible. 'Perhaps I'm wrong to try to understand her,' she said. 'Perhaps she was quite simply a monster.'

'Then she'd be the exception, Miss. I've arrested a fair few murderers in my time, and they're usually depressingly ordinary people, caught on the wrong foot. Evil isn't as common as weakness,' he added gently, and she wondered if he was trying to reassure her.

'Evil or weakness – the end result is much the same for the

victims. I don't suppose we'll ever know how many there were or what happened to the other bodies.'

'No. Kids turned up dead all the time back then – for lots of reasons, not just baby farming. It was the hardest thing we ever had to deal with – and it didn't get any easier for happening so often.'

'Although judging by what I read this morning, East Finchley had more than its fair share,' she said wryly. 'To my cynical eye, rather too many seem to have turned up there just before Sach and Walters were arrested, although no one tried to make the connection.'

'They didn't have to – they only needed one body for a conviction.'

'I wonder if Walters ever worked for other women?' Josephine said as they headed back to the car. 'Her share of the money was very small in comparison to Sach's, and it crossed my mind that she might have had a few clients on the go at the same time. Baby farming obviously wasn't an unusual crime.'

'It certainly wasn't, although there were different degrees of it. Some women – like Sach and Walters – had a thriving business going, but others were tarred with the same brush for much less.'

'Yes – I read about another woman who was in court while Sach and Walters were on remand. The stories ran side by side for a bit in the press. Eleanor Vale?'

Fallowfield shook his head. 'Doesn't ring a bell, Miss.'

'No – she wasn't as notorious because she didn't kill the babies, just abandoned them in railway carriages where they were sure to be found. But reading about her brought home to me how profitable the baby trade must have been.'

'Surely they didn't hang her for that?'

'No – two years' hard labour, I think. But it seemed ironic to me that the barrister prosecuting her was the same one who defended Sach.'

'That's the legal system for you, Miss – nothing if not consistent.'

She laughed. 'Bill, you mentioned finding me some other people to talk to – who did you mean?'

'Well, I could probably find someone who knew the coppers involved at Walters's lodgings. Seal, one of them was called – I think he's gone now, but he had a son who took after him and went into the force. Shouldn't be too difficult to track down, and he'll remember what the house was like even if he never met Walters.'

'That would be wonderful. And what about a barrister? It doesn't have to be the men involved in the trial – that's too much to hope for, I suppose – but it would be really helpful to get a legal opinion on the case. There's so much that seems odd to me, but that's probably just because I don't understand the system.'

'Inspector Penrose will help you there, Miss,' Fallowfield said, opening the car door for her. 'It's way before his time, obviously, but he'll be able to fix you up with the top brass.' He looked at his watch. 'He should be back at the Yard by now – do you want to come and talk to him?'

'Oh no, I don't want to bother him while he's at work.'

The sergeant smiled as he started the engine. 'You know as well as I do that he won't mind. You don't have to stay long – just let him know what you need and arrange . . .'

The rest of his sentence was lost as the police wireless crackled into life and a familiar voice barked angrily down the line. 'Fallowfield? Where the bloody hell are you?'

Josephine looked at him and raised an eyebrow. 'Perhaps now isn't the best time after all,' she suggested as Fallowfield hurriedly put the car into gear.

'Perhaps you're right, Miss,' he said, fumbling for the radio as he drove. 'All right if I drop you at Holborn?'

The clock on the steeple of St Mary's was just striking four when Annie Walters trudged across Whitechapel High Street towards Lockhart's Cocoa Rooms, her eyes fixed on the double row of painted white letters which left no one in any doubt as to what was served inside. The broad thoroughfare was busy – she had never seen it any other way – but she cut a determined path through the clutter of a Friday afternoon and hurried the last few yards to avoid a tram which was moving more quickly than she had anticipated. Safe on the pavement, she leaned against a lamppost for a moment to catch her breath and watched the tram go past, wishing her own life were as anchored to a fixed route as those wheels were to the curling lines in the road.

There was a smoky, dingy quality to the November air and Lockhart's – while it was never going to be the most coveted of eating places – looked welcoming enough from the outside. Having walked the streets for most of the day, Annie was glad to step out of the cold for a bit before getting rid of the baby. She shifted the weight of the bundle on to her left arm and pushed open the door, adding her own marks to the layers of grease and dirt which gathered relentlessly on the brass, a reminder that the restaurant catered for people who worked with their hands and weren't likely to stand on ceremony where food was concerned. The downstairs rooms were already full but, in any case, she preferred the comparative anonymity of the first floor and chose a table in the corner, as far from the counter as she could get. It was the usual mix of clientele – dockers, cab-drivers, stall-holders, street women and a few people who, like her, seemed not to have a job as such but who could always find the price of a meal. She sat down, nodding to one or two familiar faces, confident that her business was her own.

The service at Lockhart's was reduced to its bare essentials, and a mug of cocoa was slapped down on the table in front of her as soon as she was settled at her table. 'Anything to eat?' the woman asked gruffly, hardly seeming to care what the answer was.

'Just the usual,' Annie said, and the woman nodded.

The cocoa was sweet and hot enough to burn her lips. Annie sipped it absent-mindedly, wondering if she had imagined the knowing look that passed between the women at the counter, but when the waitress returned a few minutes later with her meal, the plate of sausage and mash was delivered without a word and she was left to eat in peace. The food was the same as it always was, straightforward and tasty, but she ate with less enjoyment than usual, conscious of the weight on her lap and sensing that the unspoken rules of the establishment were about to be broken: the staff at the counter were chatting amongst themselves, apparently oblivious to their customers, but somehow Annie sensed that she would not be allowed to leave the premises without some sort of confrontation. Sure enough, no sooner had she laid down her fork than the younger of the two women came over.

'What've you got there?' she asked, picking up Annie's empty plate but making no move to return it to the kitchen.

Annie put her arm protectively across the baby but, in so doing, unwittingly dislodged the shawl that she had wrapped so carefully around the tiny body. She looked down in horror at the face which was now revealed, still and pale under the bright lights. 'It's a baby,' she said, knowing it was pointless to lie.

'Not very lively, is it?'

Annie laughed – an unnatural, stifled sound – but, in her panic, it was all she could manage. 'No, poor little thing, but he'll be right as rain soon enough. I'm a nurse, you see,' she added, as the woman's disbelieving eyes tore into her. 'I'm taking him back to Finchley – that's where his mother's been confined.' She stood up and fumbled in her pocket for the money that Sach had given her on Wednesday night. 'I'd better be on my way.'

'I'd like to see him awake,' the waitress said, and went to stroke the baby's cheek.

Hurriedly, Annie turned away. 'Oh, I don't think you would,' she said, tidying the shawl. 'He'd be screaming the place down, and I don't know what your customers would think to that.'

A handful of coins spilled out on to the table, more than enough for the meal, but Annie made no attempt to retrieve the surplus change. Instead, she drew the baby closer to her and walked towards the door, trying not to hurry. Out of the corner of her eye, she thought she saw the younger girl take a step towards her, but she had reached the stairs by then and flew down them as fast as she could, no longer caring if she drew further attention to herself. Once out in the street, she headed east towards St Mary's, scarcely thinking about where she was going but desperate to get as far as possible from the searching eyes of those women. When she got to the crossroads, she turned left into Commercial Street and leaned heavily against the wall of the building on the corner. Her heart was pounding so fiercely that she almost believed it capable of throwing life back into the dead child which was clutched to her chest, and she had to take several deep breaths to calm herself. She knew she had said too much, and it was stupid to have mentioned Finchley, but her nerves had got the better of her. Anyway, why should she protect Sach? Annie had been a martyr for too much of her life, and there was no way that she was going to carry the blame for this on her own.

When she was feeling calmer, she walked on down Commercial Street. The vegetable market had long since packed up for the day, relinquishing its meagre shelter to the lost and the homeless, and the street in general – always so full of energy by day – had now lost its passion, and seemed pallid and lethargic. She knew how it felt. Even in her younger days, when she worked all the hours God sent, she could never remember being quite this tired, and the faint but melancholy smell of Russian cigarettes which drifted out from the alleyways seemed to underline her sense of the pointlessness of her life. She looked up at the Peabody Buildings on the corner of White Lion Street, and it reminded her of her own tenement days in Drury Lane, where she had lived for twenty-four years with her husband; that building – which had also been part of the Peabody Trust – had the same crude angles as this one, its main triumph appearing to be the elimination of beauty which characterised all buildings for the poor. She had spent her life in such places – orphanages, hospitals like the one where she had first met Sach, tenement blocks – and it seemed to her that the benefactors behind all these institutions seemed hell-bent on keeping the poor bound in ugliness, as if their lives weren't ugly enough already. Still, at least those rooms in Drury Lane had had a sense of community about them. Since her husband died, she had become just another of those shabby, transient women who moved from one narrow bed in London to another, changing their names as they went and leaving their debts behind them – so many names, so many hurried departures with the doors closed firmly on so many secrets. And for what? Perhaps it would have been kinder if someone had done for her all those years ago what she had done for the lifeless child in her arms.

Annie cut through Brushfield Street as the quickest route to the railway station. Across the way, a small girl stood in a doorway, dark-haired and pale in the light from the street-lamp, and staring out into nothing. The child must have been about five or six, Annie guessed, and she was beautiful, although it would only be a matter of time before stress and hunger would corrode her self-respect and banish the loveliness as if it had never been. Just for a moment, she understood what drove those childless women to Sach's door – the impulse to seize this fragment of childhood and take it away before contact with the streets left its permanent mark – but the understanding wasn't strong enough to block out the memory of those children who weren't adopted, who were disposed of by other means. As the child across the street looked towards her, she seemed to represent the spirit of all the lives that had been taken away. Whether her stare was accusing or thankful, Annie couldn't say.

It was heading towards rush hour at Liverpool Street, and hundreds of men and women were already pouring down the slope to the main-line and suburban trains. Annie stood for a moment on the footbridge which spanned the platforms and

111

looked down on to the black-coated crowd. It was time now, she knew that, and, in any case, the strange kind of peace which she had sometimes found in the hours spent alone with a child was getting harder and harder to come by; in her heart, she knew it couldn't last. The ladies' waiting room was over near Platform One, and she took advantage of its privacy to remove anything from the baby's body which might identify it later, then walked quickly through the arches and into the station yard. It was dark, and the air was thick with smoke and dirt, so she chose the mound of coal nearest to her. Looking back over her shoulder to make sure that no one had followed her, she placed the bundle gently on the ground, then took a nearby shovel and disturbed the bottom of the heap sufficiently to bring a stream of coal tumbling down, covering the tiny form.

She left the station without looking back, and walked around for a while with no purpose other than to put off the moment when she would have to return to Danbury Street without the child. Unable to face an evening alone in her room, she moved from public house to public house, determined to spend every penny of Sach's money on the one comfort available to her. When the only thing left in her pocket was the price of a ticket home, she caught the bus back to Islington and got off by the canal. It had just started to rain, and she hurried down Noel Road, wanting now to get to sleep before the numbing effect of the alcohol wore off. The narrow passage that led to the back of the house was dark but she felt her way along the fence, counting the gates carefully to make sure she chose the right one. She found the yard without a problem, but the tiny space was crammed with clutter and she stumbled against a policeman's bicycle, knocking it to the floor with a crash and scraping her shin badly on the pedal. She swore to herself and rubbed her leg, but she had already seen a light on downstairs and knew that there was no chance of returning home unnoticed. Reluctantly, she climbed the three stone steps to the back door, aware that she stank of gin but long past caring.

'Is that you, Mrs Walters?' called a voice from the kitchen, and Annie knew she had no choice but to brazen it out. Her landlady was sitting at the table with Mrs Spencer, one of the lodgers from the first floor. The women were drinking tea, and Annie didn't have to try very hard to work out what the main topic of conversation had been. 'The baby not with you, then?' Mrs Seal added, as if reading her thoughts.

'No. I've taken it to its new home – I told you I was going to.' Without thinking, she took the clothes that she had removed from the baby's body and threw them across the table, enjoying the shock on the women's faces. 'Here you are – you can have these for your little one. Mine won't need 'em any more.'

Mrs Seal picked up one of the knitted booties and looked at Annie. 'Poor little thing, carted round from pillar to post,' she said. 'What sort of a start in life is that?'

'Huh,' Annie scoffed dismissively. 'There's no need to feel sorry for the child. She's gone to a titled lady in Piccadilly who paid a hundred pounds for her, and she's going to be an heiress.'

'I thought you said the baby was a boy?' Mrs Spencer said, glancing across at Mrs Seal.

Annie was thrown for a moment; she had completely forgotten that she had lied about the baby's sex when she first brought it back to the house, although why she had ever thought that would protect her, God only knew. 'I didn't say anything of the sort, Minnie,' she said defiantly. 'You must have misheard.'

'I must have done,' Mrs Spencer said. 'My mistake – sorry, I'm sure.'

Annie muttered a gruff goodnight and went through to her room in the back parlour. She could tell instantly that someone had been through her things while she was out: the baby's clothes on the bed were not as she had left them, and she was sure that she had closed the drawer in which she kept the feeding bottle and the Chlorodyne. There was nothing else for it – she would have to move on soon, although judging by the look of the girl at Sach's, it wouldn't be long before she was needed again and she doubted she'd be able to find another room in time. It was dangerous, but she would have to bring one more child here and risk the consequences. If Sach knew how close they were to being discovered, she'd be horrified – but Annie had to admit to a certain pleasure in the thought of taking Sach down with her. Edwards, too, if she had the chance: she knew that Sach and that girl were up to something, that Edwards's duties were more than just cooking and cleaning. She wouldn't be surprised if they were trying to cut her out altogether, but she'd be damned if she'd let them – not now, not after everything she'd done. There were plenty of other women who wanted her services.

She picked up the rest of the milk which she had bought the day before and poured it into a mug, then added a couple of drops of Chlorodyne to help her sleep. But as she lay down, she knew it would take much more to blot out the noises in her head, the roar and clamour of a train about to depart, and the sound of a child choking in the night.

Chapter Five

Marjorie took a roll of narrow purple ribbon and carefully cut it to the right length, enjoying the peace and solitude of the workroom in the early evening. Everyone else had gone home an hour ago – most of the other women had families to look after – but she had gladly offered to stay behind and work a little longer: there was a long list of minor alterations and finishing-off touches to attend to after the various fittings that had taken place that afternoon, and she was in no rush to get back to Campbell Road to face another confrontation with her father. In any case, she had her own reasons for wanting time alone.

She shifted her chair round slightly to get more light, then selected a strong wire hairpin from one of the boxes in the centre of the table and bent it into the shape of a horseshoe, with the prongs about an inch apart. These decorative additions to the main evening gowns were often more time-consuming than the dresses themselves, but they were not difficult and, as she set about creating the fabric violets which would complete Mary Size's outfit, she found that the calm, methodical nature of the work helped to eclipse the tensions of the day. Why had the argument with her father upset her so much? she wondered, placing the ribbon over one side of the hairpin, then drawing the long end over and under the other prong, giving it a half turn to make sure that the satin stayed on the outside. It wasn't as if it was unusual – not a day went by without a row over something, and there had never been any love lost between them. Holding the ribbon taut, she repeated the process until she had made enough loops, then twisted a fine piece of wire around the centre of the material to form a stem. When she had made sure that everything was in place, she removed the hairpin and crushed the centres together to make the petals of the flower spread out, then wound the rest of the ribbon around the wire, finishing at the bottom with a tight knot. Was it because she had more to lose now, and he had dared to encroach on the new world she had created for herself? Or had she recognised a streak of opportunism which had surfaced recently in her own character?

Patiently, Marjorie cut a few more lengths of ribbon and carried on working until she had made enough single flowers to form a small corsage. She tied them together, her fingers deftly arranging the fabric to look as natural as possible and, as she looked down at her hands, she was surprised to see that they were barely recognisable as her own – comparatively well cared-for now, and with no sign of the dirt and bitten nails that she had grown used to. They were her best asset, and she needed to look after them – it was the first thing Mrs Reader had said to her when she arrived at Motley back in May, and Marjorie had surprised herself by heeding that and all the other advice which the head cutter had passed on. She was quick to learn, and as soon as Hilda Reader spotted her enthusiasm and potential she had made sure that the girl was given every possible chance to develop them, working her hard as she taught her the stitches and techniques involved in high-class couture – the hand-rolled hems and fine pin-tucks, the fringing and beading, the delicacy of embroidery by hand and machine; helping her to understand the different weights and qualities of the fabrics, and how they would be transformed by stage lighting. Under Mrs Reader's patient but demanding eye, she had gradually learned to work at the speed which a busy house like Motley required – and, for the first time in her twenty-three years, Marjorie knew what it was to be genuinely grateful. It made no difference to her now whether she was working on costumes for the theatre or more conventional clothes for the sisters' boutique range – it was the magical transformation of the materials which delighted her, the privilege of being surrounded by things which were beautiful.

So why had she risked all that with one rash decision, tricked by her father into a complicity that shamed and horrified her? Perhaps he was right – genes would always out, no matter how hard she fought against them, and a child's life was mapped out even before he or she was born. She looked around the workroom, so full of colour and individuality – walls covered with sketches of historical costumes and glamorous theatrical production shots, shelves groaning under the weight of art books and gallery catalogues from which the Motleys so often took their inspiration, small personal items left next to the sewing machines by several of the girls, implying a sense of ownership and continuity – and compared it to what she was used to: long rows of treadle sewing machines, overlooked by two prison officers, where the only embroidery to be done was the stencilling of a number on a mailbag; no banter and no company, other than a few old drunks languidly teasing out coir to fill mattresses, the joints of their hands swollen with rheumatism; and certainly no creativity or beauty – just automatic, monotonous work, the relentless blue of prison uniforms.

Sighing heavily, she put the finished violets down and walked over to the row of tall windows which overlooked St Martin's Lane. The first flakes of snow had begun to fall, fulfilling the promise of the day's cold, and Marjorie watched the people on the pavement below hurrying into theatres or public houses, shaking the weather from their Friday-night clothes and laughing as the ultimate symbol of Christmas began its gentle veiling of the city. Why did everything seem so much more desperate as Christmas got closer? The sense of disappointment and longing was even stronger than usual, the briefest moments of happiness all the more intense. December was always marked in her house by the biggest rows of the year, and the pressure to please only increased the greatest worry – money. It had peaked when she was about twelve, when they still lived outside the city; her mother belonged to a loan club, and she always drew on it a couple of weeks ahead of Christmas. Marjorie remembered how she used to love putting the money out on the kitchen table; it couldn't have been more than a few quid, but she would set some by for the kids' presents and use the rest to pay back debts from the year; the small piles of coins built up on scraps of paper – IOUs or shopping lists. Marjorie was washing up at the sink, listening to her mother hum one of the familiar carols while she did her sums; her father was by the fire, reading his paper. Then one of her little brothers called out from the next room and her mother went to see what he wanted; her father must have gone out after her, because when Marjorie turned round a few minutes later, they were both standing in the doorway, looking accusingly at her across the table, where one of the piles had disappeared. There was a hell of a row and Marjorie stormed out; she knew that her father must have pocketed the money – later, her mother had admitted that she knew as much, too, but it had been easier to blame her daughter. That was a talent her mother had, finding anyone to blame but the person at fault; it was a trait that ran throughout Marjorie's fractured family, with her parents at the centre of it – by turns resentful, uneasy, lost, as if they could no longer remember who had trapped who.

Frustrated, she turned away from her reflection in the glass and went through to the small clients' fitting room to fetch the next job on Mrs Reader's list and tidy up after the last of the appointments. In spite of her mood, she had to smile when she saw the bottle of vodka and two glasses that Geraldine Ashby had smuggled in with her earlier that evening. Marjorie was under no illusions as to Gerry's interest in her, and she saw no reason to be coy about it; what intrigued her, though, was that the feeling was mutual. She was surprised by how much she liked Geraldine – not because of her wealth or her title, but because she was unpredictable; she resisted what was expected of her, and to a girl whose petty acts of rebellion had got her in and out of trouble since she was fifteen, that sort of spirit was dangerously attractive. Marjorie picked up the bottle to throw it away before it was discovered, then thought better of it and poured herself another drink from what was left. There was a cutting from a magazine on the wall in front of her, a piece from last month's *Tatler* with the headline 'Nurses to benefit from theatrical coup'; the photograph showed the Motley seamstresses and some of the members of the Cowdray Club standing in the workroom, preparing the clothes for next week's gala, and there was a smaller picture underneath of

Noël Coward on stage with Gertrude Lawrence. Ronnie and Lettice had bought copies for all the girls to take home, and Marjorie thought again of what her father had said – her new friends were not all they seemed. She knew what he meant, and yet there was something about this world of glamour and make-believe that seemed more real to her than anything else she had ever known. The taste of it had made her reckless, and encouraged her to make promises to Lucy which she had no idea if she could keep. Lucy didn't seem bothered, though. Half the time, Marjorie got the impression that the girl was only humouring her anyway, and – emotionally – Lucy often seemed more grown up than she was; perhaps that's what having a child did for you. Still, she thought, holding up the dress that was to be altered and looking at herself in the mirror, this plan was more solid than most, and it was stupid to have doubts when it was too late to do anything about them.

As she carried the gown carefully back into the workroom, a tailor's dummy in the corner caught her eye, next to a roll of deep-blue silk. She knew it was waiting to be transformed into a cape to match one of the evening gowns for the gala, and that it would be the first job on Hilda Reader's list in the morning. She never tired of watching as the cutter worked from the designs that the Motley sisters produced, interpreting their sketches into a three-dimensional garment by pinning, draping and cutting the material, apparently without effort. It was a great skill, and Marjorie had been so thrilled when Mrs Reader said she was almost ready to try it herself. She liked Lettice and Ronnie, and was in awe of their talent; obviously she wanted them to think well of her, but it was Hilda Reader – the woman who had first had confidence in her, the mother she wished she'd had – who she really wanted to impress, and what better way than by making the cape herself, now, when everywhere was quiet? It was a risk, but it would be worth it to see the look on the head cutter's face in the morning, and it would keep Marjorie's mind off other things.

She took another sip of vodka for courage and measured out a length of material, then arranged the silk on the back of the dummy, leaving enough at the top to complete the collar work later. Carefully, she brought the selvedges round to the front and pinned them to the back cloth at the top of the shoulders, making sure that the material was not too tightly drawn across the chest. She checked the desired length against the sketch one more time, took a deep breath, and picked up the scissors – this was the moment of no return, but there was no point being half-hearted about it. She cut boldly across the bottom, allowing for a two-inch hem, and was relieved to see that the line was straight and the silk fell as she knew it should. Buoyed up by her success, Marjorie carried on patiently, so absorbed in her work that she forgot everything else. As she stepped back to examine the general shape of the material before making the final cuts, she heard the sound of footsteps on the iron stairs outside. Still exhilarated by the miraculous way in which the garment now resembled its paper counterpart, she went out into the corridor, confident that she could handle anything.

When she saw who it was, she opened her mouth to speak but, before she could utter a word, she found herself shoved hard against the back wall of the lobby. The action took her completely by surprise, and there was no chance to recover before something was sprayed in her face. She turned away, blinded for a moment, but the spray came again and whatever she had inhaled disoriented her. She stumbled back into the workroom and tried to shut the door behind her, but she was too slow. By the time she felt the tape measure tighten around her neck, she was too weak to offer any resistance.

News of Josephine's arrival in town had spread fast. She arrived back at the Cowdray Club to find a note from Ronnie and Lettice with instructions – by no stretch of the imagination could it be called an invitation – to meet them for supper at Rules after the evening performance of *Romeo and Juliet*. There was 'much to catch up on', apparently, and the envelope also included a ticket for the theatre in case she wanted to see the show. The period of coming and going as she pleased was at an end, obviously, but she found she didn't much mind.

Considerately, the girls had reserved a house seat at the back of the stalls for her so that she could slip into the performance at any point, and she was able to get some more work done before getting ready to go out. She decided to take a cab to the New and expected to have to go to Oxford Street to find one, but, as she left the Club, she noticed a taxi a few doors down, dropping someone off outside the church in Henrietta Place. The driver acknowledged her wave, and she waited on the pavement while he finished with his current fare, still thinking about what she had seen in Finchley and Islington.

'Josephine?'

The voice was hesitant and came from across the street. She looked over to where a woman was standing by the iron railings, and found it difficult to believe what she was seeing. As she stared, too surprised even to say hello, the woman left the shadows and walked up to her, apparently unsure of her welcome. 'I'm sorry to turn up like this,' she said, 'but I wanted to see you and every scheme I came up with to bump into you seemed so ridiculous that I thought I'd just come clean and say hello.'

'You don't have to come up with ways to bump into me, Marta – you could just telephone.' Josephine held out her arms, genuinely delighted to see her friend's lover after so long. 'Lydia didn't even tell me you were back.'

'She doesn't know.' Marta pulled away from the hug, and Josephine was struck by how much she had changed in the last eighteen months. She was still remarkably beautiful, but the warmth in her eyes which had prevented it from being merely a physical attribute was now hard to find, and the spark of defiance which Josephine had found so attractive had all but disappeared. It was hardly surprising, she thought: she had come so close to death, and the enforced separation from Lydia alone must have taken its toll. God knows what damage Marta's other demons had done to her in the meantime. 'I know I should have called Lydia,' she continued, 'but I just couldn't face it at the moment.' She paused, apparently trying to find a way to explain. 'You see, I didn't want her to think . . .'

'I know, I know.' Josephine interrupted, wanting to make it easier for her. 'After everything that's happened, things are bound to be strange between you, but she won't think badly of you, really she won't.' She smiled reassuringly. 'Lydia loves you, Marta, and that hasn't changed – trust me. Do you want me to pave the way for you? Is that why you're here?' She looked back down the road to where the taxi was turning round, ready to pick her up. 'I was just off to meet Lettice and Ronnie, but that can wait if you want me to talk to her now. Getting you two back together is much more important than . . .'

'Josephine – please, just listen to me for a minute,' Marta said impatiently. 'That wasn't what I was going to say. I didn't want Lydia to think we could pick up where we left off. Things have changed – I've changed – and I wanted to see you because I wanted to see *you*. It's got nothing to do with Lydia.'

'I don't understand.'

'Don't you?' Marta turned away for a moment, her frustration getting the better of her. When she looked back, Josephine was shocked to see tears in her eyes, although she spoke more calmly. 'The last time we met, we didn't have the chance to get to know each other very well.' She smiled wryly. 'I suppose you could say that things got in the way, but I don't want to talk about the past. This is a fresh start for me. I don't know if that includes Lydia. I rather hoped it might include you.'

The taxi pulled into the kerb and stopped at a discreet distance from the two women. 'Are you really saying what I think you're saying?' Josephine asked, horrified.

'God, I knew I'd make a mess of this, no matter how many times I rehearsed it.'

'Don't worry, Marta – it must be hard to be word perfect when you're asking me to betray someone we both care about. Well, someone I care about, at least.'

'Of course I care about her, but it's not that simple – you don't understand.'

A feeling which she could only describe as panic made Josephine react more harshly than she wanted to. 'Don't you dare patronise me like that,' she said. 'I've spent nearly two years watching Lydia try to pick up the pieces after you pulled her life out from under her, so I think I understand all I need to.'

'Aren't you romanticising things a little? I'm sure if Lydia's career were going better, she'd find my absence much easier to bear.' She sighed. 'I'm sorry. I'm hardly in a position to criticise Lydia, and that was a despicable thing to say.'

'Although not entirely unfair.' Josephine smiled, and some of the tension between them relaxed. 'I'm sorry, too, Marta – but I wasn't expecting this.'

'I understand that. Neither was I.'

'You hardly know me. When we met, it was the most terrible time of your life and I happened to be there. I can see why that was important to you, but it's not real – surely you must see that?'

'Now who's being patronising? Look, I've said more than I meant to already,' Marta admitted. 'I really just came here to give you this.' She reached into her bag and took out an envelope. 'I've been keeping a diary for a few months now. I thought it might help me to come to terms with what happened, and then I realised how often you were mentioned in it. I'd like you to read it.' Josephine opened the envelope and looked inside. In the light of the streetlamp, she could see a sheaf of thin, blue paper, covered in Marta's distinctive handwriting. 'It might do a better job of explaining than I've managed in person. I know it's been a shock, my turning up like this,' she added, 'but can you honestly say that it's just me? Did I only imagine that there might have been something between us if things had been different?' Josephine thought for a moment, trying to be honest with herself before she said anything to Marta, and her hesitation seemed to give Marta the encouragement she was looking for. 'Please, Josephine, give me a week – a week of your time to read this and think about it, that's all I ask. I'll be at Prunier's next Friday – if the answer's no, I won't press you and I won't bother you again.'

'And if the answer *is* no, where does that leave Lydia?'

'If?' She raised an eyebrow challengingly, and Josephine blushed at the admission that there was anything to consider. 'But in answer to your question – I can't think about Lydia until I know how you really feel.' She held up her hand as Josephine started to protest. 'I'm sorry if that sounds harsh, but I'm forty-four, and that's far too old to waste time doing the right thing, even if it means kicking kindness and sympathy out of the window. If anything good can be said to have come out of the last few months, it's that I've had the chance to be honest with myself and think about what I want. I've wasted far too much of my life over the years, and I'm afraid it's made me selfish.' She leaned forward and kissed Josephine gently. 'If you're not there, I'll know you've made your decision.'

Marta walked over to the taxi and held the door open for her, but Josephine paused before getting in. 'How did you even know I was here?' she asked.

'I saw you shopping and followed you home.'

'So the gardenia was from you,' Josephine said, the scent of Marta's perfume still heavy in the air between them.

'Yes. I thought it would be fairer than just appearing out of nowhere.'

'It would have been fairer still if you'd put your name to it.'

'I didn't think I'd have to, Josephine,' Marta said quietly. 'So perhaps I have my answer already.'

When the cab pulled up in front of the New Theatre, an embarrassed Josephine tipped the driver generously and settled into her seat just in time for the Capulets' ball. Lettice and Ronnie had designed both the stage sets and the costumes, giving the show a visual unity for which their productions were always famed, and, had she been in the mood for any sort of make-believe, she would have been instantly transported to Renaissance Italy. A narrow strip of sky ran along the back wall, suggesting sunlight and warmth, and streamers hung down from the fly tower, giving a festive air to the proceedings. The balcony stood in the centre of it all. As the play progressed, the closing of some curtains or a clever change of lighting transformed the stage swiftly and effectively into a garden or a friar's cell, Juliet's bedroom, and later her tomb, while the costumes – fresh and brightly coloured at first – faded subtly but inevitably to black, mirroring the shifting mood of the story.

Feeling as though she had already dealt Lydia one blow that evening, Josephine was determined to dislike her rival leading lady's portrayal of Juliet – but she found it impossible to do so. Peggy seemed to have walked straight out of a Botticelli painting, and the lightness and spontaneity of her performance made it a joy to watch. Larry was coming to the end of his time as Romeo, and, although Shakespeare's poetry would no doubt be better served when John Terry took over the role at the end of the month, Josephine doubted that Johnny – who was really only in love with himself – would be capable of the sort of youthful, restless passion that had the audience captivated this evening. Somehow, Larry managed to be impetuous and hesitant at the same time, and it took no great feat of imagination to believe that he was in the grip of a love so intense that he gave little thought to the consequences. It was really the last thing Josephine needed to see, preoccupied as she was with Marta, and, when the actor tenderly touched the balcony as though the stones were an extension of Juliet herself, she found herself barely able to watch.

While the actors were taking their third curtain call, Josephine left her seat and walked round to the stage door. Larry was already on his way up from the green room, and she congratulated him warmly. 'Thanks, Josephine,' he said, giving her that raffish smile which had made him such an attractive Bothwell when he stepped into her *Queen of Scots* at a week's notice. 'The girls said you might be in tonight – I'm glad you liked it.' He glanced past her to where a dark-haired woman was waiting at the top of the stairs, and his natural charm became something rather more. 'Excuse me – I have to go now, but it's lovely to see you again.' He ran up the steps, two at a time, and Josephine carried on downstairs to look for Lettice and Ronnie.

The green room was full of the usual post-show detritus – abandoned glasses of wine, half-eaten meals, cast-off modesty – and it didn't take her long to locate the Motleys amid the shrieking and hilarity coming from one of the dressing rooms. 'Vivienne was absolutely right,' Ronnie was saying as Josephine put her head round the door. 'Her make-up walks on stage and Hephzibar follows three minutes later!' As the rest of the room dissolved into rowdy laughter, Ronnie noticed her and jumped up from Benvolio's lap to greet her. 'Josephine! About bloody time! In town for forty-eight hours at least and not a peep out of you. How on earth have you coped without us?'

'I haven't. Why do you think I'm here now?' She hugged Ronnie and Lettice, then went over to kiss Lettice's fiancé, George, who had taken the role of Peter in the play. 'It's a fabulous production – you must all be thrilled with it.'

'We are,' Lettice agreed, 'but we're even more pleased with the houses. For the first time ever, we're on a percentage of the profits. Every ticket sold is a farthing to us.'

'So make sure they pay for dinner, Josephine,' said George, smiling.

'Aren't you joining us then?'

'No, but I am,' said a voice behind her, and she felt hands on her shoulders and a kiss on the back of her head.

'Lydia! I wasn't expecting ... How lovely to see you.' Josephine struggled through to the end of the sentence, hoping that she sounded more convincing than she felt. After what had happened earlier, maintaining an air of normality with the Motleys would have been difficult; with Lydia there too, it was nigh on impossible, and her mask seemed to be slipping already.

'Are you all right?' Lettice asked, looking solicitously at her. 'You don't seem quite yourself.'

'Oh, I'm fine. I've just spent the day in the company of some rather odd people, and it takes me a while to come up for air.'

'That'll teach you to stay at a women's club,' Ronnie said, stubbing her cigarette out and reaching for her coat.

Josephine laughed. 'I wasn't talking about them. I meant the people I'm writing about.'

'Even so, you should be careful. It's only a matter of time before all that female company rubs off on you.'

'I should be so lucky,' Lydia said, feigning an expression of self-pity. 'It's been so long, I think I've forgotten what to do.'

'Shouldn't we be going?' Josephine asked casually.

'Yes, we should.' Lettice looked at her watch and kissed George goodbye. 'I don't want them giving our table to someone else – I'm starving. We can catch up on the way.'

They walked out into St Martin's Lane, where the snow was just beginning to settle on window ledges and car rooftops. 'Good God, Marjorie's still at it,' Ronnie said, glancing up at the studio windows. 'Do you think we should pop in and tell her to go home?' She poked Josephine in the shoulder. 'And we could show you your outfit for next week – you're about the only member of the bloody Cowdray Club who hasn't stepped over our threshold today.' Just as she finished speaking, the lights went out in the workroom.

'Looks like she's finally had enough,' Lettice said. 'I don't blame her – she's worked hard today. We'll have to show Josephine tomorrow – Marjorie will only feel obliged to stay longer if we go up now, and we don't want her to think we're checking up on her.'

They carried on to the restaurant, and Lydia fell into step with Josephine, leaving the sisters to talk about work. 'Of course, neither of them can wear tights,' she said cryptically. 'Larry's really too thin, and Johnny's completely knock-kneed.' It was a game attempt to be light-hearted, but Josephine knew how difficult it must be for Lydia to watch a younger woman in the role she so craved, and to know in her heart that she was unlikely ever to play Juliet again. 'Johnny promised me we'd do it together one more time,' she continued, 'and then the bastard goes behind my back and gives it to Peggy without even having the decency to explain why. Tell me honestly – you'd never know there was seventeen years between me and her, would you?'

'No, of course not,' Josephine said, painfully aware that the triumph of Peggy's performance lay in the way she had preserved Juliet's youth with her passion. She remembered how often she had seen Lydia on stage, long before they ever met, and how much she had admired her; to Josephine's mind, she was a much finer actress than any of her contemporaries, but that was no consolation when the theatre belonged to a new generation. 'You know how it is, though,' she continued vaguely. 'Politics always get in the way. I'm sure if Johnny had a free hand you'd be his first choice, but he has so many people to please. And it's not as though you haven't been busy.'

'Picking up Flora's crumbs in a second-rate play at the Savoy is hardly the same thing. I really won't be sorry to see the back of this year – I feel like I've been frustrated at every turn. I hope to God that 1936 will be better.'

'At least you have the cottage,' Josephine said, knowing that the house in the country which Lydia had bought after the success of *Richard of Bordeaux* was her greatest solace in Marta's absence.

'Tagley? Yes, it's heavenly – you must come and see it.' She took Josephine's arm. 'I'm sorry to be such a miserable cow, but I still haven't heard from her. I had this stupid idea that we might be able to spend Christmas together at the cottage – use it as a place to start again. If I'm honest, I suppose that's partly why I bought it, but she hasn't answered any of my letters.'

'Has there been anyone else?' Josephine asked. 'For you, I mean,' she added hurriedly.

'Nothing serious. I haven't got the heart for anything that matters, and I never thought I'd hear myself say that.' She sighed. 'God, Josephine – eighteen months ago I had everything I wanted. You can lose it all so quickly, can't you?'

Josephine nodded. 'If Marta did get in touch, would you do things differently this time?'

'What do you mean?'

'Well, after she left, you told me that if you'd paid more attention to her and how she was feeling, things might have been different. So would you put Marta first now? Ahead of the next part?'

131

'Of course I would.' She caught Josephine's eye. 'Well, I'd try to. I'd convince myself I could. Let's face it, I'm going to have more time on my hands as I get older, not less.'

'That sounds like a choice by default.'

'Yes, I suppose it does.' Lydia was quiet for a moment. 'It worked, though, didn't it?' she asked eventually. 'You thought we were happy together?'

Josephine recalled the time she'd spent with Marta and Lydia; brief though it was, she had envied their closeness with an intensity which had surprised her and, in the months since, had found herself acknowledging her own restlessness – she refused to call it loneliness – with alarming regularity. Perhaps that was why Marta had made her so angry: by threatening to betray Lydia, she had also betrayed Josephine's fragile hope that a partnership based on love and respect and compromise might yet be possible for her. 'Yes, I did,' she admitted truthfully. 'As happy as two people *can* be.'

'Ever the optimist,' Lydia said, smiling at her, and there was a trace of their old friendship in her gentle mockery. Josephine realised suddenly how much she had missed it; they talked so rarely these days. 'Perhaps you're right,' Lydia sighed. 'Perhaps she'd be better with someone else, and I should stick to wining and dining chorus girls at the Ivy.'

'That wasn't what I meant.'

'I know, and don't worry – I'm not quite ready to give in yet.'

They reached the restaurant and Josephine opened the door gratefully, anxious to be seated at a table where the conversation would be diluted. She didn't know who to blame more – Marta for putting her in this position, or herself for allowing it to happen – but at least while she was angry, she didn't have to think more deeply about how she actually felt.

As well as having the distinction of being just across the street from the Motleys' new apartments, Rules was the oldest restaurant in London and a second home to most of the theatrical profession. In fact, it had long been crowded with celebrities from all walks of life, and past customers from Dickens to Edward VII lived on in the cartoons and photographs which lined the walls. The family had built its reputation on traditional London food, and the restaurant still specialised in game, much of which was brought in from its own estate; it was the sort of menu which would normally have delighted Josephine, but tonight she merely glanced at it perfunctorily and chose the first thing on the list.

'So tell us more about these odd people you've been hanging around with.' Lettice's tone was bright enough but she looked curiously across the table, sensing that something was wrong. 'Archie says it's got something to do with a real crime.'

'Yes, that's right.' They listened as she outlined the bare bones of the Sach and Walters case, then explained her own connection with what happened at Anstey years afterwards.

'I don't quite see her problem myself,' Ronnie said, washing her sarcasm down with a swig of champagne. 'It sounds to me like her mother had hit on a bloody good idea. I once had to look after a friend's baby for half an hour – and I would have considered thirty pounds to be a very reasonable price.'

'But how on earth did they ever think they'd get away with it?' Lettice asked, fascinated. 'Surely they should have been more careful?'

'Yes, I can't help feeling that it would have been wise to prepare a more eloquent defence than "I never murdered no babies".' Ronnie lapsed into a convincing cockney accent, and Lydia smiled approvingly at her. 'Seriously, though,' she added, leaning back to allow the waiter to place a large plate of oysters in front of her, 'isn't this gala something to do with a children's charity as well as the Cowdray Club?'

'Yes – the Actors' Orphanage. It's Noël's pet cause, and his aunt's on the club's committee.'

'It makes you wonder, doesn't it?'

'In what way?' Lettice asked, irritated by her sister's habit of never quite explaining her point.

'Well, here we are in 1935, still having to raise money for unwanted children, just so they can grow up in institutions which can't be very pleasant, even if they are supported by the lord of the London stage. It might be legal, but it doesn't exactly sound like progress.'

'It's funny – the first time I ever saw Gertie on stage, she was so pregnant she could hardly squeeze into the costumes,' Lydia said, reaching for some bread. 'It was just after the war, and I gather she did a matinee and an evening performance on the day before the birth. Of course, that all went tits up. If she hadn't had her mother to dump the kid on, I suppose she would have ended up in the orphanage as well.'

'You *are* sure it's the charities that this money is going to?' Ronnie asked, looking at Josephine with a wicked glint in her eye. 'I'd check the takings very carefully if I were you. Charity begins *chez* Lawrence with her current predicament.'

'Don't be so scandalous,' chided Lettice. 'That's all behind her now. She's paying off the debts at fifty pounds a week – they've just cleared her of the bankruptcy.'

'Bankruptcy?'

'Good God, dear – where have you been? Don't they have newspapers in Inverness? Miss Lawrence's financial embarrassment has been the toast of the press for months. Apparently, she was so busy ordering new cars and flowers that she forgot to pay her laundry bills. It's easily done, I suppose.'

'Oh, it's been simply awful for her,' Lettice said sympathetically, balancing roast potatoes around the edge of her steak-and-kidney pie. 'Gertie, her maid, even her dog – they were all turned out on to the street. In the end, her agent took them in.'

'Good to know they're useful for something,' Lydia said bitterly. 'Although I have to say, I haven't noticed any marked drop in standards now Gertie's slumming it.'

'No, she's determined not to cut back on anything.' Lettice's familiarity with the gossip columns was legendary, and Josephine wasn't at all surprised by her intimate knowledge of Gertrude Lawrence's financial affairs. 'No – she says she'll make up every penny through cabaret and extra bits of filming.'

'And charity galas.'

As the Motleys continued their bickering, Josephine noticed how often Lydia's face reverted to sadness, and she could bear it no longer. If she stayed here, she was likely to take Lydia discreetly outside and tell her everything that Marta had said, which would surely only make things worse. 'I'm afraid I have to go,' she said when there was a break in the sparring. 'I've got another appointment with the baby farmers in the morning, and I should be getting back.'

'Not so early, surely? You'll stay for dessert?'

'No, but I promise to stop by the studio tomorrow and look at my outfit. Archie assured me it's worth trying on. I'll see you then – about three o'clock?'

The girls nodded and let her go without any further argument. Outside in the street, she breathed a sigh of relief and looked up to Archie's flat, but it was in darkness. Disappointed not to find him in, she turned and walked down Maiden Lane, hoping to be lucky with a cab in Bedford Street, but she hadn't got far before she heard someone call her name. 'I couldn't possibly let you just go like that,' Lettice said, hurrying up to her. 'You've been upset all evening. What's wrong, Josephine? Has something happened between you and Archie?'

'No, nothing like that. It's Lydia – I wasn't expecting to see her tonight, and it was a bit awkward.'

'Oh God – you know something about Marta, don't you? Has she been in touch with you?' Josephine nodded. 'And she's not ready for a happy reunion, by the sound of it?'

'No, not at the moment. Perhaps not ever.'

'Shouldn't you tell Lydia?'

'Yes, I should, but I need to think carefully about what I'm going to say first.'

'Marta always liked you, didn't she?' Lettice looked at her and Josephine knew what was going through her mind, but she was kind enough not to force the point. Instead, she said: 'I'm sure you'll work it out, but if you need any help, you know where I am. No one else need ever know.'

Josephine smiled gratefully at her. 'What will you tell the others? They'll wonder why you're chasing after me in the snow.'

'No they won't – they think I found your glove under the table.' She squeezed Josephine's hand. 'It'll be all right. I'll see you tomorrow.'

When Marjorie came round, she found herself lying on the workroom floor. All the main lights in the studio had been switched off, and the only glow in the room came from a lamp on Hilda Reader's desk. It was desperately cold, and she tried to raise herself to a sitting position, but her body felt heavy and the nausea and dizziness were so extreme that she found it impossible to stay upright for more than a few seconds. Her head fell back on to the boards and she lay there in the silence, waiting for the symptoms to pass and trying to make sense of what had happened. The room was so quiet that she thought she was alone, but her relief was short-lived; a noise came from over to her left, a sound like pills being shaken from a bottle, and, as she listened more carefully, she could hear footsteps moving softly around the room. Something in their leisureliness made her afraid.

She must have passed out again. When she regained consciousness, she was dimly aware of someone standing over her, then she felt hands under her arms, lifting and dragging her like an invalid over to the head cutter's table. She was pulled roughly on to a chair, where her hands were fastened behind her with a length of soft material. Although she tried to protest, the words were thick and heavy in her mouth and the noise that came from her throat was unrecognisable even to her. A cold sweat broke out on her face and the palms of her hands, and – whilst a small part of her told her that it must be the effect of the spray she had inhaled – it felt like the physical expression of her fear, spreading slowly but irrevocably through her body. Desperately, she tried to see what was going on but there was a shadow between her and the lamp, and only when it moved away did she realise that what she had experienced so far was nothing compared to what was to come. The light from the lamp shone down on to a needle – not the sort that was commonplace on Hilda Reader's desk but a sack needle, used for hessian rather than silk and familiar to

Marjorie from her time in prison. Next to it were the beads she had bought that morning, still in their box. As the box was calmly lifted and opened, she heard again the sound which she had believed to be pills, and watched in horror as the beads poured out on to the desk in front of her, a stream of sharp, black glass.

The waiting was unbearable, eased only by the fact that she was so dreadfully tired. More than anything, she wanted to lie down again and allow unconsciousness to get the better of her, but she was tied to the chair and, in any case, what instinct for life she had left told her that she must try to stay awake. Her breathing came in deep, irregular sighs now, but she made one last effort to look this madness in the eye. It was her final act of defiance. The deadly calm was replaced in an instant by a frenzy of violence and hatred, and Marjorie felt hands on her face, wrenching her mouth open and stifling any attempts at a scream with handful after handful of glass. The sharp edges of the beads cut into her tongue and ground against her teeth, and her mouth began to fill with blood. She tried to spit the glass out before too much of it went back into her throat, but strong fingers held her nose, forcing her to swallow in order to breathe, and she felt the piercing certainty of death moving down into her stomach. Just for a second, the hands moved away and she was able to gasp for air, but the intensity of her breathing only served to aid the invasion of her body, leaving her choking and helpless, and then the torture began again. Her head was yanked back from behind and the needle tore through her skin, focusing her mind on a pain so great that nothing else existed, ripping the tissue in an outpouring of rage. The sensation of the thread moving in and out of her lips made her gag, but there was nowhere for the vomit to go except

138

through her nose or back into her throat. She felt herself slowly suffocating, and her feet beat uselessly against the floor, counting out the final seconds of her life. Just before her vision began to fade, the hands were once more at her face, but this time the violence was gone. Unable to struggle any longer, Marjorie allowed her head to be moved gently round to the right and, in the full-length mirror which had been so carefully placed, she watched the ugly, humiliating horror of her own death.

Chapter Six

Hilda Reader emerged from the underground station at Piccadilly Circus into a world transformed by freshness and light. Snow had fallen heavily overnight and into the early hours, and now there was a look in the sky which promised more. She had always thought that winter suited London better than any other season; the city was bright with the peculiar, hard brilliance of cold weather, and she was glad that she had decided to leave the stale fug of the underground a stop early in order to enjoy it. At street level, the snow had fallen victim to traffic and the games of children but it remained unspoilt on canopies and rooftops, and the upper storeys of buildings faded into blacks, whites and greys, almost as if she were looking at a photograph. The only splashes of colour came from a few resilient flower sellers who sat on the steps around Eros, their displays made suddenly more precious by the bitter weather.

She walked on down Coventry Street and across Leicester Square, looking forward to work as she always did. The Motleys were busier now than ever and she went in most Saturdays, glad of the chance to get on with jobs which the constant supervision of thirty girls often made impossible during the week. It didn't affect her home life: her husband was a buyer for Debenhams and she was lucky in her second marriage to have found a man who valued her career as highly as his own.

Widowed at thirty by the war, Hilda had been forced to accept that the prospect of building a loving home like the one in which she was raised had been buried in Belgian soil along with her husband. Grudgingly, she resigned herself to a life without intimacy, glad at least that her profession was not one which she was expected to relinquish to the handful of men who returned from the fighting, and, in her work with Motley, she found a different sort of fulfilment. Later, as her friendship with John grew miraculously into something more, she lived in fear of having to choose – but she had underestimated him: he was a good man, and wise enough to understand that, had he been tempted to force the issue, she would never have agreed to marry him.

But the marriage had worked, and the time they spent together was important to them both. They always went out on a Saturday night, and Hilda knew the West End theatres and cinemas as well as most people knew their friends. The Motleys encouraged her to see as much as possible and to keep up with the new ideas and changing fashions of the stage; that was what she loved most about them – their willingness to include others. They listened to her as carefully now as they had when they were sitting at her feet, learning to sew, and the fame of the last few years hadn't changed that. The business grew more chaotic by the day, and it drove Hilda's ordered mind to distraction at times, but it was the large, unruly family she had never had and they were blessed with a good set of workers at the moment. She would be the first to admit that the prospect of taking on ex-prisoners had filled her with horror, but she had been wrong; now, her biggest worry was how to hang on to Marjorie, how to keep her on the straight and narrow and make sure that she was sufficiently involved not to be lured away by any of the other fashion houses who knew talent when they saw it.

As Hilda turned into St Martin's Lane, the first flakes of the threatened snow shower began to fall. She fumbled around in her bag for the heavy set of keys, but was surprised to see that the wrought-iron gates which divided the street from the staff entrance were unlocked. The sisters must have come in early, she thought, but one look at the perfect covering of snow on the cobbles told her that no one had entered the premises that morning. Surely Marjorie hadn't worked all night? Or perhaps she had simply forgotten to lock the gates when she left, in which case Hilda would have to have a quiet word with her on Monday. She pulled the gates shut behind her and trudged into the yard, enjoying the dry crunch of untouched snow beneath her boots. When she turned the corner, she stopped short in her tracks: at the foot of the iron staircase, too close to the building to be visible from the street, someone was lying motionless in the snow, partially covered in a blanket of deathly white. Please God, no, she thought, hurrying forward, not Marjorie – the child must have slipped on the stairs in the darkness; if she'd been there all night, she'd have had no chance against the cold. But as she got closer, she realised that the figure was a man, and, bending over him, she saw not Marjorie but her father.

He was beyond help – she could see that instantly. He lay on his side, his eyes still open, flakes of snow frozen to his eyelashes and the stubble on his face; Hilda felt the lonely horror of his death at the same time as she thanked God for saving her from a deeper grief. There was a profound stillness about the scene, and she wondered why she had never noticed how quickly the everyday sounds of St Martin's Lane disappeared once you were in this courtyard. Here, amid the double disorientation of snow and sudden death, her mind struggled to make sense of what had happened. Had Marjorie's father come looking for her and met with an accident? Or was it worse than that? She remembered how upset the girl had seemed when she came back from lunch yesterday. Had there been some sort of struggle? Had he tried to hurt her, and had Marjorie – in putting up a fight – gone further than she intended? Hilda hesitated for a moment. She knew she must go upstairs and telephone for help, but was reluctant to leave the dead man on his own. It was stupid, she realised – no more harm could come to him, and cold and loneliness had lost their power to hurt – but it seemed wrong to abandon him now and, in truth, she longed for company herself, even that of a stranger.

Quickly, Hilda turned and went back towards St Martin's Lane, where she caught the attention of a young man who happened to glance in through the gates as he passed. Startled but keen to help, he offered to go back into the street and find a policeman, but she knew it would be quicker to call from the studio and, in any case, she had to telephone the Motley sisters as soon as possible to let them know what was happening. Leaving the man with the body, she went carefully up the steps; they were still perilous, and she clung tightly to a handrail which was slippery and far from reliable, wondering again where Marjorie was and what had happened. When she got to the top, she saw that the door to the building was open. The wind had blown some of the snow into the corridor, where it had melted into a muddy dampness. She walked quietly towards the studio, sensing somehow that she was not on her own even before she saw Marjorie sitting on the other side of the room, her back to the door.

144

'Marjorie, love – thank God you're safe. What on earth's happened?' The girl must be in shock, Hilda thought, because she didn't move or respond in any way, even when she called her name again. 'It's all right, love – whatever's gone on, you're not on your own. We'll look after you.' As Hilda stepped closer and reached out her hand, she noticed the smell but the significance of it didn't register until it was too late; by now, she was at an angle to see Marjorie's reflection in the full-length mirror which stood just a few feet away from her. She stared in revulsion and terror at the blood and bruising around her mouth, at the needle still hanging on a thread from her lips, at her own image standing over the dead girl, adding to Marjorie's degradation by the very act of witnessing it. Understanding now why there had been no response, Hilda opened her mouth and screamed for them both.

Detective Inspector Archie Penrose sat at his desk in New Scotland Yard, wondering how he could make a pact with the devil to add a few more hours to each day. He had been at work since just after seven and was only halfway through the reports that had come in overnight. Among them was Fallowfield's account of the thefts and anonymous letters at the Cowdray Club; it was not the sort of thing which Penrose would normally investigate, but the chief constable was putting pressure on him to give some time to it, and the sooner it was cleared up, the better.

He picked up the telephone to make an appointment but, before he had a chance to speak to the operator, Fallowfield stuck his head round the door. 'Sorry to interrupt, Sir, but we've got to go. Thompson's just called up from the desk – a man's reported two bodies, and I recognised the address. It's your cousins' place – and one of the bodies is a young woman.'

For a second, Penrose was numb, trying to take in the implications of what he had heard. Then he reached for the telephone again and barked Lettice's number into the receiver. 'Come on, pick it up,' he muttered as it rang and rang, but there was no answer, and the result was the same when he tried Ronnie's flat. 'What else did Thompson say?' he asked as they ran out to the car. 'Do we have a description of the dead woman?' Fallowfield hesitated, and Penrose knew that there was something he was reluctant to share. 'Well?'

'We don't have a description of the woman, Sir – only what's been done to her.'

'And? Oh for God's sake, Bill, just tell me.'

'Someone's stitched her mouth up.'

'Jesus Christ!' Penrose paused before getting into the car, and tried to rid himself of the images crowding his mind. 'Please God, no,' he said, more quietly this time.

'Come on, Sir – we don't know anything for sure yet,' Fallowfield said calmly, taking the keys from Penrose's hand and going round to the driver's side. 'She was found in the workroom. The other body's outside in the yard – looks like he fell down the stairs on his way out.'

'And who reported it?'

'Chap called Gaunt. Ellis Gaunt, I think.'

The name meant nothing to Penrose, but then very little else did either. The short journey from the Embankment to St Martin's Lane was a blur to him, and he was out of the car even before Fallowfield had brought it to a standstill in front of number 66. Just inside the gates, he saw Lettice and Ronnie comforting an older woman whom he recognised as their head cutter; another man – presumably the Gaunt who'd made the call – stood awkwardly to the side, at a discreet distance from the group of women, as if reluctant to intrude on their sorrow. All of them looked up, startled, as Penrose ran over to them. 'Thank God,' he said, scarcely caring that it was not the most professional of responses. 'I thought for a moment that one of you . . .'

'No, Archie – we're fine.' Lettice smiled weakly, but she and Ronnie both looked ten years older than when he had last seen them, and Ronnie in particular seemed to be struggling to keep her emotions under control – anger, he noticed, rather than tears, but that was what he would have expected; ever since they were children, Ronnie's response to grief or injustice had always been to rage against it rather than admit her vulnerability. The other lady – why couldn't he remember her name? – was making a valiant effort to pull herself together, but in vain: she stared down at the handkerchief in her hands, winding one of the corners repeatedly round her finger and shaking her head; she seemed grateful when Lettice saved her from having to go over what had happened straight away. 'No, it's Marjorie who's been killed – Marjorie Baker, one of our girls. Hilda found her father over by the steps when she came in to work this morning. She went up to telephone for help, and that's when she found Marjorie's body.'

Penrose glanced over to the foot of the iron staircase. 'There's another way we can get up to the workroom, isn't there?' he asked.

'Yes, through the clients' entrance at the front and up the stairs there.' Lettice opened her bag and took out a set of keys. 'Here, you'll need these.'

Penrose walked back to the street, where Fallowfield was

147

getting some gloves and other equipment out of the car, and handed him the keys. 'Have a quick look round inside, Bill – I want to get everyone out of the yard. They've had a shock and they shouldn't be out here in these temperatures, but check everywhere first. We don't want any more surprises.'

He returned to the group and spoke gently to the woman who had found the body. 'I'm so very sorry for what you've been through. My sergeant's just checking the premises and sealing off the workroom. He won't be long, and then I'll need to ask you a few questions. We can do it in one of the rooms here, or, if you'd rather not go back into the building straight away, I'm sure I can find us somewhere nearby to talk.'

'No, no – it's fine,' she said. 'I don't want to make any more work for you.'

'We'll go into the flat upstairs in a minute,' Lettice said, squeezing Hilda's shoulder. 'It's chock-a-block with materials, but it's quiet and well away from everything, and at least we can have some tea to warm us up.'

Penrose was grateful for his cousin's tact. The comings and goings of photographers, scene-of-crime officers and mortuary vans were not comfortable things to witness for anyone who didn't work with them, and he needed Hilda to concentrate without any upsetting distractions. 'You must be Mr Gaunt?' he said, holding his hand out to the man by the gates. 'I'm Detective Inspector Penrose. I gather you reported the murder?'

'That's right,' Gaunt said. 'I was on my way to work, when I saw Mrs Reader coming out from the yard. She was obviously upset about something, so I stopped to find out what was wrong. She asked me to wait down here with the man's body while she went to call the police, just to make sure that nobody else came into the yard. Then I heard her screaming, so I went straight up – I thought she was in trouble.' He paused, looking at Hilda Reader. 'When I saw what had happened, I was so sorry that I'd let her go up and make the call, but it seemed the best thing at the time – she knew where the telephone was and everything. But I wish I could have saved her from seeing that. It's terrible up there – even more so for anyone who knew the girl.'

'You weren't to know,' Penrose said, impressed by the young man's decency. 'What did you do when you got upstairs?'

'I asked Mrs Reader where the telephone was, and told her to wait in the corridor. Then I called you.'

'And you came down together as soon as you'd finished.'

'No, Archie – they did a little light dusting and finished the spring collection. Of course they came straight down – they're hardly going to stay up there with a human pin cushion, are they?' Ronnie's frustration had finally got the better of her, but there were tears in her eyes as she glared at him.

Gaunt looked uncomfortable, but Penrose nodded encouragingly at him to continue. 'More or less straight down, Sir. Mrs Reader wanted me to telephone her employers as well. So I went back to do that, and then we came down here to wait.'

'We came straight away,' Lettice explained. 'We just couldn't believe it. I suppose we'd been here about five or ten minutes before you arrived.'

'And neither of you have left the courtyard?'

'No, of course not. We knew we mustn't touch anything.'

'There is one thing, though.' Hilda Reader spoke so faintly that Penrose could hardly hear what she was saying. 'Upstairs I . . . it was the smell, you see. I couldn't stop myself. The shock of finding her there like that, seeing what he'd done to her. I'm

149

afraid I . . . I was sick. I couldn't help it,' she said again. 'I'm sorry – I hope I haven't ruined anything.'

'Oh, Hilda,' Lettice said, wrapping her arms round her. 'How bloody awful for you. There's no need to be sorry.'

'Lettice is right, Mrs Reader,' Penrose said. 'There's absolutely no need to apologise – it's a perfectly natural reaction.'

'I didn't realise she was dead at first, you see,' Hilda explained. 'She had her back to me, and when I saw her I thought that something had gone on between her and her father. If I'm honest, I thought she'd hurt him – then I realised it was the other way round.'

'Why did you think that Marjorie had hurt her father?' Penrose asked.

'Because he was hanging around here at lunchtime yesterday, asking to see her. She went over the road to meet him, and when she came back she seemed upset – angry, really. I think she was ashamed of him – she never talked about her home life. She kept apologising in case he'd been any bother to me.'

'It's us that should be sorry,' Lettice said. 'All the time it was going on, we were just across the road at the theatre. My God,' she added, remembering, 'we even saw the lights go out. We could have helped her.'

'What time was that?'

'Just after the play finished, so around ten-fifteen, I suppose. We should have gone up to see her, like we said we would. We should never have let this happen.'

'Damn right we shouldn't.' Ronnie lit a cigarette and looked provocatively at Archie, daring him to forbid her to smoke at a crime scene. 'Why didn't we know that Marjorie was in trouble? Because we never have time to talk to those girls about anything except work, that's why. We're so busy with our plays and our reviews and our fucking charity galas that we can't see what's going on under our roof. I swear to God, if that bastard hadn't cracked his own skull open, I'd be more than happy to do it for him.'

Fallowfield reappeared in the yard and nodded discreetly to Penrose. 'The rest of the building's clear, Sir,' he said. 'Nothing looks out of place except in the workroom.'

'Fine. Well, if everyone could go up to the flat now, I'll be with you as soon as I can. And Mr Gaunt – you must be very late for work, so we won't keep you any longer at the moment. We'll need a formal statement from you in due course, and there may be some further questions – let Detective Sergeant Fallowfield know how we can get hold of you, and you're free to go. Can we give you a lift anywhere?'

'No thank you, Sir – I'm only a couple of minutes away. I work at the Coliseum.'

'Stage crew?' Penrose asked, and Gaunt nodded. They watched as Lettice and Ronnie led Hilda Reader round to the front of the building. 'Thank you for what you've done this morning,' Penrose added. 'It can't have been easy for you. I'd appreciate it if you could keep the details to yourself at the moment. Miss Baker's remaining family will have to be told and I need to establish exactly what happened here – and all that will be much less painful without the help of the evening papers. Can I rely on you not to mention names to anyone?'

'Yes, of course,' Gaunt said.

For once, Penrose actually believed the answer he was given. 'Is the team on its way?' he asked Fallowfield. 'This snow's not much at the moment, but it's going to get worse.'

'Should be here any minute, Sir. I caught Spilsbury on his way out – said he'd come right over.'

'Excellent.' Penrose left Fallowfield to take down Gaunt's details, and walked over to the foot of the staircase. Standing at a distance, so as not to disturb the area immediately around the body, he looked down at the dead man. He lay with his head towards the stairs and parallel with the building, one hand close to his face, the other flung out behind him, just touching the step, as though he had still been trying to save himself when he hit the ground. In his sixties, Penrose guessed, and, from what he could see where the snow had not settled, shabbily dressed. Crouching down, he noticed the raw, red discolouration on the man's knuckles where his skin had been exposed to the cold; the snow had done its quiet work, drifting, enfolding, obliterating; imperceptibly draining his life if the fall had not killed him, and creating more difficulties for those investigating his death.

Penrose turned his back on Baker and headed upstairs through the front entrance to try to piece together the last moments of his daughter's life, stopping on the way to fetch his bag from the car. He stood just inside the door to the workroom, taking advantage of the stillness before forensics arrived to absorb the scene as a whole. Once the detailed analysis of individual pieces of evidence began, the chance to do this was lost, so he was always relieved to be the first professional to arrive at the scene of a crime; photographs were invaluable, and many a cruel murder had been solved in the photographic department high above the Thames, but, for Penrose, there was no substitute for his own first impressions. Carefully, he put his bag down on the table nearest the door and took out some gloves, then walked slowly into the room. It was a scene of nauseating horror. Marjorie was slumped on an upright wooden chair and, although he could see the extent of her injuries in the mirror, nothing could have prepared him for the trauma of looking directly into her face. It was impossible to imagine what she might have been like in life, so distorted and mutilated were her features. Blood and vomit had trickled down her nose and out through the stitches in her lips. It ran in narrow lines down her face and onto the front of her sewing smock, defacing the Motley monogram. Penrose noticed the small pieces of black glass which mingled with it and realised that Marjorie's suffering must have begun long before the needle touched her skin. As he looked closer, he could see tiny cuts and grazes all around her nose and on her cheeks, presumably from glass which had missed her mouth in the violence of the attack; some of the beads were still on the table next to the body, and he saw that they had been roughly crushed to make their edges even sharper and more deadly. Her swollen lips were bruised and discoloured, and the needle – about four inches long and angled at the tip – hung down from her mouth on a length of thick, black thread. The stitching was crudely done, and Penrose could not even begin to imagine the pain; in truth, though, he didn't have to – the evidence of that was all too obvious in her eyes. Glazed and passive in death, and fixed on their merciless reflection, they nevertheless seemed to plead with him to call a halt to the torment; as he crouched down beside her, obscuring the line of vision between the body and its grotesque mirror image, he could almost believe that she was grateful.

Marjorie's hands were clasped together in her lap, but the red marks around her wrists suggested that they had, at some point, been tied together. There was a similar chafing to her neck, and the width of the mark seemed to match the tape measure which hung over the back of the chair. Penrose had tried to prevent his mind from focusing on the stench of the body, but it was unavoidable; he would not know until the post mortem whether the incontinence was a result of some sort of toxic substance or purely of fear, but he would be surprised to find that Marjorie had not been incapacitated in some way. She was young and looked reasonably strong, but there was no sign of a struggle in the room: the work tables still stood in neat rows and the chairs and tailor's dummies remained upright and undamaged. The killer would have had ample time to tidy up, of course, but somehow Penrose did not think that was what had happened. No, he sensed something much more controlled and methodical in this determined violation of a young girl's body. He stood and looked around him at the fabrics and drawings, at the contrasts of colour and texture that filled the room. Death was always ugly, whether it came from a merciful bullet to the head or the sort of prolonged torture he saw here, but more often than not it confined itself to poorer districts and normal, even squalid, domesticity; the fact that it had been allowed to taint a place of beauty, that Marjorie had been disfigured in the most repellent way amid the trappings of class and fashion, seemed to him significant.

It occurred to Penrose that this was the first time he had attended a murder scene in a room he knew well, and he was struck by the way in which violence affected the atmosphere; it went far beyond the power of any physical damage, and he wondered how Lettice and Ronnie would cope with what had taken place here, or if Hilda Reader would ever feel capable of working in this studio again. He remembered what he and Josephine had discussed the other night: the story wasn't the crime or the investigation – the stages which concerned him;

it was how people picked up from there and carried on with their lives. If the obvious explanation here turned out to be the truth, and Marjorie's father had fallen to his death after killing her, then Penrose's involvement in their narrative was over before it really started; for everyone else – Marjorie's family and workmates, others who would be destroyed by the shame of what her father had done – it was just the beginning, and he suddenly felt an overwhelming sense of sorrow for the unrecognised victims of murder, the thousands of people for whom justice was not the same as solace, and who were left to cope while professionals like him washed their hands of one set of lives and moved on to the next.

Somehow, though, he didn't think his business with the Bakers was finished yet: the obvious scenario might be logical, but he couldn't quite bring himself to believe it. He glanced across the table next to the body, taking in the cotton reels and squares of material, the boxes of pins and needles – all the clutter which would make the necessary analysis of the scene so difficult – and stopped when he noticed an empty vodka bottle and two glasses. That might easily explain how Marjorie had been drugged, but, after what Hilda Reader had said, would the girl really have settled down for a cosy drink with her father on work premises? He doubted it. There was something else, too: on the floor by the mirror lay another sewing smock, exactly like the one which Marjorie wore. When he bent down to examine it, he could smell the faintest trace of vomit and see that it was covered in tiny flecks of blood. Clearly, the smock had been worn by the killer. Why had it been left behind? he wondered, but, more to the point, was Baker the sort of man who would bother to take such precautions? He was wary of jumping to too many conclusions before he'd heard the scientific evidence, but his instinct told him that, if Baker had killed his daughter, it would have been with a blow to the head or a hard shove down the stairs – something clumsy and unimaginative. This was altogether different; it was spiteful and emotional and – if he really wanted to speculate – the sort of crime more often committed by a woman than a man. The stitching of the mouth had obvious connotations: Marjorie had said too much, exposed a secret, perhaps, or told a lie. Then she had been made to watch herself die, taunted and mocked by her own helplessness. The evidence might prove him wrong but, at the moment, the personality of the crime did not tally in Penrose's mind with the man who lay dead outside.

Deep in thought, he heard a noise behind him and turned round, expecting to see Fallowfield or a scene-of-crime officer, but it was Ronnie. 'What the hell are you doing here?' he snapped, his concern for her making him react more angrily than he meant to. 'I told you to go to the flat.' He went over to the door and took her arm, but she shook him off.

'I want to see her, Archie,' she said, 'and don't think you're going to stop me. These are our premises and Marjorie is – was – our responsibility. Hilda walked in on this when it should have been one of us, and she's up there now in some sort of private hell created by what she's seen. I can't just hide upstairs and pretend I know how awful it must be. I won't do that. It's disrespectful to Marjorie and plain bloody cowardly as far as Hilda's concerned. Please – let me see her properly.'

She tried to push past him but he wouldn't let her. 'Does Hilda know you're here?' he asked. She shook her head. 'No, I thought not. She didn't strike me as the sort of woman who'd want to share her pain – not like this, anyway. There are ways of helping her that don't involve putting yourself through this just because you feel guilty.' He and Ronnie were alike in many ways, and he understood exactly where her anger was coming from. 'Trust me, please – I didn't know Marjorie and you did, but no woman would want to be seen like this – that's not respect. You can stay here with me for a minute if you like, but I won't let you go any closer.' Ronnie seemed to realise that she had no choice but to accept his decision. She stared across the room, bewildered and horrified by what she saw, and he watched her face as she tried to come to terms with a string of unfamiliar emotions, understanding how alienated and help-less she must feel in a space where she was usually so in control. 'Have you noticed anything out of place?' he asked after a moment or two.

'Apart from a dead seamstress, you mean?'

'Apart from that, yes.'

Ronnie looked around the room. 'The mirror's been moved,' she said eventually. 'It's usually over there by the window to catch the light. Otherwise, it's all as it should be.' She laughed bitterly. 'You could almost believe it was a normal working day, couldn't you? Oh, Archie – why did he have to pick Hilda's table to kill her at? It seems such a small thing, I suppose – what does it matter *where* she died when she died so horrifi-cally? But if it had been anyone else's, they need never have known. Now, I honestly don't know how any of us can carry on here.'

He saw no point in lying to her. 'It's going to be difficult at first, and I agree with you – Hilda may find it impossible. But it does fade, you know – that image in your mind. Perhaps it shouldn't, but it does.'

'Did he really stitch her mouth up?' He nodded, and Ronnie

seemed to search for words that would express how she felt. In the end, she simply said: 'I liked her, Archie. I really liked her.'

'Come on,' he said gently, leading her away. 'Let's go upstairs.'

They walked back along the corridor and, as they passed the open doorway which led on to the staircase, he glanced down into the courtyard, where Fallowfield was busy organising the other officers as they arrived. The snow was still falling, but only lightly, and he was pleased to see a sense of urgency in the proceedings; the sooner they could photograph both scenes and remove the bodies for post mortem, the better. He needed some preliminary results as soon as possible to confirm exactly what he was dealing with, and he knew he could rely on Spilsbury to be both swift and thorough.

Lettice had not been exaggerating about the state of their old flat on the top floor of number 66. There were rolls of material everywhere, and the living room had been transformed into a makeshift workroom to accommodate extra staff during busy times. The three bedrooms that led off it looked like the storage area for a West End jumble sale: each was packed with props, set models and costumes from past productions, and Penrose wondered how long it would take his cousins to fill Maiden Lane as well. Somehow, Lettice had found the sofa amid the clutter and she and Hilda Reader were drinking tea; he was pleased to see that both looked a little stronger than they had downstairs. As soon as she saw her sister, Lettice got up and gave her a hug, and some unspoken words of comfort passed between them. Not for the first time, he admired and envied their closeness.

'Mrs Reader – would you mind taking me through exactly

what happened when you got to work this morning?' he asked, sitting down opposite her.

'Well, I knew something wasn't right when I found the gates unlocked,' she said. 'I thought that Miss Lettice or Miss Ronnie might have come in early – we've got so much on at the moment, and they often do – then I realised that wasn't so because the snow was untouched. Beautiful, it looked.'

'So there were no footprints or marks in the courtyard at all?'

'No, nothing, so I just assumed it was carelessness. Then when I got through the arch and turned the corner, I saw someone lying at the bottom of the stairs. I thought it was Marjorie at first – she'd been working late the night before, and I thought she'd slipped on the steps in the dark – but when I got closer, it was obviously a man. I was so relieved at first, which was wicked of me, I suppose, but I was just glad it wasn't Marjorie.'

Penrose let her compose herself for a moment, and then asked: 'Why was Marjorie working on her own last night? Was that usual?'

It was Lettice who answered. 'There's been a lot of overtime recently – like Hilda says, we've been rushed off our feet and it's coming up to Christmas, so the girls are all happy to have a bit extra in their pay packets. They'll often stay late. But Friday night's different – they all want to get home to their families or go out for the evening, so they clock off at the normal time.'

'But not Marjorie?'

'No,' Hilda said. 'She seemed keen to stay. I always got the impression there wasn't much for her to go home to, although, like I said, she never talked much about her family.'

'You didn't suspect that there was something particular she wanted to stay for, though? A reason why she might want to be alone in the building?'

Hilda shook her head. 'No, I can't think of anything that would make her want to do that. You see, she always made an extra effort to show that we could trust her. We're lucky with most of our girls – they're honest and hard-working, but I think Marjorie always felt she had to try that bit harder than the rest because of where she'd come from.'

'Sorry – I don't understand.'

'She'd been in prison,' Ronnie explained. 'We took her on trial six months ago, just after she got out of Holloway – for the third time, I believe. You know Mary Size?'

'The deputy governor?'

'That's right. She's a great believer in finding prisoners some sort of meaningful work to go to when they're released. Some of the women have a talent for needlework – God knows they get enough practice – so she approached us. Marjorie's the fourth one we've had in the last couple of years. All of them have done well, actually, but Marjorie flourished.'

'What was she in prison for?' Penrose asked, surprised and impressed by his cousins' understated social conscience.

'Theft, mainly – petty stuff, but persistent.'

'And you've had no trouble like that since she's been with you.'

'No,' Lettice said firmly. 'Absolutely not.'

'Who was last to leave, apart from Marjorie?'

'I was,' Hilda said. 'We had a late fitting for the Cowdray Club gala. Lady Ashby was here and Marjorie was dealing with her, so I waited until they'd finished.'

'What time was that?'

'Seven o'clock. I'm sure about that because Lady Ashby needed to be at the Ham Bone Club by half past, and I offered to call her a taxi but she said she'd have time to walk. We went down to St Martin's Lane together. She tried to persuade Marjorie to go with her, but I think she was joking.'

'I doubt it,' Ronnie said. 'No pretty girl in London is safe when Geraldine's on heat.'

In any other circumstances, the expression on Hilda Reader's face would have been priceless. 'How did Marjorie seem when you left her?' Penrose asked.

'She'd cheered up since the incident with her father at lunchtime. We kept her busy, and work seemed to help her to forget about it. I made sure she knew what jobs were to be done, and I left her to it. She seemed impatient to get on.'

'And did you lock the gates when you left?'

'No, I just pulled them to. It's hard to unlock them from the inside, you see, because it's so dark under the arch. I thought it would be easier for Marjorie when she left.'

Penrose didn't bother to ask if anyone could have opened the gates from the street; it would be easy enough to check for himself and he didn't want to say something which might suggest to Hilda Reader that she was in any way to blame for Marjorie's death. 'And there was no sign of her father hanging around outside when you left?'

'No. If there had been, I'd never have left her on her own.'

'Of course not. Could you tell me what happened at lunchtime?'

'It was just after twelve. One of the other girls came down to the workroom from up here to fetch something, and she told me there was a man outside asking for Marjorie.'

'So he'd come into the yard?'

'Yes. When I went out to talk to him he was standing at the top of the stairs, just outside the door. I recognised him right away – he was often hanging about when the girls left on a Friday, but I never knew it was Marjorie he was waiting for. He introduced himself – Joe, I think he said his first name was – and asked if he could have a quick word with Marjorie. I told him she was out – she'd gone to the Cowdray Club to drop some samples off – but she'd be back any time. He said he'd wait across the road for her, and could I be sure to tell her? By across the road, I assumed he meant the pub. I had a quick look out the window, but I couldn't see him in the street.'

'And what was Marjorie's reaction?'

'Embarrassed. Angry. Worried that he might get her into trouble, I suppose.'

'But she went?'

'Yes, but she wasn't gone long. About ten minutes, I suppose. She didn't bother taking the rest of her lunch break.'

'And you said she was upset when she came back?'

'That's right. I didn't ask her about what had happened because she never liked you to think that she was vulnerable. She pretended to be a lot harder than she was, gave the impression that things didn't matter to her, but they did. All she said when she got back upstairs was that she was damned if she was going to be walked all over like her mother, and that she'd rot in hell before he got another penny out of her. She was talking to herself, really, and she went quiet when she realised I'd heard. I wish I'd talked to her about it now, but I didn't like to.'

'How did Marjorie get on with the other girls?'

'Well enough,' Hilda said, considering his question. 'There was never any unpleasantness. She made them laugh, and I think they were a bit in awe of her at times because she was a natural and learned so quickly. She could leave most of them standing when it came to the work we do here.'

'And didn't they resent her for that? It would have been quite natural for them to feel threatened by a newcomer, and women can be unkind if they're put in that position.'

Hilda smiled. 'That's true enough, Inspector, but if they felt that way, I never saw it – and I don't miss much. Marjorie had a charm about her, a cockiness – in a nice way, though, if you know what I mean. She wasn't arrogant – she was just young. It would have been very difficult not to like her, and I honestly think most of the girls admired her for the way she was shaking off her past, and wanted her to do well.'

Shaking off her past was an interesting phrase, Penrose thought. 'Did she still associate with anyone from prison?' he asked.

'There was one girl she saw who she'd been inside with. They'd have lunch together occasionally, go out on their days off, that sort of thing. I never saw her, though, and I can't remember her name. Miss Size would be able to tell you that.'

'Tell me a bit about the other seamstresses – have most of them been here a while? Where do you hire them from?'

Ronnie was not inclined to hide her exasperation. 'As lovely as it is of you to take an interest in our business, Archie, how can that possibly matter now? Marjorie's dead, and a full inventory of our staff is hardly going to bring her back.'

'Just humour me.'

'We take students from the trade schools each year,' Lettice said. 'Shoreditch and Barrett Street, mainly. Most of them come to us on a personal recommendation from the staff, or Ronnie and I go along to the annual exhibition and hand-pick anyone we think looks particularly promising. We're lucky – more often than not, we get the ones we want because we can offer theatre as well as fashion, and everyone thinks that's glamorous. There isn't as much call for society dress-making these days – people want more practical clothes.'

'Thank God,' Ronnie said with feeling. 'Some of the staff come to us from the department-store workrooms, as well. Hilda gets us some absolute gems from Debenhams – her husband works there, so she has inside knowledge.'

'And once they're here, they do tend to stay. Everyone seems happy enough.'

Penrose nodded. 'There's a vodka bottle on the table down-stairs, and it looks as though Marjorie was having a drink with someone before she died. Was the bottle around before you left, Mrs Reader?'

'Absolutely not. We never allow drinking in the workroom. Apart from anything else, it's dangerous.'

'So Lady Ashby didn't request it or bring it in with her?'

'No,' Hilda said, although Ronnie looked sceptical.

'Take me through everything else that happened yesterday – you said Marjorie went to the Cowdray Club in the morning?'

'Yes,' Lettice said. 'She delivered some samples ahead of the gala on Monday, then went on to Debenhams to get a few things we needed – beads, a couple of particular threads that we'd run out of. Nothing particularly unusual.'

'Black beads?'

She looked at him curiously. 'Amongst others, yes. She also delivered a note to Miss Bannerman at the club, asking her to send her ladies round for their final fittings. Four of them came yesterday afternoon, and Marjorie spent the rest of the day dealing with that.'

'Who were the four?'

'Lady Ashby, Mary Size, Celia Bannerman and Miriam Sharpe – she's the president of the College of Nursing. Don't ask me where that fits into the Cowdray Club – the politics are beyond me. We just smile and do what they ask, but she didn't seem particularly happy to be here.'

Penrose jotted down the names. 'Do you have a lot to do with the Cowdray Club?' he asked.

'Not really,' Lettice said. 'Several of the members are also private clients of ours, and we're doing the gala for them next week – at least we were. But that's because Amy Coward – Noël's aunt – asked particularly for us. Flattering, I suppose, but it's been a lot of work.'

'Yes – the sort of flattery we can live without,' agreed Ronnie. 'In return, the club has been helping us out with some classes for the girls – exercise classes, physical training, that sort of thing. People who work for years in this industry are notoriously prone to health problems.'

'And Marjorie would have been involved in those?'

'Yes,' Lettice said. 'I don't remember her being the most enthusiastic participant, but we insist that they all do it to some extent. It's important that they keep themselves well.'

'Mrs Reader, I'm sorry if this is painful for you, but there's one thing I have to ask. The needle that was used in the attack on Marjorie – it's about four inches long, and it bends slightly at the tip.' He saw her flinch, but there was no way of avoiding the question. 'I had a quick look around downstairs, but I couldn't see anything else like it. Do you keep a lot of them? Would it have been easy for someone to pick up when they got inside?'

'Four inches? Are you sure?' she asked, forcing herself to concentrate on the question rather than its implications. He

165

nodded. 'That's a sack needle, Inspector – we don't keep those as a rule.'

'What? None at all?'

'They're not delicate enough for most of the materials we use here. We've had one knocking about at some point for stage work – sail material, something like that – but not recently, and it's certainly not something that a stranger could just pick up. I wouldn't know where to lay my hands on one – and that's if we've got any at all.'

So the murderer had come prepared to humiliate, Penrose thought, more convinced than ever that Marjorie's death and her father's were more complicated than they looked. 'One last thing – was Marjorie paid today?'

'Yes, everyone got their week's money at the end of the day.'

'And as far as you know, she didn't leave the building afterwards?'

'No.'

'Is any money kept on the premises?' he asked.

'Just a bit of petty cash in the office,' Lettice said. 'No more than a few pounds.'

'I'll have to have a look round your office. I need Marjorie's address – that *is* where you keep the staff details?' She nodded. 'I'll get a car to take you home now, Mrs Reader. Will there be someone in? You shouldn't be on your own.'

'My husband's at work, but if someone could take me to Debenhams, he'll see me safely home and stay with me.' She stood up, and Penrose helped her on with her coat. 'What's to happen about the work for Monday?' she asked, turning to Lettice and Ronnie. 'There's still a lot to do if we're to be ready in time.'

'God, I hadn't even thought,' Ronnie said. 'We'll have to let the rest of the girls know what's happened somehow. But I don't see how we can possibly go on with this gala now.'

'Why not?' Hilda asked.

Lettice looked surprised. 'Well, we haven't got anywhere to work for a start.'

'There's plenty of space at the Cowdray Club,' Hilda said, buttoning her coat. 'And I reckon they owe you girls a thing or two after what you're doing for them. It is their bloody gala, after all.'

'Hilda!' Ronnie said, shocked. 'I don't think I've heard you swear once in fifteen years.'

'You've taught me a thing or two, Miss Ronnie – I just like to choose my moments.'

'But is it right to go ahead after what's happened?' Lettice asked. 'It seems so heartless, somehow.'

Hilda looked at her, then sat down and took her hand. 'It's too easy to say what the dead might or might not have wanted,' she said. 'I should know – it took me long enough to stop feeling guilty about marrying again. But sooner or later, you have to think about the living and what *they* need – and those other girls have been looking forward to this gala for weeks. They're going to be devastated when they hear about Marjorie – and they'll need something to focus on to get them through it. Making them idle won't help. And personally, I think Marjorie would have been the last to down tools if it'd been someone else.'

'Oh Hilda – we do love you,' Lettice said, giving her a hug. 'You're right, of course – we'll ask Miss Bannerman.'

'No we bloody won't,' Ronnie said. 'We'll tell her. Go with Archie now, Hilda, and we'll be in touch to let you know what's happening. And if you need anything – anything at all, promise you'll ask us.'

'There is one thing – it's Miss Bannerman's evening cape, the blue silk. Marjorie must have started work on it last night – I'd like to finish it for her. You won't let anything happen to it, will you, Inspector?'

'No, of course not. I'll make sure it's safe. We're going to have to go over everything very carefully, I'm afraid, and it will take time, but we'll be as quick as we can.' He followed Hilda over to the door. 'Whatever you pay this woman,' he said, looking back at his cousins, 'it's nowhere near enough.'

'Do you think we don't know that?' Lettice answered, but Ronnie called him back.

'You think there's more to this, don't you?' she said quietly.

'Later,' he said. 'Please take care of yourselves.' He delivered Mrs Reader into the safe hands of PC Ellis, then went to find Fallowfield. 'Pop over to the Salisbury for me, Bill. I think Marjorie and her father had a bit of a row there yesterday lunchtime. Find out what it was about if you can. I'm going upstairs to talk to Spilsbury.'

As he had known it would be, the Motleys' workroom was now a completely different place and the ominous stillness of an hour ago had given way to an organised clamour of activity. There were several photographers in the immediate crime scene, each one a trained detective, and the Home Office pathologist, Sir Bernard Spilsbury – as famous in his own right as the criminals he convicted – waited patiently for them to finish before he could examine the body. 'You don't do things by halves, do you Archie?' he said as soon as he saw Penrose. 'I gather this is your cousins' business. I'm sorry to hear that – it must be terrible for them. I suppose the logical

168

scenario is that he kills her and falls down the stairs in his haste to get away.'

'But?' Penrose asked, and his eagerness must have been obvious.

Spilsbury smiled. 'Yes – somehow I thought you'd be looking for a but. Well, I can't give you anything more than you've got yourself at the moment, and that's instinct – but the logical scenario doesn't quite add up to me either. I'd say that the man downstairs was knocked unconscious by the fall and died of exposure, which doesn't help to build any other case but the obvious one – but I'm hoping to find something more conclusive for you up here.'

'All done now, Sir,' one of the photographers called, and Spilsbury went over to the body.

'You were right about the row, Sir,' Fallowfield said, coming up behind Penrose. 'Barman said he thought he was going to have to call for help at one point – she threatened Baker with a glass, apparently.'

'Really? What was it about?'

'Money. He wanted her to hand over her wages, and she wasn't having any of it. Did you know she'd been inside?' Penrose nodded. 'Well, he got at her about that, as well – that's when she picked up the glass.'

'Anything else?'

'No. She wasn't there very long. The bloke had been in now and again over the last few weeks, the barman said – he'd never seen him before that. But he was always on his own until yesterday.'

'Right – then we need to find out if Marjorie's wages are still here somewhere,' Penrose said, and walked across to where Spilsbury was making his painstaking examination. 'Bernard,

I need to know right away if you find any money on the body.'

'I can tell you that now, Archie.' He held up a small brown envelope in a bag. 'Is this what you're looking for? It was in the pocket of her dress.' Penrose took the wage packet, which he could see had not even been opened. 'And this was with it.' The second bag held a small silver photo frame, with a picture of a young woman and baby. It was no one he recognised.

'That's interesting, Sir,' Fallowfield said, taking the bag from him. 'I'd have to check, but it matches the description of something stolen from the Cowdray Club. Why would she have that?'

'I've no idea, Bill, but I think it's time we paid the club a visit.' He brought his sergeant succinctly up to speed on what he had learned from Hilda Reader and the Motleys.

'So you think someone else is involved?'

'I think this suggests that,' Penrose said, holding up the wage packet. 'They were fighting over money, so why would he go to all that trouble only to leave behind what he came for? And for God's sake, Bill – how much do you think is in here? Twenty shillings? Thirty? It hardly warrants that sort of violence, does it? No – either someone disturbed him before he could take what he wanted . . .'

'In which case, why haven't they come forward?'

'Exactly. Or he didn't do it. I don't doubt that he came here looking for Marjorie, but I think this is what he found. No wonder the poor bastard fell down the stairs – they might not have got on, but can you imagine how any father would feel, seeing his daughter like this?'

'I suppose he might even have walked in while it was happening.'

'Indeed he might, Bill, and then we could be talking about two murders, not one – but all this is speculation until we have the post-mortem reports.' He ran his hand through his hair. 'In the meantime, we've got to break the news to her mother so I'd better dig her address out. Then we need to find a tactful way of asking if *she* thinks her husband was capable of choking their daughter with beads and stitching her mouth up with a sack needle. If you've got any ideas as to how to put that, I'll hear them on the way.'

Amelia picked up the book and settled Lizzie more comfortably on her lap. Out of the nursery window, she could see coils of smoke drifting up from the chimneys of the houses opposite, thin lines of charcoal against a slate-grey sky. The snow which had so delighted Lizzie on Sunday was long gone, and the only trace of its brief existence lay in a corner of the yard, a small mound of muddy white with twigs and buttons and one of Jacob's old pipes sunk pathetically into its heart. Her daughter wriggled impatiently on her knee, keen to get on with the story; Amelia kissed the top of her head and dutifully found the right page. 'They were indeed a queer-looking party that assembled on the bank,' she began, 'the birds with draggled feathers, the animals with their fur clinging close to them, and all dripping wet, cross, and uncomfortable. The first question of course was, how to get dry again: they had a consultation about this, and after a few minutes it seemed quite natural to Alice to find herself talking familiarly with them, as if she had known them all her life.'

As the last of the daylight drained from the world outside, Amelia read on, enjoying the sense of transporting the two of them to another place – a private, imaginary place, far away from Hertford Road, where adventures could be safely contained by the closing of a cover. Eventually, the warmth of the room and the comforting sound of her voice had its customary effect: Lizzie slept soundly, and Amelia slipped the book gently on to the bedside table. She looked down at her daughter, and wondered again what sort of life she would make for herself; she had always expected motherhood to bring with it a new sense of responsibility, but nothing had prepared her for the intensity of being relied upon by a child, the fear of failure that kept her awake at night. It was time that Lizzie had a brother or sister, she thought – she was so withdrawn at times, so self-contained, and they could afford to try for another child now. Surely Jacob would see that? There had been an uneasy truce between them since the argument last week, but perhaps another child would bring them closer together; perhaps it would be the one dream which could remain untainted by the money that made it possible. With a stab of regret, Amelia remembered how happy they had been when they were first married; now, she felt like a stranger to him. It might be her imagination, but it seemed that new alliances were forming in this house which no longer included her.

As if on cue, she heard Edwards's footsteps on the stairs, disturbing her peace. The girl knocked loudly when she got to the nursery, waking Lizzie, and, when she put her head round the door, she looked flushed and excited. 'There's a policeman downstairs, Ma'am – says he wants to talk to you. I asked him what it was about, but he wouldn't say.'

Suddenly, Amelia found it difficult to breathe. 'I didn't hear anyone,' she said defensively, as if this could somehow refute the truth of what Edwards was telling her. In her arms, Lizzie started to cry and Amelia realised that she had been gripping her daughter's hand so tightly that she had hurt her. She kissed her and wiped her eyes, then lifted her gently on to the bed.

'Look after her,' she snapped at Edwards. 'I won't be long. Is Mr Sach home yet?'

'No, ma'am, not yet.'

That was something, at least, Amelia thought as she hurried downstairs. With a bit of luck, she could clear this up before Jacob got in and he need never know about it. She had expected a uniform, but the man who stood in her parlour wore an ordinary brown suit. He hovered awkwardly in front of the fireplace, turning a bowler hat round in his hands; she smiled confidently at him when she detected his unease, but any illusions she held about having the advantage were dispelled as soon as he opened his mouth. 'Mrs Amelia Sach?' he asked, and she nodded. 'I'm Detective Inspector Kyd from the Metropolitan Police. I'm afraid I have to inform you that we arrested a woman earlier today on suspicion of the murder of a baby boy. The woman was caught with the child's body in her possession, and we have reason to believe that he was born in this establishment. What is your connection with a Mrs Annie Walters of Danbury Street, Islington?'

Amelia could have laughed with relief. If Walters had been caught with a baby today, it couldn't possibly be one of hers: the child who had left her care on Saturday would be long gone by now. Walters must have let her greed get the better of her and started working for someone else as well – she had long suspected as much; there was no shortage of opportunities. 'I don't know anyone by that name,' she said boldly, buoyed up by the knowledge that it was another woman's luck which had run out today. 'I'm sorry, but I can't help you.'

The inspector was not so easily deterred. 'Mrs Walters says you employ her, Madam.'

'Then Mrs Walters is lying. I'm a nurse and a qualified

midwife, Inspector. I take in ladies to be confined. They receive the very best of care while they're here, and I assure you that when babies leave these premises, they are most certainly alive and well.'

He smiled, and, for the first time, there was something in his expression which made Amelia afraid. 'I wasn't suggesting otherwise, Madam, but if I could just refresh your memory a little – Mrs Walters is in her mid-fifties, sturdily built . . .'

Amelia interrupted him. 'I don't know her, Inspector, and I certainly haven't given her any babies, if that's what you're implying. I have a reputation to maintain and I'm very careful about who I invite to work here.'

'So, to your knowledge, Mrs Walters has never been here?' She shook her head. 'Funny that – she's given me a very fair description of this room, but no matter. I believe a baby boy was born here on Saturday?'

'That's right. Dr Wylie attended the birth, as there were a number of complications. I'm sure he'll confirm that.'

'I don't doubt it, Madam. The mother and child – where are they now?'

'They're upstairs, Inspector,' Amelia said, her voice faltering a little.

'I'd like to see that child, Ma'am, if you don't mind.'

'I'm afraid the mother is far too ill for social calls. As I said, it was a difficult birth and they're both still very weak. I can't possibly allow anyone to disturb them.'

She had known as soon as the words were out that aggression was the wrong line to take. When Inspector Kyd spoke again, his voice had lost any trace of courtesy. 'I *will* see that child, Ma'am, whether you like it or not, and if you won't take me up there yourself, then I'm afraid I have no choice but to summon Dr Wylie and ask him to call on the mother and her baby. You can surely have no objection to a medical man looking in on them?'

Amelia said nothing as he left the room and opened the front door. She heard the sound of voices outside and went to the window to see what was happening. To her horror, she saw the inspector in the small front garden, talking to two uniformed police constables who must have been standing outside all the time. As she watched, one of them turned and hurried out to the street; the other came back into the house with his superior, and the three of them stood in silence in the parlour. Desperately, Amelia ran through a series of stories in her head; Dr Wylie only lived round the corner, and she didn't have long to come up with an explanation for the missing child. Why hadn't she done something about Walters sooner? She had known the woman was a liability and was furious with herself for allowing it to come to this; clearly Walters had told the police all about her, and now she would have to admit to their association and try to find some innocent explanation for it. After what seemed like only seconds, she heard the click of the front gate again; the policeman was back with Dr Wylie, and she was shocked to see that her husband was with them.

'What's all this about, Amelia?' Jacob asked as soon as he entered the room, but Kyd gave her no opportunity to answer.

'Mrs Sach, please take Dr Wylie here up to the woman's room,' he said, and then, turning to Wylie, 'I just need to know if the baby is safe and well, Sir.'

The doctor stared uncomfortably at Amelia and, as he turned to leave the room, she could bear it no longer. 'There's no need,' she whispered, so quietly that she could hardly hear the words herself.

'Sorry, Madam – what did you say?' Kyd asked.

'There's no need to go upstairs. The baby isn't there. It's been taken away. But it can't be the same child,' she cried, looking pleadingly at her husband. 'It just can't be.' She repeated the words again, trying to clear up the confusion in her own mind. The baby had left the house on Saturday evening – she could never bear to have a child in the house for long after its birth – and now it was Tuesday; why would Walters have kept it for three days, rather than getting rid of it at the earliest possible opportunity? What was the woman thinking of? 'Whatever child you've found,' she said at last, 'it isn't the boy who was born here on Saturday.'

Inspector Kyd nodded at the constable, who handed over a child's robe. 'Do you recognise this?' Kyd asked. It was a simple garment, probably one of hundreds, and Amelia shook her head. 'That's strange,' he continued, unfolding the robe and holding it out towards her, 'because Mrs Robertson from the laundry on Marine Parade says that this is your mark.' He pushed it closer to her, but Amelia refused to look; for the first time, she began to understand the enormity of what faced her. Obviously, she had already been the subject of gossip and speculation in Finchley, and it would only take one person in Hertford Road to notice the police at her door for the news to spread the length of the street; even if she talked her way out of trouble this time, she would never escape from the shame of what was happening to her, and how would that affect Lizzie? What would it do to her marriage? 'Do you admit that F236 is your laundry mark?' the inspector repeated impatiently. Helpless to do anything else, she nodded.

178

'Dr Wylie, did you attend a birth at Claymore House on Saturday?'

'Yes, I did – a young woman called Ada Galley had gone into labour in the early hours of Friday morning. When there was still no sign of the baby on Saturday, Mrs Sach called me in. Eventually, the child was born at around midday on Saturday, but it needed a lot of help. I had no choice but to use forceps.'

'And would that have resulted in any injuries to the baby's head?' Kyd asked. Out of the corner of her eye, Amelia noticed Jacob cover his face with his hands.

'It's likely that some bruising would develop,' Wylie admitted.

'But otherwise, the baby was healthy?'

'Oh yes, he was a bonny lad.'

'And did you come back here again to see the mother and child?'

'Yes.' The doctor glanced at Amelia. 'I came back on Sunday to check on them both, but the child was missing. I asked how he was, and Mrs Sach told me that he was well but that the mother's sister had taken him back to Holloway with her.'

'And you didn't think anything of that?'

'No, not really. I just assumed that the sister was helping out to give the mother some time to recover.'

'I see. Has anything like that ever happened here before, Sir?'

He hesitated. 'Yes – last month, in fact. That time, Mrs Sach told me that the baby's grandmother had taken the child.'

'Are you asked to come here very often, Sir?'

'I suppose I've been about a dozen times in total.'

'And of those dozen, how many times would you say that

179

the baby has been missing when you came back to check on the patient?'

'Only those two, Inspector.'

'But there are births that you're not asked to attend?'

'That's right. Mrs Sach is a perfectly competent midwife.'

'Have any other children been born here recently, Mrs Sach?'

'Another lady had a child on Wednesday – a baby girl.'

'And was that child removed from these premises without its mother?'

Four pairs of eyes tore accusingly into Amelia, and she looked round desperately at each one of them. 'Surely you don't think . . .'

But the rest of her sentence was lost as the charge was spelt out to her. 'Amelia Sach, I'm arresting you on suspicion of being an accessory to murder.'

'Murder? No! That's not possible. You're not really saying that these babies are dead? That this woman has killed them?'

'You'll be taken to King's Cross Road Police Station, where you will be remanded in custody for further questioning.'

'Jacob – please!' she screamed. 'What about Lizzie? Tell them this is ridiculous. Tell them I knew nothing about it.' The policeman took her arm and she shook him off, but he seized her again, more roughly this time, and led her out to the waiting vehicle. A small crowd had gathered further down the street, and she was almost relieved when the doors closed on her. As it pulled away, she glanced back at the house, stricken with fear at the thought that she might never see her home, her daughter, again; Jacob stared back at her from the front-room window, his face blank and emotionless. She bowed her head in shame. They turned left out of Hertford Road, and the story she had just read to Lizzie echoed again and again in her mind: "'I'll be judge, I'll be jury," said cunning old Fury; "I'll try the whole cause and condemn you to death.'"

John Kyd watched his colleagues take Sach away, and spoke quietly to her husband. 'I'm afraid we're going to have to search the house now, Sir. If you wouldn't mind waiting here until we've finished – we'll be as quick as we can.'

For a moment, he thought the man hadn't been listening because he neither spoke nor altered his expression, but then he said: 'Can I fetch my daughter down from upstairs? She'll be in the nursery with Nora – it's at the top of the house.'

'Yes, Sir, of course. If you could all wait together, that would be best. I'm going to have a word with your wife's patient now – Dr Wylie, perhaps you'd come with me?' The doctor seemed relieved to have a purpose, and followed Kyd out of the room without a moment's hesitation.

There was only one closed door on the first-floor landing, and Kyd guessed correctly that this must be the room in which Sach's unfortunate patient was resting, oblivious to the fate of her child. He knocked gently and went straight in, and was surprised to find a pleasant space, warm and comfortable and showing all the signs of good, attentive care. It was stupid of him to have expected anything else, he thought bitterly; Sach's business relied on respectability, and God knows these women had paid dearly enough for their nursing.

The girl lay back on her pillows, pale and obviously still tired, but attractive nonetheless. She must be about eighteen, he guessed, and – perhaps simply because of what he knew –

he sensed a vulnerability about her which struck him all the more forcefully for coming so soon after Sach's cold self-assurance. 'Miss Galley?' he asked, and she nodded, looking curiously first at him and then at the doctor. 'I'm Detective Inspector Kyd. I'm sorry to disturb you, but I need to ask you some questions about the birth of your baby and your time here at Claymore House. Would you mind telling me when you last saw your child?'

'It must have been on Saturday,' she said, and he noticed that her accent was not from the city; Wiltshire, he guessed, or Dorset. 'About an hour after he was born, I suppose. I wasn't really well enough to remember much of what was happening, but Mrs Sach brought him in so that I could have a look at him. Then she told me to kiss him goodbye.'

'So you were aware that your child was going to be removed from the premises.'

'Yes. Mrs Sach had found him a new home. She told me that she had five ladies who couldn't have children of their own and who wanted to adopt – the child would be well looked after, she said, and would be left a lot of money eventually. I hope she's not in trouble for that,' she added, looking at the grave expression on the inspector's face. 'She didn't force me into anything. I'm on my own, and I need to earn a living – how could I do that with a child in tow? We'd both be dead or in the workhouse. It was for the best, really it was.'

'Did Mrs Sach tell you the name of the woman who was to adopt your baby?'

'No. She said it was best that I didn't know. The mother wouldn't like it in case I changed my mind and wanted the baby back.'

'And how long have you been here?'

'Since September. I saw Mrs Sach's advertisement in the newspaper in August, and she took me in a month later.'

'And you paid her money?'

'Yes. Three guineas when I got here, then a guinea a week after that.'

'And what about the adoption?'

'She told me I'd have to give the new mother thirty pounds.'

'Even though this woman was wealthy herself?'

'Yes. Mrs Sach said she wanted to buy a present for the baby to remember its mother by. Thirty pounds was more than I could afford, though, so she said she'd write to the lady to see if she'd accept twenty-five – and she said she would.'

A present to remember its mother by – Kyd could hardly keep the disgust out of his voice when he continued his questioning. 'Twenty-five pounds still seems a lot of money for a young woman to find.'

She looked down, ashamed. 'I had to go to the baby's father,' she admitted. 'His family didn't want a scandal, so they paid up. Am I in trouble? I didn't think I was doing anything wrong – honestly I didn't.'

'No, you're not in trouble,' Kyd said reassuringly.

'Then what's happened?' she asked, beginning to cry now. 'Why do you want to know about my baby?'

Kyd looked at the doctor, who shook his head. 'Miss Galley needs to rest now,' he said. 'I'll stay with her for a bit and make sure she has something to help her sleep.'

The inspector stood up to go. The image of Ada Galley's dead son had been with him all day, refusing to go away no matter how hard he tried to expel it from his mind. There would be a time when he would have to explain to this girl what had happened to her baby, but not before he had more answers and certainly not while she was still living under Sach's roof. He opened the door to go back downstairs, but found Jacob Sach outside on the landing, a child of about three or four in his arms. He had obviously been listening – there were tears on his face which he did not bother to wipe away – but what struck Kyd most was how like her mother Lizzie Sach was; for her sake, he prayed that the resemblance was purely physical. 'Please go downstairs, Sir,' he said. 'I'll be with you in a minute.'

It would take several hours to search the house thoroughly but, by the time Kyd joined Jacob Sach downstairs, he had seen enough to gauge the extent of his wife's business. His officers had found more than three hundred items of baby clothing in the house so far, presumably made by mothers who had no idea of how briefly they would be needed. Kyd found what was left of the family in the kitchen: Sach was sitting at the table, hunched over an untouched cup of tea, while a dark-haired young woman sat on the floor with two children, one only a toddler, trying and failing to keep them amused. As soon as she saw him, the woman stood up to go, but he held up his hand to stop her. 'Miss . . . ?'

'Edwards. Nora Edwards.'

'And you work for Mr and Mrs Sach?'

'That's right.'

'Miss Edwards – may I ask how long you've been here?'

'Since July last year – well, not here, but with Mrs Sach. She was in Stanley Road then.'

'And you moved here with her?'

'With the family, yes.'

She seemed guarded in her answers, and he wondered

exactly how much she knew. It was difficult to believe that she could have lived in the Sach household for more than a year and remained ignorant of its comings and goings. 'Did you answer an advertisement for a job?'

'No, not for a job.'

'Then for what?'

'I went to her to have my baby.' She gestured to the younger of the two girls.

'And your child was born in Mrs Sach's care?'

'Yes. She looked after me herself. Sally was born last September.'

'What happened after the child's birth?'

Edwards hesitated. 'Mrs Sach asked me what I was going to do, and I said I didn't know. She told me there was a woman in Balcombe who would adopt Sally for twelve pounds. I didn't want to let the baby go and I told her as much.'

'And did she argue?'

'She said the woman would have a cot waiting for her, and that she'd be well looked after, but I couldn't do it.'

'You stayed in the house, though?'

'Yes. I paid her fifteen shillings a week at first, but then she offered me a job in return for our keep.'

'And she never mentioned adoption again?'

'No, never. She's always been good to us both, and the kids play together. You can see for yourself.'

Kyd looked down at the floor, but Lizzie's sulky expression and the tantrum threatened by the other child were no more convincing to him than Edwards's testimony of Sach's good nature. 'And what are your duties?'

'Oh, the usual – cleaning, a bit of cooking, the odd errand.'

'And did you ever meet anyone called Mrs Walters here?' He described Annie Walters, and Edwards nodded.

'I met someone who looked like that, but her name was Laming. I've seen her at both houses – here and in Stanley Road. She used to come when a child was born. Mrs Sach would send her a telegram.'

'Did you ever see money change hands between them?'

Edwards looked nervously at Jacob Sach. 'Yes, I did.'

'And did Mrs Sach ever say anything to you about Mrs Walters?'

'She told me not to tell the mothers that their children had gone with her.'

'How many children would you say that Mrs Walters had taken away with her since you've been here?'

'I don't remember. I wasn't counting.'

'Please, Miss Edwards – just a rough figure.'

'About eight, I suppose. And once Mrs Sach asked me to take a baby and three pounds to Mrs Laming – Mrs Walters, I mean – in Plaistow.'

'Thank you, Miss Edwards.' He watched as she picked the toddler up from the floor and drew her close. 'Did Mrs Walters ever speak to you about your own child?' he asked.

'Yes, she did, Inspector, quite a few times. She said I was a fool to keep her.'

The house was unbearably quiet when the police left. Jacob Sach sat in the kitchen, going over and over the questions they had asked him about his wife, trying to associate the woman they had taken away with the one he had married, but nothing made any sense to him. He poured another glass of rum and took it out into the back yard, desperate now to get out of the room which felt like the cell he imagined Amelia to be in. Had she confessed yet, he wondered? Or did she really believe herself to be innocent?

He heard a noise at the back door and turned to see Nora there, holding Lizzie in her arms. As the light from the kitchen fell on the child's auburn hair, it was like looking at his wife when she was young, and Lizzie's innocence stung him like a personal rebuke for all his failures.

'Take her away,' he said quietly, not trusting himself to move.

'But Jacob, she's asking for you. Don't take it out on her – none of this is her fault.'

'I said take her away,' he yelled, and hurled the glass towards the door. It broke against the wall, and Nora looked at him in horror, then fled back into the house with the child.

Chapter Seven

Josephine usually took breakfast upstairs in her room, but the envelope which Marta had given her had, during a long and sleepless night, come to dominate the small space to such an extent that she was glad to leave it behind for the comparative safety of the club's dining room, where, if she were forced into any conversation at all, it would at least be of a reassuringly superficial nature.

The dining room was the centrepiece of the building's architectural design, situated midway between the Cowdray Club and the College of Nursing and easily reachable from both. Breakfast was laid out along one wall, and Josephine lifted the lid on a dish of perfectly cooked sausages before deciding that coffee was all she could face. She settled down at a table in the corner, enjoying the peace and general harmony of an exquisitely conceived room. The walls were entirely faced with oak panelling, and fluted Corinthian columns and pilasters with finely carved capitals supported a magnificent ceiling. The floor, too, was of oak, finished to a rich brown colour. All in all, the wood gave the room a warm, autumnal feel which contrasted pleasantly with the ivory-white enamel that served most of the building. Strong natural light flooded in from tall windows and a glass dome overhead, illuminating the room's decorative focal points: four portrait medallions – one on each wall – of Florence Nightingale, Edith Cavell and the Viscount and Viscountess Cowdray, ensuring that, wherever you sat, you could not escape a reminder of the club's nursing origins.

'You look like I feel.' Geraldine Ashby sat down at Josephine's table without waiting for an invitation.

'As long as I don't look like you look. What on earth have you been doing? Or should I say whom?'

Geraldine grinned. 'Now that you mention it, I did get awfully scratched last night. We were at the Ham Bone – do you know it?' Josephine shook her head. She had heard Lettice and Ronnie mention the club, and knew of its reputation for glamour and the sort of carefree bohemianism that was increasingly hard to find in London, but she had never been. 'Oh, you should come with me some time – it's a riot if the right people are in. And last night, *all* the right people were in. Enid and Eileen were there, helping Toupie get over that embarrassing divorce, and then we all had to see Poppy and Honey safely home in the snow because they were absolutely wrecked. It really was the least we could do, but of course you can never get out of their flat without another drink, and the next thing I knew, it was daylight.'

Judging by Gerry's glazed, somewhat vacant expression, another drink wasn't the only thing that had kept her out all night. Josephine looked at the dark circles around her eyes, where the habit was beginning to take its toll, making her look so much older in unguarded moments than her thirty-odd years, and asked: 'Don't you ever get tired of the party?'

'Believe me, darling, you have to take your fun where you can get it these days. What I wouldn't give to have the twenties back again, before John wrote that tedious book, bless her, and everyone started to feel so bloody threatened by women having a better time without men.' Josephine had often heard Lydia

190

talk about the change in attitudes to lesbianism in recent years; it was less of a problem in the theatre but, in other walks of life, there was no question that women faced discrimination and suspicion if they tried to make a life together. She remembered herself how liberating the early twenties had been, when she and girls like her – invigorated by the female war effort and with the optimism of youth – had carved out a new independence for themselves, working together, sharing digs, never dreaming that the intensity of their friendships would be questioned. Although she was one of the lucky few who were financially and emotionally free to dictate their own lives, she was not entirely immune to a feeling that – collectively – women were being punished for getting on with things and made to feel ungrateful for a sacrifice which had never been of their choosing. 'It's ironic, isn't it?' Gerry continued, echoing her thoughts. 'The politicians wipe out all our young men by sending them to war, and then decide that the fabric of the nation is somehow at risk if we girls make our own amusement in their absence. But enough about me – what's your excuse for looking so weary?'

'Don't even ask,' Josephine began, automatically shutting down the conversation before it became personal. Then she thought better of it: she liked Geraldine, and needed to talk to someone who wasn't involved; Lettice's offer had been kind and genuine, but her loyalties were divided and, in any case, it wasn't fair to ask her to lie to a friend. 'Actually, as you've shown such an interest in my love life since that wretched flower arrived, you *can* ask.' She signalled to the waitress. 'What do you want to drink?'

Geraldine perked up immediately and twinkled at the young girl. 'Strong coffee, darling – you know how I like it –

and plenty of fresh toast. All of a sudden, I find myself with quite an appetite.' She turned back to Josephine. 'I have a feeling this is going to be good. Just let me get some breakfast, and I'm all yours.' She returned a couple of minutes later carrying two plates piled high with scrambled eggs, bacon and tomatoes, and put one in front of Josephine. 'No arguments – tell me everything.'

Josephine obliged with a verbatim account of what had happened the night before, deciding that, on the whole, it was safer to be completely truthful; Geraldine was the unofficial agony aunt to the whole club and what she didn't know she invented with flair and imagination; on the other hand, although her curiosity was insatiable, her integrity was equally legendary and Josephine had never known her to betray a secret once trusted with it. 'So this woman's written a diary especially for you?' she said when the story was complete.

'She didn't write it *for* me. She gave it to me to read because I'm in it.'

'Even so – as approaches go, I'd give her ten out of ten for imagination. It certainly beats some of the apologies for a love letter that I've received over the years.'

'It's not a love letter.'

Geraldine looked at Josephine over the rim of her coffee cup. 'Really?' she said cynically. 'Then what is it? What's she written about you?'

'I don't know. I can't bring myself to read it.'

'You haven't read it?' This time the disbelief was genuine. 'Good God, Josephine – what sort of creature are you? I'd have had it out of the envelope before the ink was dry. Just think – the chance to see yourself through someone else's eyes. If she's in love with you, it's hardly going to be anything other than flattering, is it? Unless you turn her down, of course, in which case I'd keep away from the next few entries.' She put her toast down and looked seriously at Josephine. 'I'm sure you don't need me to tell you that it must matter if you're this worried about it. What are you afraid of?'

She spoke gently, but Josephine would not even have known where to begin with the truth. 'I just thought it would be easier for everyone if I sent it straight back,' she said.

'With a rejection slip from your publisher? Come on, darling – you're better than that. I've never thought of you as unkind, but you couldn't come up with a sharper slap in the face than not even bothering to read it. I don't know the woman, but I can't imagine it was easy for her to face you and hand it over. It makes her incredibly vulnerable. So what *is* the problem? Don't you like her?'

Josephine smiled. 'And *you're* better than *that*. You make it sound so straightforward. I do like her – at least, I like what I know of her, which isn't very much. But it's complicated, Gerry. For a start, she's the lover of one of my closest friends.'

'Ah. Tricky, but not insurmountable. Is that how you met?'

'Yes. It was last year, when *Richard* was on at the New. She and Lydia had been together for a few months by then . . .'

'Lydia Beaumont?'

'Yes. Lydia wanted us to meet because Marta's a writer and she thought we'd get on.'

'And she was right. The architect of her own demise, then – how very Greek. When will we women ever learn to keep a good thing to ourselves?'

'It wasn't like that. Nothing happened – well, a lot happened, but nothing to do with that. I had no idea how she felt until she told me the other night.'

'Not even an inkling? How sweet!'

Josephine threw her napkin across the table. 'We're not all like you,' she said, laughing. 'Some of us don't expect to be adored.' Gerry grinned and poured them both more coffee. 'Anyway, for one reason and another, the two of them parted shortly afterwards. But not because of me.'

'So they're not actually together at the moment?'

'No, but it wasn't out of choice. There were things in Marta's life that meant she had to go away.'

Gerry looked sharply across the table at her. 'Is this the woman who was in the papers?'

Reluctantly, Josephine nodded. 'I don't want Lydia to get hurt so please don't say . . .'

'Of course I won't say anything. But a woman with a dark past – how splendid! For God's sake, darling, if you don't want her, pass her over here. I could do with a little excitement. And do you?'

'Do I what?'

'Do you want her?'

The waitress came over to their table to clear the plates, but Gerry waved her away. 'I don't know what I want,' Josephine said at last. 'It sounds ridiculous, but I was hoping not to have to think about it too deeply.'

'It *is* easier to cling to some sort of finders-keepers mentality, I suppose,' Gerry said provokingly. 'Lydia had her first, so that's where the poor woman must stay. God forbid that there should be any unpleasantness between the three of you – it's only happiness at stake, after all.'

'Yes, it must look like cowardice from where you're sitting, but it *is* a problem for me – a real problem,' Josephine said, refusing to rise to the bait. 'I'm afraid I've always been cursed by a sense of what's right, and I don't mean what's acceptable to other people – I don't give a damn about them; I mean what's acceptable to *me*, what feels right in here. And picking up with Marta when I know that Lydia still loves her doesn't feel right. I care about Lydia and this year's been torment for her.'

'Although on the few occasions that I've bumped into her, she's been doing her very best to get over it. We've all admired her for it.'

Josephine smiled. 'That's just Lydia's way. It wouldn't be mine, but you fall back on whatever gets you through, don't you? And anyway, most of it's bravado. I know what you're thinking,' she added as Gerry opened her mouth to speak. 'You're about to tell me that I shouldn't be putting Lydia's happiness before my own, that she wouldn't be as hesitant if it were the other way round – but it could never be happiness if that's what I had to do to get it. There'd be no peace – and peace *is* something I want. Can you understand that?' Gerry nodded, more serious for a moment. 'So no matter how much this sounds like an excuse, what I feel or might come to feel for Marta is irrelevant.'

'It sounds to me like you've made your decision already. Why are you so angry with her, though?'

'Is it really that obvious?' Josephine asked, surprised.

'Oh yes. You're livid, darling. Is that because you've found someone *capable* of disturbing your peace?'

'People want too much, then they take offence because I can't give it,' Josephine said, knowing how selfish and conde-scending it sounded. 'Give them dinner and they expect a lifetime.'

'It's human nature to be disappointed, though. If two people collide who want the same thing, it's nothing short of a miracle. And spending as much time with Lydia and her friends as you do – it was only a matter of time before one of them made a play for you. It's unfortunate that it happens to be Lydia's girlfriend, but you shouldn't mess with fire if you don't want to get burnt.' She paused for a moment to light a cigarette. 'Are you sure you're quite as blasé about what people think of you? You wouldn't be the first person to turn love down because of what it might do to your reputation.'

'Being with another woman, you mean?'

She nodded. 'It's not as easy as it used to be, although money and an artistic nature help.'

Josephine smiled, but there was a serious side to the question which she had often thought about. 'I have two lives, Gerry, and the less one knows about the other, the better I like it. You're right, of course; back home, people already think I'm peculiar but there's a limit to how far I'll push my luck, if only for my family's sake. I'd defy even you to walk down Inverness High Street with a woman on your arm, but what I do when I'm here is up to me.'

'You lost someone in the war, didn't you?'

'At the Somme, yes, and as far as Inverness is concerned, it's the only normal thing I've ever done. How did you know?'

'Oh, people talk. You're often discussed, you know – the celebrity amongst us, your fleeting visits and famous friends, the mysterious other life in Scotland and the handsome inspector from Scotland Yard. And now the exotic flowers at reception. The gossip in this place is simply shocking, but then what else do we have to do?' Her words reminded Josephine of the letters that Archie had discussed with her; Gerry would certainly have the knowledge to write them, but not the spite, she thought, nor the patience to remain anonymous, and she dismissed the idea almost as soon as it arrived. 'The war's another good excuse not to commit, of course,' Gerry added, 'if not a particularly original one.'

'You're not the first person to tell me that, and I don't suppose you'll be the last.'

'No, you'll probably hear it from Marta on Friday night, depending on what decision you come to. We girls will clutch at any straw to convince ourselves that rejection isn't our fault – trust me, I've had plenty of practice.' She smiled, then said: 'We're very alike, you and I.'

'In what way?' Josephine asked. To her mind, she and Gerry could hardly have been more different: they were roughly the same age, but their backgrounds were worlds apart and, while she was reserved and constantly questioned herself, Gerry was bold and unselfconscious.

'We have a freedom that many women would envy us for. We have money and we have independence – all right, so you've earned yours by being talented and I've fallen into mine because of who my parents are, but the end result is the same: we're not subject to the same cares as other people, and we very rarely have to compromise. I'll have to marry eventually, I suppose, if I want to inherit, but I can do what I like until then. You don't even have that pressure on the horizon.'

'I'm not entirely without ties, you know. I can't just up and leave Inverness – there's my father to think about, and a house to look after. I have responsibilities.'

'Responsibilities, yes, but not duties – that's the difference. And from what I've seen, you fulfil those responsibilities on your terms. It's a lot to give up, whether Lydia's in the picture or not. I'm not surprised you're complacent in matters of the heart.'

'Is that what I am?' Josephine gave a wry smile, which Gerry returned in kind.

'That's the nicest way of putting it.'

'You're right, of course. It's the marriage thing that scares me to death – the day-to-day with someone, the wretched domesticity of it all, the constant demands on each other.' Gerry started to laugh at the horror in her voice, but Josephine had only just begun. 'And the conversation – my God, the conversation. Can you imagine how exhausting it must be to find things to say for a lifetime? Or the effort it takes to be interesting every night at dinner? I don't know that I want that, with a man or a woman. It doesn't fit in with my life.' Satisfied that she had made her point, she spoke more seriously. 'I'll never forget what someone said during the war when I was at Anstey – it's a physical training college just outside Birmingham.'

'Yes, I know of it,' Gerry said quickly. 'I didn't realise you were there, though – not until the other night when I heard you talking to Bannerman. I didn't know she was connected with it, either.'

'It was a long time ago now, and she's done such a lot in between – I don't suppose it seems that important to her any more. But it was Celia Bannerman who said it, actually. She called us all together one day – Jack was already dead by then and nearly every girl was wearing mourning for a member of her family – and told us very gravely that only one in ten of us would marry. The rest would have to make their way in the world as best they could, because nearly all the men who might have married us had been killed. It should have been a terrible moment for all the girls in that room, but I remember looking round at them and wondering – was it just me who felt relieved?'

'Relieved? Even though you'd lost someone you loved?'

'Yes. Shameful, isn't it? I didn't dare admit it to anyone at the time, and it didn't change the grief I felt for Jack's loss or the anger at the injustice of it all, but it was definitely relief. Selfish, perhaps, but it suddenly felt like a life full of possibilities and free of obligation. And I suppose that's always been the greatest achievement for me – earning the right not to do something I don't want to do. Everybody's continually telling me that I should be writing more plays, building on last year's success – but the fact is that I don't much feel like it at the moment and I don't need to do it, so I choose not to. And there's no one at home to convince me I'm wrong.'

'I can't decide if you're a traitor to your sex or a role model for us all. Most women complain that marriage *stops* them working, not that it forces them into it.'

Josephine laughed. 'It's funny you should say that. Marta once told me that a woman's entitled to both these days – work and love. I'm not particularly diligent with either. I'm sure I'd be a terrible disappointment if she really got to know me.'

'I doubt that,' Geraldine said, seeing straight through the lightness of the comment, 'but it's natural to be terrified of failure.' Josephine felt herself redden. 'Being adored, as you put it, creates a lot to live up to. That brings me back to my original point, though. Money makes you lazy, and independence makes you lonely.'

'You? Lonely?' she said, skilfully deflecting the attention from herself. 'From what I hear, you can turn even a charity dress fitting into an opportunity for seduction.'

'You're not fooled by all that bravado, surely? I have to drink to keep that up.' Once again, Josephine was struck by how quickly Gerry's moods changed. 'Someone once told me I was too rich to care, you know,' she admitted. 'I argued at the time, but I'm not so sure that I haven't proved her right over the years.'

Josephine stirred more sugar into a cold cup of coffee, sensing that she wasn't the only one who needed to talk. 'Someone who mattered?'

'Oh yes, she mattered. At eighteen, people matter very much, don't they?'

'You were thinking about her the other night in the bar.'

'I think about her a lot when I'm here. She wanted to be a nurse like her mother.'

'Who was she?' Josephine asked, wondering if the past tense which they had both slipped into was down to a broken love affair or to something more tragic.

'She's the reason I've been wanting to get you on your own since Thursday evening.' The offer of a drink then had been casually expressed, as Josephine recalled, but perhaps she had been too preoccupied with her work and her eagerness to see Archie to notice that Geraldine wasn't simply being friendly. 'She was a girl I grew up with – I suppose I must have met her for the first time when I was five or six, but I honestly don't remember a time when she wasn't around. She came to live with our housekeeper down in Sussex. Her mother had died and her father couldn't raise her for some reason, so Mrs Price adopted her when she was four. She and her husband had been trying for a child for years without any luck, and my mother had her nose in a number of charitable causes, so she had no trouble laying her hands on a waif and stray to keep in with the servants.' Her voice had taken on a hard, unforgiving edge, and Josephine had no doubt that Gerry blamed her mother for whatever had gone wrong in her life. 'God, Josephine, those years felt like one long, glorious summer's day. I'd always taken my home for granted, but she'd come from London and, as we grew up, I saw it through her eyes – the parkland and the woods, even the sky was different, and it all seemed to belong to us. We used to dream about the day when it would just be the two of us there – no parents, no servants, just us in the world.' She laughed to herself. 'The laws of inheritance and the workings of the English class system have never been my strong points. She was beautiful, though – so wilful and independent that I believed anything was possible. It's funny – we laughed about my eye for an opportunity, but that Motley girl reminds me of her in some ways. She has the same spirit as Lizzie.'

'Lizzie?'

'Yes. The other night I found out that you knew her.'

Josephine was stunned. 'Oh God, Gerry – I'm so sorry. She was at Anstey. Elizabeth Price . . .'

'Elizabeth Sach, as it turned out.'

'Please tell me you didn't find that out from what I said.'

'No, no, I've known about that for years. I knew before she died.' Gerry reached across and squeezed her hand. 'Look, Josephine, I haven't brought this up to make you feel bad. How were you to know? But hearing her name like that just brought it all back, and I wanted to talk to you – to explain what really happened and to find out if there's anything else you can tell me. Nobody would speak to me about her time at Anstey, but I'd trust you to be honest.'

Josephine nodded. 'I'll tell you as much as I can. But what did really happen?'

'The usual stuff at first. It was fine for me to run wild with the servants' daughter as long as everyone thought I'd grow out of it, but class kicked in when we were teenagers. By the time she was sixteen and I was about to turn eighteen, an embarrassment had become a problem. My mother decided it was time for us to be separated, so she got together with some do-gooding acquaintance of hers – Bannerman, I now realise – and arranged for Lizzie to go to Birmingham. There was no room for argument.'

'That must have felt like the end of the world,' Josephine said. 'For you, obviously, but especially for her. I can still remember the shock of Birmingham after the Highlands. It was wartime as well, of course, which made things even grimmer. I longed for the air at Blair Atholl, and all I got was the smell of Kynoch's steelworks.' Gerry smiled. 'It's funny, no one seems to recognise how paralysing homesickness can be, but to my mind there's no stronger emotion. I was devastated for weeks, and that was just for a place; I wasn't leaving someone behind – in fact, my best friend from school went to Anstey with me – so it must have been so much worse for Lizzie.'

'We had a terrible row before she went. She blamed me for allowing it to happen – that's where the "too rich to care" comment came in. I'd never realised before that the class thing had seeped into our relationship, as well, but I suppose it's so much easier to be oblivious to all that when you're the one with the house and the money. Anyway, I was determined to prove her wrong, so I went to Paris with ten pounds in my pocket and drove ambulances for the Red Cross.' She reached for another cigarette, but the case was empty and Josephine pushed her own across the table. 'I couldn't wait to get out of the place. It was as if Lizzie had packed up all its magic and taken it with her.'

'Did you know all along who she was and what had happened to her mother?'

'No. My mother knew, and the Prices, of course, but that was as far as it was supposed to go. I would never have found out if I hadn't forced the issue.'

'In what way?'

'Oh, blame it on Paris.' Josephine looked curious. 'It was terrible in so many ways,' she explained. 'The city was bombed and people were dying in the streets, but we helped them, too, and there was nothing more exhilarating than saving a life. It made me think I could do anything; if I could stop people dying, I could certainly make a life for myself and Lizzie there, whether I had my parents' support or not. So I came home and told my mother what I was going to do when the war ended. By that time, Lizzie would have finished at Anstey and we could be together. She could have nursed and I – well, I would have found something to do to make a living.'

'And that's when your mother told you?'

'Yes. For some reason, she thought it would change my mind and put an end to the matter. And I suppose, to her credit, it did – but not in the way she intended.'

'You told Lizzie what had happened to her mother, didn't you?'

Gerry nodded. 'It was my fault that she killed herself. I wrote to her straight away. I was so angry, Josephine – I'd always been brought up to believe that birthright was every-thing. My parents had shoved a long line of distinguished Ashbys down my throat from the moment I was old enough to understand, and here they were, trying to deny Lizzie the knowledge that was rightfully hers. It seemed so hypocritical to me at the time – actually, it still does. I know I'm all over the place and my life's a mess, but I've always known who I am and where I fit in. Everyone deserves that much, at least.' Josephine waited for her to continue, trying to imagine how she must have felt on Thursday evening as she listened to her past being reworked by two comparative strangers, neither of whom had the slightest idea what they were talking about emotionally. 'I still think they were wrong not to tell her, but I wish I'd done it differently. I wish I'd waited to tell her myself rather than let her read it in a letter, but I underestimated the impact it would have. I honestly thought if I offered Lizzie a future that she could believe in, it would cease to matter where she came from.' She shook her head, as if she were still unable to believe her own naivety. 'I was a stupid, arrogant little bitch and I thought I was enough for her. Not too rich to care, never that – but too rich to understand.'

Josephine tried to think of something to say that wasn't either patronising or clichéd. There was little point in reminding Gerry that nobody of that age could have been expected to deal with the situation any more successfully: too young to understand was no better than too rich. Gerry seemed to appreciate the honesty of her silence. 'Tell me about her time at Anstey, Josephine,' she said quietly. 'Anything you can remember. I know so little about the last few weeks of her life.'

How easily the scars of silence were passed on, Josephine thought: Elizabeth Sach had been denied the chance to come to terms with what her mother had done and, by taking her own life, had condemned someone who loved her to years of guilt and self-recrimination. 'I didn't know her very well,

Gerry,' she said gently, wishing that she could find some small thing to ease the pain. 'I was in my final year and she was in her first, and our paths didn't cross very often. I could tell you what the college was like, how she'd have spent her days, what she saw when she got up in the morning – but that's not what you want, is it?'

Gerry shook her head. 'So you remember her for her death, and not her life.'

'Yes, I suppose I do. And you've already heard everything I know about that, although I wish to God you hadn't.'

'I could kill Bannerman for what she's done, you know – for meddling in Lizzie's life but not seeing the job through. I heard what she said to you about keeping an eye on her from time to time, but she wasn't there when it mattered, was she?'

'She did what she thought was right.' It was said half-heartedly, and out of habitual rather than genuine loyalty; privately, Josephine shared Gerry's opinion of Celia Bannerman's fated interference.

'And I suppose the college was paid handsomely for taking on a child killer's daughter.'

'You don't know that. I'm sure it wasn't a mercenary thing.'

'Really? I know how these women work, Josephine, and they're all the same. Bannerman only tolerates my presence because the Ashbys contribute so heavily to the Cowdray coffers. She's never been comfortable with my being here – I used to think it was because my louche behaviour threatened the club's precious reputation, but now I know why.'

'Will you tell Celia what happened? How Lizzie found out, I mean.'

'Oh, don't worry – I'll make sure that Celia understands everything perfectly. And there's something you need to understand, too. You said Lizzie was hard to like, but that isn't true. She was just sad, Josephine. Her world had been torn apart for the second time, and she was lost – utterly lost. Who wouldn't lash out at a time like that? Promise me you'll stand her corner when you write about her.'

'Good God, Gerry, I couldn't possibly write about her now. Too many people have been hurt – it wouldn't be right.'

'But why not, if it's the truth?'

'That's just the point – how do I know what's true and what isn't? If we hadn't had this conversation, I'd have given completely the wrong impression of Lizzie, and then how would you have felt? And God knows what lies and misunderstandings I'm spinning about her mother. You can't guess at history.'

'And you can't ignore it, either. I admit I was furious at first when I heard you talking, but then I listened to what you said about why you were doing it and it made perfect sense. It's right that we try to understand – not judge, but understand. If Lizzie had believed that more people would be willing to do that – if she'd been given the chance to do it herself – perhaps there'd be no book to write.' She held up her hands in a mock truce. 'Far be it for me to try to influence your famous sense of right and wrong – but I, for one, would feel better if Lizzie's story were told fairly. Promise me you'll think about it?' Josephine nodded, but remained unconvinced. Gerry stood up and winked at her. 'That's if you're not too busy after Friday night.'

They left the dining room, much to the relief of staff who were waiting to reset the tables for lunch, and walked slowly back upstairs. 'What's Marta like?' Gerry asked, and then, as Josephine hesitated, added impatiently: 'I don't want a carefully considered paragraph. I want an instant reaction. Put the writer down and be a normal human being for once.'

'All right. She's impossible – quick to lose her temper, brave to the point of recklessness, and irritatingly good at seeing straight through any nonsense. She's stronger than anyone I've ever met – she'd have to be to survive what she's been through – and she's never afraid to speak her mind. She's passionate, warm and intelligent, full of contradictions, and I suspect that life would be infuriating with her, but never dull.'

'And never peaceful.'

Josephine laughed. 'No, probably not.'

'And she's beautiful, from what I remember of the press pictures.'

'Anyone with that description would be, surely? But yes, in the way you mean, she's beautiful.'

They stopped outside the drawing room, and Gerry looked at her knowingly. 'I take back what I said about your having made your decision already,' she said. 'But whichever way you jump, at least talk to her. She's given you an easy way out by telling you not to turn up if the answer's no, but she doesn't mean that. Talking to someone face to face is so important – if I know anything now, I know that. And it's not for me to give you advice, but she won't appreciate any more of that false modesty you seem to have got away with last time – so don't tell her she doesn't know how she feels, and if she says she's in love with you, accept that she's in love with you. The question – the only question – is whether you want that love or not. And Josephine?'

'Yes?'

'There's plenty of time for peace, eventually.'

Chapter Eight

Except for its prison, Holloway was an undistinguished area which blended so uneventfully into the neighbouring boroughs that it was hard to identify where one ended and another began. Campbell Road, where Marjorie and her father had lived, cut out of Seven Sisters Road, dissecting a line of busy shops close to Finsbury Park tube station. Although not technically a slum, the street held some of the poorest housing in north London and, to Penrose's mind, some of the worst living conditions: his first few days in the force had brought him here – called to the death of a three-year-old girl, accidentally suffocated in her sleep by a family huddled together in one bed against the cold – and he had never forgotten the misery of that visit, fifteen years ago on a day very similar to this.

'Kids brought up in the Bunk are usually tough enough to take care of themselves,' Fallowfield said as he drove, giving the street the name by which it was best known among both locals and police, 'but I don't see how anything could have given that girl a chance.' He shook his head. 'I can't get her face out of my mind, you know, Sir. Poor kid – how old can she have been? Twenty? Twenty-one?'

'Twenty-three, according to the records my cousins kept,' Penrose said, 'and she'd done three stretches in Holloway in as many years.'

'Well that figures, coming from round here.'

Fallowfield's comment might have sat uncomfortably with the welfare officers, but it was not entirely unjust. All districts had their notorious streets, but Campbell Road's reputation was darker than most and the Bunk held a certain legendary status amongst the officers who dealt with trouble there on a daily basis. A chameleon by nature, the street was rife with domestic violence and disputes between households, yet it closed ranks at the slightest hint of interference from strangers, presenting an unfriendly but remarkably united face to the outside world.

They parked at the southern end of the street in front of a newsagent's and a small beer off-licence. A group of men stood around on the pavement talking and idling away a Saturday morning, their ragged coat collars turned up to keep out the cold, their breath mingling with smoke from their cigarettes. The air bristled with hostility as Penrose and Fallowfield got out of the car. 'Watch your motor, copper?' a small boy shouted insolently from the other side of the street, and one or two of the men sniggered as a handful of snow and mud hit the windscreen. The boy moved nearer to the car, kicking a few stones towards the vehicle as he walked, full of bravado in front of his friends. Fallowfield glared at him and seemed about to say something, but Penrose shook his head. How early the antagonism set in, he thought as he led the way up the street; the oldest of the boys could only have been six or seven.

The Bunk was broad enough to give the impression that its houses had a right to be there and, unlike most slums, the street did not crouch into the shadows of a factory or gasworks. In fact, a stranger oblivious to its history would never have guessed that the three-storey buildings housed anything other than the artisan classes they had originally been designed for.

The social face of the street may have changed, but traces of its architectural aspirations remained in the generous pavements and iron railings which ran in front of the houses, protecting a tiny sliver of private land from public footsteps. The door to number 35 was worn and neglected, the woman who answered it much the same; she looked forty but was probably younger; Penrose could smell the alcohol on her breath before she even opened her mouth. 'We're looking for a Mrs Baker,' he said. 'Is she at home?'

The woman smirked. 'Maria? I don't know where else she'd be. Top of the house – two rooms at the back. Would you like me to show you up, Sir?'

She spat the last word out sarcastically, and Penrose pushed the door open and walked past her, ignoring the mock curtsey that accompanied the offer. 'No, thank you. We'll find our own way.'

Inside, the house was in desperate need of repair: the plastered walls were peeling, the ceilings stained and dingy and, as they walked over to the stairs, Penrose noticed that the floorboards were springy with damp. Sections of balustrade had been removed for firewood, making the dimly lit, uneven steps more dangerous than ever. From what he could see through open doors on his way up, the overcrowding seemed to have got worse since he was last here. There must be more people per room than the law allowed, but that was hardly surprising; he knew from experience that what was acceptable was defined by what people were used to rather than what was legal.

'We'll just tell her the facts as gently as possible,' he said quietly to Fallowfield on the middle landing. 'Presumably she knew them both better than anyone else, so it'll be interesting to see what conclusions *she* jumps to about what happened.'

He knocked at the first of four doors which led off the second-floor corridor, and it was answered almost immediately by a dark-haired woman in her late forties or early fifties. She looked up at him with tired eyes, her face sallow and expressionless – the look of guilt or dread which usually greeted his arrival was entirely absent. 'Mrs Baker?'

'What's he done now?' Her voice was deep and roughened by cigarettes, her accent that of a born Londoner. 'It must be something serious if they've sent the busies. Or is it Marjorie you're after?'

'I need to talk to you about both of them, I'm afraid. May we come in?' She nodded and stood aside to let them pass. After the dirt and degradation of the rest of the house, the Bakers' room was refreshingly clean, but shabby and depressing nonetheless. Faded curtains with barely enough material to cover the windows hung on a piece of string, and the linoleum on the floor was scuffed and torn. The ceiling was covered in the obligatory damp stains and the bed stood at an awkward angle in the corner to avoid the three or four places where water was dripping through. A cot, an ugly deal table and chair and a chipped marble washstand were the only other significant items of furniture. A toddler with a shock of straw-coloured curls began to cry, and the woman went over to calm her down. Penrose watched as she lifted the girl from the cot, noticing the scald marks and scars on her work-sore hands; how impossible it must be to live safely in these inadequate rooms, with coal fires to cook on and oil lamps and candles for lighting; it was a wonder there weren't more fatalities.

When the toddler was quiet again, Maria Baker looked challengingly at them, daring them to surprise her with whatever news they had brought about her family. 'There's no easy way to say this, Mrs Baker,' Penrose began quietly, but he was interrupted before he could go any further.

'Killed him at last, has she?' Her matter-of-factness wrong-footed him, and it must have shown in his face. 'Nothing would surprise me about them two,' she added. 'I've lived in the middle of their fighting for too long. It was only a matter of time before it got out of hand.'

'I'm very sorry, but your husband and Marjorie are *both* dead,' he said, and for the first time Maria Baker looked shocked and confused. 'Their bodies were found earlier this morning at Marjorie's place of work, but we believe they died last night. Marjorie was murdered. Your husband was found at the bottom of some steps and his death may have been an accident.'

'He killed her?'

'Is that likely?'

She walked over to the bed and sat down, then nodded to Penrose to take the chair. 'They hated each other – always have. She stood up to him, you see – saw through his lies and his idleness and wasn't afraid to say so. Only one who ever has – but that's what girls are like today, isn't it? We were always taught to put up with what we were given, and we found our own ways round it. But Marjorie wasn't like that – she put him down to his face, played him at his own game. And Joe didn't like people getting the better of him.'

'Was he violent towards her?' Fallowfield asked.

Mrs Baker looked scornfully at him. 'He was violent to all of us – where do you think I got this from?' She parted her hair and Penrose could see where a cut was just beginning to heal. 'I don't bang my own head against the wall, although there's times when it feels like that. No, Joe's attitude was that if I wanted to run the household – bring the money in, discipline the kids – then I could take my punishment like a man, as well. He wasn't special in that – it's what men do here. They're no one on the outside, so they make their own power at home.' She thought for a moment, absent-mindedly smoothing the blankets on the bed. 'He wasn't always like that, but it's hard to love anyone when you hate yourself, when you're ashamed like he was.'

'Ashamed of what?'

'Of his life. Of ending it here. He was an old man, sixty-seven next birthday. There were a lot of things that he regretted, and he blamed me for most of them. Marjorie could look after herself, though, especially as she got older – she had a hell of a temper. She broke his nose with a poker one night. If anything, he was afraid of her. That's why I thought . . .' The sentence was left unfinished as she tried to reconcile what had happened to her family with what she knew of them. 'Are you sure he did it?'

Penrose evaded the question. 'Marjorie's murder was clearly planned,' he said, 'and I'm afraid that she was subjected to a brutal, spiteful attack.' He chose his words carefully, keen to spare her details which no mother would want to hear. 'We have reason to believe that she was killed because of something she knew, perhaps a secret that she had threatened to reveal. Do you have any idea what that might have been?'

It was a shot in the dark, based on nothing more than his interpretation of the mutilation to Marjorie's face, but Maria Baker glanced at him sharply and the guard which had begun to lift when she spoke of her husband returned more forcefully than ever. 'If that's true,' she said coldly, 'it's nothing to do with anyone in this family. It's very difficult to have secrets when you live in each other's pockets.'

'How long have you been here, Mrs Baker?' Fallowfield asked.

'Fifteen years or so. An aunt of mine lived here and she took us in. She never married, so she had room and she was glad of someone to look out for her. When she died, we kept the rent on.'

'What was her name?'

'Edwards. Violet Edwards.'

'And where were you before?'

'Essex for a bit. Joe's got family in Southend, but it didn't work out for us there.' She smiled bitterly to herself. 'In fact, I couldn't honestly say it worked out for us anywhere. We never really stood a chance.'

'Can I ask why?' Penrose spoke gently. With so little to go on, he wanted to find out as much as he could about Marjorie's family background, if only to satisfy himself that her father was innocent – of her murder, at least, if not of bringing pain and misery into her life from the moment she was born.

'Joe was married before him and me got together, but it was a disaster and it turned very bitter at the end. He never shook off the memory – it scarred him, in ways you couldn't imagine.'

'Did Marjorie know about this?'

'No, it was years ago, long before she was born, and he wouldn't have his first wife's name mentioned. As far as Marjorie knew, it'd been me and Joe from the beginning.'

'Were there any children from that first marriage?'

'Only one, but he lost touch with her when it ended. He made up for it with me, though – nothing short of a bleedin'' baby factory, we were. Eight in twelve years – it was like he had a duty to fill the place with kids.' She looked down at her hands. 'God knows why, 'cause he didn't want anything to do with them once they were here.'

'Where did Marjorie come in the family?'

'Youngest of the ones that lived.'

'And the rest of your children?'

'Couldn't see 'em for dust when they were old enough to leave home.'

'So who's this?' he asked, nodding towards the cot.

'She's from next door. I look after other people's kids – well, the ones that aren't old enough to be put out to work or lent out for begging. We all do a bit to earn what we can – some of the women do housework, some lend money; me, I look after babies – God knows I've had enough practice.'

'Did Marjorie sleep next door?'

She nodded. 'Yeah, with a couple of girls from the family across the landing. They help out with the rent.'

'Would you mind if Sergeant Fallowfield had a look around?'

'Help yourself, but you won't find anything. Marjorie never left stuff lying around – prison taught her that.'

'What did your husband do for a living?' Penrose asked when Fallowfield had left the room.

She scoffed. 'Joe and work never really got on. It was always short-term stuff with him – digging trenches for the new stands at the Arsenal, driving vans for the coal dealer down the road, the odd building job here and there.' She looked round the room and added sarcastically: 'It's not what you'd call a hearth and home worth working for, is it? And if you mention where you live to most of the employers round here, you soon find yourself at the back of the queue. That's what Joe said, anyway, but he could always find an excuse for not pulling his weight – it was one of the things that Marjorie hated him for; letting the rest of us pick up the shortfall.'

'And Marjorie's prison sentences – were they a result of her having to make up the shortfall?'

'She'd been making her own way since she was a kid. Children's wages are important – why do you think we have them?' She laughed, but Penrose realised that the comment had not been a joke. He glanced up as Fallowfield came back in, but the sergeant shook his head. 'And she was good at it, too,' Mrs Baker continued. 'She'd beg for used first-house programmes up at the Empire, then sell them back to the second houses, or buy cheap white flowers and dye them for button-holes – she was always creative, was our Marjorie.'

How easily she had slipped into talking of her daughter in the past tense, Penrose thought. 'But what did she do to end up in Holloway?'

'The first time was three Christmases ago – she got a job sorting mail at Mount Pleasant and pinched whatever was worth having. Then she nicked a handbag, and the last stretch – well, that *was* her father's fault. She started running errands for one of the moneylenders down the street – Joe stopped her one day on her way back from a customer and made her hand over the cash, but she took the flak for it.'

'Why didn't she just tell the truth?' Fallowfield's tone was incredulous. 'There was no love lost between them.'

Maria Baker glared at him. 'You don't shop your own, and anyway, mud sticks. No one had a problem believing it was Marjorie who was in the wrong.'

Penrose could see that his sergeant was having trouble

hiding what he thought of this honour-among-thieves principle. 'I gather she kept in touch with one of the girls from
prison,' he said. 'Do you know who that was?'

'You must mean Lucy – Lucy Peters. She brought her here a
couple of times. Scared little thing, she was, but then Marjorie
always did look out for the underdog.'

Fallowfield made a note of the name. 'Tell me about
Marjorie,' Penrose said. It was always so tempting to put a halo
over a murder victim. People – particularly close relatives –
were understandably reluctant to speak ill of the dead and,
more often than not, he was given a picture of a person who
had never existed, a person devoid of the very human weak-
nesses which had almost certainly got him or her killed.
Already he could see how easy it would be to dismiss Marjorie
Baker with a variety of stereotypes – the petty criminal with a
heart of gold, the mouthy upstart who didn't know her place,
the victim of poverty who never stood a chance – but he
trusted his cousins' judgement and suspected that the true
person was a complex blend of all these images. It was rare for
a mother to be able to paint an accurate picture of her child,
but Mrs Baker didn't come across as a subscriber to sentimen-
tality. 'What was she like?' he asked.

'Not like me, that's for sure. It's a different world for girls
now, they can afford to be cocky.' It was the same word that
Hilda Reader had used to describe Marjorie but without the
affection, and Penrose sensed a rivalry between mother and
daughter. 'I'm Fonthill Road rag shop, she's Islington market –
or at least she thought she was. She was too good for this life,
and almost clever enough to pull it off. She'd look at me sometimes with such pity in her eyes, and I'd know what she was
thinking – anything but a life of scrubbing doorsteps and

charring. I tell you – there's plenty round here who'd take a charring job from under your nose as soon as look at you, but not Marjorie. Oh no, she was far too proud to go knocking on doors for work, although there's been times when I could have begged her to.'

'She seemed to have settled into her new job well, though; her employers tell me she was making a success of it.'

'Well, it suited her idea of who she was, didn't it?' Mrs Baker bit her lip, and appeared to regret her words. 'You must think I'm a wicked cow,' she said, 'and perhaps there *are* women out there who are better than me, who don't grudge their daughters the chances they never had – but I'm not like that. Marjorie was lucky to get that job after being in prison. I used to say to her when she told me about all these new skills she'd learned inside – what's the point of that? Prison teaches you how to do something and makes damn sure that no one'll ever employ you to do it. But I was wrong, and someone gave her another chance. Now you walk in here and tell me she's got herself killed because of something she said and I'm so angry with her for wasting it – not for her sake, but for mine, because if things had been different, that could've been me and I wouldn't have chucked it away.'

Penrose gave her a moment before continuing, then asked: 'Did Marjorie ever talk about the people she worked with? Did she seem happy?'

'Yeah, she was happy, although Joe did his best to spoil it for her.'

'By bothering her at work and embarrassing her in front of the other girls?'

She looked surprised. 'You know more about that than I do. No – by putting her down, telling her it wouldn't last. That's

219

what he was good at – bringing us all down to his level. Marjorie brought this picture home in one of them magazines that people read who have more time than sense. She was in it, you see, her and the other girls at the factory. They were with the ladies who were having the clothes made. Ever so proud of it, she was, but that just started Joe off worse than ever. He said something to her about it that obviously upset her.'

'What, exactly?'

'I don't know – she wouldn't say. But I got the impression that he was trying to persuade her to get more out of her new job than her wage packet.'

'Do you still have the picture, Mrs Baker?'

'I suppose it's somewhere about.' She stood up and rummaged through a pile of newspapers which sat by the grate, waiting to be burned. 'Here, this is it.'

Penrose took the piece of paper and looked down at the photograph. It had been taken in the Motley workroom and Marjorie stood on the left of the group, poignantly close to the spot where she had been killed. She was holding a glamorous evening gown, draped over her arm to show the material off to its best advantage, and he was struck by the contrast between the world of the picture and the world she had been born to – and by how comfortable she seemed in the former. She was exceptionally attractive, with a smile like a young Gwen Farrar and, as he gazed at this carefree image, he felt again the full horror of her final moments.

He passed the photograph to Fallowfield, who copied down the captioned names and returned it to Marjorie's mother. 'Did she associate with anyone in particular from work?' he asked.

The woman shrugged. 'Not especially, as far as I know.'

'What about men? Was she walking out with anyone?'

The genteel phrase seemed to amuse her. 'If she was, she never told me about him, but then she wouldn't. She kept her secrets close to her, and I didn't watch her every move – we didn't have that kind of relationship.'

'So you weren't worried when she didn't come home last night? When neither of them did?'

'No, I was glad of the peace. I'm always glad if Joe stays out all night, and, like I said, Marjorie had other places to go. I don't blame them – I wish I could get away.'

'Where did your husband go, Mrs Baker? Who did he associate with?'

'Any man who'd buy him a drink, and any woman who'd give him a bed for the night.'

'Can you give us names?'

She shook her head. 'He drank in the Feathers or the Green Man – they might be able to tell you there who he kept company with. The women weren't from round here, I'll give him that – he didn't mess around on his own doorstep.'

'Were you here all night, Mrs Baker?' Fallowfield asked.

She laughed at him. 'No. Actually, Sergeant, I took a long hot bath and went out to see some friends for supper. Then we went to the theatre.' Her laughter had an edge of hysteria about it and, when it stopped, there were tears in her eyes. 'Of course I was here all night. I'm always here – you can rely on that.'

Penrose stood up to go; there was no more to be learned here for the present. 'Once again, I'm sorry for your loss, Mrs Baker, and thank you for your time. If you think of anything that might help us, I'd be grateful if you'd get in touch immediately. We will, of course, keep you informed of any developments.'

'I know what you're both thinking,' she said as they walked to the door. 'I'm not as upset as I should be. Not as shocked. But grief's a luxury I can't afford – not with Marjorie's wages to replace somehow. I don't even know how I'm going to bury them.'

Penrose knew it was futile, but he said it anyway. 'If there's anything we can do to be of assistance, you know where to find us.'

As they went back downstairs, Fallowfield said: 'Lucy Peters is at the Cowdray Club, Sir. Works there as a maid.'

'Does she? Then perhaps that's how Marjorie got hold of the photo frame we found on her body – that might have been the arrangement: Peters stole the stuff, and Marjorie sold it on. And some of the women in that picture . . .'

'Are the ones who've had the letters, the ones who saw Marjorie the day she died. Yes, I noticed that. Do you think there's a link? Perhaps it was Marjorie who sent them.'

'That crossed my mind. It's time we paid the Cowdray Club a visit, Bill, but I want to go back to the Yard first and try to get hold of Spilsbury. He might have something for us by now, and at least then we'll know exactly what we're dealing with.'

'What d'you make of the mother?'

Penrose considered carefully before answering. 'I think life's knocked everything out of her, Bill, and there's nothing left to like or dislike. These two deaths have made it easier for her in some ways, I suppose, and harder in others. I'd like another opinion on the family, though. I wonder if that woman who let us in is still about?'

They found her in the back yard, breaking up some empty wooden crates. She looked up when she heard them, and a girl of about ten with rickety legs, her skin pallid from the amount of time which she spent in a damp, cold room, moved over to stand behind her mother, peering shyly out at them.

Without giving any details, Penrose explained briefly what had brought the police to Campbell Bunk. 'Poor bitch is better off without 'em if you ask me,' she said. 'Joe Baker was a lazy, selfish bastard and that Marjorie had too much of what the cat licks its arse with – a bit of Woolworth's jewellery and some make-up and she thought she was Joan bleedin' Crawford.'

'We understand that Marjorie argued a lot with her father.'

'And her mother – believe me, there's nothing worse than two women turning on each other. We know what we're doing.'

Penrose was interested. 'They fought physically, you mean?'

'If you mean did they beat the shit out of each other, then yeah, they did. I remember Marjorie coming home not so long ago in a new coat and skirt – God knows what they must have cost her, but she didn't even get inside the house in 'em. Maria was out here in the street, tearing 'em off her back. She told me later it was because Marjorie had been earning more than she let on and spending money on herself rather than the family, but it was more than that – it was sheer jealousy. Them clothes weren't worth nothing by the time Maria'd finished with 'em, and if it'd been about money she'd have found out how much they cost and taken 'em to the pawn shop.'

Fallowfield raised an eyebrow and Penrose shared his surprise. More had changed in women's lives in the last thirty years than ever before and, in spite of what Maria Baker had said, it would take a special kind of love not to grudge that just a little. But this particular struggle between mother and daughter sounded more bitter and more violent than one generation's resentment of the chances offered to the next.

'Do you know if Mrs Baker was at home last night?' Fallowfield asked.

'Of course she was,' the woman said automatically. 'I went up to see her a couple of times.'

It was a lie, but there was no point in wasting time proving that now. 'Thank you,' Penrose said, unable to keep a trace of sarcasm out of his voice. 'You've been a great help.'

By the time they got back to the car, a long, deep scratch – admirable in its neat execution – had mysteriously appeared on the driver's side, drawing some choice language from Fallowfield and a mocking expression of innocence from the small crowd of bystanders. As Penrose opened the door and got in, the filth and degradation seemed to cling to his clothes; had it not been for the manner of Marjorie's death and the spirited image created by what people said about her, he could almost have believed that the girl was better off out of it.

Maria Baker sat on the bed for a long time after the policemen had gone, scarcely daring to believe that it was over: the shadow of that house in Finchley – which had wound itself like a shroud around her relationship with Joe, driving them apart and binding them unrelentingly together – had, with his death, finally lifted; the memories and the shame, which tracked them down no matter where they went or who they became, had lost their power to hurt.

She stood up to put the magazine back on the pile next to the grate, ready for the evening fire. As she bent down, she noticed that the date on the newspaper which Joe had left lying around yesterday was 22 November, and realised that tomorrow was her birthday. It was thirty-three years almost to the day since the nightmare had begun and now, at fifty-one, she was being offered a clean slate. Trying to remember the woman she had once been, Maria Baker walked over to the cot. The child stared up at her in astonishment as she laughed until she cried.

There was nothing from Spilsbury on Penrose's desk when he and Fallowfield arrived back at the Yard.

'I'll have to telephone him,' Penrose said reluctantly. The pathologist hated being hurried and detectives who were too impatient for results were the only thing guaranteed to disturb his equable temperament.

'Rather you than me, Sir,' Fallowfield said. 'I'll get on to the Cowdray Club, shall I? Tell Miss Bannerman we'll be over to see her.'

'Yes. Who else from the club was in that photograph?'

Fallowfield looked at his notes. 'Miriam Sharpe – she's the president of the college, Sir, and I gather from what Miss Bannerman said that she's not too happy about this gala business, even though she has to put up with it in public. I got the impression that her and Bannerman don't really get on. Then there's Lady Ashby, Mary Size and Sylvia Timpson – she's the receptionist, Sir.'

'Have you met her?'

'Yes – very prickly and a bit grander than she ought to be. You know the sort.'

'Only too well. You can tell me anything else I need to know about them on the way over. With a bit of luck, we'll be able to have an initial chat with Bannerman, Sharpe and Timpson – and Lucy Peters, too, if she works on a Saturday. I doubt the other two will be there at this time of day, so find out how we can get hold of Lady Ashby. I'd rather see Mary Size at the prison, anyway, so arrange that, will you, Bill? We'll need copies of Marjorie's prison records – and we might as well take a look at Peters's while we're there. Tell Miss Bannerman who we want to see, but don't give her any details. Let her think it's about the other business.'

'She might already know what's happened from your cousins, Sir, if they've phoned about using the premises.'

'Damn – I'd forgotten. All right – get hold of Lettice or Ronnie first and find out, and if they haven't already made contact with the club, ask them not to tell Bannerman why they need the space. And I want someone to do some digging on the Bakers – find out everything you can on the family, including the Edwards branch. Can you spare a couple of people for that?'

'Yes, Sir, I'll put Waddingham and Merrifield on it. Neither of them likes to be outdone by the other, so we should get some quick results.'

'Excellent.' Penrose picked up the telephone and got through to the mortuary in Gower Street. Spilsbury had built his reputation on a principle of proceeding slowly, taking nothing for granted and scrutinising every inch of a body before opening it up, but his insistence on doing everything himself led to occasional delays which drove the average detective – Penrose included – to distraction. But it was that very attention to detail – and a profound knowledge gained from years of experience – which enabled the pathologist to detect things invisible to others and, to Penrose's knowledge, nothing he had seen with the naked eye had ever been reversed by subsequent examination with a microscope. He knew he was pushing his luck, but he hoped that an initial examination might at least allow Spilsbury to confirm that Marjorie had not been killed by her father.

'How many times do I have to tell you, Archie? If you want miracles, you need to go to a higher authority than me.' The words were stern, but there was a note of humour in his voice which gave Penrose hope. 'Actually, I was just about to call you. I'm afraid it doesn't look as though you've caught your murderer yet – I don't know if you regard that as good news or bad.'

'I'm just grateful for any news at all,' Penrose said.

'I must stress that this is only my opinion, and nothing I've found yet would necessarily convince a jury, but a couple of things suggest to me that he didn't kill her, and, taken together with the type of crime that's been committed and your initial reaction, they're pretty conclusive. Baker had very recent scratches on his face, but there was no skin under Marjorie's fingernails.'

'But the scratches could have . . .'

'. . . nothing to do with the murder. Yes, I realise that. The second point is a little more reliable. There's a small cloakroom a few yards down the corridor from the main workshop.'

'Yes, I remember seeing it.'

'Well, we found a towel there which has blood on it and, when we looked more closely, there were tiny specks of blood on the tiles behind the sink as well. Obviously we'll have to wait for the tests to confirm that the blood is the same type as Marjorie's, but, if it is, it seems fairly clear to me that the killer went in there to wash before leaving the building. That rules Baker out – his hands and face were both filthy. There's no way that he could have wiped his daughter's blood off his hands and left behind the dirt that we found.'

'One of the other girls could have hurt herself during the day.'

227

'Yes, I thought of that, but your cousins aren't aware of any accidents and even the slightest cut has to be reported, apparently.'

'Even if it is Marjorie's blood, she could have used the cloakroom herself.'

'Think about it, Archie – there were no external injuries whatsoever on Marjorie Baker's body except for the damage to her lips and some small scratches around the mouth from glass beads which didn't go down her throat. If that blood *is* hers, she would have had to have gone to the sink after those injuries were made, and you're hardly going to nip along the corridor to make yourself presentable after suffering that sort of torture. No, I think the killer's face and hands were covered with the same specks of blood and vomit that we found on the smock, and he or she wanted to wash all the traces off before going out into the street.'

'Then why leave the smock and the towel behind, I wonder? I can understand someone missing the blood on the sink in their hurry to get out, but that seems a little careless.'

'Perhaps he or she was worried about being seen with them. Anyway, the smock and the towel don't actually tell us anything very incriminating – unless you think that the plan all along was to frame Baker for his daughter's murder.'

'I see what you mean. Baker may simply have come looking for Marjorie and turned up at the wrong moment, then had a helping hand down the stairs?'

'I don't put the story together, Archie – that's your job – but I've found nothing yet to disprove what you've just said, although Joseph Baker had enough alcohol in him to end up at the bottom of those steps on his own. It's only the scratches that suggest any sort of struggle – he was knocked unconscious by the fall and died of hypothermia, which makes the time of death difficult to establish, I'm afraid. Someone of his age didn't stand a chance left out there in those temperatures.'

'What about a time of death for Marjorie?'

'She'd been dead for between eight and twelve hours when she was found. Unofficially, I'd say towards the upper end of that.'

Which fitted with what Lettice had told him about the lights going off in the studio, Penrose thought. 'You said she had no other injuries – presumably she was drugged if she didn't put up a fight?'

'Yes, although I can't say for certain with what until we get the results of some tests. She'd been dragged across the floor at some stage – her stockings were torn, and we found matching fibres on the leg of one of the tables.'

'Was it in the vodka?'

'Perhaps. Her pupils were dilated and her skin was grey – in fact, if you discount the horror of her injuries, the picture as a whole resembles clinical cardiovascular collapse, so one of the nitrites would have done the job. Amyl nitrite's a possibility – it's a muscle relaxant and they use it to treat angina, but it's absorbed very rapidly from the lungs so making her inhale a good dose of that would achieve what the killer needed in order to complete the rest of the work.'

'Is it readily available?'

'Well, it has various medical uses and it's commonly prescribed.'

'Was she conscious throughout the worst of it?' Penrose asked, although he thought he knew the answer already.

'Oh yes. For a while, at least. She'll have lost all the power in her muscles and she'll have been drowsy, but certainly not drowsy enough. If she'd been allowed to remain lying down, she'd have recovered very quickly from the drug, but she didn't stand a chance as long as she was tied upright to that chair.'

'Medical knowledge, then?'

'Perhaps.' He sighed heavily. 'I'll get the full reports over to you as soon as I can.'

'Thanks, Bernard – I appreciate it.' Penrose put the phone down, satisfied. He had known in his heart that Joseph Baker, while having plenty to reproach himself for, was not guilty of his daughter's murder, but he tried to see where the Cowdray Club fitted into the overall picture. Had Baker persuaded Marjorie to write those notes and try her hand at blackmail, and, if so, how had she got hold of the information to put in them? He tried to remember the details of the letters, but he had only given them a cursory glance at the time. Why, though, would someone kill Marjorie to silence her when the notes had been freely handed over to the police and their contents already made public? Perhaps there was someone at the club who had never confessed to receiving one.

Fallowfield put his head round the door and Penrose brought him up to date, then asked: 'Are WPC Wyles's sewing skills up to scratch, do you think?'

Fallowfield looked curiously at him. 'Why, sir, have you got something that needs mending?'

Penrose laughed. 'No, but I'm about to tell my cousins that they've got a new member of staff – I want Wyles in that club, watching those women like a hawk.'

'Why don't you ask Miss Tey to keep an eye out, sir? She's on the spot already.'

'Because she's Miss Tey, not Miss bloody Marple. You've

been spending your evenings in St Mary Mead again, haven't you?'

Fallowfield looked sheepish. 'Seriously, sir, that sort of work's not really up Wyles's street, is it? Women coppers are all right for taking statements and looking after juveniles, but undercover work's a bit risky.'

'Oh don't be so old-fashioned, Bill. She'll suit a smock better than you will, and she's perfectly capable of looking after herself. I thought about putting her in there as a nurse, but that would mean trusting someone in the building and, for all we know, any one of them could be capable of wielding a sack needle. No, the girls' moving into the Cowdray Club is too good a chance to miss.' Fallowfield still looked sceptical. 'Cheer up, Bill – even if I'm wrong, it might get the chief constable's wife off our backs. Have you got those anonymous letters handy? I'd like to have another look at them before we go over there.'

The telephone rang while he was waiting. 'Inspector Penrose? It's Hilda Reader. I'm sorry to bother you.'

'It's no bother, Mrs Reader. Are you all right?'

'Oh yes, thank you, but I'm glad I've caught you. There's something you should know – something I've just found out from my husband.'

'What is it?'

'I told him about Marjorie – I hope you don't mind, but he could see how upset I was and it helped to talk to him about it.'

'Of course. I understand.'

'Well, it turns out he saw her yesterday when she came into the shop to get the things Miss Motley needed. A man in his department served her, and there was a bit of a scene between them. John – that's my husband – had to go over and tell them to be quiet. It turns out that this man – Lionel Bishop, his name is – had been seeing Marjorie behind his wife's back, but she'd given him his marching orders. He was trying to talk her into starting things up again, but she was having none of it. John said he heard her threaten to tell Mr Bishop's wife if he didn't leave her alone. He was furious, apparently.'

'And is Mr Bishop at the store today?'

'Yes, Inspector. All day.'

'Thank you again, Mrs Reader – you've been very helpful.'

'There's one more thing, Inspector.'

'Yes?'

'I don't know if it's important or not, but he sold her those beads.'

Penrose went to look for Fallowfield and handed him a slip of paper in exchange for the folder of letters. 'Lionel Bishop. Works in the haberdashery department of Debenhams. He's been playing around with Marjorie Baker, but she wanted to put a stop to it and threatened to tell his wife.'

'And he wasn't best pleased?'

'Exactly. Go and bring him in.'

Chapter Nine

The man waiting downstairs to be questioned stood up as soon as Penrose and Fallowfield entered the room. 'What the hell is this all about, Inspector?' he demanded angrily. 'Your lot turn up at my place of work, embarrassing me in front of my staff, and no one has the decency to offer an explanation. I have rights, you know – you might have been more discreet.'

Penrose gestured to him to sit down again and calmly introduced himself. In his experience, people who insisted on their rights so quickly were usually the sort who trampled obliviously over everyone else's, but he tried not to let cynicism cloud his judgement as he cast an appraising eye over Lionel Bishop. Marjorie Baker's would-be lover was in his late thirties, with a weak chin, pale complexion and thin, sandy-brown hair. His clothes were expensive but unimaginative, and he wore them without conviction, almost as if they spoke of an authority which even he doubted he possessed. Penrose tried to resist making judgements but, from what he'd heard so far, this was hardly the type of man whom the dead girl would notice, let alone be attracted to. 'I'm sorry to have caused you so much inconvenience, but I need to ask you some questions in connection with the murder of Marjorie Baker,' he said, trying not to take anything but a professional satisfaction from the swift erosion of Bishop's moral high ground. 'I believe the two of you were well acquainted.'

'Murder?' Bishop asked. The shock was genuine, Penrose thought, but the horror in the man's voice seemed to stem from panic at his own situation rather than any genuine sorrow. 'What's that got to do with me? I only knew her as a customer. She came into the shop once or twice a week to collect items on account.'

'And you saw her yesterday?'

'Yes, she came in around lunchtime and bought a few things – some beads and needles, and a roll or two of bias binding. We passed the time of day, that's all. Are you arresting everyone who spoke to her?'

Penrose ignored the question. 'What sort of needles?' Bishop looked incredulously at him. 'What sort of needles did Miss Baker buy?' he repeated impatiently. 'It's a simple enough question.'

'Standard embroidery needles.'

'And did you and Miss Baker argue yesterday?'

'There's not much to argue about in a list of haberdashery items, is there?' Bishop said sarcastically.

'Where were you last night between the hours of nine o'clock and midnight?'

'At home with my wife, of course. Where else would I be?'

Penrose looked at him for just long enough to make his scepticism obvious. 'You won't mind if we confirm that with your wife?'

For the first time, Bishop looked nervous. 'Will you have to tell her why? She might think . . .'

'What might she think, Mr Bishop?' Penrose demanded impatiently. 'Shall we start again? How well did you know Marjorie Baker?'

'All right, all right. I took her out for lunch a few times, and the odd drink after work. So what? There was no harm in that. You know how it is.'

'I'm afraid I don't, so why don't you tell me?'

'Look, Inspector, I met my wife when we were both very young and we got married far too quickly and for all the wrong reasons. It was during the war. She was a nurse, and I was back from the front for a bit with a smashed leg from a German bullet. We mistook compassion and gratitude for love – that's all there is to it. We weren't the only ones, but that doesn't make it any easier.'

'So you comforted yourself with Miss Baker – until she'd had enough, and told you where to go. That must have made you angry.'

Bishop shrugged. 'Not especially. There are plenty of girls like her about. Come on, Inspector – we're all allowed a little fun, aren't we? What my wife doesn't know can't hurt her.'

'Except it's not your wife who's been hurt, is it, Mr Bishop?' Penrose stood up, convinced they were wasting their time with the man in front of him. 'Give your details to Sergeant Fallowfield. If your wife confirms what you say, you'll be free to go.'

Men like Lionel Bishop brought out the worst in Penrose and he left the room seething. He was on his way up the stairs when Fallowfield called him back. 'We need to hold on to him for a bit, Sir.'

'It's a waste of time, Bill. He didn't care enough about Marjorie when she was alive to want her dead.'

'Maybe not, Sir, but I'm wondering who's giving an alibi to whom?'

'What do you mean?' Penrose asked, taking the slip of paper that Fallowfield held out to him.

'It's his wife, Sir, Sylvia Bishop. At work, she goes under her maiden name of Timpson – and she works at the Cowdray Club.'

Celia Bannerman paused halfway down the Cowdray Club's main staircase, listening to the reassuring sounds of business proceeding as usual on the floor below. No matter how busy she was, she always found time to linger here, in one of the most beautiful areas of the building. The staircase was a magnificent feature of the original mansion house which had been left unaltered during the conversion to club and college and, as such, was the only part of the organisation to have an old-world feel about it. Grandiose paintings of ancient Rome covered the walls and ceiling, arguably the work of Sir James Thornhill, Hogarth's father-in-law and one of the best known mural artists of his day. That the staircase had survived undamaged to enjoy a new existence was a tangible reminder of the past amid an ever-improving present, a symbol of earlier achievements and a firm foundation for those still to come.

Or so, at least, she hoped. The recent unrest at the club, her constant battles with Miriam Sharpe over the future of the organisation and, in a different way, her conversations with Josephine Tey about the past had made Celia take stock of her life: on the whole, she was satisfied with what she had achieved – satisfied, but appalled at how quickly the years had passed and, if she were honest, a little afraid of what the future might hold for her. Her early training as a nurse, before she went to Holloway, seemed like only yesterday but it had, she realised now, been the inspiration for everything she had done since. She could still remember the shock of those first few months on the ward, when she felt more like a charwoman than a young girl with a vocation to help the sick. Nursing at that time was little more than hard physical labour, often in nauseating conditions, and she had bitterly resented the fact that her goodwill and sense of duty had been so cynically exploited, that she and those who worked alongside her were expected to give so much of themselves in return for so little. Disillusioned and exhausted, she had abandoned her ambitions to reach sister or matron level just a few weeks after finishing her probationary period.

Ironically, it took the people she met in the prison service to restore her faith in the ideal of nursing and, although conditions were little better when she returned to the profession a couple of years later, she was, by then, armed with the determination to do something about it. After one or two administrative posts in hospitals in the north, she had been offered a senior position at Anstey and had jumped at the chance to train the nurses and teachers of the future; then came the war, and another generation of idealistic women had dedicated itself to the service of the sick and wounded, only to be financially and emotionally drained by the sacrifice. At Lady Cowdray's request, Celia had left the sheltered environment of Anstey – which had, in any case, been tainted by Elizabeth Sach's death – and thrown all her energies into the movement for reform, always with a commitment to education as the way forward. She had been instrumental in many milestones – training courses for nurses, scholarships for public health work and midwifery, the creation of a library of nursing and a student nurses' association – but nothing gave her greater satisfaction than her involvement in the College of Nursing and Cowdray Club. Thanks to the drive for modernisation, nursing was no longer an isolated, enclosed profession, but was beginning to compete with other walks of life, where women earned new freedoms and rewards every day; Lady Cowdray's death had been a blow, but it made those who had worked with her even more determined to carry on her vision – and, no matter what Miriam Sharpe said, surely they had come too far now for all that good work to be undone by those who refused to leave the past behind?

Celia moved on down the stairs, pleased to see that the foyer and lounge were busy. Saturday lunch was always popular, and small groups of women – some dressed in work clothes, others in town for a day's shopping – stood around chatting, waiting for a free table in the dining room. She recognised one or two regulars, and stopped to talk to them on her way through to the office.

'Bannerman!' Surprised, Celia turned round. 'Just the woman I was looking for, God help me.' It was barely half past one, but Geraldine Ashby seemed to have been in the bar for some time. She stood in the doorway now, making no effort to conceal her anger. 'I think you need to explain a few things to me. Starting with why you let a vulnerable young woman in your care string herself up in a fucking gymnasium.'

The silence which descended on the foyer was swift and unsettling, and Celia felt it as abruptly as if she had been suddenly plunged under water. She reddened with embarrassment and anger, but managed to keep the emotions out of her voice when she spoke. 'Whatever you've got to say to me, Geraldine, I think it would be better if it were done in private, when you've sobered up a little.'

'Yes, I'm sure you do. I'm sure that being involved in a young girl's death doesn't sit well with your professional pride *or* your social ambitions.'

'Elizabeth Price's suicide was a tragedy and a senseless waste of life, but there was nothing I could have done to stop it.'

'So it was all her own fault? You make me sick. You speak as if you had nothing to do with Lizzie until she killed herself, but let's not forget who set the tone of her life in the first place. You gave her an existence which was based entirely on lies, then tore her away from the one thing that had any truth in it. If anyone set her up to tie that rope around her neck, you did.'

'Her mother never wanted Lizzie to know who she was, and if by . . .'

'Her mother lost the right to dictate to Lizzie when she killed someone else's baby and got caught.'

'. . . and if by the one thing of truth you mean your friend-ship with her – well, a friendship like that wasn't what she needed. Sixteen was far too young to come under that sort of influence – we all agreed that, especially your parents.'

'What the fuck did it have to do with them? Or with any of you? I loved her.'

'Perhaps you thought you did, but I'm sure you don't need me to point out why that could never happen. We were simply looking out for Elizabeth's best interests.'

'So where were you when she really needed you? When she found out the truth and wanted someone who knew about her history to help her understand?'

'You're right,' Celia admitted. 'I should have done more to help, but it wasn't only me who was found lacking. At least spare some of the blame for the person who told her.'

'You think I don't? I curse myself every day for writing that letter, but she had a right to know who she was.'

'You told her?' Celia could hardly believe what she was

hearing, and the relief she felt after all these years was so great and so sudden that it made her speak without thinking. 'So you were responsible for her death,' she said, walking over to Geraldine. 'Doesn't that tell you anything about the sort of love you offered?'

She felt the sting on her cheek before she was conscious of what had happened. Someone moved across to restrain Geraldine before she could hit her again, then a voice cut through the room – stern and authoritative – ordering everyone to calm down, and Celia recognised the policeman who had been at the club the day before. 'Are you all right, Miss Bannerman?' he asked, coming over to her. She nodded, still too shocked to speak, and he introduced the man with him. 'This is Detective Inspector Penrose.'

'Inspector Penrose – I wasn't expecting you,' she said, knowing how ridiculous that sounded, but unable to think of anything else. 'I thought the sergeant and I had covered everything we needed to when we spoke yesterday.'

'I'm afraid that's not why we're here, Miss Bannerman,' Penrose said, inviting her to step away from the crowd. She noticed that his voice remained relaxed and attractive despite the formality of the situation. 'I need to ask you some questions in connection with the murder of Marjorie Baker.'

'Marjorie Baker? The Motley girl?'

'That's right. Her body was found this morning at the studios in St Martin's Lane. Is there somewhere a little more private we could talk?'

Penrose followed Celia Bannerman up the stairs and across a broad landing on to a mezzanine level which seemed to be devoted almost entirely to offices. After the elegance and grandeur of the entrance hall and public areas, the monastic simplicity of the secretary's room seemed to belong to a different building altogether. The oak furniture was tastefully expensive but minimal – just a desk, two upright chairs and a storage cupboard in each alcove. As far as Penrose could see, the only items which were decorative rather than functional were three matching Chinese vases on the mantelpiece, and he wondered if the room's austerity was a result of Celia Bannerman's personal taste, or simply a reflection of the practical economy of nursing. Her desk – usually such a good indicator of somebody's habits and preferences – suggested the former: there were no photographs, no ornaments, no books – nothing, in fact, which could have been said to belong to the person rather than to the organisation.

He took the seat that was offered to him, and waited while she removed a small powder compact from her bag and examined the red mark on her cheek, less concerned about the physical damage, Penrose guessed, than about the public embarrassment which it represented. 'If I weren't already ashamed of what happened downstairs, I would be now,' she said, snapping the mirror shut and throwing it down on the desk. 'Your business here makes our squabbles seem very petty, no matter how rooted in tragedy they may be.'

'May I ask what this particular squabble was about?'

'A mistake I made twenty years ago. How strange that it should have chosen this particular moment to come back to haunt me.'

'Strange in what way?'

'In that it may have something to do with why you're here, Inspector – although I don't see quite why Miss Baker's death should bring you to the Cowdray Club.'

241

Intrigued, Penrose answered her question first. 'I under-stand you had some dealings with Miss Baker in connection with Monday's charity gala?'

'That's correct. She'd been here a number of times to deliver or collect things on behalf of Motley, most recently yesterday. I didn't see her then, but I saw her later in the day at the studios in St Martin's Lane. She was involved in the final fittings.'

'And several of your members went for those fittings yesterday?'

'Yes, four of us. Myself, Mary Size, Miriam Sharpe and Lady Ashby.' To her credit, she spoke the final name without any resentment. 'They're not the only people who are having dresses made, but the others weren't able to fit in an appoint-ment yesterday.'

'At the moment, we're investigating a number of possible reasons for Miss Baker's death,' Penrose said, 'but, for the purposes of elimination, I do need to ask everyone who saw her yesterday where they were last night between the hours of nine o'clock and midnight.'

She looked at him in surprise. 'Are you really asking me to provide an alibi, Inspector? Well, I'm afraid I don't have one. I live on the premises, and I was alone in my rooms all evening. I had an early dinner, and came straight upstairs at about eight o'clock. After that, I didn't see any of the other members and no one saw me except the housemaid who brought me up some cocoa.'

'Who was that, Miss Bannerman?'

'Her name's Tilly Jenkins.'

'And what time did she bring the drink up?'

'Just after eleven, I suppose. I couldn't sleep, and I remem-ber hearing the clock strike the hour. Look, Inspector,' she added impatiently, 'will you allow me to save you some time?' He nodded. 'I'm sure you're being very conscientious in following every strand of Marjorie Baker's existence, but there is one which might prove more profitable than the rest.'

Being quite so blatantly patronised was a new experience for Penrose, but he was too interested to show his resentment. 'Then I'd be grateful if you'd point me in the right direction,' was all he said.

'I don't like breaking a confidence and everyone has their right to privacy, but Lady Ashby has just been kind enough to point out the dangers of secrecy and perhaps she's right. Are you familiar with the name Amelia Sach, Inspector?'

He was too surprised to continue the exchange of sarcasm. 'The baby farmer? Yes, I am. In fact, a friend of mine is currently researching the case. She tells me that you were Mrs Sach's warder in Holloway.'

'Ah, so you're Josephine's friend from Scotland Yard – the one who owes her so many favours.'

It amused Penrose to hear Josephine's public interpretation of their relationship, but he would have plenty of time to tease her about that later. Now, he needed some answers. 'What does Marjorie Baker have to do with Amelia Sach?' he asked.

'Strictly speaking, nothing,' she said infuriatingly, although he sensed that she was simply looking for the best way to explain rather than deliberately leading him round in circles. 'Amelia must have been dead for several years by the time Marjorie was born. But she *is* connected to the family. You know a little about the Sachs' story from Josephine, I'm sure, but it's what happened later that might help you find out who killed Marjorie.' Penrose nodded, keen to learn as much as he could about the Bakers' past, and sensing that he would get much more from a comparative stranger than he had been able to find out in Campbell Road. 'Well, it involves a certain amount of putting two and two together but, if I'm right, Jacob Sach – Amelia's husband – is Marjorie's father.'

'You mean the Bakers adopted her?' He was surprised. Maria Baker had struck him as someone whose own children were far too much of a burden for her to consider taking in other people's on a long-term basis.

'No, no, more than that – I'm not making myself clear. The Finchley case attracted a lot of publicity and comment, even by the standards of the crime – and if Josephine has her way, it will be resurrected for another generation.' Penrose was tempted to argue, but the story was too important to interrupt. 'Part of the strength of feeling was due to the horror which infanticide always causes, but part of it was due to Amelia Sach herself. She'd set herself up as a model of respectability, you see, caring for young women whom society judged too harshly, earning a living through her own initiative, working her way up the social scale – and it was all a front. Amelia was well known in the neighbourhood, she'd run several so-called nursing homes in Finchley – and her disgrace was an impossible burden to carry for those who were left behind after her execution. Apart from the stigma, there was also a very real possibility that one of the mothers who had unwittingly given up her child to be murdered would come looking for revenge. Sach is an easy name to trace, after all.'

'So he changed it to something less recognisable. Jacob Sach became Joseph Baker.'

'Exactly. Baker was his mother's maiden name, I believe. There was much talk at the time of how involved he might or might not have been in Amelia's business, and I can't tell you what the truth of that was. I suspect only he really knows. But he did everything he could to distance himself from his wife's crimes after the trial. He left Jacob Sach behind in that house in Finchley and moved away to make a new start as Joseph Baker. It was easy enough to do back then, and he didn't waste any time. I believe the "For Sale" notice went up on the day of the execution.'

'And you knew all this at the time?'

'Yes.'

'I don't mean any disrespect, but it seems a lot of information for a prison warder to hold.'

She took the comment as it was meant. 'I'd be the first to admit that I wasn't ideal prison officer material, Inspector Penrose. I never quite managed the art of detachment that's so important if you want to be good at the job. I got far too involved in the lives of those women – that's partly why I didn't stay at Holloway for very long. I thought I could solve all their problems.' She smiled sadly. 'In fact, all you can ever do for a woman inside is treat her like a human being and try to remain one yourself, but it's hard not to make promises you can't keep, particularly in the condemned cells – you say what they want to hear because you think they'll never know the difference. I sat for hours at a time with Amelia during the last three weeks of her life, and I got to know her – better than I knew any of my colleagues at that prison, better than I know most people here. When your time is precious, you talk about what matters – and what mattered to Amelia was her daughter.' She held up her hands when she saw his face. 'Yes, I know what you're thinking – the irony of that is quite remarkable when you consider her crimes, but Amelia would have made an excellent prison warder: her detachment from the reality of what she

245

had done never faltered. To this day, I don't know if she sensed that I was malleable and manipulated the situation or if she was simply desperate and poured her heart out – either way, I heard myself promising to look out for her child when she was gone.'

'That was very generous.'

'You mean very stupid.'

'Perhaps naive would be fairer. That was why you were in touch with her husband?'

'Yes. Amelia didn't trust him to look after Lizzie properly, although I don't think she ever dreamt that he'd give her up.'

'And why *did* he?'

'I can only guess, but I think she reminded him too much of Amelia. Lizzie was the spitting image of her mother.'

'That seems very hard on the child.'

'Perhaps, but I suppose there's precious little room in a fresh start for the mirror image of what you're running from. I never asked him why he did what he did – it wasn't my business and I was all too conscious of having overstepped the mark already.'

'So what happened?'

'I went to see him two days before the execution. It was entirely unofficial, of course – I would have been dismissed instantly for making any contact with a prisoner's family. But I'd promised Amelia that I'd talk to Jacob, offer him some help if he needed it, and I wanted to be able to look her in the eye before she died and tell her that I'd fulfilled my promise.' She got up and walked over to the window which looked out on to Henrietta Street. 'It was snowing then, as I recall. Winter is always so exciting before Christmas, and so depressing afterwards. Anyway, I found the house and knocked before I could change my mind. When Jacob came to the door, he didn't recognise me at first; he'd seen me often enough at the prison when he came to visit his wife, but people look different out of context, and he thought I'd been sent by a newspaper – he'd had several reporters hanging round the house from the moment Amelia was arrested. He let me in eventually, and there was a desolation about that place, a bleakness that I've never seen before or since. As we went through to the kitchen, I noticed that all the rooms had been stripped bare. Lizzie was nowhere to be seen, and Jacob had started drinking heavily by then. There was a box absolutely crammed with empty bottles in the yard.'

She sighed heavily at the memory of it all, and sat back down at her desk. 'To cut a long story short, I told him why I'd come and asked if there was anything I could do to help with Lizzie. He didn't hesitate: he told me that if I really wanted to help, I could take the child off his hands, the sooner the better.'

'That must have put you in a very difficult position.'

'It did. I could hardly go back and tell Amelia that her daughter was about to lose her father as well as her mother, but I could see for myself that it wasn't in Elizabeth's best interests to stay in that house.' The phrase echoed what she had said to Geraldine Ashby in the foyer, and Penrose wondered how many decisions she had made for other people over the years. 'From what I could see, Jacob intended to drink himself to death as soon as possible,' she added, 'and he wasn't about to let a child stand in his way. Then he threw a pile of papers across the table at me – letters, all from women who had contacted Amelia Sach, requesting to adopt a child.'

Penrose was astonished. 'But my understanding was that

247

there was never any truth in the adoption story. I thought it was just a front for what she really did?'

'No, Inspector. It was never as straightforward as that. Not all the children were adopted, obviously, but some were.'

'And did you show these letters to the police? It might have affected the case.'

She looked at him like a parent looks at a child who insists on the existence of the tooth fairy. 'The police knew all about them already. As far as they were concerned, they had linked Amelia to the murder of one baby and that was enough to hang her. They weren't interested in any of the other children who might have passed through her establishment.'

'What did you do?'

'I told Jacob I'd take care of it, but that he'd have to give me time. Then I took the letters, parcelled them up and sent them to one of the charities that looks after children's welfare, together with an anonymous letter explaining the situation. Please don't look at me like that, Inspector – I know I went too far. I should never have let myself become emotionally involved, but it was such a desperate situation and I just wanted to help. And sure enough, within a few days of Amelia's execution, someone had been in touch with Jacob and the adoption was arranged. None of the women who wrote got the child, of course, but Phyllida Ashby had a lot to do with that; she was on the board of the charity, and the child went to her housekeeper. But it was all done legally and it worked out well, for a while at least – Lizzie could have made a good life for herself if she'd been allowed to leave her past behind. I don't know how much you heard of what went on downstairs, but I stand by what I said to Lady Ashby – she had no business playing with things she didn't understand.'

'Although you said your mistake was twenty years ago, not thirty.'

'Implying that what I feel truly guilty about is what happened then, rather than the original act? Yes, I suppose it is. I prided myself on knowing when my pupils needed help, but I was wrong. It would have been terrible if it had been any of those girls, but it was worse because it was Elizabeth. It felt like I'd betrayed two people – her, and Amelia.'

Penrose was interested in the extent to which Celia Bannerman continued to talk of Sach as a friend rather than a prisoner, even now, but he was keen to move the story on. 'Did anybody ever find out what you'd done?'

'I admitted it to Phyllida later, when any possibility of reprimand was past. Our paths crossed on the board of several charities, and naturally I was interested in Elizabeth's progress.'

'Did you have any contact with Jacob Sach after the adoption?'

'Yes, when his daughter died. I'm afraid I didn't believe him when he said he never wanted to hear her name again – proof that naivety doesn't relate to age, I suppose.'

'You wrote to him in Essex?'

'No, I went to see him in person. He turned me away without shedding a tear.'

'But you didn't know anything about his new family?'

'No. He was hardly going to invite me in to talk about old times over a cup of tea.'

'Then how did you know about Marjorie? Baker is a common enough name – you said yourself, that was the point of his taking it – so I don't understand why you would assume that the girl doing your dress fittings was part of that history?'

'You're right. I would never have thought anything of it, but when I went to Motley last Friday, I saw a man outside in the street. I noticed him because he was talking to Marjorie Baker and I knew his face, but I simply couldn't place it. It had been driving me to distraction, but even then I don't think I'd have remembered him if I hadn't been digging up the past with Josephine. Talking about those years brought it all back, and last night I remembered – he'd aged, and life had obviously not been kind, but it was him. That was why I couldn't sleep – if I'm honest, those years are ones I would prefer to forget.'

'But you're sure about all this?'

'I'm sure that the man I saw outside Motley with Marjorie was Jacob Sach – as I said, the rest is putting two and two together, but it makes sense to assume that a young girl called Baker who associated with him was his daughter.'

It made sense to Penrose, too, and if this was the secret that Marjorie had been killed to protect, the obvious suspects were the ones closest to home. Just for a second, he doubted his instinctive dismissal of Joseph Baker as a candidate for his daughter's murder, and wondered if there was another explanation for the corroborative evidence which Spilsbury had given him; but then he thought about Maria Baker – her unemotional reaction to her daughter's death, the fight which the two women had allegedly had in the street, the jealousy and the resentment. What was her past, he wondered, and how much had she suffered because of the stigma attached to her husband's name? Did she even know about it? He wished now that he'd been firmer with her rather than trying to respect a grief which wasn't there; he would have to see her again immediately.

When he looked up, he realised that Celia Bannerman was

waiting for an answer from him, but he had been too distracted with his own thoughts to hear the question. 'I said, have you spoken to Miss Baker's father yet?' she repeated impatiently.

'I'm afraid that's not possible,' Penrose replied, and he saw in her face that his tone had told her what his words had not.

'He's not dead as well, surely?'

'Yes. His body was found at the same time as his daughter's.'

'At Motley?' she asked. He nodded, and she was quiet for a long time. 'Another life destroyed by those crimes,' she said at last. 'If only Amelia could have known how far the violence would spread. Can I ask – was he murdered as well?'

'I'm not in a position to say at the moment, I'm afraid.' Her wry glance suggested that she knew what that meant, but she said nothing. 'Did Jacob Sach recognise *you* when you saw him last week?'

'To my knowledge, he didn't even see me. He was deep in conversation with Miss Baker at the time, and he didn't seem to be taking much notice of what was going on in the street around him.'

'And did Marjorie ever give you any indication that she knew about her family background, or your connection with it?'

'No. She talked generally about the weather and the gala, and she asked me a lot of questions about myself, but that was simply professional curiosity.' She smiled. 'You couldn't be expected to know this, Inspector, but there's a certain etiquette shared by hairdressers and dress fitters which demands that they affect an interest in their clients. It gives us the impression that we matter to them, and it glosses over the more embarrassing intimacies which we have to endure to look respectable. Miss Baker was very good at it – she was always pleasant, and had a healthy appetite for inconsequential detail.'

'And you didn't say anything to her?'

Her reply was a frosty look. 'Of course not.'

'But someone must have told her.'

She shrugged. 'I can't help you there. Perhaps her father let it slip – he was obviously still a drinker. Is her mother alive?'

'Yes.'

'She probably didn't know herself, though. I can't imagine he'd feel the need to be entirely honest at the beginning of a new relationship.'

'No, although I got the impression they'd been married for a long time. Marjorie was among the youngest of eight children. Anyway, we can easily establish that now we know what we're looking for, so thank you for the information. Of course, Marjorie might have found something out in prison – I'm sure gossip has a longer life in Holloway than in most places, doesn't it?'

'Yes, now you mention it,' she said, although it seemed to take her a second to understand what he meant. 'And I suppose no one can disappear entirely – not even Jacob Sach can have rolled up every carpet behind him.'

It was an apposite phrase. 'And in all these years, you've never mentioned his new identity to anyone?'

'Absolutely not. It was never my secret to give away.'

'You weren't even tempted to point Josephine in the right direction?' he asked, imagining what she would have given for the opportunity of five minutes in a room with Jacob Sach. 'She told me that you'd helped as much as you could.'

'It's not the stuff of fiction, Inspector. I would have thought that you of all people would know enough about the debris of crime to realise that it isn't a subject for fireside entertainment.'

'That isn't my impression of what Josephine's trying to achieve.'

'Perhaps not, but her digging has already caused trouble between myself and Lady Ashby, and I can't imagine that either of us is happier now because we know more than we did last week. I'm sure Josephine's intentions are good,' she added, and Penrose resisted the temptation to mention stones and glass houses, 'but what she's doing isn't right.'

'Even if it helps people come to terms with what's happened to them? I can understand why you would want to put certain things behind you, but burying the past can hurt the victims of a crime as much as it silences the perpetrators. It isn't the best way of ensuring justice.'

She scoffed. 'When did you last read a crime novel that was about justice, Inspector?'

'That's a question for my sergeant, I'm afraid – he reads more of them than I do. But he would probably tell you that *A Pin to See the Peepshow* did more to highlight the flaws in the Thompson and Bywaters case than any amount of campaigning has managed.'

'By encouraging a popular readership to simplify a complex issue?' She shook her head, and Penrose wondered why he felt as if, of the two of them, he was the one lacking in legal experience. 'Anyway, now that the past seems to have come crashing into the present, perhaps you can discourage Josephine from taking her project too far.'

'Josephine will do as she likes,' he said, and his smile – although polite – did not entirely mask his irritation.

'Yes,' she said, softening suddenly, 'I seem to remember that she usually did.' He opened his mouth to speak, but she interrupted him. 'Please forgive me for being so harsh, Inspector, but that time at Anstey was a moment of real crisis in my life, and that's very hard to admit to a former pupil – vanity gets in the way of honesty. It's hard to explain, but I look at Josephine whenever she's staying at the Cowdray Club and I see a successful, independent woman with so much still ahead of her – and people adore her, though she doesn't look for it, sometimes she doesn't even notice it. From the way you leap to her defence, I imagine you understand that yourself.'

Penrose was furious with himself for allowing his hesitation to acknowledge the truth of what she said, and his response was uncharacteristically simplistic. 'You envy Josephine's success,' he said.

'No, not at all. Please don't misunderstand me, Inspector – I've got an enviable career of my own to look back on. The improvements in nursing and in administration which I've helped to make will last, and women's lives will be the better for it. I don't regret any of the decisions I've made about my life, and I'm content. Not happy. Content. But every now and again, respected, contented women of my age wonder what they might have missed. It doesn't last long, and we don't get hysterical about it, but it's there.'

As she spoke, she opened the top right-hand drawer of her desk and took out an envelope, which she passed across the desk to him. Penrose opened it and took out a single page of the Bible, roughly torn from the rest of the book. It was from the Song of Solomon, and, across the top, two words were written in pencil: 'Thank you.'

'Amelia gave me that on the eve of her execution,' she

explained. 'It comforted me until Elizabeth died, and it's haunted me ever since. You see, Inspector, when you make a decision that your work will be your entire life, it's important to get that right. If you don't, you feel that you've failed on more than a professional level; you feel that you've failed as a woman. When Elizabeth Price committed suicide, I had no right to mourn her, except as a teacher mourns the loss of a pupil; I wasn't her mother, I wasn't even her friend. More to the point, I couldn't think of anyone whose death would change my personal life rather than my professional one – and I suppose that made me wonder if it was all worth it. After Lady Cowdray died, things changed here, and now I find myself wondering that again.' She paused, apparently embarrassed by her own frankness, and then added more cynically: 'You press on as if it *were* worth it, though, don't you? To admit the lie would be unbearable.'

'Why are you telling me this, Miss Bannerman?' Penrose asked, unable to put his finger on why their conversation had taken quite such a personal turn.

'I don't really know,' she admitted. 'I suppose it's because what Lady Ashby said has touched a nerve. If you'd come an hour later, I might have had a chance to compose myself and you might not have had to listen to a middle-aged woman's regrets when you're trying to conduct a murder investigation.'

She smiled and stood to dismiss him, but Penrose was not quite ready to leave. He had come here to find out more about the Cowdray Club and the women in that photograph, and, although what Celia Bannerman had told him suggested that Maria Baker might only have mentioned the picture as a ploy to direct his attention away from her door, he still wanted some answers. 'I've got just a few more questions, Miss Bannerman, if you don't mind,' he said evenly. 'I won't keep you much longer.' Irritated, she sat down again. 'Do people sign in and out when they leave the club?'

'It's a private club, Inspector, not a prison. Trust me – I know the difference. We don't expect our members to report to us if they want to leave the building.'

'But there's always someone on reception?'

'Yes, all day, and we have a night porter who takes over at ten o'clock.'

'What about other ways in and out?'

'There's another entrance in Henrietta Street. Strictly speaking, it's for the College of Nursing, but there's nothing to stop members of the club using it if it's more convenient.'

'And there's no one on that door.'

'No. It's locked at midnight, so your murderer may just have got back in time.'

Penrose ignored the sarcasm; the rapid change from deeply personal information to the most basic of police questioning seemed bizarre even to him. 'So there's no way of knowing who was in the building last night?' She shook her head. 'What can you tell me about your receptionist, Miss Timpson? Or should I say Mrs Bishop?'

Celia Bannerman looked at him with a grudging respect. 'Sylvia has been with us since the club opened. She's exceptionally good at her job – conscientious, reliable and always pleasant to the members and their guests. And if she chooses to use her maiden name at work, that's really no business of mine – or, I would have thought, of yours.'

'So she's popular with your members?'

'She's polite and discreet, qualities which are much appreciated by us all. It's not the business of a receptionist to make herself "popular", as you put it.'

'To your knowledge, did she know Marjorie Baker? Other than through the gala, I mean.'

'I couldn't say for sure, but I can't imagine why their paths would have crossed.'

'What about Miriam Sharpe and Lady Ashby? Did Marjorie have much contact with them, either through her work or outside of it? You said yourself – a dress fitting can be quite an intimate affair, and I imagine there are plenty of opportunities for conversation.'

'Inspector Penrose, I have no idea what you're trying to insinuate, but I refuse to discuss the members of this club *or* my colleagues unless you give me a very good reason why I should – and so far, you've failed to do that. You're investigating the death of a seamstress on somebody else's premises. I've made it clear to you that the dead girl came from a family with a lot to hide; even if that has nothing to do with her murder, I would have thought that there were more natural paths to pursue than this one – the people she worked with, for example, or the women she was in Holloway with. Grudges breed very easily within a prison environment, and no one has a longer memory than an ex-convict. The Cowdray Club is vulnerable enough at the moment without your help and, if you persist with this line of questioning, you will leave me no choice but to complain to your superior.'

'Please feel free to speak to the chief constable, Miss Bannerman, but I know that his wife will be reassured to know that we're making good progress in getting to the bottom of the spiteful letters that seem to be disturbing her sleep at the moment.'

It was a comment made without any substance whatsoever, but it had the desired effect: for the first time in the entire interview, Celia Bannerman seemed at a disadvantage. 'What can those letters possibly have to do with the murder of Marjorie Baker?' she asked cautiously.

'That's precisely what I'm trying to find out,' Penrose said, 'but it's highly likely that there is a connection.'

'By "connection", I assume you mean that you think Marjorie Baker sent them? Why would you jump to that conclusion?'

'There are aspects of this murder which suggest that Miss Baker was killed to keep her quiet,' he began, and this time he refused to let her interrupt. 'Yes, I know what you're about to say, and I agree with you – what you've told me about her family history is a very credible motive for her murder. However, I have to investigate every possibility, and Marjorie's mother has shown me a photograph which she believes may have something to do with her daughter's death.'

'A photograph?' She looked concerned and with good reason, Penrose thought: if Marjorie had sent those letters and been killed for it, the implications for the Cowdray Club's reputation were much more serious than Celia Bannerman could ever have imagined, and she was certainly intelligent enough to realise that. 'The photograph was in *Tatler* last month. You were in it yourself.'

'Yes, I remember it – the one taken at Motley.'

'That's right. Mrs Baker seemed to think that Marjorie was being forced by her father into doing something as a result of that photograph. Obviously, in light of what you've said, I'll need to talk to Mrs Baker again to find out if she knew who her husband really was and, if so, how she fits into that history – but I can't ignore other possibilities.'

'Miss Baker might have sent the notes, I suppose, but I don't see how she'd have gathered the information. I hate to say it, but I always assumed they were sent from within the organisation.'

'She was friends with a Lucy Peters – they were in prison together and kept in touch afterwards. I understand that Miss Peters works here.'

'Yes, she's a housemaid. She's been here for a few months, but we're not in the habit of allowing housemaids access to personal information.'

'Even so, they have a way of finding out. There was a small silver photograph frame found on Miss Baker's body. It matches the description of one of the items which has been reported missing from the club, and it's possible that the two girls were involved in both the thefts and the anonymous letters.'

She thought about it, and then said reluctantly: 'It's Lucy's half day today, but I'll speak to her as soon as she comes in this evening.'

'I'd be grateful if you'd leave that to me. Just let us know as soon as she's back.'

'Fine, but please be gentle with her. These letters haven't made any financial demands on their recipients, so I really don't see what Marjorie and Lucy would stand to gain by sending them. I still believe your answer lies with the Sach family – in which case Lucy will have lost a good friend on top of everything else she's been through.' Penrose looked questioningly at her. 'Lucy got herself into trouble in more ways than one before she went to prison,' she explained. 'She had a child while she was in Holloway, and had to give it up – and it affected her very badly. She still hasn't quite got over it – if you ever do, that is.'

'Please don't worry – we're not in the habit of bullying witnesses,' Penrose said pleasantly, and was satisfied to see that his own condescension had not gone unnoticed. 'I appreciate what you're saying, but there's no reason why the answer shouldn't lie with the Sach family *and* the Cowdray Club – after all, you have a link to both, and we now know that Lady Ashby does, as well. Assuming that what you say is correct, Marjorie Baker was Elizabeth Sach's half-sister.' The idea seemed not to have occurred to her, so he let it sink in a little before asking: 'What about Miriam Sharpe and Mary Size? Could they have any links back to Amelia Sach?'

'Mary's been at Holloway for about eight years,' she said doubtfully, 'so apart from being deputy governor at the prison which hanged her, I can't see any connection.' She was about to dismiss Miriam Sharpe out of hand, then seemed to change her mind. 'Come to think of it, Amelia once told me that she had met Walters at St Thomas's Hospital – you knew they were both nurses?' Penrose nodded. 'Miriam was matron at St Thomas's for many years, and she worked her way up before that. You'd have to check the dates with her, but it's possible that they might have been there at the same time.'

Penrose shut his notebook and stood up. 'Thank you, Miss Bannerman, you've been very helpful. Either I or my officers will need to speak to the members who knew Miss Baker, and to some of your staff – Miss Peters and Miss Timpson in particular. We'll be as discreet as possible.'

'Thank you, Inspector – I appreciate that. You already know, I'm sure, that Motley will be moving into the club for a few days to get ready for the gala?'

He nodded. 'I knew they intended to ask you if that would be possible.'

'Yes. I didn't know at the time what had led to the request – Lettice said she would explain later – but, under the circumstances, I'm even more glad to be able to help. It's very good of them to go ahead with the gala at all. I assume you have no objections to the arrangement?'

'None whatsoever.'

'Good. And I'll make sure that you and your officers have the Cowdray Club's full co-operation with your investigation.'

It was an uneasy truce, but Penrose was more than satisfied with what he had learned from Celia Bannerman. The interview had taken longer than anticipated, and Fallowfield was waiting for him at reception when he went back downstairs. His sergeant listened calmly to what he had to say, but Penrose could tell that Fallowfield was as excited as he was. 'Back to the Bunk, then, Sir.'

'We certainly need to talk to Maria Baker again right away, but I'd like to do it more formally this time – she doesn't strike me as someone who'll be easily unsettled, but an interview at the station might give us the advantage. You might as well get Waddingham and Merrifield off the telephones and send them round to Campbell Road to pick her up. For God's sake tell them to be gentle, though – the woman's just lost a daughter and a husband, and we don't know that she had anything to do with it. She's not under arrest – not yet, anyway. We just need some answers. In the meantime, I've got a couple more questions here. Has Lady Ashby calmed down yet?'

'Yes, Sir. I've had a chat with her, and she seems genuinely shocked by Miss Baker's death – shocked, and upset. She's confirmed everything that Mrs Reader told you about last night, even down to asking the girl out, and it *was* her who

took the vodka in. She volunteered everything freely enough –
I didn't have to push her.'

'Not too freely, though? You believed her?'

'Yes, Sir. As far as I can see, she says what she means and
does as she likes. You know how it is with the aristocracy. She's
a bit worse for wear, though – I think that explains what we
walked in on.'

'Probably,' Penrose said, although it was his private opinion
that the temptation to slap Celia Bannerman might prove
hard to overcome whether you were drunk or sober. 'What
about an alibi?'

'She was at the Ham Bone Club until after midnight. I've
checked it out, and both the owner and the barman confirm
that she was there all night. She's also given me the names of
some friends she left with, if we want to take it any further.'

'Good, although if she's a regular there, I imagine they'll
confirm anything she wants them to. Is she still here?'

'Yes, Sir – in the bar. There's a room next door we can use if
you want somewhere more private, though.'

'The bar's fine – I want her to be happy to talk. What else?'

'Lucy Peters is off duty. She left the building just after one
and no one's seen her since. Sylvia Timpson doesn't work
Saturdays.'

'So I gather. We'll have to try her at home.'

'Mary Size is at the prison. I've made an appointment for
you at three-thirty.'

'Good.' Penrose looked at his watch. 'You told her what it
was about?'

'Yes. She'll have all the records ready for you. She was upset,
as well – you get the feeling that Marjorie was popular everywhere but at home, don't you?' Penrose remembered the

expression on Ronnie's face, and nodded. 'She asked about Peters right away, Sir. She's worried about her – the two of them were close, apparently. I've asked reception to let us know immediately if they see her.'

'Excellent. I've asked Miss Bannerman to do the same. I'll have a quick word with Lady Ashby, then I'll go to Holloway and you can take Timpson.'

'What about her husband?'

'I don't think he's got anything to do with it, but it won't hurt him to wait a bit longer, will it?' Fallowfield smiled. 'At least until I've spoken to his wife. Can't say I blame her for not wanting to take his name, though.'

He found Geraldine Ashby keeping company with a bottle of cognac. 'Is the bitch pressing charges, then?' she asked as he walked in.

Penrose sat down opposite her. 'If you mean Miss Bannerman, I seem to have forgotten to give her the opportunity.'

He smiled, and she looked surprised. 'Good God – two understanding policemen in one day. In that case, I'll forgive you for preventing me from finishing what I started. Bannerman got off lightly, which is more than Marjorie did, by the sound of it.'

She nodded towards the bottle, but Penrose shook his head. 'Not just now, thanks. Do you mind if I ask you some questions?'

'Be my guest. As you can see, I'm not going anywhere.'

She spoke evenly, and he would never have guessed the level of the bottle from her voice, but the intoxication which Fallowfield had spoken of was obvious in her eyes and in the way her hand shook when she lit a cigarette. 'Did Marjorie ever tell you anything about her family when you saw her at Motley?'

'No,' she said instantly, but Penrose's initial disappointment was short-lived. 'She didn't know anything about them herself.'

'What do you mean?'

'Just that. The first time I met her, she asked me what it felt like to be able to trace your family back for generations, because she only knew her parents and her brothers and sisters. I know she didn't get on with either her mother or her father these days, but she said even when she was younger they wouldn't tell her anything about the rest of her family.'

'So she was curious about her own history?'

'Yes – or rather about its absence. She asked me how she might find out more about it, but I told her I wasn't the best person to give that sort of advice – if I want to know anything about my family, I just go and look at a portrait on a wall. I suggested that she was better off not knowing, but she just pointed out that it was easy for me to say that, and of course she was right. She was right about a lot of things, actually.'

'Such as?'

'Such as making the most of your chances and standing on your own two feet. I don't think she meant that as a criticism, although she'd have been justified – let's face it, I live entirely on a monthly allowance which is almost offensively generous. But she was just being honest. I suppose that's what got her killed, is it?'

'Quite possibly. We don't know yet, but we *will* find out and what you've just told me helps.'

'Does it?' she asked. 'Well, I'm glad, because it doesn't help me. You know, sometimes it feels as though every bright thing in this world is snuffed out as soon as it begins to flourish.' She looked directly at him for the first time, and he was struck by how vulnerable she seemed. 'Most of us suspect that, but we spend our time trying to convince ourselves otherwise; in your job, you must know it to be true. I don't know how you do it.'

He was tempted to tell her that neither did he, but such an admission was hardly appropriate. Instead, he stood up to go. 'I'm sorry about what's happened,' he said quietly. 'To Marjorie, and to Elizabeth.'

She raised her glass sadly, and he left her to it. 'Looks like Miss Bannerman was right, then,' Fallowfield said when he was back in the foyer. 'Marjorie found out too much for her own good. Do you want to postpone Miss Size and go straight back to the Yard to see Baker?'

Penrose thought about it. 'No, she'll have a tight schedule and it'll take Waddingham and Merrifield a while to get over to Campbell Road and back. We'll stick to what we said, but don't hang about.'

He was on his way out the door when Fallowfield called him back. 'I've just remembered, Sir – it's something Miss Tey said.' Penrose looked at him curiously. 'It was the other day,' Fallowfield continued guiltily, trying to ignore his inspector's raised eyebrow. 'I bumped into her and she happened to say that she was interested in Sach and Walters – so we had a chat about it.'

'Oh yes? You never mentioned it, Bill.'

'No, Sir – you were too busy. Anyway, I might be wrong, but I'm sure she said that one of the women who gave evidence at the trial was called Edwards.'

'Edwards? As in Maria Baker's family?' Penrose was suddenly serious.

'Yes. This Edwards woman lived in the house. It was her evidence that sealed Sach's fate, apparently. You've just got time to talk to Miss Tey if she's here,' Fallowfield added, trying not to look too smug. 'She might not be Miss bloody Marple, Sir, but she's got a lot of notes.'

Penrose smiled, and went to reception to ask where he might find Josephine.

Chapter Ten

I sat in the car coming home this afternoon and wanted you so much that I stopped breathing. Are your eyes blue or grey, or grey-blue? Grey, aren't they? Perhaps I should never see you again. Perhaps it will take not one, but a hundred and one years to get over you. It's odd, this vivid physical realisation of someone whose body one has never known, and amusing to be scunnered at every physical approach to a new person by a love months old. You are like a ghost, my dear, coming between me and every other human being, but I'll lay you yet – in the accepted sense of the word. And London is lovelier when you are in it.

Josephine put the pages of Marta's diary down for a moment and walked over to the window. The snow in Cavendish Square was looking a little the worse for wear now, having been trampled underfoot by a procession of excited shop workers taking full advantage of their lunch hours, but at her level it was still fresh and magical, settling peacefully on the branches of the trees and, across to her left, providing a striking contrast to one of the city's finer bronzes. The sculpture was of a mother and child, and Josephine had found herself admiring it more on this visit than she ever had before; the stark, tender intensity of the bond between its figures resonated poignantly with the book she was writing.

For the moment, though, her work had been all but forgotten. The narrow bed was covered in a sea of blue paper, and she sat back down amongst it, curled her feet under her, and began to read again; had this been a book, she would have been fascinated by emotions so eloquently and intimately described; as it was, her confusion at being the object of them destroyed any pleasure in the writing.

I am very happy. Last night, I dreamt that we kissed. This is the first time I have dreamed of you. I have not allowed my imaginings to run riot; I have taken nothing from you in my thoughts. But last night, just after I went to sleep, you were there. You moved towards me and I knew, surprisingly, that you would kiss me. I lay looking at you and you took my face in your hands and kissed me. And then I awoke and heard the clock strike in the darkness. This morning, I know more about you than all your books and spoken words have taught me, and if you ask how one dreamed kiss could have shown me this, I cannot answer.

A knock at the door pulled her sharply back from Marta's world, and she looked up impatiently. 'Come in,' she said, and then: 'Archie! What on earth are you doing here? Why didn't you telephone?'

'Don't take this personally, but I didn't really come here to see you.'

'No?' She smiled at him, and started to gather up the pages. 'Well, you certainly know how to humble a girl.'

'Sorry, but I'm here to work and there are a couple of things that you might be able to help me with. Is this a bad time?'

'Of course not. I was just reading a letter from a friend.'

'Obviously one you haven't seen for a while.'

She looked at him sharply. 'What do you mean?'

'Nothing. It just looks like there's a lot of news to catch up on.' He looked curiously at her. 'Are you all right?'

'I'm fine. I wasn't expecting you, that's all.' As she looked around for the envelope, he picked it up from the floor and handed it to her. 'It's been a bit of a morning. Shall we go downstairs and have some coffee? You probably don't want to be surrounded by this mess.'

'I don't mind if you don't.' He pointed to the desk, which was covered in her notes for the new book. 'It's actually this mess that interests me. I need some information about the Sach and Walters case.'

'Do you?' she asked, surprised. 'Why? What's happened?'

Briefly, Archie summarised the events of the morning for her. 'Good God, how awful,' she said when he'd finished. 'How are Ronnie and Lettice?'

'Shaken and devastated, but refusing to admit quite how badly it's affected them. They're moving in downstairs as we speak.'

'In here?'

'Yes. Obviously the workroom's out of bounds so they've talked Celia Bannerman into letting them prepare for the gala on the premises.'

'I'm surprised it's still going ahead.'

'Well, the first thought was to cancel it, but I think they feel they owe it to Marjorie. There was much talk about keeping up the morale of the rest of the staff, but the same applies to them. At least if they're working, they won't dwell on it too much.'

'I suppose so. I'll go down and see them in a minute. But

first tell me what you need to know.' She picked up a sheaf of papers from the desk. 'I can't believe this is happening. I've been living with these people, and I know there's only thirty years between us, but it seemed so much longer. They felt so safe, so . . .'

'So dead?'

'Yes, I suppose that's exactly what I mean. You really think Marjorie's mother might be the Edwards who lived with the Sachs?'

'It seems too big a coincidence otherwise. Tell me what you know about her.'

'I've got all the notes from the newspaper reports of the case, but it's probably quickest if you read this,' she said, removing the most recent chapter from the rest of the manuscript. 'Everything she tells the police in there is taken directly from the evidence she gave at the trial. I've moved it forward to bring her into the story earlier, but it's pretty much verbatim. You'll see how crucial her statement was to Sach's conviction.'

Archie took the pages and read through them carefully. 'This implies that Edwards and Jacob Sach were already having an affair before Amelia was arrested.'

'Yes, but I don't know if that's true,' she admitted. 'All I will say is that the more I read about it, the more convinced I am that she's the linchpin of what went on. At best, she knew what was happening and turned a blind eye; at worst, she was involved and got away with it by providing the evidence for a conviction.'

'But you're not saying that Amelia Sach was completely innocent, and Edwards and Jacob Sach conspired to get her out of the way?'

'I wouldn't go that far, although it has crossed my mind. No, I just think that a lot of people were doing what she was doing, and punishment for baby farming was a lottery, depending on which judge tried your case, whether or not you were allowed a decent defence, and who was around to stab you in the back. Sach and Walters were convicted on the basis of one child's death, but no one bothered to look into what happened to all the other babies who passed through; on the other hand, some of their contemporaries escaped the gallows because the babies they farmed were abandoned rather than killed – but those children would have died, too, if they hadn't been found so quickly, so where do you draw the line?'

It was a rhetorical question, but it echoed what Celia Bannerman had said about the police's attitude to the crime. 'Thanks,' he said. 'This really helps, and I'll let you know how I get on. In the meantime, do you know a housemaid called Lucy Peters?'

'I've met a girl called Lucy here a couple of times – I don't know her second name. What's she got to do with it? Don't tell me – she's Walters's long-lost niece. It would be just like you to come up with a complete set of living, breathing people and leave me grubbing around in old newsprint.'

He laughed. 'No, nothing like that – at least I don't think so. She was a friend of Marjorie Baker's.' She looked thoughtful. 'What is it?'

'She was up here the other night. She said she'd brought a vase up, but she was reading something I'd written about Sach and Walters, and she was crying. She left before I could ask her what was wrong. In hindsight, I probably wasn't very kind to her – I was cross because I found her reading my work.'

'Do you know exactly what she was reading?' Archie asked.

'This, I think.' She sifted through the pages and gave him another chapter. 'You don't think she had anything to do with the murder, do you?'

'No, not really. But I'm hoping she might be able to tell me if Marjorie was up to something that could have got her killed.' He read what he'd been given, and then said: 'Of course, if Marjorie had found out the Baker–Sach connection and confided in Lucy, that would explain why this was so upsetting. Can I borrow it?' She nodded and he stood up to go. 'I'd better make a move. I need to phone the information about Edwards through to the station, and then I've got an appointment at Holloway. Sorry this has been such a hit-and-run visit.'

'Don't worry, I understand.' She thought for a moment, and then said: 'Would it be inappropriate for me to ask for a lift to Holloway?'

'Of course not, but why do you want to go there?'

'Celia told Mary Size what I was doing and she left me an invitation to look round the prison with one of her officers. I'd need to phone to make sure it's convenient, but the note said to come at any time and just to let her know. To be honest, I'm dreading it, but it seems rude not to go. It might not be quite so daunting if I turn up with Scotland Yard.'

'That's fine. I'll phone Miss Size for you now while you get ready.'

'Oh, I'm as ready as I'll ever be,' Josephine said, picking up her coat and gloves. 'What do you wear to look round a prison, anyway?'

She saw him cast a glance at the gardenia as they left, but he said nothing and she followed him down the stairs. When they reached reception, she saw that the Motleys had already made their presence felt: for the time being, the elegant, ordered atmosphere of the Cowdray Club's foyer had given way under the strain of rolls and rolls of fabric, half-made clothes on hangers and a bizarre collection of sewing machines and bric-a-brac. It was a shame that Miss Timpson wasn't on duty, she thought; the look on her face would have been priceless.

'I'll go and make the calls,' Archie said, grimacing at the chaos. 'See you back here in a minute.'

She found the girls in a spacious room leading off the foyer which was usually used for private meetings. 'I take back everything I said about this place being deathly dull,' Ronnie said, dropping the bale she was carrying and coming over to give Josephine a hug. 'The first thing we heard about when we got here was the fight in the foyer, and we half-wondered if we'd have to slap each other as some sort of induction ritual.'

'What fight? What on earth are you talking about?'

'Oh, Geraldine Ashby and the Bannerman woman decided to recreate the Battle of Bosworth in the foyer. The lunchtime queues were getting a bit restless, apparently, so they staged a distraction all of their own.'

'She's exaggerating,' said Lettice, 'but there was a bit of bother. Geraldine slapped Celia because of something she said, and it was all very public.'

'Yes, the skeletons are all so firmly out of the closet that we'll probably end up dressing them for the gala as well,' Ronnie added cynically, hauling another tailor's dummy in from the foyer. 'And if that was lunch, I think I'll book myself in for dinner now. Which is the best table?'

'God, I think that might be all my fault,' Josephine said, and both sisters turned to look quizzically at her. 'It's too long a story to go into now, but I'll tell you later if you're still here.

I've got to go out, but I'm so sorry about what's happened – you must be devastated.'

'Yes, only we could organise the best entertainment three days before the actual event,' Ronnie said bitterly, and Josephine saw Lettice glance anxiously across at her sister; as Archie had said, neither of them seemed particularly willing to acknowledge the shock of what had happened, and there was something frenetic and desperate about Ronnie's movements, as though she were afraid that standing still for too long would force her to confront her grief.

She was about to say something, but was interrupted by a voice from the door. 'Excuse me, I'm Lillian Wyles.' Josephine looked up to see an attractive woman dressed in a Motley smock standing hesitantly outside the room. 'I think you're expecting me.'

'Good God, is that what policewomen look like?' Ronnie muttered. 'No wonder Archie's so keen on welcoming them into the force.'

Lettice hit her hard on the shoulder. 'You're not supposed to say anything,' she scolded, and gave her sister a shove. 'Go and make her welcome.'

'What was all that about?' Josephine asked, as Ronnie went over to greet the new arrival.

Lettice looked round as if she expected to find peepholes in the oak panelling. 'Don't tell anyone,' she whispered loudly, 'but that girl's one of Archie's. He's brought her here to work for us undercover so she can keep an eye on the goings-on.' They were quiet for a moment as each of them looked Miss Wyles up and down. 'Ronnie's right, though,' Lettice admitted eventually. 'I can see why he chose her. You'd never guess, would you?'

'No,' said Josephine, glancing again at the woman's wavy nut-brown hair and perfectly made-up face. 'No, you wouldn't.'

'Listen – now I've got you on your own for a minute, are you all right?' Lettice asked. 'I was worried about you last night.'

'I'm fine, but you're obviously not. You're both trying far too hard to be normal, and that's ridiculous – what's happened to you today isn't remotely normal.'

'Oh, we're all right. Ronnie's worse, I think – I take what's happened as a tragedy, and she takes it as a personal affront. I wouldn't be at all surprised if she finds the culprit before that policewoman's stitched her first hem.'

While they were talking, Archie came back from making his calls and Josephine watched as Ronnie did a mock introduction between the two police officers. The woman said something which she couldn't quite catch but which made Archie laugh warmly, and then he beckoned Josephine and Lettice over.

'Where would you like me to start?' Lillian Wyles asked when the remaining introductions were over.

'You can help us set up first,' Lettice said. 'We'll worry about the sewing later.'

'Oh, that'll be fine. My grandmother was a dresser at the Lyceum – I was practically brought up on a Singer.'

'Bloody marvellous!' Ronnie said, pinching Archie's cheek. 'You'll be lucky to get this one back by the time we've finished with her.'

'I'll take my chances,' Archie said, winking at his colleague. 'We'd better go.'

'Haven't you forgotten something?' Ronnie asked, pointing

accusingly at Josephine. 'You're supposed to be having a fitting around now.'

'Sorry, it'll have to wait,' she said. 'I've got an appointment with some blue serge. Can I come and find you later?'

Lettice nodded. 'Of course you can. You won't want to rush it – I think you'll find we've surpassed ourselves.'

'Is it a surprise, then?' Wyles asked innocently, and Lettice whispered something in her ear. 'Oh, you'll look fabulous.'

'Yes,' said Josephine pleasantly, ignoring Ronnie's smirk. 'I'm sure I will.'

'Putting double agents into the Cowdray Club is a bit extreme, isn't it?' she said when they were in the car. 'It's more like something out of John Buchan than an English police investigation.'

Archie smiled, and his obvious amusement at her irritation did nothing to improve Josephine's mood. 'You sound just like Bill,' he said. 'Actually, he went as far as suggesting that you might be up for the job. I suppose you're right – it *is* much more English to allow an amateur to track down a murderer, but I think I'll stick with WPC Wyles for now.'

It was good-humoured sparring on his part, something which they often lapsed into, but Josephine couldn't be bothered to keep up with it. Unsettled by her conversation with Geraldine, shocked at the events which had suddenly overtaken her interest in the Sach and Walters case, and furious with herself for behaving like a guilty schoolgirl caught with Marta's diary, she knew it was unfair of her to take her ill humour out on Archie but couldn't seem to help herself, if only because he was there. 'Good,' she muttered, looking out of the window, 'because I've got enough to think about without your sergeant finding work for idle hands.'

She was grateful that he knew her well enough to take the hint without questioning it, and neither of them spoke again until they were close to their destination. 'There it is,' he said, pointing over to the left, and Josephine had her first glimpse of Holloway, seen through the line of trees marking the junction of Parkhurst and Camden Roads. For reasons best known to the architect, the prison had been designed to resemble Warwick Castle, complete with high wall, imposing gateway and crenellated towers; it dominated the immediate skyline like a parody of its medieval prototype, built to keep people in rather than out. Archie parked the Daimler outside the main entrance and rang the bell in the huge studded gate. They waited, listening to a jangle of keys on the other side, and eventually a small wooden door within the larger gate was opened to admit them. Two rooms lay beyond, one cosy and oddly domestic, the other more functional and office-like; straight ahead, Josephine could see a steel-barred gate which presumably led into the prison yard and through to the main building. The gate officer took their names and glanced down the pages of an enormous book, then telephoned through to announce them. 'Male officers aren't allowed any further than this,' he explained with a smile, 'but someone will be across to take you over in a minute.'

'Do you know Mary Size?' Josephine asked Archie while they waited.

'No, we've never met but I've heard a lot about her. Civil servants are notoriously parsimonious with their praise, but they have nothing but good things to say about what she's achieved here.'

'Celia's the same. I don't know quite what to expect, though – it must take a very singular sort of mind to want to spend your life in a place like this, and a formidable resilience to manage it so successfully.'

But the woman who arrived at the gatehouse a few minutes later was neither single-minded nor formidable, at least in appearance, and Josephine – who had expected to be fetched by a minion – took a moment to realise that this was in fact the deputy governor of Holloway. Mary Size must have been in her early fifties; she resembled every school teacher that Josephine had ever had, with a smart but anonymous suit, a no-nonsense attitude, and a face which defaulted to strict but was transformed easily to kindness with a smile. The gate officer wasn't the slightest bit surprised by her arrival – clearly, Miss Size often came to meet her visitors – and the genuine pleasure in his greeting told Josephine more about the woman's achievements here than a thousand civil servants could have done.

She smiled at Josephine, but dealt with the formality first. 'Welcome to Holloway isn't a phrase I often use, Inspector Penrose, and you'll forgive me, I hope, if I don't say it now. I'm very sorry that you've come here today. Marjorie Baker was a girl with real spirit, and she'd just begun to blossom. I suppose I should know better, but it's hard to believe that a personality like that can be so easily destroyed.' Her voice held a soft Irish inflection which added to the warmth of her words, and Josephine got her first real sense of the girl whose death had brought them to the prison. 'But I'm delighted to meet you at last, Miss Tey,' she continued. 'I can't think why our paths have never crossed at the club, but Celia's told me a lot about you, and of course I loved *Richard of Bordeaux*. I must have seen it half a dozen times or more.'

'Good grief – perhaps it's you who should be locked up,'

Josephine said without thinking, but Mary Size only laughed heartily.

'You're not the first person to say that, and I doubt you'll be the last.'

'Seriously, though – it really is very good of you to let me look round. I can imagine how busy you and your staff are, and writers digging up the past must be a nuisance.'

'Nonsense – I hope you'll find it valuable. As I said in my note, there's no one left to my knowledge who was here during the period that interests you, but parts of the building itself have changed very little and I've dug out some old suffragette accounts of prison life for you – they're later, obviously, but things won't have changed much. Ah, this is Cicely McCall,' she added, introducing a young woman dressed in a blue prison warder's uniform who had just arrived. 'She's writing a book about the prison, so you couldn't be in more knowledge-able hands. And it really is no trouble.'

'Even so, I appreciate it. This isn't a museum, after all – you must be more concerned about the future than former prisoners who are beyond your help.'

Mary Size looked at her, pleased, and Josephine sensed that she had just walked willingly into the subtlest of traps. 'It's funny you should say that,' the deputy governor said, 'but I do have an ulterior motive in inviting you here. I'm always keen that people in the public eye should see what we're up to, and there's still such a long way to go. We've got a good band of people on board now, many of them writers; Vera Brittain, of course, and Elizabeth Dashwood – E. M. Delafield, you know – has agreed to write a foreword to Cicely's book. I hope you might be persuaded to join us.' There was a twinkle in her eye, and Josephine could easily understand how people were persuaded to do anything she asked, but she had never seen herself as a campaigner and just smiled non-committally. Even so, she was impressed; harnessing the Provincial Lady herself to prison reform was quite a coup; it was certainly a far cry from the mannequin in Selfridge's window.

Miss Size led them over to the administrative block and up a stone staircase to the first floor. 'We'll talk in my sitting room, Inspector,' she said. 'If we stay in my office, we'll be interrupted every two minutes. Miss Tey – I hope you'll find your tour interesting and please feel free to ask Cicely anything at all. We'll see you in about three quarters of an hour.'

She disappeared with Archie, and Josephine noticed how efficiently the two visits had been managed to ensure him the discretion he needed without offending her. Left alone with Miss McCall, she felt a little uncomfortable: normally, she was too lazy or too shy to go this far in the name of research, and the bravado of her prison visit had much to do with resisting Celia Bannerman's dismissal of her work as popular entertainment. She had no idea why she was suddenly so concerned about authenticity – to be entertaining and popular had always been enough for her in the past – but she was honest enough to admit that there was a more personal reason for coming to Holloway which had nothing to do with proving anything to her former teacher. Bracing herself, she smiled over-confidently at her guide and walked through the glass door which was held open for her, feeling a little like Dante following Virgil.

Holloway had been built on the radiating principle, with four glass-roofed wings diverging from one centre like the spokes of a wheel. From where Josephine stood on the first floor, she could look down to the cells on the ground floor and up to the two galleries overhead, and her first impression was unexpectedly one of light. The afternoon sun was hazy but valiant in its efforts, and it shone through the glass on to fresh white paintwork, providing a refreshing contrast to the darkness of the office corridors.

'It's a bit of a shock, isn't it?' the prison officer said, noticing her expression. 'Apparently, the first thing Miss Size did when she got here was change the colour. This all used to be orange and brown – can you imagine how drab and depressing that must have been?'

'How long have you been here?' Josephine asked as they walked further into the main building.

'Only a couple of years. I first came here as a social worker back in '32 because I was interested in prison conditions for women, but, when I saw what they were trying to do, it seemed sensible to help from the inside. What would you like to see first?'

'Oh, I don't mind – I'll be led by you.'

'Right, then – we may as well start with the cells.'

On the way to one of the wings they passed a table full of flowers, some exotic and obviously expensive, others which looked as if they had been picked from the garden rather than ordered from a florist. Each pot or vase held a piece of paper with its owner's name and number, and Josephine exclaimed in surprise at the brightness of the display. 'Somehow I didn't expect to see flowers in Holloway,' she said.

'Well, they're not allowed in the cells so we keep them here. That way, prisoners can look at what they've been sent four times a day as they pass through to work or to exercise, and it's nice for those who never receive anything of their own. We put some in the chapel, too, but you have to be careful.' She grinned. 'Tulips are particularly good for hiding make-up.' Josephine was struck by the combination of cheeriness and practicality, and wondered – should she find herself on the receiving end of it – whether she would find it reassuring or irritating. 'This is the first offenders' wing,' Cicely continued, unlocking another glass door at the head of yet another corridor. 'You'll notice they're wearing green checked overalls instead of blue.' It seemed to Josephine a negligible distinction: the women she had seen so far had all had their individuality knocked out of them by shapeless dark dresses, a charwoman's overall, black shoes and thick, black woollen stockings; some stood at the doors to their cells, others were fetching water from a tap on the landing or queuing by a lavatory recess, but all seemed to wear an expression of resignation which suggested that the experience of prison was much the same whether your uniform was finished with blue or with green. 'Most of the women eat in their cells, but there's a dining area downstairs where those who've earned enough good conduct marks can eat together and talk or read a paper,' she added. 'It sounds grand, but it's actually a cheerless strip of landing between two rows of cells and, if I'm honest, most of the women in here have no interest whatsoever in the *Daily Telegraph*'s view of the world. Still, it keeps them in touch with things, but we've a long way to go before we catch up with the men.'

'Are men's prisons very different, then?' Josephine asked, relieved to find that Cicely McCall's view on prison reform was not as rose-coloured as it had at first seemed.

'Good God, yes. At Wakefield, they eat together, unsupervised, and they don't all look like they've just stepped out of the workhouse. I suppose it's because there are so many more male prisoners than female – they're a bigger problem, so they get more attention from those who make the decisions. But it would be nice if more people on the outside recognised that women aren't somehow less affected than men by this sort of demoralisation.' She stopped outside an open door at the very end of the wing. 'Anyway, I'll get off my soapbox and show you the cell.'

Josephine walked in, and realised too late that it had been ridiculous of her to expect the room to be empty. A woman of about thirty stood in front of a mirror. She reddened when she saw a stranger, and Josephine felt the heat of the blush reflected in her own face; it was hard to say who was more embarrassed. 'This is Miss Tey, Browning,' Cicely explained. 'Miss Size has sent her round to have a look at us.'

'What a lovely bright . . . er . . . room,' Josephine said and could have bitten her tongue out for sounding so preposterous, but Browning seemed genuinely pleased.

'Isn't it?' she said, then noticed Josephine looking at the photographs on the walls. 'That's my husband,' she explained, pointing to a picture of a good-looking young man in a postman's uniform, 'and this – this is my Bobby, but I expect he looks so different already. They grow so fast at that age, don't they?'

There were tears in her eyes when she spoke of the baby. 'Will you be away from them long?' Josephine asked gently.

'Another six months, Miss.'

'That must be very hard.'

'Yes, Miss – it'll be half his life.'

'He looks like you, though,' she said, stepping closer to the picture. 'Six months won't change that.' They left Browning to her enforced privacy and walked back down the corridor. As they neared the hub of the prison, Josephine noticed how much darker the cells became due to the close proximity of the other wings; obviously Cicely's scepticism did not entirely overcome the natural desire to make a good impression on a visitor. 'Have the cells changed much in the last thirty years?' she asked, remembering for a moment why she was supposed to be there.

'It's only in the last few months that photographs and a looking glass have been allowed, and the beds are different – they have proper springs these days, rather than old wooden planks. There's an electric light now, and it's lights out at ten to give them a chance to read or write letters. Oh, and there's a bell in case they need anything in an emergency. Sometimes it even works.'

'And the women on this landing – what are they in here for?'

'All sorts.' She pointed to each cell in turn. 'Williams was too heavy-handed with her foster child, Pears and Gregory are both shoplifters, like Browning, and Gaskell is the daughter of an admiral who somehow forgot to pay her bill every time she left a hotel. Over here, we've got a bigamist, a prostitute and a widow who lost her job and tried to steal two tins of fruit from Woolworth's.'

'So the only thing they have in common is being a first offender?'

'That's right. The only first-timers who go elsewhere are brothel keepers.' Josephine raised an eyebrow. 'For some reason, they get the heaviest sentences, they're treated like lepers and are not usually favoured by the Discharged

Prisoners' Aid Society – they never get any money when they're released. We reckon it's because the ladies on the committee fear for their husbands' moral welfare.'

'But the others are all treated the same, no matter what they've done?'

'Yes. All classes, all crimes, all ages – they get the same routine and the same treatment, no matter how long their sentence.'

To Josephine, it seemed anathema to reform that women should be herded together with so little understanding of their backgrounds or needs, and she said so. 'Or is that just naive of me?'

'Not at all – you're absolutely right, but we're battling for twentieth-century changes in a Victorian building, and even Miss Size can only do so much with the shell she's given. If she had her way, they'd knock the whole place down and start again with something more workable, but she's shot herself in the foot by achieving as much as she has. The Home Office sees that she's making life bearable in the existing prison, so we drop a long way down the Treasury's priority list.'

Bearable was a subjective term, Josephine thought, but she said nothing. 'Is anything done for their families while they're in here?' she asked, remembering the young woman's face as she had looked at the picture of her child.

'There's a group of voluntary visitors who look after families as well.' Josephine's reservations must have been obvious, because Cicely said: 'I know what you mean and, by and large, they're made up of the great and the good, but it's nothing like the old lady visitors system; they were all terribly earnest and devoted to a woman's spiritual welfare, but they had no idea how to deal with what they found here. No, these volunteers are more practical – they give money so that women can get their husbands' tools out of hock or pay their rent arrears, things that keep the family going and give the prisoner a fighting chance of not ending up back in here a week after she's released. And some of the friendships that are made last well beyond the end of a sentence.' Josephine could not help but reflect on how different it sounded from Celia's guarded comments about her own time in the prison service, when any such fraternisation would have been frowned upon. 'I know I joked about the brothel keepers,' Cicely added, 'but the Aid Society is a remarkable organisation. It's raised nearly twenty thousand pounds since it started.'

The sewing rooms and laundry were housed in separate buildings, and Josephine was glad to leave the oppressive smell of grease and sweat and general dirt behind for a while as they walked across the yard. 'I might as well show you the workrooms,' her guide said, 'but don't forget that all the work would have been done in individual cells during the period you're writing about.'

'So didn't the prisoners associate with each other?' Josephine asked, surprised. In her mind, she had created an image of Sach and Walters glaring at each other across the exercise yard as they awaited trial, or Sach and other baby farmers like Eleanor Vale talking at meal times and finding comfort in their shared fate.

Cicely smiled. 'I can only tell you what it's like now. Inside each cell, there's a card of prison rules and any woman who can be bothered to read it will find that no talking is allowed at any time.' She nodded as Josephine opened her mouth to argue. 'I know, I know – you've only been here half an hour and already you can see that's nonsense. They talk while they're standing at the doors to their cells, and while they're waiting to go to chapel. Most of the gossip happens mornings and evenings while they're queuing to empty their slops or waiting for the luxury of the lavatory. You're not telling me that fifty women on a landing with one hot tap and four toilets aren't going to talk to each other, even if it's only to suggest politely that the woman in front might like to get a move on. Then there's the exercise yard – I could show you a dozen old lags who can carry on a conversation with the woman in front without moving their lips or turning their heads. Excellent ventriloquists they'd make in another life.' She laughed. 'I'm not saying it's non-stop chatter from dawn until dusk, but they *do* speak – and I assume it was the same back then.'

'One of the women who was tried for baby farming at the same time as Sach and Walters was sentenced to two years' hard labour. What would that have meant?'

'For women, it just means straightforward imprisonment.'

'No difference at all?' Privately, Josephine had wondered if Eleanor Vale suffered more than Sach and Walters, whose punishment, although final, was at least swift.

'Don't misunderstand me. Prison isn't easy and it was far worse then – but most people cling to life at all costs, so if she got away with hard labour rather than hanging, she'll have been down on her knees thanking someone.'

There was little to see in the workrooms on a Saturday afternoon, and they didn't linger there long. The path from the laundry back to the main building took them through one of the exercise grounds, and Josephine stopped to look at the odd assortment of women walking round and round dejectedly on cement paths laid in concentric circles, each about a yard wide with snow-covered grass in between. The outside circle was occupied by an energetic prisoner who behaved as though she were tramping across the Pennines; by contrast, an elderly woman, frail and hunched low against the cold, inched slowly round the smaller circle, and Josephine could scarcely recall seeing anything more depressing than a crowd of women walking aimlessly and getting nowhere. 'You wouldn't guess it, would you, but exercise is looked forward to as a treat,' Cicely said. 'Gardens like this are a novelty for some of these women, and a sanctuary for others.'

They looked bleak enough in the fading light of a November day, but Josephine could imagine how important the lawns and carefully arranged flower beds might be to these women; in the spring and early summer, if you could detach them from their surroundings, they might even be said to be beautiful. As she looked around, her eye was drawn to an oblong bed of neatly trimmed evergreens at one end of the grounds; it stood alone, and seemed out of place next to the general scheme of paths and plants that sat between the radiating arms of the cell blocks. Cicely followed her gaze, and said: 'That's Edith Thompson's grave. She was the last prisoner to be hanged here. There's no stone or marker, but you don't need one: every woman in here knows what it is and what it means, and they'd find it hard to forget.'

'Are there many women buried here?'

'Too many, if you ask me.'

'And Sach and Walters would be among them?' Cicely nodded. They stood in silence for a moment, looking over towards the trees. 'What's that?' Josephine asked, pointing at a new building which was just visible over the top of a nearby wall.

'That's the new execution chamber – and I mean brand new.' She shook her head. 'All that trouble they've gone to to build it, and no one's had the decency to try it out yet. How ungrateful can you get?' Her sarcasm was blatant, but justified, in Josephine's opinion: there was something quietly horrifying about the close proximity of the scaffold to the victims of its predecessor. 'They pulled the old chamber down after Thompson went,' Cicely explained. 'They said she haunted it. A gang came in from one of the men's prisons to build this beauty – they arrived in a bus each day, like some sort of day trip. Do you want to see it?'

'No, not if it's not the original.' Cicely seemed relieved, and Josephine remembered what Celia had said about the burden of being the warder at an execution; to go to the chamber at all must seem like tempting fate. 'We'd better go back, anyway. I don't want to hold Inspector Penrose up.' She looked at her watch, realising suddenly how badly she wanted to leave Holloway behind.

'Why do you do this?' she asked as they walked back to the main building. 'I can't imagine it's for the money.'

'You're right there, and it's not for the social life either.' She thought before answering, and then said: 'The best way I can explain it is to tell you something about Miss Size. We had a woman in here who'd been caught shoplifting. She'd run up huge debts with her husband and she was in despair because she didn't know how he'd manage without her or what she'd do when she got out. Miss Size asked her for a list of her debts, and she wrote to each and every one of them personally, asking what they'd accept by way of payment. Everyone was paid out of money from the Prisoners' Aid Society, and that woman left prison with a clean slate, debt-free for the first time in her life.

That's just one story – I could have chosen a dozen more, but that's why I do it.'

One glance around the deputy governor's sitting room was enough to tell anyone how Mary Size spent what little free time she had: books lay everywhere, and Penrose noticed that she divided her loyalties equally between her countrymen – there was a good smattering of Joyce, Swift and Wilde – and the contemporary female writers who had been recruited into the movement for reform. Her taste for satire obviously extended to the visual: she was a keen collector of cartoons, and examples by Tom Webster and David Low lined the walls. 'David's a friend,' she explained when she saw him looking at them, 'although sometimes I wonder.' She drew his attention to a small framed drawing by the fireplace, in which a monstrous female figure towered over three caged and emaciated men, one labelled 'discipline', one 'punishment', and the third and weakest of the three, 'justice'; like all the best cartoons, the image was at once grotesquely exaggerated and instantly recognisable as her.

Penrose smiled and took the chair he was offered. There were two folders on the table in front of him, one each for Marjorie Baker and Lucy Peters, and she pushed them across for him to read. He thanked her, but left them where they were; he had liked Mary Size instantly and was interested in hearing her personal opinion before he looked at any official records. 'Tell me about Marjorie Baker,' he said.

The openness of the question seemed to throw her for a second, and she considered it carefully. 'When I first met Marjorie, she was sullen, resentful and aggressive. She showed no interest in her fellow prisoners and rejected any offer of friendship; she regarded prison officers as her deadly enemies. To prove that she wasn't afraid of anyone, she was always ready to strike the first blow, be it verbal or physical. The last time I saw her, which was only yesterday, she was in command of a responsible job where she was admired for her talent and valued for her hard work; she obviously got on well with her employers and colleagues, and was happy and excited about her future. It takes considerable courage and strength to make those changes without losing the essence of who you are, and that's probably the most important thing that I can tell you about Marjorie.'

'What do you put those changes down to?' He smiled. 'Apart from prison rehabilitation, I mean – it sounds like she benefited from her time with you.'

'Yes, she did. Her earlier behaviour was entirely down to frustration and despair, and she was terrified that she would never amount to anything. Once she could believe that she had a future other than as an outcast, she found she could look people in the eye again. It sounds terribly sentimental when I put it like that,' she added, sensing his scepticism, 'and of course there were some setbacks along the way – I can see you're about to remind me that Marjorie needed more than a second chance – but it came right for her eventually. Call it third time lucky if you're a man who believes in luck.'

'And do you genuinely believe that she wouldn't have done anything to bring her back to prison?'

'I've been in the service for thirty years now, and I've learned not to make claims which are quite as definite as that. But contrary to what some of my older officers will tell you, they *don't* always come back, and Marjorie had something to lose at last. That's the most powerful incentive I can think of.'

'Do you know of anyone who might have wanted to hurt her? Any prisoners who had a grudge against her or someone recently released who had a score to settle? You said that she didn't make friends at the beginning of her sentence.'

'No, she didn't, but that's the sort of behaviour which might bring instant retaliation: it hardly warrants the sort of violence you're talking about. I have to admit, when your sergeant telephoned and told me that her father was found dead as well, I assumed that her death had something to do with him, but, from your questions, that's obviously not the case. Can I ask how she was killed?'

Penrose outlined the barest details of the murder, and Mary Size looked both saddened and horrified. It was a long time before she spoke again. 'I honestly can't think of anything that's happened here which would make someone react like that,' she said. 'I'm not aware of everything that goes on, of course, but people will tell you that I miss very little – and I *would* tell you if there had been something, no matter how badly it reflected on the prison.' Penrose believed her and appreciated her frankness; it was refreshing after Celia Bannerman's cautious responses to his questions about the Cowdray Club, although it seemed to him that the reputation of an organisation like Holloway was much more worthy of defence than a society for privileged women. He could only suppose that the deputy governor's personal affection for the victim had influenced her desire to help, and he liked her all the more for it. 'I suppose the manner of Marjorie's death encouraged you to think of her time in prison,' she added.

'Yes, in part,' he said, surprised. 'I gather that the type of needle in question is the sort traditionally used for heavier work like sacking and mailbags.'

'I was thinking more of the glass in her mouth. It's one of the nastier forms of prison violence, and I'm pleased to say that it's never happened on my watch, but it's not unknown for glass to find its way into a prisoner's food.' That hadn't occurred to Penrose, but it made sense. 'As I say, though, I can't think why Marjorie would have been subjected to something like that.'

'When you saw her at Motley yesterday afternoon, was there anything different about her? Did she seem troubled or did she confide in you about anything?'

'I'm not sure I'd go as far as troubled, but she told me that her father had been hanging around again, making a nuisance of himself while she was at work. She was worried that he'd jeopardise her job and I think she wanted me to put in a good word for her, but there was no need; everyone at Motley was more than pleased with her, and I told her as much.' There was no new information here, and Penrose was about to move on when she added: 'She did mention one thing, though. She said that her father had told her something which she hadn't believed at the time, but which had turned out to be true.'

'Oh? Did she say what it was?'

'No. I asked her, and she seemed to be weighing up whether to say more or not, but in the end she brushed it aside.'

Penrose would have put money on the fact Marjorie had come close to telling Mary Size about her family history. It looked as though Celia Bannerman was right – the information must have come from Jacob Sach himself, and been verified by Marjorie's own investigations. If Josephine's suspicions were correct, that must have been quite a blow to Nora Edwards and he wondered if she were safely in custody yet; if his oversight had given her time to disappear again, he might as well draft his resignation letter now. 'Do you know anything about Marjorie's mother?' he asked.

'I know that neither of her parents impressed her much. From what she said, there was no love lost between any of them.'

He decided that there was nothing to lose by telling Mary Size what he knew about the Baker family history, although he stopped short of revealing where the information had come from. Her astonishment was obvious and he could tell from her face that there were hundreds of questions which she would have liked to ask, but she also had the sense to realise that this wasn't the moment to indulge her own curiosity. In the end, all she said was: 'So your investigations and Miss Tey's aren't as separate as I imagined. How strange that those paths should cross.'

'Yes. Can you think of anyone here – staff or inmate – who might know of the connection between the Bakers and the Sachs?'

'Not unless it had been handed on as gossip. When I got Miss Tey's request, I checked very carefully in case there was someone here who could help her, but I drew a blank. Celia might know – but she probably gave you the information in the first place?' He nodded. 'You're welcome to talk to anyone here, of course, but I'm afraid I can't give you a shortcut. You obviously think that her death is connected to who her family was?' Again, he confirmed with a nod. 'Well, I'm sure you're right, but I will say one thing: I would have thought it highly unlikely that Marjorie would be any keener than her mother or father for the truth to come out. Unfortunately, a shame like that spreads and Marjorie was more aware than most of how difficult it is to distance yourself from the mistakes of the past.' Penrose agreed with her, but he also thought that panic could have driven any possibility of careful reasoning from Nora Edwards's mind. 'This really was a new start for Marjorie,' she emphasised.

'At Motley?'

'Yes. Ironically, the most important thing for me is what happens to these women when they leave Holloway. We prepare them as best we can for the outside world, offer them tuition in cookery or childcare or home management, but it's organisations like Motley which really allow us to make a difference.' He smiled. 'You know Lettice and Ronnie?'

'We're cousins, for my sins.'

'Are you? Then I'm glad they have someone who can help them at a time like this – after I'd got over the shock of Marjorie, I thought of them. It must be a devastating thing to have to come to terms with – a death like that on your watch.' She spoke of Lettice and Ronnie as if they were custodians of Marjorie's welfare and in some ways, he supposed, they had been. She carried on, unconsciously echoing the sentiments expressed by Celia Bannerman. 'But what I was going to say was that it's a worthless existence without some kind of mean-ingful work, without a way to support yourself and make your own way in the world, and that's hard for ex-prisoners, partic-ularly the younger ones. Employers actively discriminate against them, and they're hounded by fellow workers or exposed by policemen with a grudge. No offence meant.'

'None taken. I know it goes on.'

'We used to bang our heads against the problem, but now we concentrate on a few forward-thinking organisations who genuinely want to do some good and it's paying off: just after the war, we placed an average of 150 prisoners in employment;

this year, it's 250. It's people like your cousins and Celia at the Cowdray Club who have made that possible.'

'How do you find the club? I wouldn't have thought you had much spare time.'

'For another claustrophobic female institution, you mean?' He was treated to the laugh again. 'I don't, really, although I can't deny that a change of surroundings is welcome, but it's a valuable contact so I sit on the committee. Some of our nurses come from the college, and lots of the ladies on the Discharged Prisoners' Aid Society are members. Cynically speaking, the Cowdray Club is a rich recruiting ground for ladies with time and money on their hands, and Celia helps tremendously – one of us, gone over to the other side; the volunteers adore that. And of course the food's excellent.' She looked down at herself good-humouredly. 'As you can see, a good dinner is a splendid antidote to incarceration.'

'And were you at the club for dinner last night?'

'What a charming way of asking for my alibi. No, I was here. I came straight back after my fitting because we had a bit of trouble in the hospital wing. When staff are off sick, it's all hands to the pump – or to the bedpan, in this particular case. There are plenty of people who'll confirm that.'

'Did Marjorie have anything to do with the club, apart from the preparations for the gala?'

'Not to my knowledge, although I bumped into her there yesterday lunchtime when she was dropping something off, and she seemed perfectly at home in those surroundings. She was certainly giving that awful Timpson woman the run-around.'

'Oh? In what way?'

'Well, you know the sort. She's a terrible snob and hates it if the likes of Marjorie get above their station, and Marjorie was clearly enjoying the fact that she had as much right to be there as Timpson.'

'But nothing more vindictive than that.'

'Oh no. It was cheeky, but I didn't blame her. In fact, I encouraged her.'

'I don't know if you're aware of this, but some of the Cowdray Club committee members have received some unpleasant letters.'

'Yes, I know. I've had one myself.'

'Really? It's not on the list that Miss Bannerman gave us.'

'I didn't bother reporting it. Someone in my position gets lots of mail; most of it's kind and most of it's signed, but not all of it. I destroyed it as soon as it arrived.'

'Can I ask what it referred to?'

'Of course. It implied that my appointment here was the result of unfair favouritism from someone in the Home Office.'

'And do you think there's any possibility at all that Marjorie was behind these letters?'

She didn't hesitate. 'None whatsoever – not mine, anyway. It simply wasn't her style. If Marjorie had a grievance, she told you about it, and she didn't give a damn about the Home Office.'

'Marjorie's friendship with Lucy Peters – did that begin in prison or did they know each other beforehand?'

'No, they met here. Lucy's a different case altogether, though – a victim, and you would never have called Marjorie that, at least not until today.'

'What was Lucy in prison for?'

'Stealing from her employer. Of course, what wasn't obvious

until she'd been in here for three months was that her employer – or rather, her employer's son – had taken something from her as well. Technically, I know that's not an excuse but she's not the brightest of girls and there was no way that she was emotionally equipped to deal with either prison or pregnancy; both at the same time could have been a disaster, so I asked Marjorie to keep an eye on her.'

'And she was happy to do that?'

'Yes, I probably didn't even need to ask. Marjorie knew when someone was vulnerable.' Penrose couldn't help thinking that Marjorie had underestimated someone's vulnerability with tragic consequences, but he said nothing. 'Have you spoken to Lucy yet?' Miss Size asked.

'No. She'd gone off duty for the day by the time we got to the club.'

'So she probably doesn't even know Marjorie's dead.'

'We'll be speaking to her as soon as she returns this evening, and I'll make sure she's taken care of; my sergeant said you were worried.'

'Yes, they were close. Will you make sure to tell her that she can come to me at any time?'

'Of course. Would Marjorie have covered for Lucy?'

'Almost certainly. Why?'

'There have been a number of thefts at the club. One of the stolen items was found on Marjorie's body.'

'What was it?'

'A small silver photograph frame.'

'And the photograph?'

'Sorry?'

'What was the photograph.'

'It was a picture of a woman with her baby.'

'That's what Lucy stole, then. The value of the frame was incidental. She's still grieving – you need to understand that. And it *is* a type of grief, you know, the pain a mother feels when she gives up her child, but it's not like bereavement; there are no certainties, no rituals like a funeral to begin the healing process. If you lose your child to adoption, you lose the right to know anything more about it and lots of women find the uncertainty very difficult. Lucy suffered a great deal – clearly she's still suffering. But Marjorie would definitely protect her.'

No wonder Josephine's manuscript had upset Lucy so much, Penrose thought. 'What is the adoption procedure here? Are prison mothers encouraged to give up their children?'

'No, it's entirely up to them. Babies are born here, in the hospital wing, and mothers are given pre-natal care and a lot of help after their confinement. On release, each mother gets a complete new outfit for the child. It's not much, I suppose, but it helps.'

'And if the mother decides to give her child up?'

'Then we arrange it for her as painlessly as possible. Our volunteers help a great deal with that, and the warders are involved to oversee the welfare of the prisoner.'

How things had changed since Lizzie Sach's adoption, Penrose thought; if Celia Bannerman had been more typical, if the support had been as open and as comprehensive thirty years ago, then at least one tragedy might have been averted. 'Miss Bannerman must have been ahead of her time as a prison warder,' he said, but there was a knock at the door before she had a chance to respond.

'Am I interrupting?' Josephine asked.

'Not at all,' he said. 'We've just about finished.'

'Has Cicely shown you everything you need to see?' Mary Size asked, offering her a seat. She looked at the expression on Josephine's face as she sat down, and said sympathetically: 'It's unsettling when you come to it for the first time.'

'Yes, it is, but from what Cicely told me, it must have been much more so thirty years ago. She's marvellous – are all your staff as receptive to change as she is?'

'Good God, no. In fact, I was just about to say to Inspector Penrose – some of the older ones are still very set in their ways and they're convinced we're giving the women a holiday rather than a punishment, but the young women coming through now are much more responsive and natural retirement is gradually shifting the balance. There's hope, as long as the girls are patient enough to wait for promotion. I've never understood why, but we're not allowed to sack people for being incompetent.'

'Sadly, the prison service isn't alone in that stipulation,' Penrose said, smiling. 'But I can see how frustrating it must have been for Miss Bannerman to be surrounded by such a rigid system.'

'Indeed. Most warders of her generation would still tell you that I molly-coddle the girls, but if Celia came back to work here now, I'm pleased to say that she'd be in the majority. I'd have her like a shot, as well, but unfortunately she's too good at what she does now.'

'You obviously admire her, but she told me that she'd been found lacking as a prison officer because she wasn't sufficiently detached.'

Josephine looked at him in surprise, but Mary Size just smiled. 'I'd dispute that she'd been found lacking, from what I know. Prison is full of marred lives and wrecked hopes –

300

that's as true today as it was thirty years ago – and, as I understand it, if Celia had a fault it was that she concentrated on the individual rather than the system. I think her lack of detachment caused *her* more suffering than anyone in her care.' She turned to Josephine. 'I know you've talked to Celia about Holloway back then, but, as I said, she certainly wasn't typical of her time. If you want to write about prison as it really was, you should talk to someone at the other extreme – Ethel Stuke, perhaps.'

'I thought she was dead?'

'Ethel?'

'Yes, Celia told me she'd been killed in a Zeppelin raid during the war.'

'Believe me, if she'd been caught in a Zeppelin raid, the Zeppelin would have come off worse. She's quite a force of nature, is Ethel. No, she was still working here when I arrived, although she left soon after.' There was something like pride in her voice, Josephine noticed, and it complemented the twinkle in her eye quite beautifully. 'As far as I know, she's alive and well and living in Suffolk – we'll have her address on file. Celia must have meant one of the other warders – there were three sets of two looking after each condemned woman.'

'Do you still keep staff records for Celia Bannerman?' Penrose asked.

'Our records go back to when the prison came over to women, so I imagine they're in the archive somewhere. Can I ask why?'

'She's the main link with the Sach case, and I wondered if her records might mention someone else who could help us.'

301

'Bear with me a second and I'll find out.' She picked up the telephone. 'Smithers? Come up to my sitting room, will you?' Her request was answered immediately. 'This is Detective Inspector Penrose. Will you take him down to the office and look in the archive for a file on Celia Bannerman? She was a warder here in 1902. And give him Ethel Stuke's address as well.'

Penrose picked up the other two files. 'I'll return these to you as soon as possible.'

'Thank you. Do you mind if Miss Tey and I talk for a couple of minutes? I won't keep her long – I know you're busy.'

He looked at Josephine, who nodded and sat down again. 'I'll see you downstairs. And thank you for your time, Miss Size. It's much appreciated.'

'You're welcome, although I don't know how much use I've been to you.'

'Apart from anything else, you've helped me to understand what happens when my job is over,' he said. 'Sometimes I think we're not sufficiently aware of the consequences of what we do.'

He left, and Mary Size turned to Josephine. 'Now, Miss Tey . . .'

'Please – call me Josephine,' she said, 'but can I ask you something first?'

'Of course.'

'Marta Fox – how did she cope?'

Mary Size looked surprised but, to her credit, she resisted the temptation to answer Josephine's question with one of her own. 'I always think the miracle is that she *did* cope,' she said quietly. 'I see every prisoner within hours of her arrival here, and I feared for Marta at first. It wasn't surprising after

302

everything she'd been through – an abusive marriage, the loss of her children in the most horrific circumstances, so many revelations which must have been impossible to come to terms with – but I don't think I've ever seen anyone quite as empty. Guilt and self-reproach, even despair – those are all emotions I'm used to seeing, and I can deal with them in whatever way is best for the prisoner concerned. But emptiness, a complete lack of concern for what happens to you – that's very hard, and it went on for some time. She refused all visits and returned all her letters unread – but you probably know that?'

Josephine nodded. 'So what changed? Or *did* it change?'

'Yes, gradually. Two things helped, I think. The gardens, strangely enough. She seemed to find peace there – peace, rather than nothingness. And her writing. I don't know what she was working on but, in the end, I think she wrote herself back to sanity.'

'And now? What does it feel like to come out the other side of that?'

'Is that really why you're here? To understand what she's been through?'

'To *know* what she's been through, perhaps. I doubt that I could ever understand. But I would like to have some idea of what she needs now.'

'Well, not the sort of help that the Prisoners' Aid Society can give, that's for sure. I'm not a psychologist, Josephine, but I'd say that Marta needs something – or someone – she can rely on. Something that isn't going to be snatched away from her. Above all, something safe.' The telephone rang on her desk. 'We'll be right down,' she said. 'They're waiting for you at the gate. I won't bother you with prison reform now; it looks like you might have your own rehabilitation project on your hands, but do think about it, and if you want to talk to me – about anything at all – you know how to get hold of me. Next time, though, we'll have a drink at the club.'

'And I'll see you at the gala on Monday.'

'You certainly will, although I considered boycotting it because I'm furious that Celia's got Noël and Gertie. I can see I'm going to have to raise my game in the fundraising stakes; perhaps you could have a word with someone for me?'

Josephine smiled. 'I'll see what I can do.'

'Excellent. And if it's appropriate, Josephine, please give my regards to Marta.'

'Do you think Celia Bannerman did mean one of the other prison warders?' Archie asked as he waited for a gap in the traffic streaming down Camden Road.

'What? Oh, no, I don't. I'm sure she said Ethel Stuke – it's not the sort of name I'd make up.'

'Says the woman who created Ray Marcable.'

She laughed. 'That's different. You're allowed ridiculous names in detective fiction – in fact, it's positively encouraged. No, Celia must have made a mistake – it would have been almost impossible to keep up with prison news after she'd changed careers. Have you got Ethel Stuke's address for me?'

'Yes. I might use it myself if I draw a blank with Edwards. Where are you going now? Back to the club?'

'Yes, I suppose so,' she said, although there was something very tempting about the overnight sleeper to Inverness. 'I don't suppose you've got time for a drink?'

'Afraid not. I've got to get back to the Yard – I hope Edwards will be there by now.'

'She fascinates me, you know. I think she's the most

interesting person in the entire case. I suppose there's no point in asking you if I can sit in on that one?'

'No. No point at all.'

'Bill would let me.'

'Which is why Bill's still a sergeant.'

'*Did* she kill Marjorie, do you think?'

Archie considered the question, although he had been thinking of very little else. 'She's certainly the main contender – she's got a motive and no alibi, and the method of killing fits with the sort of jealousy that she's supposed to have shown towards her daughter. And her reaction to the news was very odd.'

'But you're not sure?'

'Not in my heart, no. But I'll make you a promise – if she turns out to have no connection with this murder, I'll ask her if she'll see you. Are you sure I can't drop you somewhere a little more welcoming than the Cowdray Club?'

'Oh, it's not so bad, and the girls might still be there. If not, I suppose I could go and see a film later – it sounds like Geraldine needs keeping out of trouble.'

'You wouldn't rather go to Holly Place?'

She looked at him, horrified. 'How could you possibly have read the address on that letter?'

'I didn't – I just recognised Marta's handwriting. She sent me a note, too, a few weeks after she got out. Rather briefer than yours, thank God – the writing's impossible. It just said thank you, although judging by the expression on your face when you got back from your prison tour, she has precious little to thank me for.'

'I don't know about that. She was an accessory to murder, and what you did for her was extraordinarily generous.'

305

'It was right, that's all. She didn't kill anyone, and she was badly used – by everyone in her life, as far as I could see.'

'Even so, she made things difficult for you, and I didn't help.'

'I'm not in policing to get my own back.'

She stared out of the window, relieved that Archie had raised the subject of Marta but unsure of how much to say to him. 'Why didn't you tell me you'd heard from her?' she asked.

'Because I thought she'd be in touch with you as well and, if she wasn't, there was no point in raking it all up again.' He pulled over in Camden Town, ignoring the angry hooting from the car behind, and looked at her with genuine concern. 'So, what's it to be – Holly Place or the Cowdray Club?'

'The Cowdray Club,' Josephine said quickly. 'I'm not ready to talk to Marta yet.'

Amelia Sach sat in her cell on the eve of her trial, and waited for news of another woman's fate. Eleanor Vale's appearance in court was the talk of the prison, but Amelia had more reasons than most for anticipating the verdict: the similarity of the charges in their respective cases – she still refused to use the word 'crimes' – was undeniable, and she hoped that Vale's treatment would at least give her a sign of what she should prepare herself for.

She was unsure if it was the cold or the anticipation that made her shiver. In mid-winter, prison clothes consisted of a cotton frock; a thin vest and knickers made of once-white calico; and harsh, black woollen stockings with holes she could put her fist through. She had no idea if the drab uniform had a summer equivalent or if it had been carefully designed to jar with any season, but she prayed that she might be here to find out; two months ago, she would never have believed that the inhumanity of Holloway was the lesser of two evils, but the thought of her daughter made her cling to life at all costs. Beneath her feet, the stone floor made her colder still but she focused on the discomfort as an antidote to the pain which seared through her whenever she thought of having missed Lizzie's fourth Christmas, and of the Christmases yet to come which might now proceed without her. She missed her daughter even more than she missed her freedom. The sorrow of a lost child and the sound of a mother crying softly in the night were imprinted on her heart, part of the pattern of her chosen life; for the first time, she understood how that felt.

From the moment she set foot in Holloway, Amelia had made Lizzie's future her priority and it hadn't taken her long to identify an ally. Celia Bannerman was younger than most of the prison officers, and had not yet served at Holloway for long enough to soak up its cynicism; neither had she learned to hide her horror at the way in which some of the prisoners were treated, and Amelia had known as soon as she met her that Celia's sympathies could be harnessed if necessary. She had considered offering her money to look out for Lizzie, but sensed that this was not the way to deal with someone whose very desire to do good made her vulnerable; she could exploit that vulnerability if necessary and, although Amelia still firmly believed that she would be vindicated in court, she took comfort from the fact that Lizzie would not be left solely in her father's care.

It was getting late, but she was too anxious to try to rest and, in any case, the plank bed was almost impossible to sleep on. She was fighting a cold – the blue serge cloak which she was expected to wear for exercise had been greasy with dirt around the neck from its previous occupant, so Amelia had scrubbed it repeatedly, preferring to shiver in it wet than wear it dry and filthy – and her hands were so chapped that they had begun to bleed from innumerable small cracks. She had asked for some ointment to ease the soreness, but the Stuke woman only laughed; in the end, Bannerman told her that the grease from the top of the cocoa, rubbed in well, was an excellent remedy, so she skimmed it off on to a plate each evening and applied it as it set. Grease was one thing that

Holloway had no shortage of: a thin film of it covered every-thing she touched with such relentless thoroughness that she could almost believe it came from her own skin.

At least she would be allowed to wear normal clothes at the trial tomorrow, although she knew already that she would feel like a stranger in them: every last trace of her femininity had been systematically and efficiently eroded over the last seven weeks. She visualised the state of her hair after so long without attention, knowing from the evidence on her collar that her scalp was dry and full of dandruff, and that her skin would appear sickly and sallow in the harsh light of the courtroom. Not surprisingly, she had lost weight, but, more significantly, thanks to the psychological effect of appearing as a slut amongst dozens of sluts, she had lost her self-respect. What sort of impression would she make on the jury if she looked as bad as she felt? Until now, she had considered the absence of a looking glass to be a merciful omission; tomorrow, she would need all the help she could get to make herself presentable.

There was a noise outside in the corridor, and Amelia jumped up to hammer on the cell door. When it opened, she was relieved to see Celia Bannerman. 'Well?' she demanded. 'What was the verdict on Vale?'

'Two years' hard labour,' Celia said; there was the ghost of a smile on her lips, or so Amelia thought in the flicker of the gas lamp. Suddenly, she was overcome by a relief so intense that she could scarcely breathe. Hard labour – what could be harder than these hours of waiting, trying to guess what her future would be? She would gladly fill coal scuttles in the pouring rain or haul gallons of scalding liquid up three flights of stairs if it meant she could see her daughter at the end of it. 'Thank you,' she said quietly.

'You've heard then?' Ethel Stuke came up behind Bannerman and smirked at Amelia. Wearing a dark-blue bonnet with strings hanging down on either side of her long face, jangling the bunch of keys and chains at her waist, the prison warder reminded Amelia of something from Dickens which had missed its appointment with Christmas but was determined to deliver the warning anyway. 'Don't get your hopes up, Sach. Yours is a very different case. Vale hasn't killed anyone.'

'Neither have I. The jury will understand that.' Amelia tried to keep the doubt out of her voice.

Stuke laughed scornfully. 'Not when Darling's finished with them, they won't. He's not called the hanging judge for nothing, you know.' She walked over to where Amelia sat on the bed and gently straightened her collar, allowing her hand to linger for a second on the back of her neck. It was a fleeting gesture, but its significance was obvious and Amelia felt the panic well up inside her. 'Anyway,' Stuke continued, 'Vale was lucky with the prosecution – made a right mess of it, he did.' She paused to make sure that her words were hitting home. 'Trouble is, he's defending you. Sleep well, Mrs Sach.'

She forced Bannerman out of the cell ahead of her, and the door clanged shut behind them. Their footsteps faded away, and Amelia listened as the calls for attention from further down the landing grew faint from exhaustion, then ceased altogether. Left alone with Stuke's words, she was too frightened even to scream.

Chapter Eleven

Sylvia Timpson looked suspicious, then horrified when she opened her front door to Fallowfield on Saturday afternoon. Clearly policemen were as unwelcome in the claustrophobic suburbia of Westcott Road as they were in Campbell Bunk, because she ushered him over the doorstep of her small terraced house with unseemly haste, then carefully positioned herself in the hall to ensure that he could go no further without an explanation.

'I would have thought that any more questions about this unpleasant business could have been handled at the club, Sergeant. I don't appreciate being bothered in my own home.'

Fallowfield smiled politely at her. 'I'm afraid it's a different unpleasant business this time, Mrs Bishop,' he said, noticing her surprise at his use of her married name. 'Marjorie Baker was killed last night, and I need to ask you a few questions.'

At first, she seemed to struggle to place the name, and then said: 'The Motley girl? She was at the club yesterday lunchtime. But why do you need to talk to me?'

'We're speaking to everyone who saw her on Friday,' Fallowfield said non-committally. 'Might I come in for a minute?'

'Yes, of course.' She led him through to a typically unused front parlour where the only thing that caught his attention was a photograph on the mantelpiece of a young woman in a nurse's uniform, standing on the pavement outside St Thomas's Hospital. She saw him looking at it. 'That was taken so long ago now that even I don't recognise myself,' she said, and there was a note of bitterness in her voice which she made no effort to hide.

'You were a nurse, Mrs Bishop – is that how you came to be at the Cowdray Club?'

'How I ended up there, you mean? Yes. I lost my nursing career because I was foolish enough to get married, Sergeant. Now I sort mail for the women who were cleverer than me – women who've kept their independence – and the women who are too rich or too titled to care. It's funny how life works itself out, isn't it?'

'You regret your marriage?'

'I was one of those starry-eyed young women who gave themselves up to the service of the sick during the war. It was a typical nurse-and-wounded-soldier marriage, like a thousand others. We all felt as though we needed to make up to those boys for what they'd gone through, but that was all they were – boys, looking for a mother figure. The gratitude was welcome for a while, but it soon wears off.' Her description of the marriage was very similar to her husband's, Fallowfield noticed. 'But what can this possibly have to do with Marjorie Baker?'

'I believe you were on duty yesterday when Miss Baker came to the club.'

'That's right. She delivered some things from Motley for Miss Bannerman.'

'How long was she there?'

'About fifteen minutes, I suppose.'

'And who else did she talk to?'

'Miss Size was there. They obviously knew each other already.' From her tone, there was no difficulty in guessing what her opinion was on the rehabilitation of prisoners. 'And Lady Ashby made the usual exhibition of herself in the foyer.'

'In what way?'

'She made it very clear that she was looking forward to her fitting, if you know what I mean. That was it – except Baker wanted to see Lucy Peters, so I made her wait outside until Peters's break. We can't have staff fraternising in the foyer.'

'So Miss Baker and Miss Peters talked?'

'I assume so. I saw Miss Baker afterwards, waiting on one of the benches in the square.'

'And she didn't go anywhere else in the building or speak to anybody at the club?'

'No.'

'Was that the only time you saw her yesterday?'

She looked at him sharply. 'Of course it was.'

Fallowfield nodded. 'Just a couple more questions, then. Where were you last night, between nine o'clock and midnight?'

'Here.'

'And can your husband confirm that?'

She laughed suddenly, but Fallowfield could not tell whether it came from scorn or relief. 'Ah, so that's it. Was Miss Baker one of my husband's indiscretions, Sergeant? Is that what this is about? Oh, don't look so defensive. You men – you stick together through thick and thin, don't you? Must be another legacy of the war, I suppose. Well, actually Lionel *can* confirm that – we were at home together all evening. We listened to the wireless, went to bed at around ten o'clock, and said approximately three words to each other all evening. So there

313

you are – you have the alibi you came for.' She seemed almost regretful about it, and Fallowfield had no doubt that she was telling the truth. 'Anyway,' she added, 'Lionel isn't a murderer – he doesn't have the backbone for it.'

'You must see a lot of comings and goings in your job, Mrs Bishop. In your opinion, is there anybody at the Cowdray Club who would have the backbone for it?'

'Several people, I should think – although I can't imagine that a seamstress fresh out of Holloway would inspire that sort of energy. Have you tried looking in the gutter, Sergeant? One of her prison friends, perhaps – you should talk to Lucy Peters.'

'We will, Mrs Bishop. In the meantime, can you tell me exactly what Marjorie left at the club yesterday?'

'A parcel full of material samples and two letters, both for Miss Bannerman.'

'Two letters?'

'Yes.'

'Were the envelopes handwritten or typed?'

'Both handwritten, but not by the same person; one was flamboyant and written in ink, the other was in pencil, with more ordinary lettering. But the envelopes were the same.'

'So both envelopes came from Motley with the parcel?'

'I assume so.'

'Thank you, Mrs Bishop. You've been most helpful. I won't keep you any longer.'

As she showed him to the door, he glanced into one of the other rooms off the hall which was obviously used by the Bishops on a regular basis. On the centre table, there was a typewriter and a stack of paper, but the door was closed too quickly for him to see more. 'Looks like a nice machine,' he said casually. 'Do you have much correspondence?'

'It's my husband's,' she said quickly. 'He uses it for work. Good day, Sergeant.'

Lucy sat at a corner table in the Oxford Street Lyons, and watched as a young woman lifted her baby out of its pram and settled it comfortably on her lap. For some reason, children seemed to be everywhere that Lucy went; sometimes she found herself following a mother with a baby, wondering if it was the little girl she had given up. Usually, she managed to convince herself that her behaviour was down to a natural desire to find out what had happened to her child; occasionally, though, she felt in her heart that knowing would not be enough: the only thing which would stem this inconsolable grief was to have the baby in her arms again.

It was strange, this constant longing for something which was initially so unwanted. The idea of being pregnant when the shame of prison was still so new had been too intense an emotional trauma to come to terms with immediately; she had hidden the knowledge for as long as possible, pretending to others and especially to herself that all was well. Denial was followed by fear. She knew nothing about having a baby and had nobody to ask, so threw herself into the heavy labour that prison demanded, hoping against hope that something might happen to release her from this trap. Ironically, it was her sense of isolation that changed the way she felt about her child: alone at the most destructive time of her life, Lucy began to rely on her baby as the only person who made her feel worthwhile, her only friend in a hostile world. By that time, it was too late: she had already agreed to adoption and set in motion a process

315

which could not be reversed, and, as the pregnancy progressed, Lucy came to fear that her one legacy to the child would be her own sense of abandonment.

She drained the cup of tea that she had nursed for more than an hour, and tried to fight the pain which returned to haunt her whenever she thought about the weeks leading up to her confinement but, even eight months later, the memories were cruelly vivid. Expectant mothers were supposed to be moved to the hospital wing for the final month of their pregnancy but, when it came to Lucy's time, there were no free beds and she had continued in her own cell, locked in night after night with no means of summoning help in an emergency except a temperamental bell. Her sense of panic grew at the thought that the baby might come while she was alone but, in the end, she almost wished it had: there was nothing joyful or familiar about the birth, and the staff treated her so brutally that they might have been conspiring with her baby to punish her for what she was about to do.

Afterwards, she was given twenty minutes with her daughter. She spent them trying to memorise the child's features, wishing that people would stop talking so that she could take in everything about this small part of her which was about to be removed, angry at them for wasting her time. The emotions she felt were so new that it was impossible to know how to respond to them, but she remembered that her hands were like ice, and she had desperately tried to warm them so that her baby's only memory of her would not be this cold, unfamiliar touch. Then she heard the door open, and knew that someone had arrived to separate them. She tried to ignore it, and moved over to the far side of the bed, turning her body to the wall to protect the child, but it was no good. For some ridiculous reason, she had tried to smile when they took her away, had made an effort to look nice, as if this moment could somehow be stamped on her baby's consciousness as deeply as it was on hers. But she felt the scream start up inside her before the door closed, and it had never gone away.

The woman with the pram got up to go, and Lucy followed her out into the street. She walked a few paces behind, and then, as the mother paused in front of one of the sparkling Christmas window displays which were beginning to appear along Oxford Street, Lucy grabbed her opportunity. While the mother was distracted, she reached gently into the pram and pulled the blankets down to take a closer look at the baby's face, but she had underestimated the other woman's vigilance. She stared at Lucy in horror, and snatched the pram away; realising how this must look, and with no way of explaining that she just wanted to find her child, Lucy hurried off into the anonymity of Oxford Circus.

She slipped into the Cowdray Club through the Henrietta Place entrance, hoping to get down to the kitchens before anybody noticed she was late. 'Lucy – wait a moment, please.' Celia Bannerman was standing by the carved oval balcony which overlooked the lobby from the mezzanine level. 'I'd like a word with you before you start work.'

Celia had thought long and hard about what to do when Lucy Peters returned from her afternoon off, and had decided that she was unwilling to let the girl face the police without some sort of gentle warning. She didn't doubt that Lucy was behind the thefts at the club and she would have to be disciplined accordingly, but Celia had no intention of allowing it to get out of hand in light of what else had happened; Lucy was fragile at the best of times, and there was no telling what she would do if the news of Marjorie's death were sprung on her by an unknown and unsympathetic police inspector. The reputation of the Cowdray Club was at stake, and containment was to be fought for at all costs.

She looked down at the girl's anxious face through the oval well-opening and cut off her apologies for arriving back late. 'Don't worry about that,' she said reassuringly. 'Come upstairs with me for a moment – your evening duties can wait. I've told Mrs Lawrence that I'll be needing you for a while.'

Lucy's apprehension turned to suspicion, and Celia wondered what sort of impression she usually made on the girls if this was their reaction to a few words of kindness from her. She led the way up the back stairs to her own rooms on the third floor, and asked Lucy to sit down. The girl perched uncomfortably on the edge of the settee, and Celia tried not to be irritated by her timidity. 'Now, Lucy – there are some serious matters that I need to speak to you about. I don't want you to be alarmed, and I promise to take care of you, but it's vital that you're honest with me.' Lucy nodded. 'The police were here this afternoon, asking about some of the items that have gone missing from the club recently, in particular Lady Weston's silver photograph frame. Do you know anything about it?'

'Just because I've been in the nick before, you assume it's me?' Lucy said angrily, but the defiance was half-hearted.

'Did you take it, Lucy?' Celia asked patiently. Lucy nodded. 'And the other things? The scarf and the money.'

'Yes.' She looked up, and Celia saw the panic in her eyes. 'What will happen to me, Miss? Will I have to go back inside?'

'Not necessarily, Lucy. The police will have to know, of

course, but I'll help you all I can if you're honest with me now. Tell me why you took those things. None of them were worth much, so why put your job here at risk?'

The girl shrugged. 'It's hard to explain, Miss. I don't really know myself why I took them, but the little girl in that photograph – she looked so much like mine. I know it was wrong, but I just wanted something to remind me of her, something that I could keep.' She looked up at Celia, desperate to make her understand. 'These women – they've all got children to love, and someone out there's got something of mine – I just wanted to take a little bit back for myself. The baby made me feel special, you see – she's the only person who's ever looked to me for help, who's ever made me think that I might have something precious to give.'

She began to cry, and Celia moved over to sit beside her, angry with herself for having been too busy to notice Lucy's distress before now. 'Why did you give her up if you were so attached to her?' she asked gently.

'It didn't feel like I had an option, Miss. Everyone said it was for the best, and I just got carried along with it. It sounds daft, I suppose, when I already had a prison record, but I was worried about what people would think of me and what that would do to the baby. Anyway,' she added, as if trying to convince herself, 'how could I ever have looked after a little girl?'

How, indeed, Celia thought. 'What about the father? Couldn't he have helped, at least financially?'

Lucy scoffed. 'He denied she was his – the family told him to. They said it was my word against his, and no one would ever believe a con.'

'And your own family?'

'Oh, my mother believed me all right. She said I'd brought disgrace on the family twice, and there was nothing she could do about the prison sentence, but she'd bloody well do something about the kid. She wouldn't tell my father, said the shame would finish him off if he ever found out – he still doesn't know he's got a granddaughter out there somewhere.' She wiped her hand across her eyes. 'It's probably best – he doesn't deserve to feel like this.'

'And neither do you.'

'Don't I? That's not what my mum says. She told me it was my own weakness that got me into this, and she was right, I suppose. You get used to doing what you're told in prison, but that wasn't new for me. I've been doing it all my life. That was what got me into trouble with the baby in the first place, and that was what made me give her up – I was too weak to argue. I used to dream that somebody would come in at the last minute and save us from being separated, but dreaming doesn't get you anywhere, does it? The prison brought some woman in to arrange it all. She always seemed to be in a hurry, rushing it all through in case I changed my mind. I hated her, you know, for making a living out of taking my baby away from me.'

'I expect she was trying to help, Lucy. She was just doing a job, like the rest of us – providing a service that she thought you needed. It's easy to blame the messenger, but it wasn't her fault.'

'I know, I know – and it was myself I really wanted to punish. It sounds wicked, Miss, but I almost wished the baby was dead. It would have served me right.'

Celia knew that it was impossible for women to understand or even to imagine the disgrace of an unwanted pregnancy if

320

they hadn't been through it themselves; even so, she was shocked. 'Surely you didn't really think that it would have been better if she'd died, Lucy?'

'At least then I'd know what had happened to her. As it is, I don't know if she's happy or sad, rich or poor, ill or healthy. I don't know what she looks like, or what she's been told about me – if she's been told anything about me at all. She *could* be dead, Miss, for all I know.'

Uncertainty was, perhaps, the cruellest form of grief. During the war, Celia had known women who, having given boys up for adoption earlier in their lives, had scanned the newspapers every day, terrified that their son had been lost in the trenches: it was a hopeless task, with no familiar name to look for, but they scarcely seemed to care, so great was the suffering caused by ignorance. Lucy had lost her child, but the fact that the girl lived on with someone else had obviously added a bewildering twist to the grieving process; what she didn't know, and what Celia could not bring herself to tell her, was that her feelings were likely to intensify with time, that the guilt and sense of self-blame would get worse rather than better. Instead, she just listened, sensing that Lucy had rarely had an opportunity to talk about how she felt. 'I'll never forgive myself for not saying more to her when I had the chance,' the girl continued, 'but it didn't feel like she was my baby to say anything to. I should have insisted on knowing what sort of life she was going to have, at least. Anything could have happened to her. I read what that woman upstairs is writing – I know I shouldn't have looked at it, but I couldn't stop myself. What if something like that happened to my baby?'

There was a hysterical note in her voice now, and once again Celia cursed Josephine for her interference in the past. 'It's fiction, Lucy – she doesn't understand what she's writing about and anyway, it was a long time ago. Things like that don't happen these days – there are laws and systems to make sure they don't. You have to believe in your heart that what you did was for the best.'

'You sound just like the rest of them,' Lucy said scornfully. 'Everyone told me to put it behind me and pretend it never happened, but they only did that so I wouldn't embarrass them any more. No one would talk to me about it afterwards, not even Marjorie. You could almost hear the sighs of relief from everybody that life could go back to normal – they don't seem to understand that mine never can.'

'You're still very angry, aren't you, Lucy?'

'I'm angry with all of them, yes. They made everything worse.'

'In what way?'

'By being so unkind. Sometimes I think I might never have grown attached to her if people had been more understanding, but it was just me and my baby against the world. In the end, I dreaded her being born because I knew I'd lose her; while she stayed inside me, we were together and nobody could do anything about it. If I hadn't landed myself in prison, things might have been different.'

'Oh, Lucy,' Celia said, and put her arm round the girl, noticing that she trembled with grief and rage. 'People think that cruel to be kind is the answer, and it's not just because you were in prison – only someone who had experienced what you were going through would have been any use to you.' She remembered thinking at the time that Amelia Sach's weakness had been exactly that: she understood the pain of women who longed for children, but not the distress of those who were talked into giving them up; if she had, she could never have put the babies so callously into Walters's hands. 'You can't torture yourself with what might have been.'

'But it's the unfairness of it all. When my sister had her little boy, my mum worked her fingers to the bone knitting shawls and boots. She was so excited, but she never even saw my baby – and would it really have hurt her to try to understand? Would it have hurt any of them? I wanted to scream at them, Miss, and worse. Because of them, that barren bitch had my child – I wanted them all to suffer like I have, teach them what pain really feels like.'

Celia looked down at her, surprised and unsettled by the strength of feeling. 'Even Marjorie?' she asked.

Lucy nodded. 'Yes, even Marjorie, with her job and her prospects and a string of people after her. And what do I have? Nothing. Sometimes I hate her more than anyone, because she seems to have so many choices. Me, I was still trapped even after we got out of the nick – not by bars any more, but by what was going on in my head.' Lucy's grief had a desperate quality to it, and it occurred to Celia that this might drive the girl to go further than stealing trivial souvenirs of someone else's life. She knew she would have to tell Penrose that he was right about the thefts, no matter how badly it reflected on the club, but should she also tell him what Lucy had just said about making people suffer? What would he read into that, and how would he treat her? Lucy would never have the wit to defend herself if the police suspected that she had killed Marjorie, and there was no guarantee that they would take into account her state of mind after the loss of her child. Could she really bring herself to set all that in motion? 'It's mean of me, I know,' Lucy continued, embarrassed by her outburst and beginning to calm down a little. 'It wasn't Marjorie's fault and she's always been good to me. She took me for a day out last weekend, you know. Bought the train tickets for us both, and took me to the seaside to cheer me up.'

'That sounds nice. Where did you go?'

'Somewhere in Suffolk. I can't remember what the place was called – it had a funny name. She wanted to talk to somebody who lived there, and I remember thinking how lucky they were. I'd never seen the sea before, except on postcards, and I walked along the beach, waiting for Marjorie to finish, and tried to imagine what it must be like to live there all the time and see it in summer as well as winter.' She smiled to herself, thinking back to the day, and Celia let her talk, wanting her to make the most of the happy memories before she broached the subject of Marjorie's murder. 'We had tea before we came back, and it was like we'd left all the shit behind. We weren't ex-cons or girls who couldn't keep out of trouble or any of the other names they call us – we were just Lucy and Marjorie, out for a day by the sea. I even forgot about the baby for a bit – it seemed easier to do that when I was somewhere else.'

'You should have more days like that, Lucy,' Celia said gently. 'Life's very short. Just try to put the past behind you a little more each day. It *will* get easier – trust me.' Lucy looked at her gratefully. 'Now, why don't you go downstairs and get the cocoa for the drawing room, and we can have a cup together and decide what to say to the police. There's something else we need to talk about before you see them.' The girl's face clouded over. 'Don't worry – I'll look after you. Go now, or Mrs Lawrence will haul me over the coals as well as you, but be as quick as you can. The lift's broken again, I'm afraid, so use the main staircase – if you bring it up the back way, it'll be cold by the time you've walked down all those corridors.'

Lucy smiled and Celia watched her leave. Then, with a heavy heart, she reached for the telephone.

Penrose was losing his patience with Maria Baker, as the woman sitting in front of him still insisted on being called. Like most people, she looked much less sure of herself now she was away from her home ground and in a police interview room but, since Waddingham and Merrifield had brought her in, she had steadfastly refused to speak other than to state her name; a flicker of surprise when he first mentioned the alternatives 'Sach' and 'Edwards' was the only indication she had given him so far that he was on the right track at all.

'Mrs Baker – there are ways and means of proving your husband's real identity and your own, but that will take days, perhaps weeks. By forcing us to go down those routes rather than helping us now, you are giving your daughter's killer the advantage of time. Is that really what you want to do?'

Still, there was no answer. She stared down at the table between them as if oblivious to what he had said. Exasperated, Penrose glanced across at Fallowfield and decided to try a new tactic. So far, he had deliberately avoided going through all the horrific details of Marjorie's death: if Mrs Baker had killed her daughter, she would reveal herself eventually and he liked to keep some things close to his chest; if she had had nothing to do with it, then it was information which no mother needed to hear. But reason and firmness had got him nowhere, and shock seemed to be the only route left to him. 'Marjorie was

choked to death with glass,' he said bluntly. 'Her killer incapacitated her with drugs, waited for her to come round, and
then tortured her in the most horrific way possible. While
Marjorie was still conscious, he or she took a needle four
inches long and sewed her lips together so that the glass and
the vomit went back down into her lungs.' The woman covered
her ears with her hands, but Penrose continued relentlessly,
loathing what he was doing but determined not to lose the
upper hand now that he had finally forced a reaction. 'The
needle tore through Marjorie's skin and caused severe damage
to her mouth, and the pain must have been more extreme
than we can begin to imagine. As if that weren't enough,
Marjorie was made to look at herself in a mirror while all this
was going on. It was a slow, ugly and humiliating death, and
someone must be made to answer for that.' He had used
Marjorie's name repeatedly in an effort to break down the
extraordinary detachment which Maria Baker had managed
to maintain since receiving news of her daughter's death, and
it seemed to have worked. She was crying now, and Penrose
drove home his advantage. 'I think your husband told Marjorie
about his past, either deliberately or when he was drunk. I also
believe that you discovered the secret was out, and were horrified to think that the shame which you'd been running from
for years was about to catch up with you.'

'No,' she insisted angrily. 'Marjorie knew nothing about all
that. If she had, she would never have kept quiet.'

'But that's the trouble, isn't it, Mrs Baker? Marjorie needed
to be kept quiet, so you made sure that she was. And when
your husband turned up, you saw the perfect opportunity to
silence both of them.'

'No,' she screamed, standing up and slamming her hand

down hard on the table in front of him. 'That's not what I meant. Marjorie didn't know who we were.'

'Shall I take that as an invitation to call you Mrs Sach?'

'Call me what you fucking like, but I didn't kill my daughter.'

She was so close to him now that Penrose could feel her breath on his face, but he resisted the temptation to sit back. 'There was no love lost between you, though, was there?'

'So? You try playing happy families with the sort of life we had. What sort of world do you live in, for Christ's sake? Walk down a street like ours, and you can count the loving mother-and-daughter relationships on the fingers of one hand. But there's a difference between that and what you've just told me. I could never do that to another human being, and I didn't do it to Marjorie.'

'What about your husband? Could you have pushed him down some stairs?'

'He wasn't my husband. I didn't marry him. He never asked me. He always loved Amelia.'

Penrose was astonished that she would tolerate the life she had led for a man who didn't love her, but he wasn't going to give her another chance to point out his naivety by questioning her about it. Instead, he just said: 'But you are Nora Edwards?' She nodded. 'Right, Miss Edwards – I'm going to give you a few minutes to compose yourself, and then I'd like you to answer my questions as honestly and as fully as you can. Let the constable outside know if you need anything.'

In truth, it was Penrose who needed the break. He closed the door to the interview room and leant against it. 'Well done,

Sir,' Fallowfield said quietly. 'I began to think she was never going to admit the connection.'

'At what cost, though?' Penrose asked. 'You know, Bill, sometimes I hate this job. If she's not guilty, she didn't need to know all that.'

'She left you no choice, Sir. Do you think she is guilty?'

'I really don't know. Somehow I doubt it, but that could just be because I don't want to believe that a mother could do that to her child.' He smiled bitterly. 'It must be the sort of world I live in. We'll give her five minutes, then go back in. Right now, I need some coffee.'

Fallowfield obliged, and returned with two mugs and a piece of paper. 'A message for you at the desk, Sir. Miss Bannerman's just telephoned – Lucy Peters is back at the club, and she's keeping an eye on her.'

'Then God help the poor kid,' said Penrose. 'But that's good news – we'll finish with Edwards first, and then go over there. Lucy won't be disappearing again if she's under that sort of surveillance.'

Celia stood at the top of the staircase and waited for Lucy to come back with the cocoa. The club was always quiet at this time of the evening, particularly on a Saturday, when most of the members had either gone out to the theatre or to dinner, and she enjoyed the peace of the old house as it must have been when it was a family residence. It wouldn't last long, she knew: she had done her duty and left a message for Inspector Penrose, and he was bound to arrive soon to speak to Lucy. She only hoped that she was doing the right thing.

Voices drifted up from the bottom of the stairs, and Josephine appeared with the two Motley sisters. Celia greeted them warmly. 'I hope you've had a peaceful evening after such a terrible day.'

'Hardly peaceful,' Josephine said wryly. 'We've been all over the Highlands, and witnessed a shooting at the London Palladium.'

'We went to see the new Hitchcock,' Lettice explained. 'It's really terribly exciting.'

'Although I'm not sure playing a sex-starved crofter's wife counts as Peggy's finest hour,' Ronnie said, and continued in a dreadful Scottish accent. '"You should see Sauchiehall Street, with all its fine shops." Lydia will die laughing when she sees it.'

'I thought she was rather good, didn't you, Josephine?'

'Not bad for someone who's clearly never been north of Camden. But I think Lydia would happily play the croft if it meant getting a film role, so my advice is not to mention it.'

Celia walked with them along the corridor to the drawing room. 'Make yourselves at home. The hot drinks are on their way up.'

'Bugger the hot drinks,' Ronnie said, grimacing. 'I want something a bit stronger after all that bracing Highland air.'

Celia laughed. 'Take a seat, then, and I'll have something brought up to you. Large brandies all round?'

'Lovely. And thank you for letting us take over your hall downstairs. I honestly don't know what else we'd have done.'

'Nonsense. It's me that should be thanking you for all you're doing for the club – especially after what's happened. It must be terrible for you. I know what it's like to feel responsible for your staff, and Marjorie seemed to fit in so well at Motley.'

'Yes, she'll be very hard to replace,' Lettice said. 'But we're determined to make the gala a success, if only to do her justice.'

She and Ronnie chose some chairs by the window, but Josephine lingered at the door for a moment. 'I'm so sorry about what happened earlier,' she said. 'I can't help feeling responsible for stirring things up with Geraldine. Are you all right?'

'Of course I am,' Celia sounded more convinced than she was. 'Please, Josephine – think nothing more of it. Go and enjoy the rest of your evening. I might join you for a nightcap later.'

Thank God the lift didn't let them down very often, Celia thought when she got back to the staircase and saw Lucy on her way up with a large pan of cocoa, concentrating hard to make sure that none of the liquid spilled out over her feet as she climbed: this might be a common enough sight in prison, but it was hardly appropriate in the Cowdray Club. The container was heavy and awkward, and Celia smiled encouragingly down at her. 'Be careful, dear. Don't burn yourself.' She waited until Lucy was just a few steps from the top, then added: 'By the way, I forgot to tell you. That little bitch Marjorie is dead.'

The shock and confusion in Lucy's eyes told Celia that she had the advantage she needed. While the girl was caught off guard, Celia put her foot against the side of the pan and pushed with all the strength she had. She had judged the angle correctly. Lucy lost her balance and tumbled backwards down the stairs, and the scalding contents of the pan poured all over her upper body. The cocoa spilled everywhere – two, three times as much, surely, as could possibly have been held by one vessel – and the sugar in the liquid made it stick to Lucy's face and neck like a deadly second skin, scorching her flesh and

330

splashing back into her eyes. She came to rest awkwardly on the middle landing, the pan at her side, but, to Celia's dismay, she remained conscious, and there was something primitive – inhuman, even – about her screams; it was the sound of an animal begging for death, the physical expression of a torment which, until now, had only touched Lucy emotionally.

In a few seconds, the staircase would be full of people. Celia was by the girl's side in an instant, trying to calm her down, but still she struggled and Celia was amazed and horrified by her strength, even as her body writhed in agony. Panic welled up in her as she realised that she only had a few seconds left to make sure of what she was doing. Her hands went automatically to Lucy's throat, red and blistered already from the heat, but she stopped herself just in time; that would be suicide – this was supposed to look like an accident. Instead, she grabbed Lucy's hair and banged her head hard against the stone wall of the staircase, desperate to subdue her cries. The force of the blow splattered hot liquid all over the delicate paintwork, but at last the girl was quiet and Celia looked for a pulse, feeling so sick with relief that she remained oblivious to the injuries on her own hands and lower arms where the cocoa had made contact with her skin. Lucy was alive, but only barely, and Celia knew enough about burns to be sure that the shock would kill her in a few hours, long before she regained consciousness. As the panic subsided, her head cleared and she reached down to pull one of Lucy's shoelaces undone. Behind her, she could hear people hurrying up from the foyer and down from the drawing room; satisfied that it would do no good, she turned and screamed for someone to fetch help from the College of Nursing.

* * *

'What happened after Amelia Sach's execution?' Penrose asked. 'Where did you go?'

'We moved around a lot at first – Kilburn, Stockwell, the East End, but somehow people always found out who we were, or at least who Jacob was. It seemed like there was no one who didn't know about that trial, and they tormented him, as if he'd been behind it all. They threatened him in the streets, drove him out of any job he tried to hang on to. Sometimes they'd leave stuff at the house – kids' clothes and old newspapers. Once we came back from the pub and found a baby doll with a rope round its neck on the doorstep. All because that bitch was never satisfied and couldn't see what she had already. As the years went on, people forgot about us and moved on to some other poor bastard. It got easier for us then, but the damage was already done.'

'How involved *was* Jacob in what was going on?'

'He wasn't,' she said quickly. 'Oh, he knew about it all right – he wasn't stupid. But like I said, he loved her. When he couldn't get her to stop, he just shut it out. Most men would have come down hard on her, forced her to do what she was told and remember her place, but not Jacob – he turned all that resentment in on himself instead. Sometimes I think that's what I was to him – a punishment, a second-rate version of what he'd lost.'

'So why did you stay with him?'

'How many options do you think I had? I was nineteen and unmarried, with a bastard to bring up – the sort of fool who made the Amelia Sachs of this world possible. And it didn't take him long to saddle me with more children and make sure I couldn't go anywhere.' Her tone was scornful, but she softened slightly when she added: 'Anyway, it's taken years for me to work out what was going on. You don't realise when you're young, do you? We were bound together by what happened in Finchley, for better or worse.' She laughed bitterly to herself. 'And in sickness rather than in health. I thought I loved him.'

'Is that why you gave such damning evidence against his wife?' She glared at him, but said nothing. 'Surely what you said about Jacob also applies to you, Miss Edwards? You weren't stupid. You must have known how Amelia Sach made her money.'

'Which crime are you putting me on trial for, Inspector?'

It was a fair point, but Penrose was not about to admit that. 'I'm not putting you on trial for anything, Miss Edwards. I'm just trying to establish what happened all those years ago and assess its relevance to this investigation. Marjorie discovered something that got her killed. We know from another witness that the information came from her father, and that she had checked it out herself and found it to be true. It's reasonable to assume that the secret which made her vulnerable is connected to your family's past history, and the only person I can think of who would care about protecting that secret now is you.' He paused, and she stared at him defiantly. 'You tell me you're innocent, so now I have to go back over the facts to see who else might kill to keep the past in its place. Jacob's daughter, Lizzie – she was adopted by a couple in service in Sussex, I believe.'

She shrugged. 'I don't know who they were. It was all done in such a hurry, and Jacob wanted a clean start so he insisted on not being told the details. Some prison warder sorted it out.'

'The same prison warder who came to see you during the war to tell you that Lizzie had died.'

'Lizzie's dead?'

She seemed genuinely shocked and saddened by this, and the contrast with her attitude to Marjorie threw Penrose for a second. 'You know she is,' he said, confused. 'Celia Bannerman came to tell you when you were in Essex.'

'I don't know what you're talking about. Nobody told us anything about Lizzie from the moment she was taken away.'

'Well, she told Jacob. He must have kept it from you.'

'Why would he do that? I tell you, this Bannerman woman never came near us. Apart from anything else, we weren't in Essex during the war.'

Thinking back, Penrose realised it was he who had said Essex, although Celia Bannerman hadn't corrected him. Perhaps she hadn't heard, or simply thought it insignificant. Even so, he couldn't see what Nora Edwards stood to gain by lying about it. 'When did you go to Essex?' he asked.

'January 1919, straight after Jacob came out of Pentonville. He did a four-year stretch for assault which conveniently coincided with the war. He was a bit old to fight, but they were getting desperate so he thought he'd make sure.'

Essex and Pentonville were difficult places to confuse, Penrose thought, but he couldn't see why Bannerman would lie about it, either. Whether or not she had broken the news of Lizzie Sach's death to her father made no difference to anything, except perhaps her own conscience. 'Can you think of anyone else who knew your past history?' he asked.

'No. In my experience, when anyone found out about it, they couldn't wait to throw it in your face, so I think I'd know.'

'Your first child – what happened to her?' he asked.

'Him,' she corrected, and Penrose reproached himself for

forgetting that not everything in Josephine's manuscript was fact. 'I don't know. Jacob made me give him up. When he said we'd make a clean start, he meant it.'

Whatever the truth of her life was, Penrose could see why Edwards was bitter. As he understood it, she had withstood a great deal of pressure from Sach and Walters to keep her baby, not to mention the social ostracism which she faced as an unmarried mother, only to lose her child to another man's selfish guilt. Was that why her relationship with her other children had been so strained, he wondered? Because they reminded her of what she had given up and the man who had made her do it? Just as he was about to ask, there was a knock at the door. 'Sorry to interrupt, Sir,' Waddingham said nervously, 'but there's an urgent phone call for you at the desk. It's about Lucy Peters.'

'Hardly bloody urgent, Constable,' Penrose said impatiently. 'Sergeant Fallowfield gave me that message half an hour ago.'

'No, Sir, this is a different one. The girl's had an accident on the stairs, and they don't know if she'll pull through.'

Chapter Twelve

By the time Penrose and Fallowfield arrived at the Cowdray Club, Lucy Peters had been moved to one of the treatment rooms on the second floor. Without waiting for an invitation, they went through the foyer into the separate staircase hall. Two maids were hard at work on the stairs, trying in vain to remove the mess caused by Lucy's accident, but there were still enough traces left for Penrose to guess at the extent of her burns.

'Get them to stop that until we've established exactly what happened here,' he said quietly to Fallowfield, 'and have Peters's room locked. Then get statements from anyone who was close by when she fell. I'm going to find out how she is.' He turned to go back to reception, then added: 'And if my cousins and Miss Tey are here, make sure they're all right, will you, Bill? The last thing Ronnie and Lettice needed tonight was another shock.'

A nurse was waiting at reception to show him through to the college. 'Shouldn't Miss Peters have been taken straight to hospital?' he asked, as he followed her down a short corridor past the dining room and up another staircase, less ostentatious than its Cowdray Club equivalent but just as graceful. The newer building which housed the college had, he noticed, been carefully designed to conform to the type of the older one with which it was connected; it was a great architectural feat, achieved without a hint of awkwardness, and a visitor might easily pass from one house into the other without realising it.

His guide smiled at him reassuringly, as if he were a concerned relative. 'She really won't get better treatment than we can give her here,' she said. 'With injuries like hers, it's best to be moved as little as possible, and the faster those burns can be treated, the more chance she stands of making a reasonable recovery.'

'And you have the facilities to do that?'

'Oh yes. Not on any great scale, of course, but the college is superbly equipped and you won't find a greater concentration of knowledge anywhere in the country. Good, practical nursing knowledge, I mean, and that's what's needed here. We wouldn't perform major surgery, but cleaning wounds and preventing infection, monitoring her blood levels and managing the pain as best we can – that's all second nature to everyone here, and we have excellent contacts with the local hospitals. A doctor will check on her at regular intervals and oversee the treatment. Please don't think I'm making light of what's happened, Inspector, but if I were going to scald myself, I'd rather do it here than anywhere else.'

'How serious is it?'

'Extremely serious, but Miss Sharpe will explain everything to you. Wait outside, please. I'll let her know you're here.'

Left alone in a long, barrel-vaulted corridor, Penrose glanced through the glass in the door and saw Lucy Peters lying on a hospital bed; her injuries were hidden by a bed-cradle which had been placed over her upper body, preventing the sheets and blanket from touching her skin and ensuring that her wounds were protected but remained exposed to the air. Three nurses stood at her bedside, including one in a matron's uniform whom he presumed was Miriam Sharpe. There was no sign of Celia Bannerman.

He watched, impressed, as Miss Sharpe calmly lifted the sheet to examine the girl's body, then whispered some instructions to one of the other women. When she came out to greet him, she said nothing at first but gestured to a narrow space at the end of the corridor which had been furnished as a sitting room, with upholstered chairs and a Sheraton bookcase. When she spoke, her words held the same composed economy as her actions. 'How can I help you, Inspector?' she asked, and he detected a lingering note of Yorkshire in her voice.

'I was intending to come here later tonight to question Lucy Peters in connection with the death of Marjorie Baker,' Penrose said, pleased to see that their conversation was unlikely to be punctuated with time-consuming formalities. 'Obviously, events have overtaken me. How is Miss Peters?'

'Her condition is critical. Surprisingly, she escaped the fall without any serious damage other than a blow to the head, but the burns to her face, neck and chest are extensive and severe, particularly those on her chest where the cocoa soaked into her clothing and was kept in contact with her skin for longer. We've cleaned the wounds, drained the blistering and removed any loose rolls of epithelium – that's the thin tissue on the outside of the skin – but her body is in shock and her blood pressure dangerously low. The next two hours will be crucial, and even if she survives those, there's still plenty to worry about – secondary shock, anaemia, infection. I can't offer you any guarantees at the moment, I'm afraid, except with regard to her care.'

There was no point in beating about the bush. 'Assuming

the best possible outcome, when will I be able to speak to her?'

'Not for some time. If she regains consciousness – and I do mean if – she will still be in no state to be questioned by the police. The stress of that alone might kill her, and I couldn't possibly allow it. Apart from anything else, she has extensive burns to her lips and tongue which will make speech painful, if not impossible.'

'Can you tell me what happened?'

'I wasn't there, but I understand she tripped and fell down the stairs with a pan of scalding liquid. Quite what she was doing in that situation in the first place, I couldn't say. The running of the Cowdray Club is entirely Celia Bannerman's domain, but if you intend to ask her what the hell she thinks she's playing at by allowing that sort of thing to go on, then you have my full support. My girls have enough to do in their day-to-day work without wasting time on accidents that could have been prevented by common sense.'

Penrose detected a degree of animosity in the outburst which went back further than current events. 'Where is Miss Bannerman now?' he asked.

'Having her own injuries treated.'

'Oh?'

'Just minor burns on her hands from trying to help. After that, I advised her to go to her rooms to lie down – she was in shock herself.'

'Was she first on the scene?'

'By a matter of seconds, I gather. It was just as well that she was – someone without a nursing background might have done more damage by trying to help. Celia might have spent years in administration, but you never forget your practical training.'

'I'll need to speak to her as soon as she's free, but do you have time to answer some more questions first? I wouldn't keep you if it weren't important.' She nodded. 'You knew Marjorie Baker?'

'I'd met her once or twice. This wretched circus on Monday night has been somewhat forced upon me – if it were up to me, it wouldn't be happening at all, but as it's done in the name of the college of which I'm president, I feel obliged to take part. Anyway, I met Miss Baker at the fashion house. She helped at the fittings. Please tell me that Lucy Peters is not a suspect for her murder.'

'Would that shock you?'

'Quite frankly, Inspector, it would horrify me. I'm sure you're already aware of recent shameful events at the Cowdray Club which have involved the police and which invariably reflect on the college. If you're now going to tell me that one of the club's employees is suspected of murder, I may as well hand in my resignation immediately. We're supposed to be two organisations devoted to the care of the sick and the professional needs of those who look after them. We prolong life. We do not take it.'

Penrose thought about Sach and Walters and others like them, and wondered where their crimes fitted into Miriam Sharpe's view of her profession. 'Miss Peters isn't a nurse, though.'

'That's hardly a distinction allowed for by the headline "Killer arrested at the heart of nursing". And you haven't answered my question. Is she a suspect? I have a right to know how much disgrace Celia Bannerman has brought on us, if only to try to limit the damage.'

That antagonism was there again, and he was interested to

see that she made no attempt to hide it. She was right, of course: the papers would go to town on a story like this. 'I'm not ruling anything out at the moment,' he said cautiously, 'but I want to talk to Lucy Peters primarily because she was Marjorie's friend and I hope she might give me an insight into aspects of her life which other people can't. Nothing more than that at this stage.' He paused, thinking back to the *Tatler* photograph which he had been about to discuss with Nora Edwards again; Miriam Sharpe had been in that picture and, if Bannerman was right, she might have had a connection to Amelia Sach early in her career. 'You spent some time at St Thomas's Hospital, I believe?'

She seemed surprised by his change of direction. 'That's correct. I did my probationary period there and stayed on afterwards, first as a staff nurse and eventually as matron.'

'When was that?'

'From 1896 until 1916, when the college was established. Why?'

'Did you know Amelia Sach and Annie Walters?'

'What can that possibly have to do with anything?'

He repeated the question, although the expression on her face had already given him his answer, and, when she said nothing, added: 'Marjorie Baker's father, who was also found dead last night, was Jacob Sach, Amelia's husband. I believe that Marjorie's death has something to do with the crimes and execution of those two women. Anything you can tell me about their history may help, no matter how irrelevant it seems.'

'I knew *of* Amelia Sach, but that's all. Annie Walters, on the other hand, worked with me for a while. I assume by your question that you know they met at St Thomas's Hospital?'

'I'd heard as much, yes.'

'They were both trained midwives – Sach was young and ambitious, I gather; Walters was very much of the old school, a time when nursing was not the caring profession which it is today. Some people may tell you that I belong to that school myself, Inspector, but they confuse discipline with hard-heartedness; one does not necessarily lead to the other.' Penrose nodded; he had already seen enough of Miriam Sharpe's style to know exactly what she meant, but he wondered where she was going with her story. 'Walters was the product of an emotionless regime, one which trained women to be psychologically robust, particularly in their dealings with patients. I'm not excusing what she did later on; plenty of nurses were trained in that way, but very few of them, to my knowledge, went on to be killers. But that environment blended with her particular mentality to create devastating results. In the late 1890s, we had a number of stillbirths at St Thomas's; that was not unusual in itself, but the number continued to escalate and the authorities were obliged to investigate. Walters was in attendance at many of these births, and it was thought that she may have been responsible.'

'In what way?'

'If a baby is suffocated at the point of delivery, before it has a chance to take its first breath, then the death will appear to all intents and purposes like a stillbirth. She was reported by one of her colleagues, but there was no proof and of course she denied it. She was dismissed, but no criminal charges were brought because of the lack of evidence. Gossip was rife amongst the nurses, as you can imagine, and there's no question that Sach would have heard about it. She left shortly afterwards to have her own child, but I often wonder if it was that incident which sowed the seeds of the scheme which she developed later, and I feel to a certain extent responsible. You see, Inspector, I reported Annie Walters to my superior and began the chain of action against her. It's a turning point, in hindsight, which disturbs me a great deal.'

'You could hardly have kept quiet, though. Who knows how many more lives might have been lost? More, probably, than Sach and Walters took.'

'Oh, I know, and I have no doubt that what I did was right. But the lesser of two evils is still evil, Inspector. You must see that all too often.'

He nodded, intrigued by a connection with the past which he had certainly not expected but unable to see how it aided his present concerns. 'Indeed I do, Miss Sharpe, and thank you for being so frank. Now, I'd like to see Miss Peters's room.'

'I'll get someone to show you where it is.'

'Please don't worry. I've got to go back to reception – I'll ask there.'

There was no sign of Fallowfield in the foyer, so Penrose collected the key to Lucy's room from the night porter and followed the directions he was given to the servants' area on the third floor. The bedroom he wanted was just along the corridor from Josephine's, but it lay at the back of the house and, without the enviable view across Cavendish Square, its modest size made it oppressive and gloomy – not a great deal different from Lucy's Holloway accommodation, he thought wryly, looking at the narrow single bed and basic furniture.

There was no great sense of belonging in the room, and it did not take him long to establish that the wardrobe and bedside chest of drawers held nothing of any interest. There was nowhere else to look except the bed, and there he had more luck: underneath the blanket, tucked by the pillow so that it wasn't obvious at a glance, he found the most valuable thing that Lucy Peters owned – a Box Brownie camera. He picked it up, surprised, and wondered if she'd come by it honestly or if it was another item missing from the club. Either way, it wouldn't take long to find out if anything helpful was on it. He checked the rest of the bed, then felt under the pillows and drew out two picture postcards, one of a row of beach huts and some sand dunes, the other of a lighthouse. There was no writing on either one, so he guessed that Lucy had bought or been given them as a souvenir of a visit. He looked at the location names printed on the back, and found that they were pictures of the Suffolk coast – one from Walberswick, the other Southwold. It was the second time he had seen Walberswick mentioned in a matter of hours; the first had been on Ethel Stuke's address card, and somehow he didn't think that was a coincidence.

He slipped the postcards into his jacket pocket and picked up the camera. Just as he was about to leave, the door opened and he was surprised to see Celia Bannerman. At first, he thought she had been told that he wanted to see her, but the look of astonishment on her face soon told him that whatever had brought her to Lucy's room, it wasn't him. 'I'm sorry to barge in on you, Inspector,' she said, flustered, 'but I didn't expect to find anyone in Lucy's room.'

'Can I ask why you're here?'

'It sounds silly, I suppose, but I thought she might appreciate some familiar things near her when she comes round.'

Penrose glanced at the bare walls and surfaces. 'She doesn't strike me as the type to collect much,' he said, a little sarcastically. 'And my understanding is that she may not come round at all.'

She stared defiantly at him, having regained her usual composure. 'It's wise to stay positive, in my experience.' She pointed at the camera in his hand, and he noticed that her hand and wrist were bandaged. 'You've found that, I see. The owner will be pleased to have it back.'

'In due course, Miss Bannerman. I need to hold on to it for now. It's fortuitous that you're here, though – I wanted to ask you a few questions about Lucy's accident. Did you see what happened?'

'No. I'd just left the drawing room and was coming down the corridor to the stairs when I heard Lucy's screams. I ran to the staircase immediately, but she was already lying in the stairwell.'

She had the sense not to offer more information than was asked for, Penrose noticed. 'And you assumed she'd fallen?'

'I didn't assume anything at first – I just went to help her. But afterwards, of course that's what I thought. What other explanation could there be? Her shoelace was undone, and she'd obviously tripped over that on her way up the stairs or lost her balance through the weight of the pan. Lucy should never have been carrying something like that up the stairs on her own,' she added, taking the words right out of Penrose's mouth, 'but the lift is out of order and I suppose she thought she had no choice.'

'Did you touch the pan?'

'I moved it when I went to help her. I blame myself for what's happened, I'm afraid – I should have been more vigilant.'

'Why didn't you call me as soon as Lucy returned to the club?'

Her demeanour changed instantly when she saw that he had no sympathy with her self-recriminations. 'I left a message as you'd instructed, Inspector, so please have the decency to acknowledge your own shortcomings as I have mine. Cowdray Club business can hardly be brought to a standstill while we wait for the left hand of Scotland Yard to communicate with the right.'

'No, Miss Bannerman, of course it can't. A girl has been murdered and another one lies at death's door, but evening cocoa must still be drunk.' He ushered her into the corridor, locking the door behind him. 'There will be a police presence outside the treatment room until Lucy regains consciousness,' he said, as he walked with her back to the stairs. 'I'll take your advice, and remain positive that we'll be able to speak to her very soon. There's no doubt in my mind that she holds the key to Marjorie's murder.'

It was said with a confidence which he certainly didn't feel, but he thought he saw a flicker of fear pass across Celia Bannerman's face. On their own, the lies that she had told signified nothing; taken together, though, they painted a rather different picture, and the possibility that she had simply been mistaken on so many accounts was slim. He wondered if he should confront her with them now, but decided against it; there was nothing that he could relate directly to Marjorie's murder, and the other reason for bringing things to a head – ensuring Lucy's safety, albeit a little late – could be easily achieved by the police presence he had warned her of. No – before he talked to Celia Bannerman again, he wanted to find out if Marjorie and Lucy had been to see Ethel Stuke, and, if so, what she had told them.

Downstairs, he met Fallowfield just coming up from the

kitchens. 'Anything interesting your end?' he asked, after telling him about Miriam Sharpe and Celia Bannerman.

'No, Sir. Nobody saw what happened – only Miss Bannerman trying to help the girl, and then the business of getting her moved upstairs.'

'I wonder how hard she really *was* trying to help Lucy?'

'What do you mean?'

'We're missing something, Bill. Think about it: the only motive we've got at the moment for Marjorie's murder – *and* her father's – is what they knew about the Sach family history. Put Edwards to one side for a minute. There are three people in this club who freely admit a connection with that story – Geraldine Ashby, Miriam Sharpe and Celia Bannerman – but none of them has a reason to kill because of it. To our knowledge, though, only one of them's lying; Bannerman lied to Josephine about Ethel Stuke's death, and to me about going to see Jacob Sach; now she's first on the scene at Lucy's accident. I can't help feeling I made a terrible mistake in sticking with Edwards rather than coming straight here when we heard Lucy was back.'

'I'm not sure about that, Sir. What if Edwards was more involved in the baby farming than anyone realised, and lied in court to save her own neck? She told us herself – Sach loved his wife; if he found out later that Amelia had been made a scapegoat, he'd have been more resentful of Edwards than ever. He might have told Marjorie, maybe even threatened to go to the police – that would give her a powerful motive to shut them both up.'

'You think Edwards did it?'

'I wouldn't rule it out. She lied, too, remember – she's been lying for years.'

'Yes, but I can understand why. I bet what she told us about the backlash they had to put up with after the trial only scratches the surface. On the other hand, Bannerman's lies seem senseless – that's what makes them interesting. There's a significance in them that we haven't seen yet.'

Fallowfield looked doubtful. 'I spoke to the kitchen girls just now, Sir. Lucy was telling them how kind Miss Bannerman had been to her this evening. Said they'd had a long talk.'

'Does Bannerman honestly strike you as the kind of woman who has cosy chats with her staff?' Penrose asked impatiently. 'Patronise or discipline – those are her codes, and there's nothing in between.'

'You don't like her, do you?'

'No, but that's not the point,' he said, a little more emphatically than was necessary. 'Surely you don't, either?'

'Not especially, but I admire what she did as a prison warder. There's obviously more to her than posh clubs and committees. And I do think she's got more sense than to try to kill a girl in the middle of the Cowdray Club on a Saturday night. It's a bit risky.'

Fallowfield's defence of Celia Bannerman was beginning to grate on Penrose, not least because it made sense. 'It didn't have to be risky – that staircase is effectively a separate room, and it can't be seen from the foyer or the public rooms above. And perhaps she had no choice – perhaps that little chat you mentioned was about establishing what had to be done. If Lucy had been to see Ethel Stuke with Marjorie – those postcards aren't a coincidence – and learned something about Bannerman, then Bannerman would have been forced to act before we got to her.' Fallowfield remained unconvinced, but Penrose pressed on. 'Try this for a scenario – Sach sees that

349

picture in *Tatler* and tells Marjorie something about Celia Bannerman that he thinks he might be able to make some money from, something she might pay to keep quiet. He wants Marjorie to do the dirty work because of her connections with Bannerman through Motley, but she doesn't believe him. Why should she? He's got her into trouble in the past, and this time she's got more to lose. So she verifies it for herself. Remember what she said to Lady Ashby – her father told her something that turned out to be true; we assumed that was about his own history, but perhaps it wasn't.'

'What would Jacob Sach have on Celia Bannerman? She's freely admitted that she interfered in his daughter's adoption when she shouldn't have done, so she's hardly likely to bother to keep that quiet, and I don't see what else he could have known?'

'Maybe that's what Ethel Stuke will tell us. I'm going to Suffolk first thing in the morning to talk to her, while you clear the decks on everything else. Go back to Campbell Road and try to establish once and for all if Edwards was at home last night – that house is so crowded that I refuse to believe we can't find out for sure, no matter how hard they try to fob us off. Mary Size will need to be told what's happened to Lucy, and she may have more to say about Celia Bannerman – but be careful there; don't alert her to anything. I'll brief Wyles and tell Ronnie and Lettice to come up with something that will keep her here round the clock. Did you find them, by the way?'

'Yes, Sir, in the drawing room upstairs. They're all right – shocked, of course, but to be honest, they both still seem so numb after what happened this morning that I don't think this has touched them like it might have done otherwise. Anything else?'

Penrose thought about it. 'Yes. It might be worth trying to find out a bit more about Lizzie Sach's death – get on to the boys in Birmingham in the morning and ask them to look up a suicide at Anstey Physical Training College in 1916.'

'Right-o. And Miss Tey should be able to help us with that.'

'Is she still up?'

'Yes, Sir – with your cousins.'

'Good. I thought I might ask her along tomorrow. I want to know everything she can tell me about Bannerman, and I'm not happy about her being here at the moment anyway.'

Fallowfield nodded at the camera in Penrose's hand. 'Do you want me to get that developed?'

'Yes. Was the girl who confirmed Bannerman's alibi for last night down there when you talked to the staff just now?'

'Tilly Jenkins? Yes, Sir.'

'Good. Nip back down and double-check with her to make sure, and tell them they can get that staircase cleaned up. I'm going to talk to Josephine, and I'll find out how Lucy is before we leave. I want to look through those prison files again when we're back at the Yard, just in case I missed something. We'll leave Edwards until tomorrow, when you've been back to the Bunk and I've seen Ethel Stuke.'

He found Josephine in the drawing room with Lettice, Ronnie and Geraldine Ashby. Like the other public areas of the club, this room struck a peculiarly feminine note; even if it had been empty, he would have known somehow, through the refinement of detail, that it was a place where women assembled, one in which he would not, as a matter of course, be welcomed. Unusually for Penrose, who was egalitarian by nature and comfortable in the company of either sex, he felt a small stab of resentment at the female solidarity which the building proclaimed in its every feature. It struck him all the more strongly for coming at a time when Josephine's friendship with Marta Fox had created a part of her life from which he was similarly excluded, and he wondered if he would feel the same if she became close to another man. Probably not: as much as he hated the way in which his emotions were suddenly reduced to an antiquated stereotype, he realised that his resentment stemmed from the fact that, with Marta, there was simply no level on which he could compete.

Josephine smiled when she saw him, and he beckoned her over to the door. 'Aren't you coming to say hello to the girls?' she asked.

'In a minute, but I wanted a quick word with you first. Will you do me a favour?'

'Of course, if I can.'

'Will you come to Suffolk with me tomorrow morning? I'm going to see Ethel Stuke.'

'Isn't that you doing me a favour?'

He looked sheepish. 'I can't let you sit in on an interview like that, I'm afraid. I can't even promise you'll get to meet her. It depends on what she's like and how much time we have. Sorry.'

'It's all right – I understand. But why do you want me to come with you? As nice as a day out in Suffolk sounds, I can't see a favour – unless it's purely the pleasure of my company.' She smiled self-mockingly. 'That's understandable, I suppose.'

'It goes without saying. But I need to speak to you about the past – the Sach and Walters case and Anstey, and I don't know when else I'll have time to do it. If we can talk on the way, it'll kill two birds with one stone.'

'Two jail birds, you mean?' she said, but it wasn't meant as a joke and she added, concerned: 'How is Lucy?'

'Not good. I gather the next few hours are crucial, but even if she pulls through, it'll be a long haul to recovery. So you'll come?'

'Of course I will. I could do with a change of scene and a bit of sea air. It might clear my head.'

He refrained from asking why that was necessary. 'It'll mean an early start.'

'That's fine. Just tell me what time I need to be ready, and if you're going to grill me too thoroughly, you'd better get the Snipe to send breakfast. I'll tell you anything you want to hear for a flask of tea and a sausage sandwich.'

He laughed. 'I'm sure she'll do you proud.'

'I don't doubt it. Is Bill coming with us?'

'No, there's too much for him to do here, but he's downstairs now if you want to see him.'

She shook her head. 'No, it's not that. I was just wondering if I'll have you to myself.'

As Penrose had requested, a car was waiting at Ipswich Railway Station, courtesy of the Suffolk police. Provincial train connections were few and far between on a Sunday, and, in any case, he had wanted to speak to the local force to establish that Ethel Stuke was still living at the address he'd been given, and that she was at home and happy to see him; it was a long way to go on a hunch, and even further if the hunch had decided to visit her sister in Bournemouth for the weekend. He and Josephine had used the train journey to go through everything she knew of the Sach and Walters case, but nothing fresh had come to light and he wondered now how much to tell her about his suspicions. There had been nothing in Celia Bannerman's prison file except a record of exemplary conduct and a copy of her resignation letter prior to her taking an administrative post in a hospital in Leeds. Her alibi for the night of Marjorie's death was solid, although, if the earlier end of Spilsbury's estimate for time of death proved to be the correct one, she would still have had time to carry out the murder and get back to the club. If he was wrong, he didn't want to compromise Josephine's relationship with her former teacher; and if Bannerman did have something to hide, the last thing he needed was for Josephine to put herself and his case in danger by finding it impossible to behave normally around her.

He collected the keys from the station master as arranged, and they drove away from the town and out into open countryside. The East Anglian landscape was already scarred by the starkness of winter. With no leaves on the trees or crops in the fields, it appeared as a negative image of its fertile summer self, a world governed by absence, bracing itself for the long, dark months ahead.

'Tell me about Anstey and what you remember of Lizzie Sach's suicide,' Archie said, handing her the map on which he had marked their route.

'What do you want to know?'

'Who found her?'

'The games mistress, I think. Her body was in the gymnasium. She'd used one of the ropes to hang herself.'

'And were there any signs leading up to it? How long had she known about her mother?'

'I don't know, Archie. You'd have to ask Geraldine when she sent the letter. My impression at the time was that Lizzie killed herself as soon as she found out, but I don't know that to be true. And as for tell-tale signs, I didn't know her well enough to notice. I know it happened in the summer term, because we were all preparing for exams, so she'd have been at the college for nearly a year, but she'd never settled in from what I could see – and that makes sense now I've heard what Gerry had to say about it. But I doubt there was any warning of what she intended to do. The teachers at Anstey were very good, on the whole, and they genuinely seemed to care about our welfare. I think they'd have noticed and done something about it if she'd shown any sign of depression.'

'How did Celia Bannerman react?'

Josephine thought before she answered, careful to distinguish between Celia's reaction at the time and what she had said about the incident more recently. 'She was shocked, obviously. I think she felt guilty because it happened while she was in charge, and because she brought Lizzie to Anstey in the first place.'

'But it was professional sorrow rather than a personal sense of loss for a particular girl?'

'You make it sound rather self-centred but yes, I suppose it was.' She looked out of the window at a mill, admiring the way the light reflected off the sails. 'It was so strange for us all – I've never known an atmosphere like it. Anstey was such a noisy place, you know, at every hour of the day – with so many girls crowded into it, it was bound to be. Yet the next morning the whole school seemed to be populated by ghosts. It didn't last long, although it shames me to say it: I look back on her death now and I see the tragedy of it, particularly since I've talked to Gerry about it, but I think that's an age thing. I hate to admit it, but there was a scandalous fascination about it for us girls. The teachers really felt it, though. I imagine there was an awful lot of black coffee drunk in the staff room that day, and a few recriminations handed round.'

'I'm surprised Lizzie didn't go to Bannerman when she got the letter. Wouldn't that be the automatic reaction if you found out something like that – disbelief? A need to have it confirmed?'

'It depends who told you, I suppose – she trusted Gerry and would have believed her. And we don't know how much she remembered, do we? She wasn't a baby when it all happened, so perhaps the story fitted with something she had a dim recollection of. Adults think they're clever enough to keep things from children, but that's often an illusion.'

'All the same, you'd think she'd seek some sort of clarification, but she didn't, as far as you know?'

'No, not as far as I'm aware. If she'd gone to Celia, the suicide would have been prevented, I'm sure. Of course, I have no idea if she knew what an influence Celia had had on her life.'

'I suppose it *was* suicide?'

'For heaven's sake, Archie – what else would it have been? She left a note.' Penrose wondered if Fallowfield would be able to trace that note through the Birmingham police. 'And it seemed significant to me that she'd chosen to die like her mother. Surely that would have been very hard to fake?'

'Yes, I suppose so,' he agreed reluctantly.

They passed a sign to Framlingham, and Josephine turned back to look in that direction. 'We really are getting close to my roots now,' she said.

'What? You're a Suffolk girl?'

'On my mother's side, a couple of greats ago. They brewed beer somewhere between Framlingham and Saxmundham, apparently.'

'Just think – you could be related to Bill. That really would make his day, especially if there's a free pint involved.' He slowed the car to take a sharp right-hand bend. 'Do you know it, then? Did you ever come here with your family?'

'No, and as an adult I'm afraid my Suffolk travels begin and end in Newmarket. I'm easily waylaid by the Rowley Mile. I'd like to get to know it better, though,' she added, as they drove down a high street flanked on either side by handsome houses and small shops. The sun finally broke through the clouds for a second, burnishing the pavements as if cued by her enthusiasm, and she exclaimed in delight. 'This is lovely. I may have to move south after all.'

'You don't think it's all a bit too perfect?'

'Is there such a thing? What makes you say that?'

He pointed at a picturesque gabled building with a walled garden, set back a little from the road. 'What would you say if I told you that a young servant girl of dubious morals was found murdered in that house after a violent storm, stabbed several times in the chest and with her throat slashed from ear to ear?'

She laughed at the melodramatic note in his voice. 'I'd say it was a nice house, and I hope they cleaned up well. Who killed her?'

'Supposedly a man called William Gardiner. He'd got her pregnant, despite having a wife and two children.'

'Good God, was that here?'

'You know about it?'

'I read about it recently. It was in the newspapers at the same time as Sach and Walters. Didn't they have to have two trials or something?'

'That's right – the jury couldn't agree. It was eleven to one

357

guilty first time round, and eleven to one innocent when they tried again.'

'Why was it so contentious?'

'The evidence was confusing. They found a bottle by Rose Harsent's body which contained paraffin that someone used to set light to her clothes, and it was labelled as medicine for Gardiner's children. The prosecution said it was incontrovertible proof of his guilt; the defence claimed that only someone certifiably insane would have been stupid enough to leave a clue like that there, and they said it was a set-up.'

'I'm inclined to agree with the defence, although I suppose it could have been an extremely audacious double bluff. What happened in the end? Did they have a third trial?'

'No, the judge tried to force a conviction based on the evidence, but the jury wasn't having any of it and Gardiner was released. He caught the first train to Liverpool Street and disappeared in London.'

'I can't decide if that makes him more likely to be innocent or guilty. How could he have just disappeared, though? Surely he was notorious all over the country.'

'Disappearing off the face of the earth was easier than you think back then – it happened all the time. Newspapers didn't carry photographs the way they do today, and people only had his word for what his name was. There were far fewer official records than we have. Look at what you told me about Annie Walters – she went from place to place with a different name each time and got away with it, and she only moved from street to street. Walters's trouble started when she stayed in one place for too long, but Gardiner wasn't as careless and London was a long way from Peasenhall.' He looked at his watch. 'It feels like a long way today, too.'

'That must have been a terrible existence for him,' Josephine said. 'Surely he spent the rest of his life looking over his shoulder, never quite knowing if he'd got away with it? It must have been like that for Jacob Sach and Edwards, too, I suppose.'

'Yes, and all happening at the same time. You should build it into the book.'

'You've got to be joking. One real crime is more than enough at the moment, thank you. Don't give me something else to worry about.' She fumbled in her bag for a lighter and lit them both a cigarette, hoping that Archie hadn't noticed Marta's diary in amongst the clutter. 'It's interesting, though – Rose Harsent sounds like exactly the sort of girl who Sach took in. It makes you think, doesn't it? These girls or their children – all given a death sentence because men couldn't take the consequences of their actions. I don't get any sense that the twelve men on Sach's jury were quite so analytical of the evidence. If it had been Gardiner's wife on trial for murder, they'd probably have hanged her first time.' She had a point, Penrose thought; he had been surprised by what he had heard of the lack of evidence put up in Sach and Walters's defence and, while he doubted they were innocent, he could see a number of loopholes in the prosecution which a good barrister would have used to save them from the gallows. They reached a junction and Josephine looked at the map, intrigued by the names of the villages. 'Left here,' she said, 'then right in about five miles.'

They turned off the main road just as a magnificent church appeared in the distance, and the landscape changed once again. Closer to the sea, the rolling, arable countryside gave way to heathland covered with a patchwork of heather, scattered fir trees and gorse bushes. Miraculously, one or two of

359

the gorse bushes were still in flower, and the flash of yellow, though tired and faded, made a refreshing change after the muted greys of the journey so far. At the edge of a small patch of woodland, a red deer moved shyly through the rhythms of light and shade created by the sun and the trees. 'This must be stunning in summer,' Josephine said, enchanted by the way in which such rich and varied scenery could exist in close proximity.

Walberswick itself was charming, too, perched on the Suffolk coast where the River Blyth joined the North Sea. The village obviously had a long history, Josephine thought, as they wound their way slowly into its heart: the variety of its architecture was fascinating, ranging from small cottages and converted fishing huts to large, rambling villas. Many of the houses had been built in the Arts and Crafts style which she loved and, by the time they passed the church, which sat defiantly in the ruins of an older, grander place of worship, she had identified at least three properties which she would have been very happy to own. 'Not a bad place to retire to,' she said.

'Very nice,' Archie agreed. 'It's hardly Holloway by the sea, is it? She lives on the green, so it must be quite central.' The road offered no choices, and they found the heart of the village without difficulty. He drove a short distance further on, and parked outside the Bell Hotel, a welcoming, thatched building which looked out towards the estuary. 'I don't know how long I'll be,' he said. 'What are you going to do?'

'Have a look at the sea, I think – it's a wonderful day for a walk. And we passed a tea shop opposite the green. I'll wait for you there when I can't stand the cold any longer, but don't feel you have to hurry – I'll pace myself with the scones.'

He smiled and watched her go, then headed back the way they had come. Ethel Stuke's house was the last in a row of small, red-brick cottages on the left-hand side of the green, and he wondered whose sense of humour had named it after a famous siege. He closed the wooden gate softly behind him and knocked at the front door, although the fierce agitation of the downstairs curtains had already told him that he did not need to announce his presence. It was a minute or two before he heard the key turn in the lock, and he remembered that the former prison officer must be in her early seventies at least; when he saw her, though, he realised that it was not age but arthritis which had caused the delay. She was a tall woman, but bent low over two walking sticks, and her arms and legs were so thin that any sort of movement without injury seemed a small miracle in itself. 'Miss Stuke?' he said. 'I'm Detective Inspector Archie Penrose from the Metropolitan Police. It's very good of you to agree to see me at such short notice.'

She looked at him for a moment before speaking, and he tried to decide if hers was a hard face or if he had simply been influenced by what he knew of her style of pastoral care; in either case, Ethel Stuke was clearly not the type to indulge in social niceties. 'Your colleagues weren't very clear on what you wanted,' she said, standing aside to let him into the sitting room. 'I hope you've got a better idea of why you're here.' Her years on the Suffolk coast had done nothing to erode the harsh London edges of her speech. 'Tea?' she asked, with an economy born, he guessed, of years spent barking out monosyllabic orders; she managed to make the offer sound more like a challenge, and he was about to refuse when he noticed a tea tray in the corner of the room, carefully laid with cups and saucers and a selection of cakes. Perhaps Ethel Stuke's bark was worse than her bite, or perhaps loneliness was too powerful an emotion these days for her reputation to matter. 'That would be very nice,' he said. 'Thank you.'

She went slowly through to the kitchen next door, and he took advantage of her absence to look around the room. It was fussier than he would have expected from someone who had spent most of her career in an institution like Holloway, but she could simply have been compensating in her later years for the trinkets and clutter which had been denied her until now. Most of the surfaces were covered in ornaments and pot plants – African violets, mostly, with a couple of aspidistras – but it was the bookshelves which interested him most. They were stacked with crime novels – Christie, Sayers and Allingham, interspersed with Freeman Wills Crofts and a Ngaio Marsh – and, although he couldn't see a copy of Josephine's book, *The Man in the Queue*, Ethel Stuke's tastes seemed to bode well for the request he wanted to make on her behalf.

'Have you been here long, Miss Stuke?' he asked when she eventually came back into the room, her progress made even slower now by having swapped one of her sticks for the teapot. 'It seems a lovely village.' He resisted the temptation to help her, sensing that it would be looked upon as an insult; the last thing he needed to do was offend her before she had had a chance to tell him anything.

'Sit down,' she said, nodding to one of the armchairs by the fire. 'I'll bring your tea over.' She added a slice of fruit cake to the saucer and put it down on the table next to him. 'I came here to live with my sister when I retired eight years ago. It's not so bad, I suppose. Full of people with too much time on their hands, and nothing better to do than worry about other people's business, but I've met enough like that in the past to know how

362

to deal with them, and they've not found quite such a warm welcome here recently. Mabel died in January, you see.'

'I'm sorry to hear that.'

'Don't be. We weren't close. She never liked what I did for a living. Having to tell people that her sister was in Holloway created the wrong impression, if you know what I mean.'

It was impossible to tell if she meant the comment as a joke or a simple statement of fact. 'It's your time at Holloway that I'd like to talk to you about,' Penrose said, 'and some of the prisoners you looked after and the officers you worked with.' She seemed to brighten at the prospect of talking about the prison, and he understood for the first time that she had lived for her job in exactly the same way as Celia Bannerman, Mary Size or Miriam Sharpe; no wonder she was bitter about the other villagers; to her, a retirement home by the sea must seem like a cruel parody of the institution she had reluctantly left behind. 'But first I want to check – have two girls come here recently asking about the same thing?'

'No,' she said, and Penrose's heart sank; had he really come all this way to learn nothing except that he was wrong? 'There was only one girl. She came last week.'

'Was her name Marjorie Baker?'

She smiled. 'I knew she was a wrong 'un as soon as I clapped eyes on her. Far too sure of herself – she'll be in and out of that place all her life.' Penrose noticed that the force of nature to which Mary Size had referred was much more evident when the former warder was sitting down and the physical frailty of her body was less noticeable. 'What's she done this time? Must be serious for someone like you to be interested.'

'She hasn't done anything, Miss Stuke, but I would like to know why she came to see you.'

'She wanted to know about a warder I worked with at Holloway, a woman called Bannerman. She's gone on to far loftier things since, of course.' There was a note of resentment in her voice which she made no effort to hide, but Penrose was too satisfied to pay it much heed. 'The Baker girl was interested in the early days, though, just after the prison had been turned over to women.'

'What did she want to know?'

'What Bannerman was like, what sort of prison officer she made – I got the impression that she didn't really know herself what she was looking for. She didn't ask anything specific – just let me talk.'

'Would you mind if I did the same?' She shrugged. 'Start by telling me when you first met Miss Bannerman.'

'1902. She found it hard to fit in, right from the start. Most of us at that stage had gone into the profession because it was in the family – it was just like going into domestic service in that respect – but Bannerman had chosen it. She came from nursing, which is what she eventually went back to, because she'd heard some lecture on the terrible medical conditions for women in prison and she thought she could make a difference.'

'And she was wrong?'

'Of course she was. She might get away with that nonsense now – there's no such thing as discipline these days, as far as I can see – but she was fighting a losing battle back then. She was soft on the prisoners, and far too kind to them – most of us start that way, but it soon rubs off. No, Bannerman was too good for us – I don't mean she looked down her nose like she does now, by all accounts; I mean she was genuinely a good person.' She said it in the incredulous tone which most people

364

reserved for extraordinary feats that were beyond the capabilities of an average human being. 'There was no place for sensitivity in Holloway, and it was only a matter of time before she got herself into trouble.'

'In what way?'

'She got too close to the women – didn't report them when they broke the rules, tried to interfere in their lives outside.'

'Are you talking about Sach and Walters?'

'Sach could twist Bannerman round her little finger, but then she was a manipulative bitch at the best of times – that's why she was in there. Got someone else to do her dirty work and thought she'd get away with it. Smarmed her way round the chaplain and the prison doctor, and had Bannerman eating out of her hand. She honestly thought she'd get off, too – right until we took her to the execution shed. That soon wiped the smile off her face.'

It was the first indication of an attitude which went beyond duty and discipline, and it sickened Penrose; Mary Size's efforts at reform became all the more admirable when he saw what she was up against. 'I understand that Miss Bannerman found their execution difficult to deal with,' he said.

'She didn't understand like we do, Inspector. She was like all these abolitionists who wouldn't dirty their hands by talking to a real criminal; she couldn't see that some crimes are so abhorrent to decent people that there's only one answer.'

She assumed his complicity because he was a policeman, and he didn't correct her. Rarely did Penrose allow himself to think about the morality of taking a human life in the name of justice – he would never be able to do his job if he did – but there was a more practical reason why he questioned the sense of the death penalty: the reluctance of witnesses to appear in a hanging case, and of juries to convict, meant that there were far fewer guilty verdicts in the courts than there should have been. Privately, he believed that justice and the families of the victims would often be better served by an alternative – but this was not the time for a debate on abolition. 'Did Marjorie ask you anything about Sach and Walters?'

'No. I might have mentioned their names in passing, but she didn't recognise them and she certainly wasn't interested in finding out more about them.'

'So what did interest her?'

'Bannerman's relationship with Eleanor Vale. That's what I was saying – she was soft on the women, then wondered why they threw it back in her face.'

The name was familiar to Penrose from Josephine's work. 'Eleanor Vale was another baby farmer, wasn't she? But she wasn't condemned.'

Ethel Stuke nodded. 'That's right.'

'What do you mean by their relationship?'

'It started shortly after Sach and Walters's execution. That caused a lot of trouble amongst the other prisoners, and some of them took against Vale – taunted her, told her she should have gone to the gallows as well. Some of them said she was even worse than Walters, leaving babies to die rather than finishing them off quickly. You have to understand – most of the women in Holloway then were just drunks or prostitutes. They stuck together, and they didn't look too kindly on people who took advantage of girls like themselves. They set out to make Vale wish she *had* been hanged, and they did a bloody good job of it. One night, she couldn't put up with it any more and she started to smash her cell up. Bannerman was one of the warders on duty, but officers don't carry cell keys – they have to be fetched from the chief officer, and that takes time.' God help any woman with a genuine medical emergency, Penrose thought, but he didn't interrupt. 'By the time they got there, Vale had managed to break her windows with one of the planks from her bed. Bannerman was first inside to stop her and Vale cut her with a piece of glass, right down here.' She made a slash from her left shoulder down across her breast. 'A couple of inches higher, and she'd have cut her throat. As it was, she nearly bled to death.'

Penrose looked doubtful. 'Nothing like that appears on Celia Bannerman's prison record.'

She gave his naivety the expression of contempt it deserved. 'Record is a contradiction in terms. Things like that tend to be omitted – they don't look good at the Home Office.'

'Is that why Celia Bannerman left the prison service?'

'Partly, yes, but let's not forget who we're talking about. Most of us would have hated the woman for something like that, but Bannerman took her animosity on as a personal challenge. She forgot that a prison officer's weapon is power, not reason, and she just redoubled her efforts at kindness. She was religious, I think, brought up in a convent or something – but whatever went on in her head, she went out of her way to forgive the woman. Set out on her own private rehabilitation scheme, she did; looked out for Vale in prison, and even took her into her own home when she got out. That's the other reason she left, I suppose; officers weren't supposed to associate with ex-prisoners.'

Penrose didn't quite see why this would have satisfied Marjorie's curiosity; kindness and naivety were hardly crimes to be kept quiet, and the shame of the incident was not Celia

Bannerman's. An affair with a baby farmer, however, would be something worth hiding from the circles in which she moved these days. 'Were they lovers?' he asked.

Ethel Stuke glared at him as though he had deliberately tried to offend her. 'Of course not,' she said. 'Prisoners might occasionally get that sort of thing into their heads, but it's knocked out of them before it starts. It's certainly not something an officer would get involved with, not even Bannerman. But it did backfire a little – Vale ended up sticking to her like glue, which probably wasn't convenient once Bannerman started aspiring to better things.'

'Who else did Miss Bannerman associate with? Was she close to any of the other warders, or anyone outside the prison?'

'No. You say goodbye to a social life when you take that job on. That comes hard to most people at first, but not her. The prison was her life – she didn't seem to need anything else. A career was all she cared about.'

'And what happened to Eleanor Vale?'

'Bannerman cast her on the scrap heap as soon as she got this new job up north. I took over the lease on her house in Holloway, as it happens, but I told her I wouldn't have Vale boarding there so she must have asked her to go. She gave me a note with her new address and wished me well, but she didn't say anything about Vale, and I never heard anything more about her. I don't know where she went. I wrote to Bannerman a couple of times in Leeds, but she never bothered answering. The next thing I know, her name starts turning up in the newspapers and she's more important than the Queen.'

'I don't suppose you still have that Leeds address, do you? And the London house which you took on after she left?'

'It's probably somewhere about.' She left the room and went next door, where Penrose guessed she slept; he doubted that she managed the stairs very often these days. When she returned, she was carrying a photograph album stuffed full of pictures and newspaper clippings; from what he could see, most of them were reports of major trials, and it seemed surreal to him to look down at the faces of convicted criminals where he would normally have expected to find family photographs or souvenirs of treasured holidays. 'Here it is,' she said, and handed him a piece of paper.

'May I borrow this?' he asked, and she nodded curiously. 'Did you give this to Miss Baker?'

'No. She wasn't interested in anything else after I told her about what had happened in the prison.'

'And did she show you a photograph from a magazine?' She shook her head. 'Then I've taken up enough of your time, Miss Stuke. Thank you – you've been very helpful.' She looked almost sorry to see him go; in spite of her protestations, she clearly welcomed company if it involved the past, and that augured well for Josephine; the least he could do was pave the way for her. 'A friend of mine is writing a novel based on the Sach and Walters case,' he explained. 'I wondered if you'd be kind enough to help her with her research.'

'If it's a novel, she's hardly likely to be interested in the truth, is she?'

He was surprised by the vehemence of the response. 'The two things aren't mutually exclusive. Anyway, I couldn't help noticing that you like crime fiction.'

'I can't bear it.'

'But it takes up an awful lot of space on your bookshelf.'

'Most of the things in here are what my sister left. I have

read them, but they're full of mistakes – not unlike her outlook on life in general.'

He couldn't help the note of irritation in his voice. 'So you read them to find fault with them?'

'No one who's touched real crime would give them the time of day,' she said, and he wondered what she would say if she knew how much like Celia Bannerman she sounded. 'So I'm afraid I can't help your friend.'

As he stood up to go, his hat caught one of the plants and he remembered what Josephine had said to him. 'Did Celia Bannerman put violets on the bodies after Sach and Walters's execution?' he asked as she walked him slowly to the door.

'No. I did.'

He was astonished. 'After everything you've said about punishment and paying for their crimes, you offer them a final mark of respect like that. Why?'

'Because by that stage they were innocent again in the eyes of God,' she said. 'That's the point – they'd paid the price and *earned* my respect.'

Josephine was pleased to feel the air on her face after the long journey, and even more pleased to discover that she didn't have to share it with a crowd of people; the narrow lane down to the estuary was almost deserted, and she was able to stand at the water's edge and take in the view without any distraction other than her own thoughts. The tide was out, exposing wide expanses of glistening mud, much to the delight of the wading birds and wildfowl which wintered there, and across the river she could see the lighthouse and church tower which marked the boundaries of a nearby town. The ferry which might have taken her there was shut up for the winter, but she had no intention of gravitating towards anything busier than the bank she was standing on; instead, she set out along the beach, enjoying the crunch of the shingle beneath her feet and the unassailable sense of solitude.

The Suffolk horizon was dominated by the energies of sea and sky, and by the endlessly fascinating play of light on water. At first, the sea seemed flat and grey, but she soon noticed that if you looked at it closely, the water was flecked by hundreds of metallic shades of silver and gold, and she felt that it was the sea of childhood – felt it so strongly, in fact, that she wondered if her parents *had* brought her here when she was young and she had simply forgotten. If not, the affinity she felt with this particular landscape would have to be put down to an innate recognition of some remote part of herself, of roots that could never be completely dislodged by time or distance. It was one of the miracles of the natural world, she thought, that you could invariably use it to gauge who you really were.

When she could stand the cold no longer, she turned inland and used the imposing chimneys of a red-brick manor house to guide her back to the village. The Old Cottage Tearooms occupied a pretty, single-storey white building opposite the village green. The beams and floorboards were ingrained with centuries of living and, as she took a table next to the fireplace, she relished the smell of home cooking which filled the room. A bell over the door had rung when she walked in, and she sensed the proprietor hovering behind the kitchen door long before she emerged. 'What can I get you, Madam?' she asked, stoking up the fire.

'Some tea, please – and crumpets if you've got them.'

'Jam or cheese?'

'Oh, just butter, thank you.'

She smiled, and Josephine knew what was coming next. 'You're not from round these parts with an accent like that,' the woman said, brushing some imaginary crumbs from the table.

Josephine was tempted to claim her Suffolk heritage, but she didn't want to encourage any more conversation than she had to. 'No, I'm only visiting,' she said. 'A friend of mine's calling on someone in the village, so I thought I'd have something to eat while I'm waiting for him. I don't expect he'll be long.' The woman took the hint and disappeared into the kitchen, and Josephine breathed a sigh of relief. From where she sat, she could see across the green; there was no sign of Archie yet, so she took the envelope from her bag, found her glasses, and began to read. The handwriting was – as he had said – impossible, but she was growing used to it by now, and its quirks and idiosyncrasies were almost as familiar to her as her own.

'*Josephine, I'm really tired and life seems a bit grim,*' Marta continued, and the sudden directness of the address unsettled her as it had throughout the diary. '*I thought how lovely it would be to have four whole free days to write in, but my brain goes back on me. I want to do nothing but idle. There is so much I want to tell you about things that . . .*'

'There you are – crumpets with plenty of butter, and a nice pot of tea.' She unloaded the tray, and stood back to admire her own handiwork. 'It's something sweet you're missing. I've just got a lovely cinnamon and walnut cake out of the oven – how about a nice slice of that?'

Josephine smiled stoically back at her. 'Perfect,' she said, willing to try anything that might keep the woman busy. She went back to her reading, conscious now that her time was limited and wishing she'd braved the cold to sit in a sand dune.

There is so much I want to tell you about things that – like the strata in a rock – have lain in me since long ago. I have been writing this diary for five months and have said so little – nothing that can interest you. A shaming little record of a shameful little personality – arrogant and unsure. I cannot talk about my work in capital letters, nor theorise about it; I just want to do it, and the lack of opportunity – the result of my own inadequacy – makes me afraid to think about it with anything but flippancy. I do not even pray now the way I did when young, because that prayer would become a drop of water to wear away my heart.

'I know I shouldn't say it myself, but you won't find better anywhere in the county.' A large slice of cake was slapped proudly down on top of the rest of the diary and, to Josephine's horror, the woman sat down in the chair opposite. 'I'm Mrs Reynolds,' she said, obviously hoping for an introduction, but Josephine just nodded. 'What brings your friend to Walberswick, then? Who's he gone to see? You did say "he", didn't you?'

Josephine put the pages down, abandoning all hope of getting any further before Archie turned up. 'A lady called Ethel Stuke,' she said through gritted teeth. 'I believe she lives somewhere on the green.'

'Ethel? Oh yes, that house just up on the left,' she said, pointing out of the window. 'She's very popular all of a sudden, I must say. Two girls were here only the other day – they sat where you are, in fact. One of them had been to see Ethel, and very pleased she was with herself, too. Can't think why – Ethel's nothing like her sister, Mabel – now she enjoyed a good chat, but Ethel's not the friendly type at all. She's the sort of woman who's never allowed herself a piece of cake in her life, if you know what I mean, so I'm surprised she's having so many visitors.'

'What were they like, these other girls?' Josephine asked through a mouthful of sponge. The cake was exceptional, she had to admit, and almost worth the sacrifice she was making for it.

'In their early twenties, I should think – they'd come all the way up from London, just for the day. I remember them because they ordered a piece of every cake we had, and I had to ask them to pay up front – well, you can't be too careful, can you? The pretty one paid – said it was a sort of celebration, and there'd be plenty more where that came from.'

That was interesting, Josephine thought; there was no doubt that the girls were Marjorie and Lucy, and it saddened her to think of how short-lived their celebration had been; perhaps by now Archie had discovered its cause. The bell rang as an answer to her prayers, and Mrs Reynolds bustled off to settle another table, leaving her in peace for a moment. Rather than trying to get any further with the diary, Josephine let her mind go back over what she had already read, and her thoughts drifted back to one particular phrase which she remembered from the first few pages. *'Always when I think of you, I feel we might be together without talking or doing anything in particular, and be happy.'* Thank God Gerry hadn't read it, Josephine thought; the look of triumph on her face as Marta unconsciously countered Josephine's objections, offering her the peace she sought, would have been unbearable. She glanced up and saw Archie on his way over the green; hurriedly, she gathered the papers together and shoved them back into her bag. Mrs Reynolds looked at her curiously and, for once, she couldn't blame her: her behaviour was ridiculous, and it would simply have to stop.

'Crumpet?' she asked, as Archie sat down.

'No thanks,' he said. 'I've had enough of Ethel Stuke's cake to keep me going.' Josephine could not resist a sly glance at Mrs Reynolds, who had come over to take his order and was obviously not as omniscient as she thought. He smiled at the proprietress, and Josephine watched, amused, as she was temporarily wrong-footed by his charm. 'But perhaps you'd be kind enough to tell me where the nearest public telephone box is?'

'My brother'll help you out there, Sir,' she said. 'He's got the grocery store on the main street as you come into the village. He won't mind opening up for you.'

'Oh, I couldn't possibly put him to all that trouble,' Archie said. 'A public one will be fine.'

'Near the village hall, then. Turn left out of here, and it's about a hundred yards ahead of you.'

Josephine stayed behind to pay while he put his call through to the Yard. 'Bill, I need you to find out what happened to Eleanor Vale – she's the link between Bannerman and what happened to Marjorie and Lucy.' He explained briefly what Ethel Stuke had told him, and passed on the addresses. 'Something happened between those two women which Bannerman wants to forget – I'm convinced of it. Check on the Holloway house and make sure it was passed on as Stuke says, then find out if Vale ever turned up in Leeds. I know, I know,' he added, cutting the sergeant off. 'It's a needle in a

375

haystack, but just do your best. And if you have no luck, look for suspicious or accidental deaths between . . .' – he checked his notes – 'between March and August 1905. That's the time span between Vale's release and Bannerman's departure for Leeds.'

'Do you really think Bannerman got rid of her, Sir?' Fallowfield asked, and distance did nothing to moderate the scepticism in his voice. 'I thought you said she was full of the milk of human kindness?'

Penrose considered the contradiction for a moment, imagining a young Celia Bannerman, ready to start a new job and a new life but saddled with an ex-convict through excessive kindness and bad judgement: could she really have taken the ultimate step to press on unhindered with her career? Then he thought about the same woman thirty years later, the woman who had, in her own words, made a decision that work would be her entire life; could she kill to justify that decision? With the image of Marjorie's bruised and bloody lips still in his mind, Penrose rather thought that she could.

He was impatient to get back to the Yard, and the journey through Suffolk seemed interminable. Neither he nor Josephine spoke much; both seemed preoccupied by their own thoughts, and he sensed that Josephine was censoring how much she said in exactly the same way as he was, although on a very different subject. At Ipswich, he was relieved to find the London train half-empty, and they had no trouble in getting a compartment to themselves. 'I'm sorry she wouldn't see you,' he said as the train left the station.

'Don't be. To be honest with you, Archie, I'm losing heart with the whole thing. Ethel Stuke and Celia probably have a point – I shouldn't put real people into a novel and manipulate them for the sake of the story. It's not right.'

He lit a cigarette and looked out of the window. 'You don't really believe that. You just think you *should* believe it.' She smiled and ignored him, and he took that to mean she conceded the point. 'Do you know anything about Celia Bannerman's personal life?' he asked casually. 'Did she ever talk about her family?'

Josephine considered the question. 'Now you mention it, I've never heard her talk about her family at all. That may not be as strange as it seems, I suppose – we were pupil and teacher, so there was always a distance between us, but when I think back to Anstey, I could tell you something personal about most of the other teachers there. For a start, we were all homesick when we got there, so they'd share things about their own families to make us feel better, and we got to know them quite quickly. It was that sort of school. But I think I can honestly say that I've never heard Celia talk about anyone who wasn't connected with the job she was in at the time.'

Her reticence would make sense if she had been raised in an institution, Penrose thought; even now, there was a stigma attached to that sort of upbringing. 'And did she ever mention being attacked by a prisoner?'

She looked at him, startled. 'No. Is that what Ethel Stuke told you? Sorry – I know I shouldn't ask. I'm trying so hard to be discreet and respect the confidentiality of your case, but it's not easy when I know some of the people involved.'

'It's *because* you know them that we can't talk about it. Sod's law, really – I'd value your opinion, but I simply can't put you in that position. And please don't mention it to her – the attack, I mean.'

377

'Of course I won't.'

'Actually, I'm not terribly happy about your being at the Cowdray Club at all at the moment. Couldn't you come to Maiden Lane and spend a couple of nights with the girls?'

'They seem to be spending most of their time at the club right now. Ronnie told me she's developing quite a taste for the institutional life, and Lettice has booked herself in for lunch every day until next Wednesday.' His smile was half-hearted. 'You mean it, don't you? If it will stop you worrying, of course I'll stay with them, although I can't imagine they'll thank me – they're frantically busy.'

'It's all right – the Snipe will sort it out. She'll be pleased to see you. Don't make a big thing of it, though – you don't have to tell anyone if you stay out all night, do you?'

She laughed. 'It's not a boarding school, Archie. I can come and go as I please.'

'Fine. I'll tell the Snipe to make up a bed.'

'All right. There's no hurry, though – I thought I'd pop in to Holly Place first if there's time when we get back. You were right yesterday – I do need to speak to Marta.' She waited, but he said nothing. 'You haven't asked me anything about it.'

'Perhaps I just don't want to know.' The remark came out more abruptly than he had intended, but it had the advantage, at least, of being honest.

'It isn't what you think.'

'I'm glad you know what I think, because I don't.'

'Oh come on, Archie. This isn't like you. Can't we at least talk about it?'

'No, Josephine, I don't think we can. Who you see and what you do is entirely up to you – you've always made that abundantly clear. But surely you can't expect me to sit here like some sort of passive sounding-board while you work out where your heart is? I'm not a bloody saint.' He could see he had shocked her; in truth, he had shocked himself, but there was no point in trying to retract his words now. 'This is something you're going to have to work out for yourself. I can't help you.'

They sat in silence as the train snaked through the East End. When they got off at Liverpool Street, he was surprised to find Fallowfield waiting for him on the platform. 'I've got some information, Sir – I thought the sooner you heard it, the better.' He smiled at Josephine. 'Can I drop you somewhere, Miss Tey?'

'Thanks, Bill, but no. I'll get a taxi.'

'No, Josephine, don't be silly,' Penrose said. 'At least let us take you to Hampstead. I didn't mean that we can't ever . . .'

She cut him off abruptly. 'No, Archie, it's fine – you're busy. And you're right. I need to sort this out for myself. Tell me one thing, though: Marjorie's murder and what happened to Lucy – is it because I've been digging up Sach and Walters?'

'No. Marjorie knew nothing about her family history – I'm convinced of that.'

'Good. I'll see you at the gala.' He nodded and moved to kiss her, but she had already walked away.

Chapter Thirteen

The taxi jolted slowly but steadily up the hill, and Josephine sat in the back, wondering what on earth she was doing. The driver's first few efforts at conversation had met with such a brusque response that he soon lapsed into silence, but the peace did nothing to help her make sense of her thoughts, or to form any sort of rational decision on what she was going to say when she knocked at Marta's door. Archie's words had hit a nerve, and not only because she recognised how upset he must be to make his feelings so obvious; in truth, she was at a loss even to understand the situation she found herself in, and she certainly had no idea how to resolve it. The only thing she was sure of was that the longer she hesitated, the more damage she would do.

Hampstead rested on higher ground than most of the city, and had a clean, country feel to it, even on a grey, November afternoon; the church clock which struck the half hour as she got out of the car had little other noise to compete with, and the spire which nestled among the trees just ahead of her could easily have graced any village in the south of England. When she turned into Holly Place, she found it quieter still; as she rang the bell at number 8, only the poignant song of birds about to roost and the dry rustle of leaves along the pavement disturbed the peace. She waited, but there was no answer, so she rang again, relief mingling with disappointment at the prospect of finding no one in. Still, the house refused to come to life, and she was just about to leave when a woman ran down the steps of the house next door. 'She's in the garden,' she called to Josephine over her shoulder. 'Try round the back.'

She did as she was told, following a narrow path around the side of the house. Her heart sank when she heard Marta's voice – the last thing she needed was to walk uninvited into a crowd of strangers – but she resisted the temptation to turn back. In fact, Marta was alone. She stood next to a pile of earth by the far wall, wrestling with a large ceanothus root which stubbornly refused to budge from the ground. On the lawn next to her, there was a wheelbarrow piled high with dead branches, stones and bits of brick, and a motley collection of spades, trowels and secateurs, none of which seemed to be of much use in the task she had set herself. 'Come out, you bastard,' she swore loudly, oblivious to the fact she had any company other than the tree.

'Do you want some help?'

Marta let go of the wood as if it had burnt her. 'Josephine! What on earth are you doing here?'

'Is this a bad time?'

'No, of course not. Well, yes, but only because of my pride. Look at me – I'm such a mess.' She gestured at the mud on her face and the twigs caught in her hair, but, if anything, she looked more striking than ever, and it occurred to Josephine that this was the first time she had ever seen Marta truly at peace with herself. 'Muck and dirt wasn't exactly what I envisaged wearing when we met. If we met.'

The contentment left her face, and Josephine knew that Marta was trying to work out if her appearance five days ahead of their scheduled meeting was good news or bad. 'It doesn't matter,' she said. 'Muck and dirt suit you. What do you want me to do?'

'Don't be ridiculous. You're hardly dressed for gardening.'

'No, I'm not. It was probably short-sighted of me, but I didn't expect to be digging up trees in November in virtual darkness. If you insist on it, though, I might as well join you.' She took off her hat and fur, and threw them down on a wrought-iron table, next to her bag. 'Anyway, they're only clothes.'

Marta smiled. 'At least let me get you a coat.' She disappeared into the house for a moment, and returned carrying an old tweed jacket, gloves and a pair of boots. 'I'll feel better if we both look ridiculous. I can't be seen in rags while you stand there in Chanel.'

Josephine slipped the jacket on, noticing that it smelt faintly of cigarette smoke and Marta's perfume. 'It's a lovely house,' she said. 'How long have you been here?'

'Only a couple of months, and it was the location I chose it for.' She picked up a spade and started digging again. 'I couldn't be in the city, Josephine – I've had enough of being hemmed in by bricks and mortar day after day. I took a flat in Kensington when I got out, but I soon realised that a place doesn't have to *be* a prison to feel like one. I couldn't face the loneliness of the country, either, so this is a perfect compromise – solitude in the middle of London. And you're right,' she added, touching the crumbling red brick which enclosed the whole garden, 'there's something special about these walls. Think how many summers' worth of sun they must hold.'

'I must try something like this one day,' Josephine said, raising her voice slightly as an aeroplane clattered lazily overhead. 'I've never made a new home in my life.'

'You've always lived in the same house?'

'Not in the same house, no, but always the family home. I've got an encyclopaedic knowledge of digs, boarding houses, hotels and other people's homes, but that's not the same as choosing something for yourself.' She dug a fork deep into the earth and lifted it so that Marta could cut through the sinewy roots that had spread towards the wall. 'It's pure laziness, I suppose. I could easily have had a flat when I was teaching, but I preferred even the ugliest of rooms to doing anything for myself.'

'You should try prison,' Marta said drily. 'It doesn't get much uglier than that, and you never have to cook a thing.' They worked in silence for a while, each preoccupied with their own thoughts. 'Do you have a garden in Inverness?' Marta asked eventually.

'Yes, and it's full of every sort of shrub and tree, from hydrangeas to monkey puzzle, all painstakingly cared for and agonised over each year, but if you were to ask me what I love most about it, I'd say the daffodils that fill the drive in the spring without a moment's work from me. I know it's not a very original observation, and if I were a proper gardener, it's probably the last thing I'd single out, but I don't care. I look forward to them every year, and every year they surprise me.'

A thin trail of smoke rose up from a pile of burning leaves in a neighbouring garden and the smell filled the air, at once nostalgic and bitter, the final goodbye to summer. 'That's the point of a garden, though, isn't it?' Marta said, wiping soil off her face with the back of her hand. 'Something to look forward to, something permanent. That's what I want to create here – markers of a year. You can keep your flower pots and your annuals – they're all far too temporary for me. No sooner has something flowered than you're deciding what to replace it with, and I can't cope with that at the moment. I need something that promises to come back, something that convinces me I'm going to be here to see it.' She glanced up, embarrassed at having strayed into the emotional territory which they both seemed to have been avoiding. 'Something like your daffodils.'

Josephine crouched down and took off her gloves, then gently brushed the mud away and let her hand rest on Marta's cheek. 'I can't be what you want me to be,' she said.

Marta smiled sadly at her, and covered Josephine's hand with her own. 'But you already are – that's the problem. None of this is about changing you.' The encroaching dusk brought a melancholy aspect to the garden, and the lights from the house combined with the smoke and the evening mist to create an atmosphere of pale ochre. Marta stood up. 'It always gets depressing at this time of night,' she said. 'Let's go inside.'

Josephine followed her into the house, and waited alone in the sitting room while Marta went to change. Inside, the house was very much what she would have expected – elegant, although not particularly tidy, and furnished according to individual taste rather than fashion or expectation. In two months, Marta had managed to create the illusion of a much longer occupancy, and Josephine could imagine how much time she had invested in the house, seeking the safety that Mary Size had talked about in a home rather than another human being.

The weather had taken a turn for the worse, and she walked over to the French windows, looking out into the darkness and enjoying the sound of the rain against the glass. 'It's a lovely view when you can see it,' Marta said, putting an armful of logs down in the hearth. 'Just trees beyond the wall, with the odd roof or gable, and the spires of the city in the distance.' She waved dismissively at the garden. 'Shame about the no-man's-land in between.'

'It won't look like that forever. You'll have it beaten into shape by the spring.'

'Damn right I will. Beverley Nichols is moving in round the corner, apparently, so the challenge is on.'

She took longer than was absolutely necessary to lay the fire, and Josephine noticed that she was much less relaxed than she had been in the garden, as if coming inside had forced her to focus on the awkwardness between them. Being here with her was a different experience entirely from reading the diary, where the strength of Marta's emotions and her ability to analyse them had left Josephine feeling like a gauche, inexperienced schoolgirl. Shy and reticent when it came to anything other than her work, Josephine so very rarely made someone else uneasy; now, she seemed to be more in control than Marta, and she was ashamed to acknowledge that she found it gratifying.

Marta poured them each a large gin and sat down by the fire. 'So what did you dress for, if it wasn't gardening?'

'A day by the sea. Archie had to go to Suffolk for something to do with a case he's investigating, and he asked me to go with him.'

'Doesn't he have sergeants any more?' Marta asked, and her expression was so like Archie's whenever her own name was mentioned that Josephine would have laughed had she not found the inevitable triangle so tiresome. Right now, she would gladly have absented herself from the whole situation and let the two of them fight it out between themselves. 'Does he know you're here?'

'Yes.'

'I bet that made his day.' Josephine said nothing; she refused to be drawn into a conversation which would reflect badly on Archie, and to defend him felt like protesting too much. 'Is there anyone else?' Marta asked, and Josephine shook her head. 'You know, I often wondered if you and Lydia would get together after I left. She's always admired you.'

'We're friends, that's all,' Josephine said impatiently, wondering if she would be asked to justify every relationship she had. 'It will never be anything more than that.'

'And where do you draw the line? Spending time together? Enjoying things more together?' She finished her drink and got up to fetch another. 'Having sex?'

She was being deliberately provocative, and Josephine realised that she was simply adopting the best form of defence, but her question was less straightforward than it sounded. Even as it stood, her relationship with Marta was unlike anything else in her life: she and Lydia shared a creative bond and a mutual admiration, but she increasingly felt obliged to be somebody else whenever they were together and, if you removed the theatre, they had very little in common; Ronnie and Lettice's friendship was an uncomplicated joy, which was picked up and put down again with no damage to its significance; and Archie – well, there was no question that she loved Archie and would choose his company over any other; if he pushed her like Marta was pushing her, she had no idea what she would do – but she knew that he never would. None of those relationships risked anything, none of them made the slightest difference to the world she returned to in Inverness – to her real life, she supposed. But Marta was different: she threatened to blur all the boundaries that Josephine had so carefully drawn. Although they had spent very little time together, most of it had been on their own without the safety of numbers, and they had been thrown together in circumstances which demanded an intense emotional honesty; she knew that Marta was capable of awakening something in her which her life would be happier – or at least more content – without. Complacent, Gerry had called it, but frightened would have been more accurate.

She took the diary out of her bag and put it down on the table. Marta said nothing, wanting her to speak first. 'This is all so foreign to me that I don't even know how to begin to respond to it,' Josephine said quietly.

'Because it comes from another woman?'

'What? No, don't be silly. Why should that make a differ-ence? No, it's not that.' She hesitated, realising that any attempt at an explanation would expose flaws in her own character which Marta might scorn, but she owed it to her to be honest. 'It's the intensity of it, Marta – the strength of how you feel. I'm not hard-hearted, I don't lack imagination, but I've never felt like that about anyone. This love that you have for me – look how unhappy it's made you. I haven't often made people unhappy in my life.'

'Perhaps they just didn't tell you. But I didn't hand it over for you to beat yourself up with – making you feel sorry for me was the last thing I wanted.'

'I know, and that's not what I meant.' She left the sofa and sat down by the fire next to Marta. 'I'm being much more selfish than that. You're writing about emotions that terrify me – because of what they might do to both of us.'

Marta took her hand. 'You really didn't know, did you? I

388

thought at first that you were just trying to brush it aside, but you had no idea how I felt until I told you.'

'No, I didn't. And I suppose, in hindsight, that makes me very stupid.' She laughed. 'Even Lettice had spotted it, for God's sake.'

'You've spoken to her about us?'

'No, not really, but she saw I was upset the other night at dinner and I told her you'd been in touch. Lydia was there as well, much to my surprise. As you can imagine, it wasn't the easiest of evenings.'

'Surely you didn't say anything to Lydia?'

'Of course not, but I felt vile about it and we can't go on like this.' She took her hand away and stared resolutely into the fire. 'Go back to Lydia, Marta. She loves you, and she'll accept all the love you can give her in a way that I don't think I ever could.'

'So that's still your answer? To come here as some sort of selfless ambassador for someone else?' She got up and placed herself in front of the hearth, forcing Josephine to look at her. 'And what if I did go back to Lydia? How would you feel? Tell me honestly, Josephine.'

There was no need to think about it: she had asked herself the same question many times. 'Jealous, I suppose. Resentful. But mostly relieved – relieved that things could go back to normal.'

'And what does normal mean? Sitting in Inverness where no one can touch you? God in heaven, Josephine – what on earth is the matter with you? Why submit to being half alive when life is so short? Don't you ever want to watch the sun rise from somewhere that isn't Crown Cottage or Cavendish Square? Breathe some different air for once?'

Josephine was used to Marta's sudden bursts of anger by now, and it wasn't that which unsettled her. 'You don't understand,' she began hesitantly. 'I'm perfectly happy as I am.'

'I'm sure you are, but just remember – a dying man often says leave me alone, I want to die, but when he recovers, he trembles every time he remembers his foolishness.'

'So being with you is a matter of life and death, is it? Jesus, Marta, I thought I was arrogant. Why don't you just listen for a moment? I don't want the things you think I should want, and telling me that I want them won't make me change my mind.'

'No? Then perhaps this will.' Marta moved forward to kiss her. As Josephine tasted the gin on her mouth and felt the softness of her skin, she realised that she wanted more than anything to understand what it was like to lose the rest of the world in the sheer joy of one person. She felt Marta hesitate, surprised by her response; tenderly, she put her hand up to Marta's face, pulling her closer in the hope that the sudden wonder of their intimacy would be enough to prevent her from coming to her senses. For a moment, the simple disbelief of what was happening was enough to convince her that nobody could be hurt by what they did, that she herself would remain unchanged by it; as hard as she tried to forget it, though, Josephine knew that Marta *would* change her, no matter how much she claimed not to want to, and she pulled away.

Confused and upset, she got up to leave but Marta reached the door first and slammed it shut. 'I'm sorry,' she said. 'Please don't go. Just stay and talk to me; we haven't finished this yet. Please, Josephine – don't leave like this.'

* * *

'Let me get this straight. You want to arrest the secretary of a prestigious private club – a woman with a distinguished career in nursing and welfare, who is admired and respected by all and sundry, who was Lady Cowdray's right-hand woman – on two counts of murder and one of attempted murder without any evidence at all? Are you out of your mind, Penrose?'

The chief constable glared across his desk, and Penrose took a deep breath. 'I wouldn't say that we're without any evidence at all, Sir. Sergeant Fallowfield has traced three women who died just before Celia Bannerman left for Leeds and whose bodies were unidentified at the time. Two of them were recovered from the Thames, and the third went under a tube train.' Penrose was convinced that one of these women was Eleanor Vale; certainly, there was no trace of her in the Leeds area as far as they could tell, and while this was in no way conclusive – people disappeared all the time, as he had explained to Josephine – he had not yet found anything which disproved his theory. 'So it's three counts of murder, really, and one of attempted murder. I think Celia Bannerman killed Eleanor Vale, and the current crimes . . .'

'I'm not interested in the death of an ex-convict from thirty years ago, and neither should you be. From what you tell me, she should have hanged anyway and the pressure on us from the Home Office is rather more contemporary than you seem to realise.'

'But that's my point, Sir – there *is* a direct connection to what we're investigating now. I think the Baker murders and Lucy Peters's fall happened because Marjorie and her father found out about Vale's death and were foolish enough to try to blackmail Miss Bannerman.'

'Yes, yes, Penrose – I understand what you *think*. You've

made that very clear. But I'll ask you again – where's your evidence? I don't count three unidentified bodies who happened to depart this world just as Celia Bannerman was catching a train as incontrovertible proof. London's full of women who disappear without leaving anyone behind to care – God knows it was even worse back then. And apart from anything else, the picture you paint of Bannerman's well-intentioned interference in prison hardly fits with someone who could take a life simply because it was convenient to her.'

That was true, and the contradiction had made Penrose doubt his own theory at first; but, in his conversations with Celia Bannerman, he had detected a streak of steel, the kind of dedication and self-righteousness which occasionally blurred the boundaries between right and wrong, and he was willing to believe that her crusade to do good had, in her own mind, justified evil in its progress. The chief constable was clearly not in the mood to discuss the finer points of human nature, however, so he stuck to the basics. 'Then there are the post-cards I found in Lucy's room,' he said. 'She and Marjorie had obviously been to see Ethel Stuke – the woman in the tea shop in Suffolk confirmed as much.' It's just as well she had, because the miraculous piece of evidence which he had hoped to find on Lucy's camera had failed to materialise: all that the film would testify to was a girls' day out, poignant in hindsight because of what had happened since, but nothing more than that.

'A day out by the seaside and some idle gossip are hardly enough to warrant an arrest, though.'

It sounded thin, even to Penrose's ears, but he pressed on. 'Not in themselves, perhaps, but taken together with Celia Bannerman's lies and the fact that she was on the scene at

Lucy's accident, I think we have enough to bring her in for questioning.'

'Has Bannerman got any connection to this Baker girl other than having her frock made?'

'No, but her father . . .'

'And has she an alibi?'

'A partial alibi.'

'But there's absolutely nothing to put her at the scene after two-thirty that afternoon, when she readily admits to being there?'

'No, but she has a history with the family . . .'

'And that's all it is, Penrose – a history. What about the girl's mother? Am I right in thinking that she has no alibi for the murder, that she was on bad terms with her family, and that she and Marjorie had been fighting in the street? Or did you make all that up just to pad out your report?'

'Of course not, Sir.'

'Then I suggest you concentrate on the woman you already have in custody and get a result before some do-gooder from a welfare organisation starts suggesting that we're hounding the socially disadvantaged without good cause.'

'I questioned her again this afternoon when I got back from Walberswick, Sir.' He omitted to say that the interview had consisted mostly of questions relating to Eleanor Vale and Celia Bannerman, and that it had got him nowhere; if Jacob Sach and Marjorie knew something about that relationship, they certainly hadn't shared it with anyone else in the family. Fallowfield had still been unable to establish a clear alibi for Edwards but, whilst this was a blow to the sergeant's professional pride, it created no problematic doubts for Penrose: after the interview, he had taken her downstairs for the formal identification of Marjorie's body and there was no question in his mind that her grief – which seemed to have gained strength from being denied for so long – was genuine. She had touched her daughter's bruised and violated lips with a tenderness which Penrose doubted she had ever expressed while Marjorie was alive and, of all the regrets which he saw pass across her face, remorse at having killed her was not one of them. 'The truth is we *don't* have any good cause to keep her here,' he said as patiently as he could. 'I really don't think it's her.'

'But you don't *know* it's not. You seem to be confusing the issue, Penrose. I asked you to take a look at the Cowdray Club because of some anonymous letters and a spate of petty thefts; I did not ask you to investigate the private lives of its members, and in particular of its secretary.'

'I think they're connected, though.' It was a half-truth; he agreed with Fallowfield that Sylvia Timpson was likely to be behind the spiteful letters, driven by bitterness about her own abandoned career, but that didn't exclude the possibility that Bannerman had received a threatening note from a different source. 'Marjorie delivered two letters to the club on Friday morning,' he explained, 'and only one of them was from my cousins – I've checked that. I think Marjorie wrote the other one herself and challenged Celia Bannerman to . . .'

'Can you prove that?'

'Not yet, sir, but it seems reasonable to assume . . .'

'It's not reasonable to assume anything when you're dealing with something as sensitive as this. I hope to God you haven't been stupid enough to tell anyone else what's in your mind. When I asked you to look into the matter, I told you to be discreet.'

'To be fair, Sir, we weren't investigating two murders at that stage. Sudden death does rather limit the opportunities for discretion.'

He knew he'd pushed his luck too far: sarcasm was never the right tack to adopt with the chief constable, and certainly not with an issue that contained such a strong political subtext. 'Do I need to remind you, Inspector, that the murders to which you refer happened half a mile away on someone else's premises?' The rank was spoken in such a way as to suggest that it was a temporary arrangement which could easily be dissolved. 'Premises owned by your family, in fact. Perhaps I should take you off this case. The fact that one of the victims was your cousins' employee creates an obvious conflict of interests.'

The comment wasn't worth addressing seriously and Penrose ignored it; he was arrogant enough to realise his value to the force, and he knew that the Chief would never risk insulting his integrity without a better reason than the one he had just given. 'But Lucy Peters wasn't half a mile away, Sir.' He had checked regularly on the girl's condition with Miriam Sharpe and there had been no marked improvement; she may have survived the immediate trauma but, as Sharpe had warned him yesterday, there was still plenty to worry about. 'She was well and truly on the Cowdray Club premises.'

'And she fell down the stairs. It's all very tragic, I agree, but it can't be helped.'

'But just suppose for a moment that I'm right, Sir. Peters is in danger, because the killer will try again.' He was careful to avoid using Bannerman's name; it would only antagonise his superior even further. 'Do we really want to risk that? A young girl's death caused by our negligence – that really would be a scandal.'

'You've got a man posted outside her room around the clock, haven't you?'

'Yes, of course.'

'Then I don't quite see your problem.' The Chief hadn't met Celia Bannerman in Lucy's room and seen the fear in her eyes, Penrose thought; the longer Lucy survived the accident, the more desperate Bannerman would become. 'Look, I understand what you're saying to me and normally I admire your flair – you know I do.' Penrose accepted the condescension through gritted teeth, but he knew that the battle was over for now. 'This time, though, I honestly think you've got it wrong. There's the gala tomorrow night to consider, and the minister's going to be there. I really can't allow you to make waves unless you've got the facts to back it up. Go back and talk to Baker or Edwards, or whatever her name is.'

Penrose knew that he could talk to Edwards until he was blue in the face, but the answer would still be the same: she hadn't killed her daughter or her husband. Understanding now exactly how Miriam Sharpe felt about society getting in the way of the job, he tried one more shot. 'And if I can bring you evidence that Bannerman is involved somehow?'

The chief constable looked at him as though he were a weapon which had fallen into dangerous hands. 'Then of course I'll allow you to bring her in,' he said cautiously. 'Good God, man, we're not in the business of hushing things up. But don't waste time that should be spent on the Baker woman, and if you can get a confession out of her before tomorrow night, it would reflect well on us all.'

Never mind that it's the wrong one, Penrose muttered to himself, but he recognised a dismissal when he heard one. 'I'll do my best, Sir,' was all he could manage to say with any degree of courtesy.

'And you're at the gala tomorrow night?'

'Yes, Sir. I wouldn't miss it for the world.' He smiled, enjoying the nervous expression on his superior's face.

'Then I hope I can rely on you to put on a good show. There'll be lots of important people there, and it wouldn't do your career any harm to make a good impression. No nonsense, Penrose.'

'Of course not, Sir.' Still seething, Penrose shut the door behind him and went to look for Fallowfield. Perhaps the chief constable wasn't entirely wrong after all, he thought, remembering the half-finished evening cloak which Marjorie had been working on for Celia Bannerman: a good show tomorrow night might be exactly what was needed.

'I thought I might publish it, you know – the diary.'

'You should do. It's beautifully written. I imagine that people who can read it without feeling guilty will be fascinated by it – there's a big market for angst by proxy.'

Marta laughed. 'You wouldn't mind?'

'No, not really. Are you writing anything else?' She and Marta had arrived at a fragile peace and, by an unspoken agreement, had lapsed into pleasantries to protect it. Josephine sensed that they both needed time to reassess what was going on between them; Marta had disappeared for ages on the pretext of getting them something to eat but, when she finally returned with plates of cheese and fruit, neither of them had touched it. While Josephine had been glad of the breathing space, she knew that sooner or later they would have to face their feelings or something precious would be lost; superficial chats on social occasions were not what she wanted from Marta, and she was surprised again by how important the relationship had become to her. 'What about another novel? I can't imagine you idle.'

'I've started something, but I haven't got very far with it. And you? I kept an eye out in the papers for a new play, but there hasn't been anything.'

'No, I've gone back to crime. It'll be out early next year.'

'Please tell me I didn't drive you to it.'

'Not to the crime, no, but there's a character in it you might recognise – an actress. I gave her your name and Lydia's personality.'

'Determined to couple us in one way or another, then,' Marta said, turning the bottle in the grate to warm the other side. 'How is Lydia?'

'Up and down. Work's dismal, but the cottage is heavenly. She spends as much time there as she can, I gather.'

'You gather? Don't you see her much?'

'We drifted apart a bit after what happened at the end of *Richard*, and it didn't help that *Queen of Scots* wasn't quite the career boost that she'd hoped for. We're still friends, but it's all a bit superficial at the moment. She's never really forgiven me for being the one who was there for you when you needed someone. I get the feeling she doesn't trust me any more.' She gave a wry smile and poured the wine. 'With good reason, as it turns out.'

'You saved my life, Josephine – literally. Lydia couldn't have done what you did to make me believe in a future; she would never have said the right things. And I haven't even thanked you for that, have I? All those pages of pouring my heart out to you, and I never once mentioned it. It must seem ungrateful of me, but it felt like the sort of thing that I should say to your face – if I ever got to see your face again. So thank you.'

They sat in silence for a while, listening to the soft crackle of the fire. 'Sometimes I think it would have been kinder to let you do what you intended,' Josephine said at last. 'What you went through instead can't have been easy. I was at Holloway yesterday.'

'What on earth for?'

'It started out as research for a new book, but really I went for you.'

Marta lit a cigarette and stared at her. 'Why would you do that?'

'Because I wanted to understand. There's so much that I don't know about you, Marta. I met you as Lydia's lover, and we've hardly seen each other – yet here we are, talking about love and deciding whether or not we should go to bed together.'

'What do you want to know before you have your wicked way with me?'

Josephine took the cigarette out of Marta's mouth and made her light another. 'Don't be so glib,' she said irritably. 'You know what I mean.'

'No I don't. I'm astonished and touched that you would bother to walk round Holloway just to understand what I've been through, but I don't see why anything else matters.'

'So if you could ask me anything at all, you wouldn't bother?'

She shook her head. 'Not if it was about the past, no. I don't need to. How I feel about you won't change just because I know what school you went to.'

Josephine flushed, and felt like a naive child who had failed to understand the simplest of life's truths. The control she had marvelled at earlier was now all but gone and the power between them had shifted: at the beginning of the evening, it was Marta who had laid her soul bare, Marta who wanted something; now, Josephine wanted it too, and that made her vulnerable, as Marta clearly recognised. 'Do you ever do what's expected?' she asked angrily.

Marta held up her hands in apology. 'I'm sorry. I didn't mean to make you feel like a Victorian parent scouting for a suitable daughter-in-law, but are you really so surprised that I don't want to dwell on things that are over and done with? My whole past is dead, Josephine. There's no one left to testify to the person I've been for most of my life – no parents, no lovers, no children. Lydia is the longest connection I have, and I've only known her for two years.'

'That sounds quite liberating to me – you can be anyone you want to be.'

'It's not liberating, it's terrifying. It's almost as if I never existed, because my whole history died with the people I loved. I used to think that was the peculiar hell of the very old, you know, to be the last of your generation; now I know how easily it can happen. I want someone who can testify to my future, not my past. Is that really so unreasonable?'

'No, of course it isn't, but if Lydia is the longest relationship you have, why not try to make it last?'

'Because everything's come to pieces in my hands, Josephine. How could I inflict that on her?'

Josephine couldn't resist raising an eyebrow. 'But you're happy to inflict it on me?'

'You're different – you can take it. Lydia's not as strong as we are – she glosses over things. It's a useful talent to have and I love her for it, but it's no good in the end. She just hands me a plaster and sings while I bleed; you amputate the arm and tell me to get on with it.'

It was an insightful comment, and Josephine was reminded of why she admired Marta's writing. 'So you do still love her?'

'Yes. Not in the way I love you, but I still care about her.'

Josephine remembered what Mary Size had said about Marta's needing something to rely on, and she knew in her heart that it wasn't these extremes of emotion and snatched hours spent with her. 'Then put the pieces back together, Marta,' she said quietly, hoping that the sadness didn't show in her voice. 'The way you love me won't help you do that. There are only so many limbs you can lose.'

Marta sighed impatiently. 'You make it sound so straightforward. Apart from anything else, why should Lydia even think of taking me back after everything that's happened?'

It was the first hint of acquiescence, and relief was the last of the emotions which Josephine felt. 'Coy really doesn't suit you,' she snapped. 'Of course she'd have you back. Surely you've read her letters?' Her jealousy took her completely by surprise, and she realised suddenly that many of her reasons for bringing the couple together were utterly selfish: as long as Marta was with Lydia, there was no danger of losing her completely. 'Anyway, it's not up to me to tell you to make a go of it with her. I'm just saying don't make me a reason not to.'

'But you are. Damn you, Josephine – my head tells me to go to Lydia, but still I cling to this ridiculous dream that you and I might have a future together. I never dreamt when I started that bloody diary in February that by November I'd still be incapable of looking at anyone else because of you, but it's true. Even then, I thought that seeing you would be a kill-or-cure method. That's all very well, but you forget that sometimes those methods do actually kill.' She drained her glass and rubbed her hands across her eyes. 'You got me through prison, too, but if I'd known then what I know now – what your coming here today has taught me – I think I'd have turned my face to the wall and given in.'

'What has it taught you?'

'That there's no such thing as pride any more. I used to think that my feelings for you were all or nothing, that if I ever had the guts to declare myself to you, I'd also have the strength to walk away. I meant what I said, you know – if the answer was no, I vowed I wouldn't bother you again.'

'And now?'

'Now?' She put Josephine's glass down and took both her hands. 'Now I think that just to be in the same room as you is adventure enough, that your friendship would be more exciting than most people's love. All my good intentions left me the minute I set eyes on you today, and I know that even if I tell you to go now, sooner or later I'll come crawling back like a spaniel begging for any crumb you might throw me. I know that my love for you will make me lie my way into your friendship, that I'll deny the very fact of its existence just for the joy of seeing you.' She looked away, suddenly self-conscious. 'It's ironic, isn't it? I don't want you to change at all, but I'll become whatever I have to just to be near you – I'll even be your friend.'

'Don't you think there's more permanence in that, though? If we were lovers, you'd soon get tired of it.'

Marta laughed scornfully. 'You think I only want you

402

because I can't have you? That's really not worthy of you, Josephine. I'm forty-four, but even when I was sixteen I didn't confuse those issues. I've told three people in my life that I love them, and each time I've known that it would always be true, no matter what happened. I meant it when I said it to Lydia, and I mean it when I say it to you.'

'But Marta, you can't go around collecting lovers – that's not worthy of *you*.' Josephine looked at her in disbelief and pulled away. 'If you're always going to love Lydia, I don't quite see where I fit in.'

'That's not what I meant. I was just trying to convince you that this isn't about a cheap conquest. And anyway, if it's about fitting in, I have no illusions about the fact that *I'll* have to fit in with *you*. I know you have a life. I know you have responsibilities. I look at you sitting there and I know that whatever we do or don't do, you'll have to go away some time. If you stay the night, morning will call you back to Cavendish Square; if you stay a week, you'll still go eventually, and I'll be left longing for you to return.'

'And you really want that sort of life?'

'I want you. If you come with that sort of life, then so be it. I can accept that.' Marta sat as close as she could without touching her, and Josephine had no doubt that she realised the power of that restraint. 'If you're holding back because you really don't want me in your life, then go – I won't stop you again. But don't do it for my sake. This sort of thing doesn't happen very often, Josephine, or with many people. If we ignore it, we're missing something splendid, and I think you want it as badly as I do.'

'How can you have any idea of what I want if I don't know myself?'

403

'Because we're alike, you and I. We both want peace and freedom. The only difference is that I believe you can find them in another human being – that we can find them in each other – and you've yet to be convinced.'

'And you think you can convince me, I suppose.' Josephine stood up and put her empty glass down on the table. For once, Marta seemed to have no arguments left; defeated by Josephine's resolve, she sat staring into the fire, saying nothing. 'Well?' Josephine asked impatiently.

Confused, Marta looked up. 'Well what?'

'Do you think you can convince me? I don't want to be right about this, Marta, so if there's the slightest chance that you can prove to me what you say you can, then what are you waiting for?'

'I don't understand.' Marta spoke hesitantly, scarcely daring to believe what she was hearing. 'Are you sure?'

'Of course I'm not. I'm not sure about anything, and the more we talk about it, the less sure I become.' Fear made Josephine antagonistic, and she took Marta's hand to soften the words. 'It's going to kill us, all this talking,' she said. 'We analyse everything and it's one of the things I love about us, but there are times when that isn't necessary, and perhaps this is one of them.' The truce had been so long in coming that Josephine was reluctant to place any more obstacles in its way, but she spoke anyway. 'I need to know that you meant what you said, though – about understanding my life and not changing anything. If you're just saying that, and you're going to come to me in a week or a month or a year and want more, then I should leave now.'

'A year?' Marta grinned wickedly. 'If you're giving me a year, this must be serious.'

'Don't joke about it. This has to be between you and me, and no one else.'

The grin faded, and Marta looked at her for what felt like an age. 'I was right,' she said eventually. 'They are grey.' Gently, she touched Josephine's cheek, just below her eye. 'I'm not joking, Josephine. I know this isn't a competition, but you're not the only one who's vulnerable. We both need to be sure of what we're doing.'

For the first time, Josephine recognised how much Marta stood to lose by loving her, and somehow the fact that their bond was based on a mutual fragility gave it strength. 'I'm sorry. That was selfish of me. It's just . . .'

Marta interrupted her. 'I know what it is. You need to be safe, and I understand that. But this isn't Inverness, Josephine. It isn't the West End. What happens between us, in this house, has nothing to do with anyone.' She smiled and stood up. 'Wait here – I won't be long. I don't have to lock the doors, do I?' Josephine shook her head, and listened as Marta's footsteps faded. When she came back a few minutes later, she stood at the door and held out her hand. 'Come on.'

The bedroom was a beautiful, high-ceilinged room at the back of the house. Marta had lit a fire, and the flames threw a muted reflection on to the mahogany of the bed, turning the wood an even richer red. The only other colour in the room came from a painting on the far wall, an oil of a village street which reminded Josephine of somewhere in France she had visited as a girl. Everything else was white, and there was a stillness about it which seemed to underline Marta's promise to her of peace. Suddenly unsure of herself, Josephine walked over to the window and looked out into the darkness; Marta's reflection stared back at her, vague and insubstantial in the lamplight, and she put her hand up to touch it. The glass was cold beneath her fingertips.

'Are you all right?'

Josephine nodded. 'None of this feels very real, though. It sounds ridiculous, but I'm half afraid to turn round in case you're not there.'

Marta kissed the back of her neck. 'Where else would I be, now I've gone to all this trouble?' She took Josephine's hand and led her over to the bed. Slowly, they undressed each other. Transfixed by the curve of Marta's back as she leaned forward, by the way her hair washed over her shoulders, Josephine was forced to acknowledge a need which had been suppressed for more years than she cared to remember. They lay down together and Marta pulled her close, kissing her hard as she became more aroused, then gently guiding Josephine's mouth towards her breasts; as Josephine felt the nipple harden against her tongue, she had to fight the rush of her own desire to prevent her from hurrying anything about this moment. Aware that the first time would always be special, she explored Marta's body inch by inch, tenderly stroking her skin, then allowing her hand to move softly across her pubic hair. Her touch – hesitant at first – grew more urgent, and she heard Marta whisper her name with a longing that both moved and frightened her. For a moment, she tried to deny the emotional impact of what was happening, but, as Marta cried out and pressed against her, Josephine knew it was useless to pretend that the joy she found in their bond was simply a physical attraction.

The strength of her feelings took her completely by surprise. Struggling to make sense of them, she ran her fingers back across Marta's stomach and traced the contours of her breasts, noticing that her skin was flushed with desire. Marta kissed her fingertips one by one, then turned and took Josephine in her arms; her hand moved lovingly down Josephine's body, and Josephine felt a combination of exhilaration and safety which she had never thought possible. Her instinct was to close her eyes and submit all her other senses to the joy of Marta's touch, but it was impossible: Marta's gaze held her as steadily as the arm around her shoulders, and she couldn't have looked away even if she had wanted to. She lifted her hand to Marta's cheek, a silent apology for having doubted her, and Marta drew her closer as she came, softly kissing tears from her face and neck. In the peace of the moments that followed, Josephine wondered how she could ever have believed Marta to be dangerous.

For a long time, they lay together without speaking. 'What are you thinking?' Marta asked eventually.

Josephine glanced away, reluctant to answer. 'You don't want to talk about the past.'

'I'll make an exception. You look so sad.' She tried to keep her tone light, but it sounded forced and unconvincing. 'Is it someone you've loved and lost?'

'No, of course not.' Josephine kissed her. 'What more could I possibly want than this? No, it's not my past I was thinking about – it's yours, and what you had to go through when you were married. I can't bear what he did to your body, how he must have hurt you.'

'It's my mind he fucked with, not my body. That's where the real scars are.' She smiled sadly, and ran her fingers through Josephine's hair. 'And even they're fading. Every time you look at me like that, he takes another step back.'

Josephine found it hard to believe her, but she didn't argue;

if Marta wanted to convince herself that her past could recede so easily, she wasn't about to disillusion her, but she doubted that the memory of her husband – and in particular the things he had driven her to do by separating her from her children – would ever allow Marta to live her life entirely without shadows. 'Even so, I can't imagine that Holloway is the best place to lay your ghosts,' she said.

'I don't know; at least I had plenty of time to think about what happened. I remember wondering if that was why I loved you – because you understood, and you gave me the only connection I had with the daughter I'd never known.' She smiled, 'It didn't take me long to realise there was more to it than that, but you met Elspeth before she was killed and that made you precious to me, regardless of anything else. I tried to get in touch with Elspeth's adoptive mother,' she added hesitantly. 'I wrote to her from prison, but the letters came back unopened. Then when I got out, I went up to Berwick to see her.'

'What happened?' Josephine asked softly.

'Nothing. I couldn't do it. There was a little park at the end of their street, and I sat for hours trying to find the courage, but I couldn't even go to the door. In the end, I just caught the train back again.' She rubbed her hand angrily across her face. 'If I'd given up so easily on other parts of my life, things might have been very different.'

Josephine caught Marta's hand and wiped the tears away more gently. 'What did you want from her?'

'I told myself I wanted to know about Elspeth's life,' she said. 'I had some bizarre notion that sharing the loss of a child might bring us together, that we could help each other, but really that was nonsense. I wanted forgiveness, Josephine.

Actually, more than that: I wanted someone who mattered to hold me and tell me that what happened to Elspeth wasn't my fault. I must have been insane. Why would that poor woman lift a finger to comfort her daughter's killer?'

'You didn't kill Elspeth, Marta.' She said nothing, but Josephine felt her body stiffen in an effort to control her tears. 'And she was *your* daughter, nobody else's.' The words were a trigger for Marta to submit to her grief. Her sobs – raw, violent and intense – shook them both, and Josephine clung to her as if she could somehow absorb some of Marta's pain into her own skin, desperate to help but at a loss to know how. Coming so soon after their closeness, it was a shock to her to realise that a degree of separation would always exist between them, regardless of love: no matter how well she grew to know Marta, she would never understand what it was like to lose a child. It was a lesson which all lovers had to learn, she supposed, different in each case but carrying a universal sense of regret; even so, Josephine had not expected to be faced with it quite so early in their relationship.

'I'm sorry,' Marta said at last, following her thoughts. 'You must wonder what the hell you've got yourself into.'

'I know what I'm doing, Marta. And you have nothing to be sorry for. You've apologised enough.' As the night went on, they made love again, and this time the intensity was replaced by a tender assurance which seemed to Josephine to hold its own excitement, if only because it hinted at a past and a future. Afterwards, she lay awake for a long time, her body pleasurably tired, her mind weary with guilt at having unlocked in Marta a grief which would be with her long after Josephine had returned to Inverness.

Chapter Fourteen

Celia Bannerman opened the leather carrying-case carefully, and took out its contents one by one: a tape measure and a two-foot rule first, followed by a roll of twine and some copper wire, a pair of pliers, two leather straps, a white cap and, of course, the rope. She was surprised to see a bundle in the corner of the bag, wrapped in what looked like a baby's shawl. It wasn't something she remembered packing, but she took it out anyway and laid it on the table. Satisfied that everything was in order, she turned to fetch the prisoner but her exit from the cell was blocked by two men in suits who stepped quickly towards her. Before she realised what was happening, her hands were clasped behind her back with one of the straps and she was swung round and led from the cell. The rope which she had laid on the table only seconds before was somehow now hanging from the ceiling in a chamber at the end of the corridor, and she felt herself pushed inevitably towards it. She tried to speak, to explain that she was the warder and not the prisoner, but it was no good: a white hood was pulled over her face and she began to suffocate, choking on the cloth which moved in and out of her mouth as she tried to gasp for air. Someone shoved a bundle hard into her hands, then, when she could bear the suspense no longer, she heard the sound of a lever being pulled and felt herself falling.

She sat up in bed, trying to breathe calmly until the panic of the dream subsided. It was hard to say which was worse: the long hours spent lying awake, or the short snatches of sleep, when thirty years of denial and suppressed fear came back to haunt her with twisted versions of her past. Someone had once told her that to dream of the gallows was a prophecy of good fortune, but nothing felt further from the truth; whenever she dropped her guard, the images took advantage of an exhausted mind to play themselves out like disjointed scenes from a film which should never have been made, and she fumbled for the lamp on her bedside table, praying that the night was almost over. It was only 3 a.m.

Damned either way if she stayed in bed, she put on her dressing gown and went through to the telephone in the sitting room. The nurse who answered sounded surprised to be disturbed at such an early hour, but she gave Celia the information she asked for: no, there was no change in Lucy's condition, but, with every night that passed, there were more reasons to be positive; she was obviously stronger than she looked. That was something Celia didn't need to be told: every time she thought back to those moments on the stairs, she remembered Lucy's scorched and blistered body struggling beneath her hands. It was the first time in her life that she had underestimated someone, and it would be the last.

She walked over to the window and stared out into the darkness. Cavendish Square lay somewhere beneath her, invisible at this time of night, but Celia needed neither daylight nor streetlamps to be able to plot each individual feature because the familiarity of a view was perhaps the greatest luxury in a life which she had only recently allowed herself to take for granted. She thought she had finally put it all behind her, this need to be continually moving on, but she had begun to look over her shoulder again, and her nerve was not what it used to be. Knowing that to hesitate would be fatal, she took a piece of paper out of the drawer and began to write.

It was just after ten o'clock when Penrose left the canteen, a snatched cup of coffee still burning the back of his throat. He took the lift to the third floor, ready to brief his team. The public sharing of information and progress on a case was normally something he enjoyed tremendously but this morning, as he walked down the long corridor to the CID office, he realised to his surprise that he was nervous. Usually, when he stood in front of his officers, he had the backing of the Yard's chemists, pathologists and photographers, not to mention a well-tested system of analysis and procedure; today, he was asking them to trust him rather than the evidence. This time, the experts had been unable to help, and even Spilsbury's typically thorough post-mortem report on Marjorie Baker and her father had only told him what could not have happened. His case against Celia Bannerman was based on his personal dislike, as Fallowfield had pointed out, and on a pieced-together narrative gleaned from unreliable sources, one of which made no attempt to hide the fact that it was fiction. The chief constable had hit the nail on the head – he must be going out of his mind – but his attempts to shrug off the seriousness of what he was doing did not entirely blind him to the reality of the situation: if he was wrong, his career and everything it meant to him were on very shaky foundations.

The sane, businesslike atmosphere of the CID room reassured him a little, if only by its familiarity. Fallowfield had already gathered the rest of the team together, and they looked at Penrose expectantly as he walked in. 'Right, everyone,' he said, perching on a desk at the far side of the room, his back to a wall covered in maps of the different London divisions, 'you all know why you're here and you're all familiar with the details of the two murders in question. Some of you have put good work in on the case already, but patience and persistence hasn't got us anywhere, so it's time to step things up a gear. Before we go any further, though, I have to stress that what we talk about in this room today goes no further than the people present.' He saw one or two of the men exchange glances. 'The Cowdray Club and the College of Nursing are respected organisations with high-profile connections. WPC Wyles is already working at the club under cover, and I'll brief her later this morning when I go over to Cavendish Square, but she's the only other person who will know what's going on.' He smiled wryly at his colleagues. 'We don't want to upset the chief constable's evening, do we?'

A ripple of laughter ran through the room. Penrose opened the file he was carrying, and passed the contents round. 'There are some plans of the club here, and photographs from a recent *Tatler* which show some of its key members and the victim, Marjorie Baker. I want you all to familiarise yourselves with the faces in the picture and the layout of the building – you'll need both this evening. The woman I'm most interested in is Celia Bannerman, second from the right. She's the club's secretary, and a key figure in nursing administration and welfare. I won't bore you with her list of achievements, but suffice it to say that she's shaken Queen Mary's hand often enough to have calluses.' He paused, anticipating the impact of his next sentence. 'I believe that Bannerman killed Marjorie Baker and her father because they discovered something about her past which she wanted to keep quiet. I also think that she tried to kill Lucy Peters on Saturday night and that, given the opportunity, she'll endeavour to finish what she started. That's where we come in.'

He nodded to Fallowfield, who gave a brief résumé of the past which Celia Bannerman wished to forget – or at least Penrose's version of it. To his credit, the sergeant showed no sign of the doubts which he had expressed privately to Penrose; loyalty was one of his many fine qualities and, if he still favoured Edwards as prime suspect, none of the younger officers would have guessed as much. Penrose was grateful: if tonight was to be a success, the whole team needed to believe in what it was doing, and he knew that the officers had as much respect for Fallowfield's opinion as they did for his. 'Thompson and Daly have been through the records office with a fine-tooth comb,' the sergeant said, referring to the storehouse of past misdeeds at the Yard, where hundreds of thousands of files were kept on all types of convicts and their associates, 'but there's nothing to help us at all with Vale. Of course, it may be that her sentence did the trick and she turned over a new leaf when she got out, or it may be that she just happened to disappear off the face of the earth when Bannerman left London. On the other hand, Bannerman's employment record since she took the job in Leeds is exemplary, as Inspector Penrose says. No one can speak highly enough of her. I don't say that as a testament to her good character, but merely as an indication of how much she's got to lose.'

Penrose took over again, and held up his copy of the club's floor plan. 'The gala will take place on stage in the Memorial Hall,' he said. 'That's where Bannerman will be for most of the evening so we'll concentrate our efforts there, although we'll also have some of you positioned amongst the guests in the bars and dining room. I want her under close surveillance at all times, and Sergeant Fallowfield will tell you all where you're to be in a minute. Lucy Peters is being cared for in the treatment rooms on the second floor, which is actually part of the College of Nursing. You don't need to worry about the distinction between the two organisations; as you'll see from the plan, they're linked architecturally, but it's a complicated building and I want you to know it like the back of your hand before tonight. Bannerman does, and that's the one advantage she has on us. There are two staircases and lifts between the floors; the stairs by the Henrietta Street entrance are the most direct route to Peters's room, but don't take anything for granted.' He glanced down at the timetable that Wyles had given him for the evening. 'The champagne reception starts at seven, and the show itself at eight-thirty, but the highlight of the evening doesn't come till later, after the interval. If Bannerman is going to do what I think she is, she'll choose the moment when Noël and Gertie take to the stage – that's when everyone will be in the hall.'

'Don't blame them, Sir,' chipped in one of the officers. 'That Miss Lawrence is a bit of all right.'

Everyone laughed, including Penrose. 'I couldn't agree with you more, Ben,' he said, 'and if we get the job done, no one will be heading for the front row faster than me. But this is where it gets serious. At that point, if nothing untoward has happened, the policeman on watch outside Peters's room will come down for a drink and a look at the show. He'll make sure that Bannerman sees him – she's been up to check on the poor girl every hour or so, I gather, so there won't be an issue about her recognising him.' He took a deep breath and sounded as confident as he could. 'That's when she'll leave the room and go upstairs.'

'Will there be someone in the room with the girl?' Merrifield asked.

'Absolutely. There must be no risk whatsoever to Peters's condition – it's fragile enough as it is. I wish we could put someone in her place, but Bannerman's not stupid. Whichever one of you is in that room, wait as long as you can to make sure that our murderer incriminates herself, but do not – I repeat, do not – put the girl in danger. And if it's a choice between the two, for God's sake do the right thing. I'm going to have enough trouble persuading Miriam Sharpe to let us do this at all, so don't let me down.'

'Can she be trusted, Sir? Miss Sharpe, I mean.'

It was Fallowfield's question, and something that Penrose had already thought long and hard about. 'I'm as sure as I can be, Bill,' he said, 'and we have no choice. I don't doubt that she's capable of keeping this to herself and she's no great fan of Celia Bannerman; my only concern is that she'll object to the ethics of the thing. I know what she means, but if I can convince her that Lucy's in no additional danger, I think she'll go along with it. Any other questions?'

'How will Bannerman do it, Sir?'

'Suffocation, probably, or perhaps an injection. It depends how prepared she is for the right opportunity.'

Another hand was raised hesitantly, and Ellis glanced nervously at his colleagues before speaking. 'What happens if you're wrong, Sir?'

Penrose smiled. 'Good question. If that turns out to be the case, then I'll be introducing you to Detective Inspector Fallowfield on my way out of the building.' The joke eased the tension in the room, and only Penrose realised that there was a serious side to it. 'I'll leave you with him now to go over the details for later, and don't be afraid to ask any questions you like. We need to be as prepared as possible. So best bib and tucker, everyone, and good luck.'

On his way over to the Cowdray Club, Penrose thought about how best to approach the subject with Miriam Sharpe and decided that honesty was the only way to convince her. Even so, as he sat across the desk from her in her office, he realised that he had a long struggle ahead of him. 'Of course she's in danger, Inspector. The girl has third-degree burns on a large percentage of her body, and all the other complications which that involves. I hardly think you needed to come all the way from the Embankment to tell me that.'

'That's not quite what I meant, Miss Sharpe,' Penrose explained patiently. 'I must ask you to keep this strictly confidential, but I don't think Lucy Peters's fall was an accident and I think there may well be another attempt on her life during the gala tonight.'

'Not an accident? That's impossible, surely. Celia was on the scene immediately, and there simply wouldn't have been time for someone to push the girl and get away without her seeing them.' As Penrose remained silent, he could see Miriam Sharpe reading between the lines of what he had said. 'Oh, that's ridiculous, Inspector,' she said, horrified. 'There's no love lost between Celia and me, as you know, but she's built a career – a life, if you like – on improving things for women. Cold-bloodedly pushing a child down the stairs simply isn't something she'd be capable of.'

'I gather she's shown an avid interest in Lucy's condition since the accident.'

'Well yes, she has, but that's only natural. She's as worried about the organisation's reputation as I am, and her own position may well be in question if Lucy dies – the girl should never have been doing what she was doing in the first place.'

'I think she has rather more at stake than her position, Miss Sharpe.'

'But why on earth would she want to harm a servant?'

'I'm afraid I can't tell you that at the moment,' he said, and marvelled at how this simple expression of honesty invariably conveyed a greater significance to the listener. Miriam Sharpe was no exception.

'Very well, Inspector,' she said. 'I suppose I have no choice but to trust you, but please explain to me what you intend to do. I'll agree to nothing which goes against the interests of my patient.'

'Of course,' Penrose said, and outlined his plan with as much reassurance as he could. 'When the policeman leaves the door outside Miss Peters's room, I want the nurse on duty to leave, too, and wait in one of the other rooms down the corridor.'

'You think the girl is in danger so you leave her entirely unprotected?'

'Not unprotected at all. As soon as the nurse leaves, one of my officers will wait behind the screen in . . .'

'Yes, yes, Inspector – we've all read *The Murder at the Vicarage*. But how do I know that I can rely on your officer to put my patient's safety first? How does the life of a servant girl – particularly a life that is already hanging in the balance – rate against your conviction?'

'You have my word. There will no additional risk to her life. I don't make sacrifices, Miss Sharpe, particularly the human

419

sort, and I don't take it upon myself to decide the value of a life any more than you do in your work.'

His self-righteousness won him the day. She nodded reluctantly, but said: 'I must stress, Inspector, that if anything goes wrong I will personally do everything I can to ensure you never have the opportunity of making another mistake.'

If anything went wrong, Penrose thought, she would have to get in the queue, but he thanked her and stood up to leave. 'And I can rely on you not to share this information with anyone?'

'Yes. I'll take care of Lucy myself tonight. I have no desire to be at the circus, but my nurses will be only too glad to go. In any case,' she added as he got to the door, 'this is hardly something that I'd wish to broadcast, is it?'

Lettice and Ronnie were taking a break in the bar when he got downstairs, and he was pleased to find them on their own. 'Coffee?' Lettice asked, pushing the pot towards him across the table.

He shook his head. 'Sorry – I haven't got time. I was hoping to have a word with Wyles if you can get her for me?'

'I'm not sure we can spare her,' Ronnie said, and grinned. 'Seriously, Archie – she's been an absolute gem, and she's really taken Hilda's mind off what's happened. If you ever decide against women in the force, you know where to send her.'

'You'll be lucky,' he said. 'I need all the help I can get, especially today. As do you, it seems – you both look exhausted.'

'It's the coffee that's keeping us conscious,' Lettice admitted. 'We've been here all night. It's the only way we stand any chance at all of being ready by this evening.'

'Then you can't tell me how Josephine is,' Archie said. 'I was hoping you might have seen her at breakfast.'

'Josephine?' Ronnie asked, confused.

'Yes. I sent her back to Maiden Lane last night – there's too much going on here at the moment, and I'd rather she was safely out of the way. And you should be careful, too, if you insist on wandering round the building in the dead of night.'

'But I popped back to Maiden Lane at around two to fetch something to eat and Josephine . . .'

'And Josephine was asleep by then,' Lettice interrupted, glaring at her sister. 'But she's fine, Archie – we saw her this morning when she came to try her dress on. It was sweet of you to be worried, though. I'm sure she appreciated it.' Ronnie looked at her, bewildered, but said nothing more. 'We'll go back to the girls now and find an excuse to send Lillian out to you. Will you be here?'

Archie looked round, and changed his mind about the coffee. 'Yes, this is private enough and I won't keep her long. And if you see Josephine again, tell her I'll be here at six-thirty.'

'All right. See you later.'

'What the fuck was that about?' Ronnie asked peevishly as they made their way out into the foyer.

Marta sat by the window for a long time after Josephine left, half afraid to go anywhere else in the house. It was a neat trick, this conjuring of loneliness from solitude, restlessness from peace, and she couldn't quite put her finger on how Josephine had managed it in just a few hours, but all her carefully constructed self-sufficiency had disappeared in a taxi to Cavendish Square, and what she was left with now felt empty and desolate.

Tired of the silence, she walked over to the gramophone to put some music on, then changed her mind and made some coffee instead. Her head ached from too much wine and too little sleep, and she turned the bathroom cabinet inside out looking for the aspirin before remembering that she'd left the bottle on the terrace the day before, when her back had lost the war against the ceanothus. Throwing a coat on over her pyjamas, she went out to fetch them. The garden looked worse than ever this morning: it had that weary, dirty feel that always follows snow, and her efforts to clear the borders had only succeeded in trampling mud into the grass and creating piles of dead wood and rubble wherever she looked. As she stared out over a barren, bleak stretch of earth, a wasteland with no hope of spring, she wondered why she had ever imagined that there was a point to all this.

She picked the bottle of pills up and put it down again, afraid of how comforting it felt in her hand. By now, she had lost count of how many times this particular routine had played itself out in her life, but she was surely running out of excuses. She turned to go back inside, the tablets once again in her pocket, but something caught her eye by the wall – a flash of brilliant yellow which hadn't been there yesterday. Bending down, she looked in delight at the winter daffodil, and smiled to think that it should have chosen today to arrive.

Before she could change her mind, Marta walked back to the house, wrestling with the lid of the bottle as she went. She swallowed two aspirin with a mouthful of cold coffee, then took a card out of the wastepaper basket and went over to the telephone.

* * *

Josephine stared at her reflection in the looking glass on the back of the door, and decided that it wasn't going to get any better. There was no question that Ronnie and Lettice had excelled themselves on her behalf: the dress was modelled on a design by Lucien Lelong which she had casually admired when last at their studios, never suspecting that they would recreate it for her. Cut low at the back, and made of a soft satin which clung to the waist and hips and draped in sinuous folds from the thigh, the gown was predominantly black except for a twisted column of scarlet and emerald ribbons that extended down the spine to the floor. It was stunning, and normally she would have been thrilled, but dressing to be on show was the last thing she wanted to do this evening; she only hoped that she had appeared more gracious than she felt when she tried the dress on earlier.

She fastened a single string of pearls around her neck so that it hung down her back, emphasising the low-cut line of the dress, and left the room while she could still resist the urge to crawl between the sheets and hide. Going down the stairs, she was careful not to tread on one of the club's more idiosyncratic features – a silver cross, embedded into one of the steps as a memorial to an unfortunate resident of the old house who had died from a fall and was supposed to haunt the first-floor landing. It was all nonsense, of course, but it fascinated some of the members and Celia had always been happy to exploit any legend that brought in more subscriptions – in fact, Josephine had once joked that she probably put it there herself. After the tragic accident at the weekend, though, the remark had ceased to be amusing. She wondered how Lucy was, and remembered how nervous and clumsy she had seemed at their two brief meetings; with the luxury of hindsight, it seemed inevitable that something would happen to the girl sooner or later, but Josephine had never envisaged the horror of the injuries which Celia had described to her.

Archie was waiting at reception, and she smiled nervously at him, wondering how quickly they would be able to leave yesterday's argument behind. 'You look beautiful,' he said, bending to kiss her. 'Gertrude who?'

The words were warm, but Josephine saw her own anxieties reflected in his face and she led him over to the door, out of earshot of the group of women by the desk. 'Archie, I'm so sorry about yesterday,' she said. 'I should never have expected you to counsel me on what to do about Marta, or about anyone else for that matter.'

'I should be apologizing, not you. I didn't mean to be so impatient with you, but this case is . . .'

She raised her hand to interrupt him. 'Don't blame yourself or the case when I'm at fault. Please, Archie.'

He smiled. 'All right. Shall we go in?'

She took his arm, relieved that he seemed as reluctant as she was at the moment to return to the subject of Marta, but they hadn't got far before Lettice came hurrying out of the dining room. 'There you are,' she said. 'I've been looking out for you. Sorry, Archie, but I just need a quick word with Josephine – you can have her back in a minute.'

'All right, but let's get a drink first,' Josephine said. 'I'm dying for one.'

'No, I need to speak to you before you go in,' Lettice insisted, then added more quietly: 'After that you can have as many drinks as you like – you'll probably need them.'

'What on earth are you talking about?'

Before Lettice could answer, Lydia came up behind them

and threw her arms around both of them. 'Josephine – how lovely to see you.'

'Lydia, I need to speak to Josephine in private for a moment,' Lettice said impatiently, and Josephine looked at her in surprise: she rarely lost her temper with anybody; the pressure of the gala and the shock of Marjorie's death seemed to have taken their toll.

'Of course,' Lydia said, 'but I wanted to say it as soon as I saw you. Thank you, Josephine.'

'You're welcome. What for?'

Lydia laughed. 'Don't be so modest. For Marta, of course. She's here tonight, and she told me that you spoke to her and encouraged her to get in touch. I'm so grateful, Josephine.'

Lettice mouthed an apology behind Lydia's back, while Archie looked as if all his Christmases had come at once. Wondering if she had inadvertently walked on stage in a farce at the Vaudeville, Josephine heard herself give the sort of nervous laugh which usually made her want to slap someone. 'Marta's here tonight?' she asked, the voice barely recognisable as her own. 'Gosh – she doesn't waste much time.'

'No. I sent her an invitation weeks ago, never dreaming that she'd say yes, but she phoned this morning, completely out of the blue.'

'I'll meet you inside in a minute,' Josephine said to Lettice and Archie. 'Lydia and I will just have a quick chat out here while it's peaceful.'

'No, no – Lettice needs to talk to you and I don't want to interrupt.'

'It's fine,' Lettice said, defeated. 'I can wait.' She disappeared into the crowd with Archie, glancing back apologetically over her shoulder.

425

Lydia took Josephine's hand and led her over to the window. 'Let's sit down here for a minute,' she said. 'I owe you an apology, as well as a thank you.' Her words came so soon after Archie's unwarranted contrition that Josephine began to suspect some sort of conspiracy, designed to make her feel worse than she already did. 'I haven't been a very good friend to you since Marta and I split up, have I?' Lydia began hesitantly.

'It's been hard for you – I understand that. You love her, and you've been apart – you're bound to feel bitter at times.'

'It's more than that, though.' She looked away, and Josephine guessed that she was considering how much to say. 'The fact is, I blamed you because we didn't get back together again the moment she stepped out of prison. I'm ashamed to admit it, but I thought there was something between you – something on her side, at least – that was keeping us apart.'

'Why didn't you tell me what you were thinking?' When I could have denied it truthfully, was what Josephine wanted to add, but she simply said: 'We should have talked about this months ago.'

'I know, but I was angry and hurt and bewildered at Marta's silence, and the last thing I wanted to do was show any vulnerability to you.' She smiled, embarrassed. 'And rather more childishly, I didn't want to find out that you were in touch with her if I wasn't. Jealousy isn't a very generous emotion, is it? Or a very attractive one.'

'No, and it has a habit of creeping up on you when you least expect it. I don't suppose I would have behaved any more generously in your position. And I'm sorry if I've made things worse for you – I never meant to.'

'You didn't. It was just the shock of it all, and knowing that Marta felt able to talk to you about things that she'd never

426

discussed with me. I never thought I'd hear myself say this, but it's not just about sex, is it?' Josephine shook her head. 'I began to wonder how close we'd really been. And then there was Archie, and everything he did when she gave herself up.'

'What do you mean?'

'He found her a lawyer, spoke up for her in court, made people take into account her mental state – you're surely not telling me he did that for Marta? He did it for you. And I thought to myself – why would that be such a gift? Why, by helping Marta, could he hand you something precious?' Josephine was too shocked to speak: she had honestly never considered that Archie might be doing anything other than what he believed to be right and just, but she knew now that what Lydia said was true, and Marta's words came back to haunt her: how many times had she made Archie unhappy without even realising it? 'It was stupid of me,' Lydia continued, 'but the longer the silence lasted, the more significant all these things became in my imagination. I blew them up out of all proportion, when I should have had the sense to realise that Marta just needed time to get over what happened to her, to leave prison behind.'

'Is that what she said?'

'Not in so many words, but she's changed, Josephine, and even I can see that things are different now. I suppose I'll just have to be patient.'

'You'll never be able to pick up where you left off, but that's not always a bad thing.' She looked at her friend, knowing how fragile Lydia's new-found happiness was. 'You can build something new – something stronger.'

'I hope so. We haven't actually talked about getting back together and I don't want to rush her, but friendship's a start, isn't it?'

Josephine was too tired to do anything but give Lydia the hope she was looking for. 'Yes, it's a good start. And you're right to give her time. Take her to the cottage. Find some peace together.'

She stood up, afraid to test her public generosity any further, and they walked together into the Hall. Lydia disappeared to find Marta, and Josephine looked round for Archie, but he was nowhere to be seen. She was about to head for the bar, when someone shoved a glass into her hands. 'Coward,' Gerry said, 'and I'm not giving you a run-down of the play bill. I see you've decided to play Cupid after all.'

'It's not as straightforward as you think.'

Her voice was less ambiguous than her words, and Gerry looked at her with genuine concern. 'Christ, Josephine, I'm sorry – are you all right?'

'I'll be fine as long as I stay angry.'

'With her or with yourself?'

'That's not a distinction I want to make at the moment.' She drank the champagne and looked at Gerry. 'How are you? I notice that Celia's still on her feet tonight.' They both stared across the room to where the secretary was deep in conversation with Amy Coward, Mary Size and the rest of the club's committee. Archie was standing nearby, talking to a man she didn't recognise. 'I'm sorry about Marjorie,' Josephine said, more seriously. 'You've had a bitch of a weekend.'

'Haven't we both? Losing someone is losing someone, no matter how it happens.'

'Did you know her very well?' As soon as she asked the question, Josephine realised that Gerry was probably still oblivious to the fact that Marjorie had been Lizzie's half-sister; Archie was unlikely to have shared the details of the case

during his questioning, and he wouldn't thank her for inter-
fering now before everything was resolved, but Gerry would
have to know eventually and Josephine doubted that it would
make things any better.

'No, not really. Not well enough, anyway.' She pointed
across to the bar. 'If you're still angry, now might be the
moment to show it. She's on her own. And Josephine?'

'Yes?'

'If you want someone on your arm later – purely to get your
own back, of course – I'm happy to oblige.'

Gerry grinned, and Josephine laughed properly for the first
time that day. 'Thanks. I'll bear it in mind.' The hall was
beginning to fill up with guests, and it took her a few minutes
to get to the bar, but Marta didn't seem to be going anywhere.
'What the hell are you doing here?' she asked angrily.

'You look beautiful. Champagne?'

'Don't mess about. Why are you here?'

'I wanted to see you.'

'So you just turn up on Lydia's arm without even warning
me?'

'If I'd warned you, as you put it, you'd have found an excuse
not to be here.'

'Jesus, you move quickly. It's a wonder that any of us can
keep up with you. I thought after . . .'

'After what, Josephine?' Marta turned to look at her for the
first time, and Josephine was startled to see tears in her eyes.
'After you left, and I wandered round the house wondering
what to do with myself? After I stopped trusting myself to be
on my own?' She waited until her voice was more under
control, and then said: 'I know how this looks, and I know
how angry you are, but please try to understand – being with

429

you last night made me realise how isolated I've become, and how damaging that can be. I need company, friendship, love – whatever you want to call it, and I need it more often than I could ever demand it from you. You were right. I can have that with Lydia, and I can make her happy – really happy. But none of that changes how I feel about you. Everything I said last night, everything I asked of you – it still stands. I just can't be on my own while I wait for you to come back to London.'

Marta's vulnerability made Josephine long for the privacy they had shared the night before, but it was impossible to hold her in a hall full of people. Casually, she slid her glass a few inches along the bar until her fingers rested against Marta's; it was the subtlest of touches, imperceptible to an onlooker, but sufficient to dispel everything else in the room. Denied the possibility of anything more, they allowed this one small gesture to become the focus of everything that was miraculous and fated about their relationship, and the moment was so surprisingly intense that it was a while before Josephine could speak. 'What are we going to do?' she asked quietly.

'I love you.'

'That's not an answer.'

'It's the best I can do. Can you think of a better one?' Josephine shook her head. 'You have to go,' Marta said, squeezing her hand. 'It looks like you're needed for the cameras.'

'That can wait. This is more important.'

'Yes, but this could take a lifetime to resolve, and we have approximately fifteen seconds.' Marta hugged her, and Josephine felt her hand trace the line of pearls down her back so fleetingly that she might have imagined it. 'You're about to be fetched.'

'What?' Josephine turned round to see Celia Bannerman bearing down on her and beckoning her over to the other side of the room, where a couple of reporters were lining up guests to be photographed. She groaned. 'That's just what I need.'

'Before you go, take this.' Marta held out an earring. 'You left it at Holly Place. I was going to keep it, but when you start holding pearls to ransom in the hope that someone will come running for them, you really are lost.' She smiled. 'I don't have any more tricks up my sleeve, Josephine. You'll come, or you won't come. I hope you do.'

She disappeared into the crowd and Josephine fought her way reluctantly across the room to smile for *Tatler*. 'Nice to see you back in London, Miss Tey,' called one of the reporters. 'You've got a new Inspector Grant book out soon, we hear.'

'Yes – early next year. It's called *A Shilling for Candles*.'

'Let's hope it raises a bit more than a shilling, eh? You're donating the proceeds to charity, aren't you?'

'That's right, to a cancer hospital.'

'And is there a personal reason for that?' He must have seen the look on her face, because he added quickly: 'I'm not trying to pry, but it'll make a nice little story to go alongside the Cowdray Club piece. It all helps to get the public on side, doesn't it?'

It was a cheap trick, but Josephine felt obliged to answer, as he had known she would. Remembering why she hated the press, and why she never gave interviews, she said: 'My mother died of breast cancer twelve years ago.'

'That must have been a sad time for you.' She didn't even dignify that with a response: in truth, her mother's death had devastated her, but she wasn't about to share that with the world, not even in the name of charity. Smiling politely, she tried to excuse herself, but the reporter hadn't finished. 'A lot of people say that one of the characters in Mrs Christie's new book is based on you,' he said with a sly grin. 'Muriel Wills – the woman who writes plays as Anthony Astor. Is there any truth in that, do you think?'

'I wouldn't know. I don't often read Mrs Christie.' It was the best snub she could think of at short notice; she had, in fact, bought the book as soon as she heard the rumour, and had been furious to discover a ghastly creation who simpered and giggled and cluttered her home with nick-nacks; the fact that the playwright was observant and deadly with a pen did nothing to soften her anger.

'No harm in a bit of friendly rivalry, though, is there?' the reporter continued. 'I just wondered if we might find a little cameo in your new book for Mrs Christie?'

'What?' Josephine was distracted by a commotion at the door. 'A cameo for Mrs Christie? I couldn't possibly say. If you look carefully, though, you'll find a tramp with a very similar sense of humour. Now, if you'll excuse me, there are some people I have to talk to.' This time, she didn't have to work very hard to get away: the commotion signalled the arrival of the real stars of the evening. As the dignitaries and charity ladies clamoured for position around Noël and Gertie, Josephine found her table and sank gratefully into a seat next to Lettice. 'I feel like I've gone ten rounds with Jack Dempsey,' she said. 'What have I done to deserve a night like this?'

'Looked gorgeous in that dress?'

'You're the third person to tell me that tonight, and you can probably guess who the other two were. The dress is stunning, though – thank you.'

Lettice poured her a drink. 'I'm sorry I didn't get to you

first,' she said. 'I wanted to let you know what you were walking into, but Lydia was too quick for me.'

'Don't worry – it was nice of you even to try. Where's Archie?'

Before Lettice could answer, the lights in the hall were lowered and Celia Bannerman walked on to the stage. 'That's it, then, girls – fun over,' Ronnie said, slapping two more bottles of champagne down on the table. 'Sweet charity's arrived.' She leaned across to Josephine. 'And where did you spend the night? You could have had the whole of Scotland Yard out looking for you if it hadn't been for our discretion.'

'You? Discreet?' Luckily for Josephine's self-respect, a ripple of applause drowned out the rest of her reply. Celia held up her hand for silence. 'Ladies and gentlemen, welcome to the College of Nursing and Cowdray Club on what promises to be a very exciting occasion for us all. Before we go any further, I'd like you to join me in giving a warm welcome to our special guests this evening, Miss Gertrude Lawrence and Mr Noël Coward, who have taken a break from the tour of their latest production to be with us.' The spotlight moved to a table at the front of the hall. 'Later on, they'll be treating us to two short pieces from *Tonight at 8.30*. You'll be the first London audience to enjoy the new show, and I'm sure it will whet our appetites for when it comes to the West End early next year.' There were cheers around the room and, when they subsided, Celia said: 'Clearly neither of our guests needs any introduction from me, but I will, if I may, tell you a little about one of the charities that we're all here tonight to support.'

'Here we go,' Ronnie muttered. 'It'll be *Tomorrow at Bloody Six* by the time she's finished.'

'The Actors' Orphanage, of which Mr Coward is president,

started nearly forty years ago and now offers a home and a school to sixty children at a time. I need hardly stress to you that today, even with the vast improvements that have taken place in social welfare over the last few years, one of the casualties of a modern city is still the unwanted child, or the child who is left without anyone to care for him. Hard times press hardest on our children: now that the winter has come, and the days are dreary with fog and the streets are cheerless, now that Christmas approaches, it's only natural that we turn our thoughts to bringing some brightness into their lives. But Mr Coward and his colleagues work tirelessly to do that all year round; thanks to them, and to other organisations like the Actors' Orphanage, women are no longer driven to the desperate measures with which they were once faced, and children find the fabric of their lives immeasurably improved each day. I'm sure you'll agree that money donated to such a cause is money well spent.'

Archie slipped into the seat on Josephine's right, and she poured him a glass of champagne. 'I've got to hand it to Celia,' she said, 'this is quite a performance.' He nodded, but seemed too intent on the stage for any further conversation.

'Before we move on to the night's other very good cause, I have one more organisation to thank. You will all know the name of Motley; through their splendid designs for the stage and the high street, they bring romance into our lives and glamour into our wardrobes, and I'm sure I'm not the only woman here who offered them up a prayer when she was getting dressed tonight.' A murmur of appreciation ran through the audience. 'Tonight, though, our thanks are tinged with sadness when we think of the appalling tragedy which took place just a few days ago, and which would have brought a less stoical organisation to its knees. Lettice and Ronnie tell me that the dress I'm wearing this evening was the last that Marjorie Baker worked on before she died, and I feel humble and honoured to own it. The money from tonight may go to our charities, but the spirit of the occasion belongs to Marjorie, and to her colleagues and friends who must continue without her.'

Ronnie made a great show of rummaging under the table for a napkin, but Archie seemed less moved. 'Jesus Christ,' he muttered under his breath, and Lettice looked questioningly at Josephine; she shrugged, completely bewildered by his reaction.

'Now to the organisation closest to my own heart and, I know, to many of yours. Of all the people I've met in my life, the one I feel most privileged to have known and worked alongside is the lady who has given her name to this club – her name, and so much more. Annie, Viscountess Cowdray, was one of the most sincere and true friends that it is possible for a body of professional women to have. She had a wonderful grasp of business matters, a great ability to make quick and wise decisions and, above all, a deep compassion and desire to be of use to those who needed help.' She pointed upwards, to three stained-glass windows built into one of the walls, each depicting a cherub in a different pose. 'Tonight, we're watched over by the three symbols of the nursing profession, Love, Fortitude and Faith – although some would say that to those three should be added a good sense of humour and a strong back.' The laughter was most appreciative amongst the nurses in the room, Josephine noticed. 'Lady Cowdray had more than her fair share of all of them, and it is to her that we owe the success and good standing that her club and this college enjoy all over the world today. If I may, though, I'd like to finish on a more personal note.' She paused, and looked slowly round the room. 'Tonight will be my last public event as secretary of the Cowdray Club. The last thirteen years have brought me great joy and satisfaction, but, while I hope my reserves of love, fortitude and faith are as strong as ever, the apocryphal qualities let me down increasingly in the face of old age and it's time to hand over the reins to younger hands. I hope that my successor, whoever she is, will find this job as rewarding and fulfilling as I have. Thank you, ladies and gentlemen – please enjoy the show, and give as generously as you can to our causes.'

She relinquished the stage to the first act of the night, and Archie turned to Josephine. 'Did you know she was going to do that?' he asked, almost accusingly.

'No, I had no idea. I've hardly seen her over the weekend.' She looked at him, a little put out by his tone. 'I suppose she wants to leave while she's still got the respect of most of the members. That scene with Gerry on Saturday must have been the last straw for her, don't you think?' Archie said nothing and, although she made several more attempts at conversation, he seemed far too preoccupied to listen to a word she was saying. Exasperated by his silence, and able to think of only one explanation for it, she took his face in her hands and made him look at her. 'Archie, would you be happier if we didn't see each other?' she asked.

'What?' At least now she had his attention. 'Don't be ridiculous. This is about yesterday, isn't it? I'm sorry, Josephine, but that's not why I'm so distracted. Forgive me.' He kept her hand where it was with his own, and smiled at her. 'But in answer to your question, I can't imagine a world in which you and I don't see each other. Nothing would make me *un*happier. I know it's

436

not always easy, and I know that there are bound to be things in both our lives that get in the way, things that can't be shared, but there will never be a time for me when your absence is preferable to your company, and I hope you feel the same.'

She was about to say something when a waiter came over to their table and passed Archie a note. 'Shit,' he said, standing up to leave. 'I'm sorry, Josephine – I've got to go. We'll talk about this later.'

'I thought you'd want to know immediately. She died ten minutes ago. There was nothing I could do. Her heart was so weak that there was insufficient blood-flow to the vital organs, and the kidneys never regained their function. I'm sorry.'

Penrose realised that Miriam Sharpe was expressing regret at Lucy's death rather than its inconvenience to his plans, and normally his priorities would have been the same, but Celia Bannerman's resignation speech had created a sense of urgency which left him uncharacteristically tactless. 'Who knows about this?' he asked.

'Only you and one other nurse, and the policeman who was on duty. But I can't keep this quiet, if that's what you're about to ask. There are procedures to follow and next of kin to be notified, not to mention the small matter of common decency.'

'I know, and I wouldn't put you in this position unless it were absolutely necessary,' Penrose said, desperate to buy himself some time: if Celia Bannerman found out that Lucy was dead, she would have no reason to take any more risks and could happily sail off into a glorious retirement, leaving him with absolutely no proof whatsoever. 'Please – just give me an hour.'

Miriam Sharpe thought for what seemed like an age to Penrose before saying: 'I won't hold up what I need to do, Inspector, but neither will I go out of my way to let anyone know about Lucy's death. Everyone is preoccupied downstairs at the moment, and that should give you the time you're asking for. But I hope I don't need to tell you that I can't have policemen crawling all over what is sadly now a place of rest.'

She didn't: even in his desperation to trap Celia Bannerman, Penrose had no intention of offering up a young girl's body as bait. He thanked Miriam Sharpe, and went to tell Wyles and Fallowfield about the change of plan.

The lights dimmed again after the interval, and an audience which had responded to the entertainment so far with polite applause stood and cheered as the curtain rose on the stars of the night. Noël and Gertie, dressed as music-hall performers, stood in front of a painted street scene which could have been the backdrop to any provincial theatre in England; both wore curly red wigs and sailor clothes with exaggerated bell-bottomed trousers, and each carried a telescope. They launched into their first number, and Archie raised his glass to an older man on a nearby table, who smiled suspiciously as he returned the greeting. 'Who's that?' Josephine asked.

'The chief constable.'

'Why's he looking at you like that?'

'Because he thinks I'm about to disgrace him with the Home Office.'

She stared at him. 'And are you?'

'I hope not.'

They turned back to the stage, where Gertrude Lawrence was taking particular delight in mocking the seedy touring life which she had known earlier in her own career; Coward's music, and the banter which ran in between the songs, perfectly captured the half-desperate atmosphere of a struggling music hall, an atmosphere that Josephine remembered herself from her early introductions to theatre. The piece was a light-hearted affair, both loving and cynical, but even the ridiculously exaggerated outfits couldn't hide the magic of the partnership on stage; it was a radiant, if fragile, glamour which had sustained people since the war and which continued to keep them spellbound now, even as most of them feared that their lives were once again held to ransom by politics, and Josephine doubted that there was a single person in the room who wasn't thankful for it.

As the orchestra picked up the refrain and the on-stage husband and wife lapsed into a series of terrible jokes, Josephine noticed Mary Size leave the room, followed swiftly by Fallowfield. She watched him go, surprised that he was willing to miss a second of the performance; he glanced quickly at Archie as he passed, but she thought nothing of it. His departure left an empty seat by the Snipe, who seemed to be finding the performance a vast improvement on *Romeo and Juliet*; the Motleys' housekeeper smiled when she caught Josephine's eye, and Josephine hoped to God that she could rely on her to be discreet about the bed which sat redundant in Maiden Lane. She didn't want to have secrets from Archie, but she wasn't ready to face her own feelings for Marta yet, let alone discuss them with anyone else.

The fading music-hall couple attempted a snappy finale, but Lawrence's character dropped her telescope and ruined the whole effect. As her husband glared at her, the curtain fell, then rose again almost immediately on a squalid dressing room. Noël and Gertie reappeared, still breathless from the number and looking furiously at each other; they flung their wigs down and ripped off the sailor clothes, and the sight of Gertrude Lawrence clad only in brassiere and silk knickers drew the loudest cheer of the night. 'I bet you're not saying "Gertrude who?" now,' Josephine whispered to Archie, but he was still miles away. He nodded at someone, and she followed his gaze to the door and to Lillian Wyles; as she watched, Wyles walked over to the committee table and whispered something in Celia Bannerman's ear, then handed her a note and left the room. 'What's going on, Archie?' Josephine asked, suddenly afraid. 'First Mary Size and now Celia.' As if on cue, Bannerman got up and hurried from the hall. 'You surely can't think . . .'

'Don't worry,' he said. 'Just stay here. I'll explain later.' Without another word, he got up and went after the two women.

From the doorway to Memorial Hall, Fallowfield watched Mary Size walk across the college foyer to the stairs, then followed her at a discreet distance up to the first floor. She hesitated at the mezzanine level, and he held back, waiting for her to make a move; for a moment, he thought she was simply looking for the ladies' cloakroom and he breathed a sigh of relief, but then she turned and hurried up the stairs. He quickened his pace, hoping that the muffled cheers and applause from the hall below would mask the sound of his footsteps, and followed her over the next landing and up to the treatment rooms on the second floor. There was only one place she could be headed for now, and he could think of no legitimate reason why she should have left the performance to see Lucy Peters. But a prison governor? Could they really have got it so wrong?

He arrived at the door to Lucy's room just in time to hear her remonstrating with Miriam Sharpe. 'Oh come on, Miriam – just let me see her for a moment. I won't stay long and surely it won't do her any harm? From what I hear, it can't get much worse for the poor girl.'

The nurse looked questioningly at Fallowfield, and he nodded. 'You're right, Mary,' she said gravely. 'I'm afraid it really can't get any worse at all. Lucy died earlier this evening.'

Fallowfield watched Mary Size's face as she took in the news, but there was no hint of relief, only a deep sorrow which she made no effort to hide. He introduced himself, and then asked gently: 'Can I ask why you wanted to see Miss Peters, Ma'am?'

She took a moment to register the question, then held out a photograph. 'Yes of course, sergeant – I came to leave this by her bedside. I wanted it to be the first thing she saw when she came round.' He took the picture and looked down at a beautiful baby girl, less than a year old. 'I'm afraid I've broken all the rules and accepted procedures to get hold of it. You should never contact the new parents once an adoption has gone ahead, but I don't regret it. The one thing Lucy wanted was to know that her baby was all right. I thought if she had that peace of mind, she might have the strength to pull through this terrible thing that's happened to her, but it seems that I've come too late.' She unpinned the silk violets from the front of her dress and handed them to Miriam Sharpe with the photograph. 'I hope she may have found some peace of a different sort now, but will you give her these anyway?'

Fallowfield was about to offer what words of consolation he could find, but, before he had the chance, a scream came from the floor below.

* * *

441

By the time Penrose left the hall, there was no sign of Celia Bannerman, but he knew exactly where to go: he had instructed Wyles to lead her to the first-floor drawing room, where two other officers were already concealed, and he hurried up the stairs and along the corridor, past the glass dome over the dining room and into the Cowdray Club part of the building. The door was ajar, but there was no sound of voices from inside. Impatiently, he waited a few seconds, then cautiously pushed the door open. As he had feared, the room was empty.

'Where is she?' he shouted, panic driving him quickly to anger.

Swann and Christofi emerged from their respective hiding places, looking bewildered. 'She hasn't come anywhere near here, sir,' Christofi said. 'When did she leave the gala?'

'A few minutes ago,' Penrose snapped as he headed back to the door. 'Come on. If she's on her own with that bitch, God knows what might be happening.'

The scream from further down the corridor offered more possibilities than any of them wanted to hear.

Wyles had not expected Bannerman to follow her so quickly from the hall; before she had a chance to climb the stairs, she heard a voice behind her, calling her back.

'Not the drawing room,' Bannerman said calmly, her voice showing no trace of anger or fear. 'Someone may come in. If you want to talk to me, we'll go to my office.'

Wyles hesitated, knowing that to obey would be to go against everything that she had been taught in her fifteen years of policing; by the same token, a chance like this was what she had been waiting for all that time. She weighed Penrose's anger against his approval, and the latter won. After all, the woman in front of her was in her fifties or sixties; if she was no match for that, she shouldn't be in the police force at all. Hesitantly, she nodded at Bannerman, and followed her up to her room.

Once inside, Bannerman locked the door and removed the key. Without a word, she walked over to the other side of the room, took a piece of paper out of her evening bag and placed it with Lillian's note on the desk between them. 'Your letter implied that you know what happened to the last person who sent me a threatening message,' she said. 'If that's the case, I'm surprised you would wish to risk following in her footsteps.'

This veiled affirmation of everything that Penrose had suspected sent a shiver of triumph and fear through Wyles. She looked defiantly at Bannerman, determined to force her into a more direct confession. 'I'm smarter than Marjorie,' she began cautiously, 'and I'm not greedy. Anyway, you can't go on like this forever, can you? Sooner or later, it's got to stop, and it might as well stop with me. I can keep my mouth shut for a fair price, without the help of a needle.'

It was a gamble, but it seemed to give Bannerman the proof she was looking for. She nodded, and unlocked the top drawer of her desk. 'I see. And what would you call a fair price?'

'Two hundred should do it.' Wyles looked over at the pile of notes that Bannerman had removed from the drawer. 'Or as near as damn it. Like I said, I'm not greedy.'

'And how do I know that if I give you your money today, you're not going to come back tomorrow for more?' Bannerman walked towards her, the money in her hand.

'Because you can trust me. Why would I push you when I know what you're capable of?'

'A good answer, but not quite the right one.' She held out the notes, and only spoke again when Wyles had committed herself to taking them. 'You see, I'll know you're not coming back because you simply won't be able to.' Even as her fingers closed around the money, Wyles was conscious of Bannerman's other arm moving rapidly upwards, drawing a line across her chest; she saw the glint of a knife before she felt the pain, and looked down to see blood already seeping through her dress. The cut was mercifully shallow, but the shock of the attack and the sudden realisation of the danger she was in were enough to make her feel faint, and she struggled not to lose consciousness. Bannerman came at her again with the knife. It was a surgical instrument, Wyles noticed, small but deadly, and it struck her as ironic that something which had been created to save lives should so easily be put to the opposite purpose. Using her strength while she still had some to use, she grabbed hold of Bannerman's wrist and smashed her arm down on the desk. The woman yelled in pain and let go of the knife, and Wyles used her temporary advantage to kick it across the room. The respite was only brief: Bannerman's anger fuelled her strength, and Wyles was astonished and horrified by the ease with which the older woman pushed her to the floor. She tried to resist, but the brief amnesty on pain which follows any wound was well and truly over now, and Wyles felt increasingly weakened by the loss of blood. Sensing victory, Bannerman pinned her to the floor and put her knee on Wyles's chest, twisting it hard against her skin and aggravating the injury until she screamed to be released from the torture; she thought she saw her attacker smile as she took the scarf from her own neck and wound it round Wyles's throat.

Then there were shouts in the corridor outside. For the briefest of seconds, Wyles was overcome with relief – until she realised that the prospect of help was just the impetus Bannerman needed to finish what she had started. As desperate shoulders pushed against the heavy oak door, she felt the scarf tighten around her neck and knew that the struggle was all but over. Seconds later, she heard Penrose's voice calling her name and felt him dragging Celia Bannerman away from her, but she lost consciousness before she was able to thank him.

'Loving you is hard for me – it makes me a stranger in my own house. Familiar things, ordinary things that I've known for years like the dining-room curtains, and the wooden tub with a silver top that holds biscuits and a watercolour of San Remo that my mother painted, look odd to me, as though they belonged to someone else – when I've just left you, when I go home, I'm more lonely than I've ever been before.'

Josephine had tried not to look over to Marta's table too often, but the music-hall sketch had given way to an exquisitely written piece set in a railway station cafe, and, as Gertrude Lawrence's character continued with an understated but affecting monologue which seemed so accurately to express the situation they found themselves in, she was compelled to look to Marta for some solidarity, if only to reassure herself that she wasn't suffering alone. Lydia chose that moment to stand up and walk to the bar; as she passed behind Marta, she let a hand rest on her shoulder and Marta squeezed it affectionately. It was an unconscious gesture, not designed to be provocative in any way, but its very ordinariness was the last thing that Josephine wanted to see: it spoke of a bond that didn't need to be continually questioning itself, a life too busy being lived to find its way into the pages of a diary, and it was so different from the connection which she and Marta shared that she could stand it no longer. She stood to get some air, wondering if Noël and Gertie had ever had to put up with so much disruption during a performance. The mood at supper afterwards was likely to be deadly.

The door to Henrietta Place stood open and she watched the comings and goings in the street for a while, too glad of the anonymity to worry much about the cold. Putting Marta from her mind, she wondered where Archie was; she had long given up trying to work out what was going on – the conclusions she came to were simply too bizarre to contemplate – but she was worried about him, in spite of his reassurances that everything was fine. As if in response to her concern, the noise of an ambulance cut sharply across the murmur of night-time traffic in Oxford Street; to her horror, it rounded the corner a moment later and pulled up by the kerb, followed shortly by two police cars, and she moved back into the foyer to allow the men through unhindered.

One or two people began to drift out of the hall when they heard the commotion. 'What the hell's going on?' Gerry asked.

'I have absolutely no idea,' Josephine shrugged. 'I just hope that everyone's all right.' It seemed a ridiculous thing to say as people in uniform continued to pile into the building, but she had nothing else to offer. Ronnie and Lettice joined her, but she had barely begun to explain when Archie appeared at the top of the stairs. 'Thank God,' she said, then looked on, astonished, as he held the door open for Celia Bannerman to be brought through; Fallowfield and another officer led her carefully downstairs, her dress stained with blood, to where a crowd was gathering in the foyer.

'Are you all right, Celia?' Josephine asked, but her voice faded as she saw that Bannerman's hands were cuffed behind her back, and she looked apprehensively at Archie. 'What's she done? Who's been hurt?'

'It's WPC Wyles, but she'll be fine, thanks to Miriam Sharpe. They're taking her to hospital, but there's no danger.'

'And what else?' In her heart, Josephine already knew the answer; still, she clung to the possibility that there might be some other explanation, but Archie's silence said it all. She turned to Gerry, but it was too late to stop her.

'You fucking bitch,' she screamed, throwing herself at Bannerman. 'Did letting Lizzie die give you a taste for it? What did Marjorie ever do to you?'

Archie pulled her away and held her until she was calm. 'She *will* pay,' he said quietly. 'It may not seem like justice, but I promise you – the pain that Marjorie suffered will come back to haunt her when she's waiting in that cell, and the fear will be a thousand times greater than anything Marjorie had time to know.'

Ronnie looked at Celia Bannerman in disbelief. 'Marjorie? You did that to Marjorie?'

Fallowfield tried to move on, but Josephine caught his arm. 'Why, Celia?' she asked softly. 'I've looked up to you since I was eighteen. All the people you've taught and cared for, every woman you've given a start to in life – does that count for so very little that you just trample all over it as if it never existed?'

Celia Bannerman stared back at her. 'You can't rewrite history, Josephine, no matter how hard you try. Those achievements still stand, regardless of anything else I've done.'

'Of course they don't. They were tainted the moment you

447

started choosing between lives to build and lives to destroy.' She looked at her old teacher, wondering how she could possibly remain so unchanged by what she had done. 'I don't even know who you are any more.'

Bannerman laughed and took a step towards her. Josephine flinched as she felt the woman's breath on her face and Archie stepped forward to intervene, but she waved him away; her pride refused to let her pull back, and, in any case, she was still hoping for some sort of explanation which would help her to understand how she could have been so wrong. 'And do you know who *you* are, Josephine?' Bannerman asked, her voice low, almost gentle. 'The lives you separate, the names you hide behind – one day, they'll all come crashing down and you'll be left on your own, trying to work out where the real person went. If I've taught you anything, let it be that.'

She turned and allowed herself to be led away. Fallowfield headed for the Henrietta Street entrance, but Penrose stopped him. 'No, Bill,' he said, unable to resist a quick glance in the chief constable's direction. 'Take her out the front. She inflicted as much humiliation as she could on Marjorie Baker – let's show her how it feels.'

Chapter Fifteen

Penrose glanced through the small window of the interview room where Celia Bannerman was waiting for him. She seemed calm now, with no trace of the frenzied anger that had prompted her attack on Wyles, and, when he opened the door, she simply lifted her face and gave him a steady, faintly scornful stare. He sat down opposite her, Fallowfield next to him, and took two pieces of paper from the file in front of him.

'Before we start, Miss Bannerman, I understand that you've chosen not to have any legal representation present during this questioning. It's my duty to advise you against that, and to ask you to reconsider.'

'I'm my own counsel, Inspector. I've never relied on anyone else for help, and I have no intention of starting now.'

'Very well. You have already been charged with the attempted murder of a police officer. This interview relates to the murders of Marjorie Baker and Jacob Sach – also known as Joseph Baker – on Friday 22 November at 66 St Martin's Lane.'

Before he could continue, Bannerman interrupted him, showing no more sign of agitation now than when he had sat down at the Cowdray Club to question her as a witness. 'I imagine you have no proof of my involvement with those murders, Inspector, or that little stunt with your policewoman wouldn't have been necessary.'

She was absolutely right, of course: there was no evidence as yet to place her in St Martin's Lane on Friday night, or to prove that Lucy's fall had been anything other than an accident. A meticulous search of her living accommodation had revealed nothing of any significance, but Penrose never expected it to: one look around her office had told him that she was not the sort of woman who left her life lying around for others to read. He had one more gamble up his sleeve, though, and he chose his next words cautiously, careful to avoid a lie: 'That may have been true last night, Miss Bannerman, but I'm pleased to say that things are very different this morning. Perhaps you've forgotten Lucy Peters? She's only a servant, I know, and probably not very important in the scheme of things as you see it, but she was close to Marjorie Baker and the two of them shared some very interesting information.'

She laughed, but he was encouraged by the first flicker of doubt in her eyes. 'You're bluffing, of course. People with mouths as badly scalded as Lucy's are incapable of talking, no matter how interesting the information they have.'

'Indeed. But they can write things down.' He let the suggestion sink in, then pushed the two letters across the table towards her. 'These notes, one written by Miss Baker and found in your desk, and one by WPC Wyles, refer to a secret in your past which you would prefer to forget. Would you care to tell me what that is, Miss Bannerman?'

She stared at him for a long time. 'You're talking to a dead woman, Inspector,' she said eventually.

Her voice was soft, but the calm acceptance of something too horrific for most people to contemplate unnerved him. 'I'm glad you can look at your fate so stoically,' he said, 'particularly as you have such an intimate understanding of what the process of justice involves.'

Bannerman smiled, and settled back in her chair. 'That wasn't quite what I meant, but do go on. Why don't you tell me what you think you know about my life?'

Refusing to let her condescension frustrate him this time, Penrose said: 'With pleasure. Let's start thirty years ago, when you left Holloway and moved on to your new job in Leeds. By that time, you were involved with a former prisoner called Eleanor Vale. Vale had attacked you in Holloway, but you were young and dedicated to your work, and you genuinely believed that you could rehabilitate her and turn her life around. You meant well, but your efforts were misguided,' he continued, satisfied to see that *his* condescension was beginning to irritate *her*. 'Not content with forgiveness, you took her into your home, and by the time you realised your mistake, Vale had become so dependent on you that it was impossible to free yourself of her. The only way out, as far as you could see, was to leave her behind once and for all, so you accepted a position in Yorkshire and made sure that she was unable to follow you. Eleanor Vale made the ultimate sacrifice for your career. She died for it.'

When he had finished, she began to applaud. 'You tell a good story, Inspector, and a far more accurate one than your friend. Accurate, except for one important detail: Eleanor Vale isn't dead.'

Her words threw Penrose for a moment: if Vale was still alive, the whole foundation of his case was destroyed. Why would Bannerman start to kill so suddenly if not to hide a past crime? As he struggled to make sense of what she was saying, she stared at him impatiently, incensed by his confusion. 'Someone like Celia Bannerman could never have killed Eleanor Vale. Do you understand that?' She slammed her hand hard down on the table, making him flinch. The force of the blow must have damaged skin which was already burnt and sore from Saturday, and he saw a trickle of blood seep out from beneath the bandage, but she seemed oblivious to the pain. 'Do you understand that, Inspector, or do I have to spell it out for you? Celia Bannerman did not kill Eleanor Vale. Eleanor Vale killed Celia Bannerman. She pushed her under a tube train, to be precise, and walked away with her life.'

Penrose heard Fallowfield draw his breath in sharply, and suddenly he understood exactly why he had found it so difficult to reconcile the compassionate prison warder whom Ethel Stuke had described with the woman he was convinced was a killer. 'You're Eleanor Vale, aren't you?' he said, shaking his head in disbelief, 'and you've lived as Celia Bannerman for thirty years. How the hell have you managed it? She was a respected prison officer and a qualified nurse with a great future ahead of her.'

'And Eleanor Vale was just a convict? A baby farmer with no right to any other identity, branded with one mistake for life? I was a qualified nurse, too, Inspector. I had a future, and those thirty years were only the life that I would have had if circumstances had been different.'

'You mean if you hadn't served two years' hard labour for leaving babies to die in railway carriages.'

'Don't even begin to talk about things you don't understand. I did what was necessary to survive. All my life, I've done that. Nothing more, and certainly nothing less.'

'And why was it so necessary to kill the woman who tried to help you?'

'Help me? She picked me up and dropped me. How do you

452

think it feels to be taken on as a project until something better comes along? To spend your life being grateful, only to find out that it's all been for nothing? Yes, I was dependent on her, as you put it, but only because she made me that way. And if I was that disposable to her, why should she be any different to me?'

'So you planned to kill her.'

'No, not at all. It had never occurred to me that I was capable of killing anybody. I begged her to change her mind and either stay or take me with her, but she said it was impossible. On the morning she was due to leave, I watched her pack her whole life into two suitcases and stow away all her private papers and precious letters of reference, and I walked her to the underground station. It was the middle of August, and so hot in those tunnels. The platform was busier than usual because London was full of summer visitors, and I remember feeling more and more desperate as we waited. Even then, I don't think I'd have done anything about it, but when we heard the train coming and she turned to kiss me goodbye, she looked at me and she said: "However will you manage without me?"' She rubbed a hand across her eyes, and Penrose could see that she was making an effort to suppress a thirty-year-old rage. 'I'm afraid that was more than I could tolerate, Inspector – not just the smug, self-righteous arrogance of it all, but her complete inability to understand what she'd done. I must have pushed her, because the next thing I knew, she was under the train and people were screaming, but I have absolutely no recollection of that moment. I was eaten up with anger and resentment, and I just wanted to be rid of her. Please don't misunderstand me – I'm not trying to make excuses, and I'm not sorry for what I did. She played with my life, then taunted

453

me with my own weakness, and I killed her for it. But if she's looking down now, she'll see exactly how I've managed without her.'

Penrose stared doubtfully at her; in his heart, he believed what she was saying to be true, but it was an enormous risk to take, and he said so.

'What did I have to lose? I picked up those cases automatically and walked away, half expecting someone to come after me, but it was too crowded for anyone to have noticed what happened. I suppose I was in shock, because I walked around for ages before it occurred to me that I had a chance, that I was holding the possibility of another life in my hands. I went back to that house one last time to pack up Eleanor Vale's things, and I sent them to a charity – Celia would have approved of that, and most of the clothes were her cast-offs anyway. Then I went north.'

'And what about the death you left behind?' Penrose had been involved in enough clear-up operations on the underground to know that the usual identification of a body might not have been possible; during the last few years, the country's dire economic situation had led thirty or forty people a year to view the trains as a way out of their despair, and many of the stations had begun to install deep pits between the tracks to minimise their chances of success and to keep those still alive safe while the train was being moved. Even so, something tangible was usually found at the scene. 'Were you really so confident that there was nothing on the body which would expose the lie?' he asked.

'Everything that testified to Celia Bannerman was with me, in her luggage. The one thing she was wearing that was remotely personal was a locket I'd given her when she first took me in; it was the only thing of any value I had to give at the time. She didn't wear it very often, but she made a big thing of putting it on that day – asked me to fasten it for her, as if I'd feel better about being abandoned if she left me wearing my jewellery.'

'Your family – didn't they wonder what had happened to you?'

'They disowned me as soon as I was arrested. I went to them when I got out of prison, but they turned me away. Celia was all I had, God help me.'

'But surely someone must have missed her?'

'The only people she associated with were connected to her work,' she said, echoing what Ethel Stuke had told him. 'Even I was a mission, as it turned out. And nobody who knew her professionally had time to realise she wasn't there any more; as far as they were concerned, Celia Bannerman left one job and reported when she was supposed to for the next. No one in Leeds knew what she looked like. If someone from Holloway or the hospitals we were in before had turned up, that would have been it, but they didn't; Leeds was a long way from London in those days, and it worked in my favour that she'd tried to get as far away from me as possible. Of course, I made sure I kept a low profile for the first few years,' she added, smiling. 'Very self-effacing was our Celia – she never wanted the limelight, and she always refused any public recognition for what she did. A living saint, you might say.'

'Until now. That was a very stupid slip, Miss Vale – allowing yourself to be photographed in that way. No wonder you were so angry with Marjorie. I suppose she paid for your arrogance.' She said nothing, but the look in her eyes and the tight clenching of her hands told him that he was right, and he guessed that the rage which had led to such a spiteful murder had remained with her in the days since Marjorie's death. 'I can see how you killed Celia Bannerman and got away with it,' he said quietly. 'What I still find astonishing is that you managed to live as her.'

'I had all I needed to be Celia Bannerman in those two cases and in here,' she said, tapping the side of her head. 'She may have had the references, but I certainly had the qualities to live up to them, and in all my life I've never let anyone down the way she did. What I start, I finish.'

'As Marjorie Baker learned to her cost. She and her father knew all this, I suppose.'

'Good God, no. Don't be ridiculous – you give them far too much credit. I doubt that either of them had ever heard of Eleanor Vale. They knew enough, though. Marjorie's father saw the photograph in the *Tatler* she took home, and he told her I wasn't Celia Bannerman.'

'Because he remembered the woman he'd given his child to?' She nodded. 'And that's why you lied about going to see him during the war – to give yourself some sort of continuity with the person you were pretending to be. But Marjorie didn't trust her father's word – she had a lot to lose, and she wanted to make sure that what he said was true.'

'Yes. I'm afraid Ethel Stuke sealed Marjorie's fate as effectively as if she'd hanged her.'

At last, Penrose understood what Stuke had said that seemed so conclusive to Marjorie. 'She knew you'd never been attacked, didn't she? She'd handled your fittings at Motley, and she knew there was no scar.' It was a simple, feminine thing, but irrefutable, and Marjorie could have had no idea of the danger she was putting herself in by using her knowledge. Her death, he realised now, was a vicious, sadistic parody of the means by which she had gained that fatal piece of information. The peculiarly female intimacy of the dress fitting had come back to haunt her.

Vale nodded approvingly at him. 'Yes. She was measuring me for silk and piercing me with steel. The letter came just before the final fitting.'

'She wanted money?'

'Of course. Nothing more imaginative than that. All the women I've taught and nurtured, all the people I've fought for to ensure they get a decent working life – and that stupid little bitch wanted everything handed to her on a plate. When I went to Motley on Friday afternoon, I promised her she'd have what she asked for later that night. I kept my word.'

'And you got her to make sure that her father was there as well?'

'No. I knew nothing about her father until he turned up drunk at Motley. Marjorie hadn't mentioned him or how she'd come by her information in the first place, and I certainly had no idea who was in her family. He was waiting for her outside, and he caught me leaving the building. He slurred something about seeing me in that photograph, and that's when he told me how he knew the real Celia Bannerman.'

'Did he find out what you'd done to his daughter before you pushed him down the stairs?'

'Does that really matter?'

Penrose looked at her for a long time before speaking again, astonished at how little remorse she seemed capable of. 'Don't you regret any of it?' he asked eventually. 'If you could go back to that underground platform, would you really do it all again?'

'Yes, if it enabled everything that I've achieved during the years in between. People aren't good or bad, Inspector – their actions are, and everyone is capable of both. Take Amelia Sach – a good mother, by all accounts, yet capable of destroying that sacred bond in others to advance her own position. And Celia Bannerman, of course – such an asset to society, so selfless in her efforts to help people, and yet she dropped her little rehabilitation project like a stone the minute a better offer came along. Ambition – that's what it was about. That's what it's always about. Everyone in public life says it's the work that counts, and what does it matter who does it – but deep down we all want the credit for our little piece of progress.'

'Even when those achievements are undermined by the very violence on which they're built? What about the people whose lives you've destroyed?'

'A convict who would have been in and out of jail for the rest of her life? A drunk who made no contribution to society and couldn't even keep his wife from the gallows?'

'A police officer?'

'Who was herself involved in an act of deception.'

'You're surely not comparing that with the lie you've lived for thirty years?'

'I'm not the one making *any* judgements. I'm saying that we all fool ourselves and others to get by. Some of us even making a living out of it.'

The barbed reference to Josephine wasn't lost on Penrose, but he refused to be drawn by it. 'Let's talk about Lucy Peters,' he said, confident now that they were far enough along with the questioning for his own deception not to matter. 'Did she know that killing Marjorie wasn't enough for you? That you had to torture and humiliate her first?'

Vale looked at him warily. 'Surely you know what I said to Lucy if you've been exchanging letters at her bedside?'

Penrose just smiled. 'Eleanor Vale, you will now be formally charged with the murders of Celia Bannerman, Marjorie Baker, Jacob Sach and Lucy Peters, and taken to a . . .'

'You bastard,' Vale shrieked, standing up and shoving the table hard into his stomach. She lashed out at his face, but Fallowfield was too quick for her, catching her by the wrist as her arm came down. She screamed in agony as the sergeant's fingers tightened around the blistered skin, but somehow she still managed to pull away, her rage exploding in a stream of abuse as she grabbed hold of a chair and went for them again. This time, though, Penrose was expecting the attack: he moved to one side, and the chair crashed harmlessly into the door while he held Vale's arms behind her back, pinning her against the wall for long enough to give Fallowfield time to get the handcuffs on. Later, he would regret showing any emotion at all, but as he walked her into the corridor and gave instructions for her to be taken downstairs, his anger was the mirror image of hers: 'I hope you rot in hell for what you've done,' he said.

Josephine sat at the front desk of New Scotland Yard, wondering what Archie wanted. She had been surprised to get his message, but relieved to have any excuse to get out of the Cowdray Club for an hour or two. The atmosphere there was unbearable: crime reporters given a tip-off by their society-page colleagues were the latest addition to Cavendish Square, and the arrival of the mortuary van to remove Lucy's body was an image that no one was likely to forget, but the sadness ran deeper even than that. Everywhere she looked, Josephine saw her own sense of betrayal reflected in the faces of the other members; a professional mourning ran throughout the building, a feeling amongst the women that they had battled governments and legislation for so many years, only to see what they had worked for tarnished from within. They had been let down by one of their own, and it left them all feeling angry and foolish and guilty; personally, Josephine couldn't remember a time when her trust had been more comprehensively destroyed.

When Archie came down to fetch her, he looked pale and exhausted. 'I won't bother to ask how you are,' she said. 'You'll only lie, and anyway, I can see it in your face.'

'Let's just say it's been an eventful night.'

'How's your policewoman?'

She saw him smile at her phrasing of the question. 'She'll be fine. She's shaken, obviously, and she took a nasty cut to the chest, but thank God for the College of Nursing. Miriam Sharpe was wonderful.'

There was so much she wanted to ask him about what had gone on overnight, but she knew it would put him in an impossible position. 'So why have I been summoned to the Yard?'

'Come with me a minute.' He led her out on to Victoria Embankment and pointed across the road.

'What am I looking at?'

'Do you see the woman on the bench over there?' She nodded. 'That's Nora Edwards.'

Josephine stared in astonishment. 'What's she doing there?'

'We released her straight away last night and took her home, but she was back a few hours later. I noticed her when it started to get light, but God knows how long she'd already been sitting there. I can only suppose it's because she knows we've got her daughter's killer here.'

'I thought you said she didn't care about Marjorie?'

'Either I was wrong or she was. And going back to that place on her own with everything that's happened can't be easy. She's had enough gossip and prejudice in her life, and now people are going to start on her all over again.' Josephine knew exactly what he was going to say, and she tried not to look as horrified as she felt. 'Anyway, I thought you might want to talk to her. I can't arrange it – it wouldn't be right now – but there's nothing to stop you going over there and striking up a conversation.'

Josephine was torn between grabbing the only chance she would ever have to speak to someone who had been at Claymore House, and a cowardly reluctance to put herself through what was bound to be an ordeal. 'I'm sure she's been through enough without an interrogation from me,' she said doubtfully. 'Anyway, I was going to drop the whole thing. It's too painful now; too many people have been hurt.'

'Have you told your publisher that?' he asked cynically. 'You've got the story of the decade. It's up to you, though: if you don't think it's appropriate, that's fine, but I didn't want you to miss the chance to satisfy your own curiosity, whether you go ahead with the book or not.' As she hesitated, he added: 'Just don't tell her that I sent you. She's hardly likely to be open with you if she knows you're a friend of the person who's spent the last two days accusing her of killing her daughter and her husband.'

'So how will I explain who I am?'

'You'll think of something.' He smiled, recognising that she had made her decision. 'Come and see me before you go, and

461

let me know how you get on. I'll tell the chap on the desk to expect you.'

Josephine crossed the road, and played for time by buying two cups of coffee from Westminster Pier. She went towards the bench, but lost courage and walked straight past, then realised how ridiculous her behaviour would seem if she finally did announce herself. Before she could change her mind again, she retraced her footsteps and stopped in front of Edwards. 'This is going to sound very odd coming from a complete stranger,' she said quietly, 'but I'm so sorry about Marjorie.'

The woman looked up at her in astonishment. 'What do you know about it?'

She must have been in her fifties, and it took Josephine a second or two to remove herself from the moment in which she had been so absorbed and add thirty-odd years to the Nora Edwards of her story. Feeling self-conscious as Edwards continued to stare at her, she held out the coffee. 'Marjorie worked for some friends of mine,' she said. It sounded feeble, even to her, but it was the best that she could do. 'Can I sit down for a minute?' Edwards shrugged, and took the cup. 'I never met your daughter, but I gather she was very talented.'

'Was she? You know more than I do. Everyone seems to be talking about someone I don't recognise.' She laughed bitterly. 'And no one talks about Joe at all, as if his life counted for nothing.' Josephine was silent: it was true, she thought – Marjorie's father had hardly been mentioned over the last few days, except with regard to his true identity. They had all been happy to condemn Celia's valuing of one life above another, but everyone betrayed their own innate prejudices at a time of grief. 'Who are you, anyway?' Edwards asked.

'My name's Josephine, and I realise how this may look, but

I'm writing a book about Amelia Sach and Annie Walters.' Edwards put the coffee down and started to get up, but Josephine caught her arm. 'I knew Lizzie,' she said. 'We were at a school in Birmingham together, and I was there when she died. It seemed to me that she was another victim of Amelia's crimes and all the publicity that followed, but there were plenty of other people whose lives were ruined by what happened – you and your husband more than most, I imagine. That's what the book's about. If you don't want to talk to me, I understand and I'll leave you alone – but let me be the one to go, not you. Please, sit down.'

'Just passing, were you?' Edwards asked sarcastically, glancing back towards Scotland Yard, but some of the suspicion had gone from her face and Josephine sensed that she'd chosen the right approach.

'Something like that. Look, Mrs Baker, I don't presume to know anything about your life or your relationship with your husband, but it must feel very lonely to be the only one left who knows what it was like to live through that time. I imagine an experience like that creates a bond which is difficult to break, for good or bad.'

'It's broken now, that's for sure.' Her tone was still aggressive, but she sat down again and looked at Josephine with a new interest. 'It was a relief at first, but I was stupid to think that it could ever be over. You're obviously clever enough to say the right things, but I suppose it's Amelia you really want to know about, rather than Joe.'

'Is it possible to know about one without the other?' Josephine asked. 'Surely she made him whatever he became. You must have felt as if she were still in the room with you all these years.'

463

'It was finding out what happened to her that really destroyed him,' she said, so softly that Josephine could hardly hear her. 'We might have been all right eventually if it hadn't been for that, but he always blamed himself for allowing Amelia to carry on with what she was doing until it was too late. When he heard about the hanging, it was as if she'd come back to torture him herself. He never got rid of that image once he knew about it, awake or asleep.' That was understandable, Josephine thought, remembering how she had felt as she stared at Holloway's brand new execution shed: there could be few things more horrific than imagining those last terrible moments for someone you loved. 'I suppose you've been told the official version,' Edwards continued bitterly. 'Everything mercifully quick, Amelia calm and dignified until the last – an efficient job all round, in other words.' She laughed scornfully. 'It wasn't like that.'

'How do you know?'

'One of the hangmen got himself into a lot of trouble after the execution, drinking and brawling and shooting his mouth off. They say that hanging Sach and Walters was the start of it all, but I don't know how true that is. Anyway, Joe got to hear the rumours that were going round. Of all the ways that people found to taunt us after what had happened, that was the most damaging. Like I said, he never got over it.'

'And what were the rumours?'

'The whole thing was a bloody mess. None of the officials at the prison were used to executions, and they had no idea how to cope. Amelia collapsed screaming as soon as the hangman and a couple of warders dragged her up and told her to pull herself together. Then they brought Walters through her cell to get her to the ropes, and that set her off again.' Edwards shook her head, and Josephine wondered how she had lived with this knowledge herself, knowing that it was her evidence which had effectively sent Sach to the gallows in the first place. 'Mad with fear, she was, and Walters couldn't have been calmer.'

'I can't help feeling that a calm woman going to the gallows is the insane one.'

Edwards nodded in agreement. 'Amelia couldn't even walk the few paces to the scaffold,' she said. 'She was helpless and barely conscious, and the warders had to drag her there. There was no last-minute peace before she died, no standing calmly on the trapdoor waiting for someone to pull a lever. They virtually had to throw her down the hole.'

How could anyone ever say that death was instantaneous, Josephine thought, trying to imagine the terror that Amelia Sach must have felt, the humiliation of dying so close to the woman she had grown to hate, knowing that – at the last moment – their roles had been reversed and she was now the weak one. 'They must have been the longest few minutes of her life,' she said. Glancing to her right, she saw how deeply the story had affected Edwards, despite the effort she had made not to show it; God knows what it had done to Jacob Sach's mental state. 'And you knew all this at the time?' she asked gently.

'Soon afterwards. Everyone made sure we did. I suppose the hangman was only trying to ease his own conscience by talking about it, but people should think about how it will affect those left behind before they open their mouth. Amelia might have been dead, but we weren't.'

Josephine couldn't decide whether this last comment was directed at her or not. 'No wonder there was such a backlash against hanging women,' she said.

'Some women, perhaps. No one worried when it was just drunks and prostitutes who got desperate, but the minute that middle-class women started getting convicted for murder, people started to say that hanging was wrong.' She shrugged. 'I didn't notice any clamour of indignation on Walters's behalf, not that I'm defending her.'

'Was Jacob – Joe – the reason you stayed in that house, even after Amelia tried to get you to give up your own child?'

'I wasn't exactly flooded with offers,' she said, and there was a trace of the old sarcasm back in her voice. 'I had nowhere else to go. But yes, I would have been sorry to leave him, not that I could compete with her in his eyes.'

'Did he ever ask you to lie to save her?' The fact that Jacob Sach had spent the rest of his life with the woman who testified so convincingly against the wife he supposedly loved was one of the many things which Josephine had never understood about the case. 'And would you have done it if he had?'

'I offered to, but he said no. He said he didn't know how else to stop her doing what she was doing.' She noticed Josephine's expression, and added quickly: 'I don't mean he wanted her to hang – of course he didn't. But neither of them ever believed it would come to that, and Joe thought that if she had to go to prison for a bit, it would frighten her so much that she'd knock it all on the head and they could go back to the way they were, just the three of them. I'm not trying to make excuses for him: he was a bastard to me and a bastard to his kids, and if he hadn't been such a waste of space, then perhaps Marjorie would still be alive. But nothing would ever convince him that he hadn't put the noose around her neck himself.'

Josephine hesitated, wanting to move the conversation from Jacob Sach to his wife, but reluctant to aggravate Edwards.

'You must have got to know Amelia very well,' she began cautiously.

'I was her servant, not her friend.'

Precisely, Josephine thought: if someone ever wanted an accurate picture of her, they'd be much better off talking to her maid in Inverness than to Lydia or even Archie. 'Even so, you lived under her roof. What was she like?'

She realised that it was a simplistic question, but there was no point in trying to dress it up: Edwards would simply see straight through her. It seemed to take her a long time to decide how to answer, or even whether to answer at all, but eventually she said: 'You could say that she was kindness itself. When I turned up on her doorstep, I was seven months pregnant and desperate. There was nobody I could turn to, and I knew nothing about having a baby. Have you got kids?' Josephine shook her head. 'Then you won't understand what it's like to feel trapped by your own body. She took me in and looked after me, she explained what was going to happen when the baby's time came, and she made sure that I wasn't frightened any more. When I think about Amelia Sach, I think about giving birth to my first child. She was so gentle, so caring, and so in control – it's the only time in my life that I've ever felt truly safe. And she was a devoted mother. Lizzie adored her. So did my son. Nothing was too much trouble for her where they were concerned.'

Josephine had expected to hear that Sach was a good mother, but she had never dreamt that Edwards might regard the woman as some kind of sanctuary. She barely had time to consider the information before Edwards continued: 'Or you could say that she was an obsessive, manipulative bitch who set out to destroy innocent lives and made a half-decent job of

467

it. I watched her with those other girls, you know, and she was so protective until the moment the baby was born; after that, there was no warmth, no compassion – just a cold, detached process until the kid was safely out of the house. She held those babies as though they were already dead.'

Edwards must have seen the confusion in Josephine's eyes, because she added: 'There's no sense in trying to work out the truth from what I've just told you. The point is, you can never know what Amelia Sach was like because you weren't there. Just ask yourself – how would you feel if someone wrote a book about you in fifty years' time? Would that be an accurate picture? Would I know what you were really like if I read it?' She finished her coffee and put the cup down. 'Don't think I'm trying to put you off what you're doing – it makes no odds to me, because things can't get any worse. But if I were you, I'd forget all about it. It'll only ever be half a story.'

Josephine looked at the woman she had cast as the pivotal figure in the Sach and Walters story, and saw only another casualty. 'What will you do now?' she asked.

'Bury them and move on. Find somewhere else to hide and live the lie again until someone else finds out.'

Josephine stood to leave, but this time it was her turn to be held back. 'You said you knew Lizzie,' Edwards said, and there was an uncomplicated affection in her voice which hadn't been there when she spoke of anyone else. 'I didn't know anything about her death until the police told me. What happened?'

Josephine hesitated, then chose the half of the story which was likely to give Edwards peace rather than further torment. 'She had an accident in a gym. It was a physical training college, and she was practising on one of the ropes.'

'But she was happy? I've never really forgiven myself for letting her or my son go just because Joe wanted a new start.'

'Yes, she was very happy. From what I understand, she'd had a fabulous childhood and a lot of love. As hard as it must have been for you to give her up, she never suffered because of it. I'm sure it was the same for your son.'

Uneasy with the lie, she left Nora Edwards to her thoughts and headed back towards Scotland Yard. Archie must have been watching them, because he was already waiting for her on the steps. They walked in the other direction along the Embankment, and found a bench overlooking the river. 'How did you get on?' he asked.

'I think I learned more than I ever wanted to know,' she admitted, and told him about Amelia Sach's execution. 'I'm not sure I want to live in a world where that can happen.'

'I know what you mean, but if you try to take responsibility for something like that, you'll go insane. Believe me, I've lost enough sleep over it in my time.'

'We're all responsible, though, aren't we? We've just come through a general election, for God's sake, and we're supposed to live in a democracy.' She waved a hand in the direction of parliament. 'If that lot can't sort out a more humane way of punishing people, isn't that my problem? Shouldn't there be basic rights for everyone?'

'And Marjorie? What about her rights?'

Josephine sighed. 'I know what you're saying, and I don't have any arguments to that one.' She waited for a pause in the traffic over Westminster Bridge, and then asked: 'Has Celia admitted everything?'

'Yes and no. I'm afraid it's rather more complicated than

469

that. This is strictly confidential, but the woman we have in custody isn't Celia Bannerman.'

'What?' Josephine looked at him as though he'd lost his mind. 'Of course she's Celia Bannerman. I should know – I spent enough time with the woman at Anstey.'

'With the woman, yes, but not with Celia Bannerman.'

She listened, incredulous, as Archie explained. 'So you're telling me that half her life has been a lie?'

'In the fundamental sense of her identity, yes; the personality and the achievements aren't an act, though – they're who she really is, as she went to great lengths to point out to me. We're waiting for Ethel Stuke to get here from Suffolk to confirm what she's saying, but I've no doubt that she's Eleanor Vale.'

'But what about the information she gave me for the book? How could she have known all that?'

'She'd spent enough time in Holloway to know how prison worked, and she lived with Celia Bannerman – they must have talked. I had another look at what you'd written, though; if you analyse it very carefully, there's not much there that isn't generally available, and as you've just found out yourself, a lot of it isn't even true.' He accepted a cigarette gratefully. 'It's that speech I can't get out of my head, you know. All that talk about the nation's children, and she ends up being a bloody baby farmer.'

Josephine stared out across the river to the crescent-shaped façade of County Hall. 'Do you think she had anything to do with Lizzie Sach's death?' she asked quietly. The thought that Lizzie might somehow have discovered the truth about her mother's execution as well as her crimes had haunted her from the moment Edwards described it to her.

'I don't know. The police were satisfied at the time that it

470

was a straightforward suicide, if you can ever have such a thing.'

'I'm not saying that Celia killed her – well, not Celia, but you know who I mean. I can't think of her as anybody else. I just wondered if she might have had good reason to want Lizzie dead – she was a link with the past, after all. She might have seen the real Celia Bannerman.'

'She was four years old, Josephine. I doubt she'd have remembered anything that could threaten Vale's lie.'

'I was thinking about what you said on the way to Suffolk, though, and you were right: the natural thing for Lizzie to do when she first heard about her mother was to seek confirmation from the woman who had shown such an interest in her life – not take every detail on trust and hang herself in the gym. Wouldn't you ask questions before you did something like that? What if Celia knew what she was going to do and didn't try to stop her?' He said nothing, but Josephine could see that he agreed. 'Archie, Gerry's life will never be settled as long as she believes that it was her fault, and only her fault, that Lizzie died. If there's the slightest chance that Celia was in some way responsible, couldn't you at least question her about it?'

'I can't guarantee I'll be questioning her about anything else with the state she's in at the moment,' he admitted. 'And the three recent deaths have to be my priority. I'm not even sure that I can get her for the murder of Celia Bannerman after all this time.'

'I thought you said she'd confessed?'

'She has, but we still need corroborative evidence if we're to get a conviction, and she knows that.'

'So what you're trying to tell me, in the nicest possible way, is that you can only hang her once.' She was quiet for a moment, trying to make sense of everything in her life that had been thrown into doubt over the last few days. 'How far would she have gone, do you think?'

'She'd have done whatever was necessary to protect the lie,' he said. 'I'm sure of that, at least.' He looked at his watch. 'I'm sorry, but I've got to go. Can I get Bill to drop you back at the club?'

'No, I'd rather walk. I'll be stuck on a train for long enough later.'

Archie looked surprised. 'I thought you were staying until the weekend?'

'Not any more – I've managed to get a sleeper for tonight.' She stood up, hoping to avoid a long explanation. 'London's lost some of its loveliness for a bit, and I need to get away.'

He knew better than to try to change her mind. 'Do you know when you'll be back?'

'Not at the moment.'

'But you'll call me when you do?'

'Of course.' She smiled, and bent to kiss him. 'Perhaps you'll have got those bloody boxes unpacked by then.' She was almost at Westminster Bridge when she heard him call after her. 'What did you say?' she asked, shouting to make herself heard over the traffic.

'I told you to think about yourself.' He threw his cigarette stub on the ground and stood up. 'Not me. Not Lydia. Not even your family. Just you.'

Chapter Sixteen

Josephine walked slowly up the hill to Crown Cottage with the latest *Film Weekly* tucked under her arm. Inverness was grey and quiet and misty in the late morning, and the weather seemed to have settled on a compromise, halfway between the absurdly March-like sun which had lit the Grampians on her journey south and the snow which had turned them white to their roots by the time she travelled home. But if nature had righted itself to usher in December, her world remained strangely at odds with itself. She glanced down towards the railway station, with the bleak, dark mass of Ben Wyvis in the background, and watched as the Edinburgh train pulled lazily out into the countryside; just a fortnight ago, she would have considered the sight of a train headed for London as a lifeline; now, she was not so sure.

'You're popular today,' called a cheerful voice from across the road.

Josephine waved to the post girl, but her heart sank as she envisaged a pile of bills, begging letters and catalogues. The mail was always so dull after a trip away, and it was only a matter of days now, surely, before the first Christmas card dropped smugly on to the mat. 'Couldn't you just tell them I've moved, Jenny?' she asked drily. 'How bad is it?'

'Eight letters and a parcel. I've left them in the porch for you.'

Josephine thanked her and climbed the narrow set of steps which led directly to the back of the house, saving her the bother of greeting her neighbours as she went down the drive. What could the parcel be, she wondered? Something back from the laundry, perhaps, although she couldn't immediately remember sending anything to the laundry. When she picked it up and saw the label of an Oxford Street bookshop, she smiled and looked for the explanatory letter; there it was, in Marta's handwriting; in fact, two of the envelopes were from Marta.

She barely had a chance to close the front door behind her before her maid emerged from the kitchen, clutching a wet towel. 'Miss Tey – thank goodness you're back. The sitting-room grate's fallen out and now we've got a leak under the kitchen sink. I've mopped it up as best I can, but the whole place will be flooded if it's not fixed this afternoon.'

How quickly reality came crashing back in, Josephine thought, listening to the catalogue of domestic disasters that seemed to have befallen Crown Cottage in the space of an hour and a half. She took one look at the girl's worried face, and knew that she just wanted to be on her own. Putting the mail down on the hall table, she took the towel from her gently and led her back to the kitchen. 'Why don't you take the rest of the day off, Morag. You've had a lot to deal with while I've been away, and you deserve some time to yourself.'

Morag looked at her in astonishment. 'But I haven't even started your unpacking yet.'

'I'll take care of it later,' Josephine said firmly. 'Go and do some Christmas shopping or something.'

'But what about the leak?'

Just in time, she stopped herself saying something about the leak that Ronnie would have been proud of. 'Stick a bucket under it before you go, and I'll make sure it's dealt with.' She helped Morag on with her coat. 'Were there any messages while I was out?'

'Your sister telephoned. She and Mr Donald are coming up on Thursday instead of Friday next week. And your father won't be in for supper – he said to go ahead and eat without him.'

Josephine breathed a sigh of relief as Morag's footsteps faded down the drive, and tried to remember the last time she had had the house to herself for eight glorious hours. The rooms were still fragrant with Marta's flowers; the scent had followed her to Inverness from London, filling the sleeper and reminding her – if she needed reminding – that whatever she was running from was not so easily shaken off. She picked the post up, walked through to the tiny sitting room at the back of the house where the grate was still intact, and settled down with her feet on the hearth to look through her mail. The book was a copy of *Wuthering Heights*, a beautiful leather edition with gilt lettering, its pages yet to be cut; Marta had looked at her in disbelief when she said she hadn't read it, almost as if it were a personal affront, and Josephine knew that it would only be a matter of time before the novel found its way to Inverness. With apologies to Emily Brontë, she put the book aside and turned to Marta's letters. One envelope contained some more pages from the diary, which Marta had promised to continue to send her; the other, a short note.

You left me no time to give this to you in person, so I throw myself upon the mercy of His Majesty's post and hope that it slips through those hallowed defences at Crown Cottage, even if I can't. It seems that we're destined to spend our lives at railway stations, you and I, and hurried departures are becoming a habit. Once again, you've blighted my life by going out of it, but tonight, somehow, Inverness feels closer than it used to.

Lydia tells me that she's writing to suggest you join us at Tagley for Christmas. It will be amusing to see whether you accept or refuse. In your place, I should wickedly accept for the fun of seeing what the other fellow would do, but perhaps your Scottish code doesn't allow that? Stop being so glib, I hear you say – but Josephine, sometimes it's the only way. Don't ever be fooled by it; don't doubt that I love you.

That, at least, was no longer in question: Josephine had known it from the moment that Marta first touched her, had felt the truth of it in every hour they spent together, and she was ashamed to remember how easily she had dismissed Marta's feelings as something less than real. And if the looker-on in her still insisted that there was no sense in loving someone you couldn't be with, there was, for the first time in her life, another voice which accepted that the loving itself was not a matter of choice.

She glanced through the rest of the mail – sure enough, there was the card from Lydia – and put it down to open later. There was something she needed to do first, something for Gerry which she would have found impossible when they had talked that morning at breakfast. Consciously or not, she had underestimated Gerry's love for Lizzie Sach, too, and had written it off as some sort of adolescent passion which would have passed with time, but she realised now that it was her imagination which had been lacking, not Gerry's feelings.

Determined to make it up to her, she settled down at her typewriter to lay the Sach and Walters case to rest once and for all. The final chapter would only ever be read by one person; even so, it was the one that mattered most.

(untitled)
by Josephine Tey
First Draft
Anstey Physical Training College, Birmingham,
Wednesday 14 June 1916

Lizzie knocked loudly on the door of Celia Bannerman's office and went straight in without waiting for a reply. Miss Bannerman was at her desk, and made no acknowledgement of any interruption until she had finished the letter she was writing. The arrogance of her unhurried progress across the page sickened Lizzie, and she could barely contain her anger; eventually, the teacher looked up at her and smiled.

'Miss Price – what can I do for you at this time of night?'

'Don't you mean Miss Sach?' Lizzie was gratified to see that her words had temporarily ruffled Bannerman's composure, and she pressed home her advantage by throwing the letter down on the desk in front of her – Gerry's letter, which she had waited all day to open, holding on to it as some sort of salvation from the misery of her daily life, only to find that its contents destroyed the very fabric of her existence. She waited impatiently while Bannerman read it through, taking her time and going back over some of the earlier paragraphs, and wondered how she could ever have trusted or respected the woman in front of her.

'Geraldine shouldn't have told you any of this,' she said calmly when she had finished. 'It was irresponsible and reckless of her, and I'm sorry you've had to find out in this way.'

'Of course she should have told me,' Lizzie shouted, incensed by the lack of remorse in Celia Bannerman's voice. 'Don't transfer all your shortcomings on to her – she's not to blame. It looks like she's the only person in my life who's ever told me the truth, and thank God she did. At least there's someone I can trust.' She paused, then said more quietly: 'I assume by your attitude that it *is* all true? And you knew all the time?'

'Yes, it's true, and I know how hurt you must feel, but . . .'

'You have absolutely no idea how I feel – none of you. You all think you've been so clever, managing my life for me and treating me like a child, but this is where it stops. You can keep your precious school and your career – I won't stay another day in this bloody prison.'

'Stop being ridiculous, Elizabeth, and calm down. Where on earth would you go?'

'To find Gerry. We're going to be together – she's got money, she'll look after me until I can find a job.'

'That won't be possible, I'm afraid,' Bannerman said, and there was a coldness in her voice now that frightened Lizzie. 'This is the last time you'll be hearing from Geraldine.'

'What do you mean? What's happened to her?'

'Nothing, as far as I know, but your parents' – Lizzie looked scornfully at her for using words which no longer applied, but she carried on oblivious – 'your parents *and* Lady Ashby all agree that your relationship with Geraldine isn't . . . well, appropriate. I have to say, I think they're right.'

Lizzie stared at her in disbelief. 'You really think you can keep us apart, don't you?' she said, snatching the letter and holding it up to Bannerman's face. 'But she means what she says in here, you know. She loves me.'

The older woman laughed softly. 'Oh, my dear, you're so young, but you must understand – Geraldine Ashby has responsibilities. Money doesn't solve problems in the way you think it does. It creates them.'

'Don't fucking patronise me,' Lizzie said, shocked by her own anger, but Celia Bannerman continued her relentless denial of everything that Lizzie had ever taken for granted, slowly eroding her confidence and her ability to fight back.

'Geraldine has no more control over her origins than you do. She may think she's free to do as she likes at the moment, but her future is already mapped out for her, and it doesn't include the servants' daughter.' She paused, making sure that she had Lizzie's attention. 'And it certainly could never include the child of a convicted murderer. I'm sorry to have to speak to you in this way, but, since you've raised the subject of your past . . .'

Before she could hear the rest of the sentence, Lizzie stormed out of Bannerman's office. Fighting back tears, she ran down the corridor, past the notice board where she had collected the letter that morning, and back to her own room. On the landing outside, a group of third-year girls paused in their conversation to look at her, but no one said anything and Lizzie shut the door behind her, relieved for once to have made herself too unpopular to bother with. She tore open the top drawer of her desk and rifled through it, desperate to find the only thing which could convince her that her past and her future were more tangible than she now believed them to be. The pile of letters and photographs was tucked right at the back, and her instinctive decision to hide them as if they were something to be ashamed of seemed to Lizzie to underline the truth of Bannerman's words.

When she left the room again an hour later, she thought only of Gerry. In all the years she had known her, Lizzie had never questioned their love; now, by analysing what it meant to her, she had let it slip through her fingers, and the loss of innocence was more painful and more final than any revelation about her mother could have been. Since coming to Anstey, she had understood what it was to miss someone: Gerry's absence was like a constant fog over her life; it was there when she went to bed and when she opened her eyes again in the morning, and it lifted only when she saw the handwriting on an envelope. To miss someone with hope was bearable, but to have that dark ribbon of grief stretching endlessly ahead of her with no prospect of a reprieve was more than she could bear. As she opened the door to the gymnasium and walked quietly across the floor, she hoped that Gerry would forgive her.

Author's Note

Two for Sorrow is a work of fiction, inspired by real lives and events.

Amelia Sach and Annie Walters were hanged at Holloway Gaol in London on 3 February, 1903, having been sentenced to death by Mr Justice Darling at the Old Bailey, despite a recommendation of mercy from the jury. Theirs was the first execution at Holloway since its conversion to a women's prison the year before, and the last double female hanging in Britain. The bodies of both women were removed from the prison grounds in 1971 and taken to Brookwood Cemetery in Surrey, where they are buried together.

Most of the material included in Josephine's untitled novel is reported in or suggested by the various newspaper accounts of the arrest and trial. When she died, Amelia Sach left behind a husband and young daughter, but their names were not Jacob and Lizzie, and their fates as depicted in *Two for Sorrow* are entirely fictional.

In 1927, Mary Size became the first female deputy governor of Holloway Prison. Although her improvements fell short of her own ideals, the reforms she introduced – mirrors and photographs in cells, a system for prisoners to earn their own money and a prison shop, financial aid to help with debt and the provision of clothing on release – brought a new humanity to the incarceration of women and did much to bring the standard of women's prisons more in line with those for men. Her story is told in an autobiography, *Prisons I Have Known*. Cicely McCall's book on Holloway, *They Always Come Back*, was published in 1938, and I am indebted to her for providing the details of Josephine's guided tour.

Josephine Tey was one of two pseudonyms created by Elizabeth Mackintosh (1896–1952) in a successful career as playwright and novelist; it first appeared in 1936, paying tribute to her late mother and her Suffolk great-great-grandmother, and it is the name by which we know her best today. As Josephine Tey, although her output was small, Mackintosh wrote some of the most original and modern crime novels of the 1930s, 40s and 50s, including *The Franchise Affair*, *The Daughter of Time* (both re-workings of historical crimes) and *Brat Farrar*. One of her finest books, *Miss Pym Disposes*, takes its setting and some of its characters from Anstey Physical Training College near Birmingham, where Mackintosh studied during the First World War. The other alias, Gordon Daviot, was reserved mainly for plays and historical fiction, and was the name most widely used by her friends.

For most of her life, Elizabeth Mackintosh lived in her hometown, Inverness, where she kept house for her father, but she loved England and spent a good part of each year south of the border or, occasionally, in Europe. Her time in London was usually spent at the Cowdray Club, a club for nurses and professional women where she was a member from 1925 until her death in 1952. As well as providing a convenient and comfortable base in town, the club gave Tey the names of many of her characters; look through the membership lists for those years, and you will find a Grant, an Ashby, a Blair, a Farrar and a Marion Sharpe. The club no longer exists (not because of murder or scandal, which are all my invention), but the building in Cavendish Square is still the headquarters of The Royal College of Nursing.

Mackintosh is widely believed to have lost a lover at the Somme in 1916; although her early work supports this, her lifelong friend from Inverness, who was with her at Anstey during the war, knew of no such relationship, and Mackintosh shied away from close emotional entanglements. The most significant attachments of her later life were almost exclusively with women, many of whom she had met during the West End run of her phenomenally successful play, *Richard of Bordeaux*. From April 1935 to March 1936, one of those women – the actress, Marda Vanne – kept a diary, a year-long love letter written to Gordon Daviot. The words which Marta asks Josephine to read here are Marda's, an eloquent expression of a real and lasting love.

Acknowledgements

It would take a lifetime to do justice to the creative contribution which Mandy Morton makes to this series: her ideas, research and suggestions along the way have made each book – and the joy of writing it – far richer than it would otherwise have been. And a lifetime's fine.

Many people have been generous with their time and knowledge, and I owe particular thanks to: Jenny Elliott from the Royal College of Nursing for helping to recreate the Cowdray Club as it would have been in 1935, and Susan McGann, Archives Manager, Royal College of Nursing, and staff at the London Metropolitan Archives for further information; Birmingham Archives & Heritage Service, and all who have given information on Anstey Physical Training College; staff at Cambridge University Library for tracking down so many accounts of the Sach and Walters case; Peter Cox for taking us in off the street in Finchley and helping with the history of Hertford Road and the Sach family; Fiona and Catherine Cameron, Pat Wythe, Julia Reisz, Richard Stirling and Sally Morgan for supplying details of Inverness, pre-war Walberswick and other locations in the book; and to Sir John Gielgud, who was kind enough to talk to me at length about Josephine Tey and, in so doing, created one of the mysteries on which this book is based.

The history of crime and execution in the first half of the

twentieth century is widely documented, but nowhere more vividly than in Albert Pierrepoint's *Diary of an Executioner*, and I'm especially grateful to Stewart P. Evans for his extensive work on the subject. Books by Judith Knelman, Jerry White, Cicely McCall, Lilian Wyles, Sheridan Morley, Michael Mullin, Alison Bruce, Richard Clark, Harriet Devine and Virginia Nicholson have all provided invaluable research for various aspects of the novel and, once again, I'm indebted to help and advice from Dr Peter Fordyce, Margaret Westwood, Dr Helen Grime, the staff at The Highland Council, and to John Stachiewicz and The National Trust for continued permission to quote from Elizabeth Mackintosh's work and correspondence.

Love and thanks to everyone who continues to care so much about these books: Walter Donohue and everyone at Faber; P.D. James; and, of course, my family, whose support and encouragement now is as important as it has always been.

And to Gordon Daviot and Marda Vanne, whose correspondence and friendship are at the heart of *Two for Sorrow*, and who continue to inspire the series; some of the author's proceeds from this series will go to the Daviot Fund to support the work of The National Trust in England.